The
Witkiewicz Reader

The

**Edited, Translated and with an
Introduction by Daniel Gerould**

Witkiewicz
Reader

Quartet Books

First published in Great Britain by
Quartet Books Limited 1993

A member of the Namara Group
27/29 Goodge Street
London W1P 1FD

First published by Northwestern University Press
copyright © 1992

A catalogue record for this title is available from
the British Library

ISBN 0 7043 0203 9

Printed and bound in Great Britain by
The Cromwell Press Ltd, Broughton Gifford, Wilts

**To the Memory of Konstanty Puzyna,
First Editor and Best Critic of Witkacy**

CONTENTS

ILLUSTRATIONS

Following page 152

PREFACE

The aim of this collection is to present Stanisław Ignacy Witkiewicz in the full range of his artistic and intellectual activities: as a playwright, novelist, aesthetician, theorist of the theater, philosopher, cultural critic, experimenter with drugs, painter, portraitist, and photographer. Although in his lifetime he occupied only a marginal position in the cultural life of his country, he was rediscovered after 1956 and became a major force in shaping the flowering of Polish drama and theater in the second half of the twentieth century. He is now recognized both in Poland and abroad as a creative personality of unusual dimensions and one of the most colorful figures in the European avant-garde. More than that, Witkiewicz has achieved the status of a cultural hero. In the name of creative freedom he defended the individual against the collective. Even before it came into existence, he foresaw and warned against the Communist regime in Poland. But he was no less an opponent of the hypocrisies and injustices of liberal democracy and capitalism. In his life and in his death he stood for untrammeled art and inquiry.

The best way to introduce Witkiewicz's works is, I believe, through a presentation of the artist himself and his dramatic relationship to his own creativity. My introductory essay develops these ideas and places the author in the context of the historical avant-gardes, modernism, and postmodernism. The separate introductions to the five chapters provide brief biographical and critical commentary on the unfolding story of Witkiewicz's life. Here my aim is to draw near the author in all his human complexity rather than to glorify and mythologize.

The works in the collection represent the diverse aspects of Witkiewicz's creativity. Drama occupies a central place. In addition to two childhood plays, I have selected *The New Deliverance*, an accessible and often-performed one-act work, and the more esoteric *Janulka*, a four-act tragedy of singular weirdness and a special favorite of the author and of his modern enthusiasts. It appears here for the first time in English. Witkiewicz's fiction is represented by newly translated excerpts from *Bungo*, *Farewell to Autumn*, and *The Only Way Out* (*Insatiability* has already appeared in Louis Iribarne's fine translation).

I have also included a wide range of essays and philosophical and critical works in abridged versions. Witkiewicz's rambling prose works were written without regard to form, and they benefit from condensation.

Of the thousands of letters written by Witkiewicz to many different correspondents, I have chosen to give several dozen of those to his best friend, the anthropologist Bronisław Malinowski. This correspondence constitutes a coherent block and comes from all periods of Witkiewicz's life. The bulk of these letters (supplemented by several related items to the playwright's family) focus on the journey to the tropics, a decisive moment for both writers. I regard Witkiewicz's friendship with Malinowski as key to understanding his life and work. The correspondence enables us to see the playwright in relation to a member of the same generation of Polish artists and thinkers who by changing language and country was able to escape the limitations of minor-culture nationality and achieve world fame at a much earlier point. The appendix contains comments by contemporaries and moderns on Witkiewicz. Also included is a chronology of the parallel lives of Witkiewicz and Malinowski, charting the different creative paths followed by the two friends, and some biographical notes on people mentioned in the text, mainly Polish, who may not be generally known.

ACKNOWLEDGMENTS

Earlier versions of some of the material included in this volume appeared in the following publications: *Cockroaches* and *Comedies of Family Life* in *yale/theater*, vol. 5, no. 3, 1974; *The New Deliverance* in *The Polish Review*, vol. 18, no. 1–2, 1973, and in *New Directions in Prose and Poetry*, New Directions, 1975; "Rules of the S. I. Witkiewiz Portrait-Painting Firm," "Report about the Effect of Peyote," and portions of *New Forms in Painting*, "Interview with Bruno Schulz," "Bruno Schulz's Literary Work," and *Unwashed Souls* in *The Beelzebub Sonata*, PAJ Publications, 1980; several of the letters to Malinowski in *Performing Arts Journal*, vol. 7, no. 3, 1983.

The translations of *Cockroaches, Comedies of Family Life, The New Deliverance,* and *Janulka, Daughter of Fizdejko* are by Daniel Gerould and Jadwiga Kosicka.

The photographs and drawings in this volume come from the collections of Ewa and Stefan Okołowicz and Anna Micińska and from Wojciech Sztaba's book, *Stanisław Ignacy Witkiewicz. Zaginione obrazy i rysunki sprzed roku 1914 według oryginalnych fotografii za zbiorów Konstantego Puzyny* (Warsaw: Auriga, 1985).

I have received invaluable help in preparing this volume and wish to thank the many friends and colleagues who have shared their knowledge and their collections and archives with me: Janusz Degler, Anna Micińska, Ewa and Stefan Okołowicz, Bohdan Michalski, Lech Sokół, Irena Jakimowicz, Alain van Crugten, Jan Witkiewicz, Helena Wayne, George W. Stocking, Jr., and James Lingwood. I should also like to express my gratitude to Jane House, Pamela Billig and the Threshold Theatre, Robert Pucci, Stuart Baker, Scott Walters, Jerry Leo, David Willinger, Jan Heissinger, and David Goldfarb, who read and commented on the translations.

The Witkiewicz Foundation in Warsaw has given its moral support and full cooperation to the creation of this volume.

INTRODUCTION
WITKACY AND THE CREATIVE LIFE

■

"Witkiewicz is by birth, by race, to the very marrow of his bones an artist; he lives exclusively by art and for art. And his relationship to art is profoundly dramatic; he is one of those tormented spirits who in art seek the solution, not to the problem of success, but to the problem of their own being." Such was the opinion of Tadeusz Boy-Żeleński, the only critic in the interwar years to gauge accurately the extraordinary vocation of his friend Witkacy (the pen name and persona by which the writer was known to his inner circle). Boy's perception, I believe, offers a key to understanding both the life and work of the multitalented Polish artist who was at one and the same time a painter, playwright, novelist, photographer, philosopher, and aesthetician.

This collection of his writings—with accompanying photographs, drawings, portraits, and compositions—explores the drama of Witkacy's relationship to art over almost half a century, from his debut as a seven-year-old playwright in the crumbling Austro-Hungarian Empire at the fin de siècle to his final essays on the eve of a catastrophic war that would bring about newly independent Poland's extinction and the author's suicide.

From earliest childhood young Staś had been urged by his charismatic artist father, Stanisław Witkiewicz, to develop his individuality in as many directions as possible, and for the rest of his life Witkacy wrestled with the problem of his own creativity. The artist himself proved to be his most daring

I

work. "I live constantly on the edge of the abyss," he confessed. Forever constructing new selves out of nothingness, Witkacy gave a perilous auto-performance that pitted creation against destruction—until he finally succumbed to the attractions of the void.

Nietzsche points out that man is the only animal who must strive to explain his own presence on earth. This never-ending need to justify one's existence was for Witkacy the source of all creativity. The Polish artist attempted to place himself, his art, his entire life and work within the critical framework of a theory that could explicate his being. The central philosophical question for Witkacy was the problem of the one and the many, or in his own formulation, of unity in plurality, comprising both the existential issue of the solitary individual confronting the external world of otherness and also the aesthetic task of giving cohesive form to diversity. On a personal level, a multiplicity of selves impishly subverted his quest for self-definition and identity, which he sought within the fluid construct: Witkacy, variously depicted in the numerous "auto-Witkacies" (self-portraits), mugging photographs, and playful signatures, such as Witkas, Witkrejus, St. Witkacy à la fourchette, de St. Vitecasse, Witkatze, Vitcatius, Witkoś, and Mahatma Witkac, among others—not to be confused with the unsavory Onanisław Spermacy Wyfiutkiewicz, one of his low-down antithetical alter egos and doubles.

In 1904 Witkacy characterized his existence as "imaginative self-commentary." He was a great observer of himself, making precise notations with camera, pen, and brush, quite willing to record every aspect of his own psychic disorders. Autobiographical revelation was a game or form of play. In all Witkacy's creativity, performance aspects of life and art were accentuated; every moment became a staged scene, whether recorded by the camera or acted out in "reality." He delighted in disguising himself. "We have a complete choice of masks," the playwright declared. Intense awareness of his own multiple possibilities and potential roles made him loath to abandon any of them. In his dealings with others, Witkacy resorted to tricks, jokes, and conscious manipulations to reveal the unknown lurking in the obscure depths of the human personality.

According to Witkacy's aesthetics, based on his ontological system, true art intensifies one's feelings of individuality and affirms one's existence in the face of an alien cosmos, thereby restoring a lost sense of childlike wonder and anxiety. In the modern age, such metaphysical feelings of strangeness—the same for all humankind, regardless of class, time, and place—are threatened by the historical evolution of society toward perfect anthill utilitarianism. Nurtured on the apocalyptics of turn-of-the-century decadents and symbolists, Witkacy was drawn to a menacing theory of the irreversible decline of Western culture, which he elaborated before World War I (several years before the appearance of Oswald Spengler's monumental *Decline of the West*) and subsequently published in *New Forms in Painting* (1919).

The acutely paranoid artist feared that humanity would lose its individual features and tragic sense of life in the name of social progress and the necessary pragmatic adjustments to the demands of the masses. The myth of the death of art, which became his obsession, led Witkacy to take steps in his own career that would constitute evidence corroborating his gloomiest predictions. In 1924 he stopped painting pure compositions and thereafter devoted himself to portraits, which he regarded as a form of commerce, creating in the "Witkiewicz Portrait-Painting Firm" a miniature one-man business that reflected and parodied the degraded status of art in a philistine society. As time passed—and the rebellious 1920s, more receptive to formal experimentation, changed into the gray 1930s, a period of sober neorealisms and drab totalitarian art—the aging writer, by his own admission formerly an elitist schizoid, now ironically proclaimed his own "pyknicization" and wrote almost exclusively articles and essays expounding his ideas on philosophy and society. Witkacy had often sought for strong stimuli to creativity in alcohol and drugs, but art had always seemed to him to be the best narcotic. In his last years the playwright lost faith in art as a powerful drug, seeing it rather as a tame and ineffectual accommodation, designed to hide the true horror of existence. Perhaps the only way out was to cut one's throat.

1.

The artist must forge his own reality by creating new, endlessly proliferating forms that serve him as masks. The formal impulse is primordial, whereas mimesis has been only a temporary aberration in the history of aesthetics. Pure Form was Witkacy's expression of the modernist ideal of an autonomous art freed of referentiality. Art became an epiphany, transcending everydayness and putting one in direct contact with the structure of the universe. Unlike anything in real life, the eternal forms revealed, as in a dream, something hidden and ungraspable, beyond or beside what was actually depicted in the work. As with Clive Bell's significant form and Roger Fry's formal design, Pure Form created its own absolute meaning, independent of content. In a world of shifting appearances, it could be a refuge, a place of no compromise, a source of ontological certainty.

Yet despite insistent and repeated expositions of his theory, Pure Form seemed constantly to elude Witkacy; in his own artistic practice, it was in perpetual danger of being invaded and overrun by reality. "The purest form is always sullied by life," the writer was forced to admit. Pure Form served Witkacy as a mask, through which life kept peering. Like one of the "faces" or "mugs" that the artist adopted and had photographed, like his constructed persona as Witkacy, Pure Form was a theoretical gesticulation, a polemical stance, a dominating pose by which the playwright attempted to control and set the terms for the public perception of his work. But the theory could not effectively limit Witkacy's imaginative production, as witness the list prepared by the author himself indicating which of his plays illustrated his own aesthetic precepts and which of them fell short of these absolute demands.

In making art out of theory (and not simply according to theory) and in playing with many forms and styles rather than choosing a single one, Witkacy joined early modernist exaltation of Art (with a capital A) to postmodern eclecticism and frivolity. Interaction between theorizing and artistic practice were in his case productive. The critical and creative faculties coexisted within Witkacy, unbounded by sharp division, the one feeding the other; a manifesto could be a histrionic performance, or a theatrical work could play with theory and dramatize aesthetic discourse.

Yet these impulses sprang from quite different sources and developed on distinct psychic planes. The polemical sometimes spilled over into the creative and attempted to usurp its prerogatives. Just as his father had once looked over young Staś's shoulder and been his guide, so Witkacy himself became a fascinated observer of his own creative endeavor, but also at times a rational censor who was either unwilling or unable to investigate its unconscious origins. Although he grudgingly allowed that in a theatrical work the author cannot eliminate his ideas and feelings, his experiences, and his worldview, Witkacy did not examine the role of these elements in shaping the aesthetic response or discuss how they contributed to possible interpretations of his own work. Rather, he recognized only in the most general way the impossibility of rigidly separating art and life and acknowledged the wrenching oppositions between form and content that lie at the basis of all creative work.

In the light of these contradictions, Witkacy's aesthetic orientation is anomalous, and it is difficult to place him in the context of his times. He was a total outsider. The cultural and literary establishments in Poland between the wars dismissed the playwright as the deplorably eccentric son of a revered father and attacked his theatrical theory and practice as the ravings of a maniac. Witkacy, on the other hand, did not feel himself a part of any of the radical artistic movements of the time and was hostile to abstract art, futurism, cubism, dada, and constructivism. He stood only on the fringe of the avant-gardes of the period, remaining true to the doctrines of the early modernism of his youth.

Witkacy was a doubly marginal figure, denied a place in a culture that was itself in constant danger of eclipse; for the first thirty-three years of the playwright's life Poland was a nonexistent nation, partitioned among Russia, Prussia, and Austro-Hungary. Such extreme marginality left Witkacy in an existential limbo that accorded well with his ontological views of man's position in the universe, heightened his consciousness of cultural dislocation and impending disaster, and sharpened his susceptibility to the absurd. Precariously located at the edge of what was at best a disintegrating world, Witkacy benefited from the dynamic tensions produced by fear of falling through the cracks and made his "boundary situation" into a source of creative strength for a number of years.

Even though he was without allegiance or filiation to the new schools and fashions that dominated the art world in the 1920s, Witkacy was avant-garde in his personal style, the hallmarks of which were an aggressive blend of provocation and exhibitionism, extreme vulnerability concealed beneath the bravado of a self-chosen role as buffoon, and a marked propensity for immolation and martyrdom.

Although from a country and a culture peripheral to the main currents of European art and thought, Witkacy had in abundance the forward-looking experiences characteristic of the new age and fundamental to the formation of twentieth-century sensibility. The range of his exposure was neither provincial nor specifically Polish. He took part in the generational battle, not by rebelling against philistine parents, but by struggling with an enlightened, liberating father who represented the most advanced late nineteenth-century ideas and ideals; he confronted the principal revolutions in art, music, and science, seeing congruence between the new perceptions offered by physics and mathematics on the one hand and by cubism, dissonance, and atonality on the other; he underwent psychoanalysis and responded personally and idiosyncratically to Freud's ideas; he discovered the primitive and exotic through travel to a non-Western civilization; and he directly participated in a war and revolution that toppled old empires and radically changed the map of Europe, psychically as well as geographically. Because he synthesized and internalized all these experiences—and yet did so as an outsider, as a Pole—Witkacy can be viewed as a vanguard artist several decades ahead of his time, overburdened with all that he had absorbed and spewing it out in the form of parody and caricature, which functioned for him as modes of aesthetic control.

As emerges from his letters to Malinowski following his fiancée's suicide, for which he held himself responsible, Witkacy cultivated a "crisis" imagination, thereby exacerbating a natural proneness to foreboding anxiety and inciting hysteria. Like the young Freud, he had a superstitious obsession with numbers and dates that might foretell his doom. Yet at the same time the genuinely lacerated author developed a protective response in the form of an ironic sensibility directed against himself. The death-of-art myth, the apocalyptic historiography, the prophesied demise of the individual are dramatized by the playwright with such grim and ghoulish nonchalance that the pathos of these disasters is deflated and we as spectators are placed in a detached position of horrified amusement. In particular, Witkacy felt doubts about himself and his calling, and ultimately about the nature of art—at least in its present degraded state. In his later days art ceased to be Witkacy's beloved mistress and became a fat old whore, her legs spread wide, and he himself was the "old portrait prostitute," who, as his sight worsened, dared not wear glasses for fear of losing customers.

Crisis was also the basis of Witkacy's view of the evolution of the stage. A new theater arises at moments of decay and decline, taking the place of old cults and rituals, as had happened in ancient Greece and in the Middle Ages. Witkacy likewise saw the origins of modern theater in the crisis of contemporary European culture. Europe was experiencing in realism the death throes of a degeneration of art that had started in the Renaissance with the doctrine of imitation—and its attendant vices of perspective, illusion, symmetry, and in-depth character. The stage, which had lagged behind the other arts, still had before it a brief moment of creative greatness in which to blaze up in a splendid final conflagration. Such a nonrepresentational theater, confronting man's metaphysical dread in the face of the universe, can oppose the mechanization of life—"the petrification of everything into one uniform, gray, undifferentiated pulp."

Genius, as a form of insanity, involves breakdown and exhaustion. Witkacy seized upon the prevalent fin-de-siècle representation of the artist as a solitary and exceptional individual driven to self-destruction by the nervous acceleration of life and the incomprehension of society. Recourse to ever stronger stimuli to creativity in drugs, alcohol, cigarettes, and other forms of systematic derangement quickly consumed the lonely creator's talents and left him a burned-out shell. Imprisoned, mad, enslaved, the artist must break out of the straitjacket in which society and the cosmos have confined him. As with the other early modernist stereotypes, such as the demonic woman and the Nietzschean superman, which were part of Witkacy's youthful experience of literature and life, the self-image of the *poète maudit* was incorporated by the mature writer into his repertory of popular icons that he mocks and ironically deforms, even while recognizing that they contain a fundamental truth as debased mythic characters with High Art pedigrees who have become déclassé and begun to frequent trash novels and sensational film serials.

Always ready to put on a new "face" and adopt another mask, Witkacy tried to avoid all modes of social identification and came to dread the multiplicity of interchangeable roles and functions imposed by society. Hence his fear of the many doubles who pursued him and threatened his indeterminacy with definition. "The whole charm of life lay in staying undefined," his alter ego Bungo had asserted. As a condition for creativity, Witkacy felt the need for the unforeseen, the uncaused, the unrepeatable. The greatest threat posed by the approaching psychic mechanization of mankind was boredom. "Better to end in beautiful madness than in gray, boring banality and stagnation," the writer declared in 1919, not long after his experience of the Russian Revolution and his glimpse of its deadening bureaucracy and regimentation. "The fall of man as a unique entity," he warned, would lead inevitably to a "mechanized, hopelessly dull humanity devoid of creativity."

2.

The future anthropologist Bronisław Malinowski was from the 1890s until 1910, when he settled permanently in England, Witkacy's principal companion, and he remained through the playwright's life his closest friend, notwithstanding the distances that separated them and their increasingly infrequent meetings. Except for the bonds to his parents, none of Witkacy's early attachments was as deep and enduring as his affection for Malinowski, despite—or perhaps because of—its stormy nature and the dynamic tensions resulting therefrom. The mutual influence on each other of these two opposed but complementary types was profound, psychically as well as intellectually, and at one point their relationship became a potentially dangerous experiment in self-exploration, taking the form of a brief love affair. Sensing these murky undercurrents, Witkiewicz senior repeatedly warned his son to be wary of too sustained contact with Bronio (referred to in the correspondence by such nicknames as Lord Douglas and Edgar, Duke of Nevermore—*commedia* masks inspired by Wilde and Poe). "Like you, he is in the process of self-creation," the elder Witkiewicz wrote of the future anthropologist in 1905 when his son was living in Cracow with Malinowski and his mother, "and may be passing through phases that could arouse apprehensions as to whether he is the best companion for you." In 1912 (the year after Witkacy had visited Malinowski in London) the father wrote asking the son why he considered Bronio his best friend and how he would define young Malinowski's state of mind at present, since "he had been heading for total submersion in total egotism. His antisocial theories were both narrow as a conception of life and also expressed the narrowness of his own feelings."

Witkacy's own representations of this friendship offer different perspectives on an unfolding drama. In the Edgar, Duke of Nevermore, sections of *The 622 Downfalls of Bungo; or, The Demonic Woman*, Witkacy's youthful *Bildungsroman* (published only posthumously in 1972), as well as in the early letters to Malinowski, we see the two talented young men at the beginning of their careers, planning their future lives, expounding ideas on art and science, imagining erotic possibilities. One account is fictional, the other confessional—different tonalities on Witkacy's palette of colors that constituted a continuous spectrum ranging from make-believe in life to Pure Form in art, with scarcely perceptible transitions along the line. "We apparently cannot define where art begins and life ends," Witkacy himself acknowledged. Commenting on his own work, Malinowski would later observe that it is not easy "to make a distinction between what is mere mytho-poetic fiction and what is . . . drawn from actual experience."

In 1914 when Malinowski was teaching at the London School of Economics in the department of sociology and preparing to do fieldwork in New Guinea, his mentor, C. G. Seligman, a professor of ethnology, secured for his Polish protégé the position of secretary in the anthropology section of the British Association for the Advancement of Science, which would enable him to attend the summer congress to be held in Adelaide, Australia, all expenses paid. When he learned of the tragic death of Jadwiga Janczewska and his friend's suicidal despair, Malinowski immediately proposed that Witkacy join him on the expedition—an offer finally accepted, but only after Malinowski had come to Zakopane on a rescue mission.

When the two "pals" sailed from London on the SS *Orsova* of the Royal Orient Line, heading first for Colombo, Ceylon, Witkacy at twenty-nine and Malinowski at thirty were embarking as not-quite-so-young adventurers on a voyage of self-investigation and conquest. Each had his own strategies and stratagems, as seen in their diverse reactions to the British and their differing uses of Conrad, an older compatriot who had become a famous English novelist. Already launched on a brilliant career, Malinowski was determined to become "the Joseph Conrad of anthropology," having, like his model, emigrated to Great Britain and adopted English as his public language. Still unformed and unfocused, without profession or direction, Witkacy was poised on the brink of self-destruction, struggling to master himself. Alienated by the pragmatic British passengers, he kept to his cabin, reading Conrad's *Lord Jim*, the story of a man who—like himself—felt obliged to expiate terrible guilt for an act of betrayal. With a loaded revolver held to his temple (Conrad too had attempted suicide in his twenties), Witkacy sat staring at his own nothingness.

These distinct styles of auto-performance corresponded to the contrasting theories of the two friends. For the purposeful Bronio, art had to serve life in order to produce a unified, efficient self, capable of concentrated effort. One must be the same in all situations and not adopt different personas according to circumstance. On the other hand, Witkacy, endowed with a different histrionic consciousness and a natural gift for diversity, believed that life should be transmuted into art, into an endless play of forms whose absolute priority is such that they do not express content but exist independently of it. Witkacy seemed most devastated by Jadwiga Janczewska's suicide because it had destroyed any possibility of his becoming an artist. Confronted with an experience that could not be transformed into art, he was unable to remake himself. Aesthetic justification of his being proved impossible; life kept forcing its way into the autonomous forms designed to exclude it. Witkacy acknowledged the contradiction at the heart of existence: "Everything that exists negates the principle by which it exists."

3.

Witkacy's theory of the theater is radical in three respects. It is nonmimetic, calling for artful construction instead of faithful imitation; it is noncathartic, denying emotional identification through the use of ironic distancing; and it is nonliterary, asserting the primacy of performance as created by director, designer, and actor, for whom the playwright provides what is little more than a scenario. Accordingly, the actor must cease being an impersonator pretending to be someone else, faking Stanislavskian "life experiences," and instead become a true creator using all his tools of expression—words, gesture, and body—with mathematical precision to produce formal values.

Although not excluded by the theory of Pure Form (as is shown by Witkacy's use of bizarre scenarios as illustrations), what seems most characteristic of the playwright's theatrical style—humor, playfulness, free borrowings and chance associations, parasitical and parodic structures—is neither explained by the theoretical formulations nor in keeping with their tone. Witkacy's theory is solemn and severe, his theatrical practice unbridled in extravagance and weirdness. Beneath the mask of formal art there lurks the grimace of demonic laughter.

Recognizing that the exhaustion of forms in twentieth-century art was being accelerated by an "insatiable craving" for novelty, Witkacy sought renewal by means of neither tabula rasa innovation nor a safe return to the past, but rather through the dissolution of old structures. From the decomposition of inherited shapes, out of cultural "leftovers" (largely from the property rooms and storehouses of European modernism and its antecedents), the playwright created new forms. He ransacked the history of drama for the raw matter of his art. Rather than avoiding worn-out themes and devices, Witkacy displayed a marked preference for shabby material, obsolescent character types, and outmoded stereotypes. His technique with the threadbare was to pull apart the fabric, display the threads, expose the weave. Making no attempt to conceal his borrowings, the artist gave virtuoso performances, flaunting his sources at the same time that he ostentatiously parodied them and himself. Even as an eight year old, in his *Comedies of Family Life*, Witkacy was adept at the self-conscious revelation of his own intertextuality.

MOTHER   Have you seen Staś's comedies?

MISS JASTRZĘBSKA   No.

[*Mother shows her Staś's comedies.*]

MISS JASTRZĘBSKA   [*Reading.*] Mrs. Witkiewicz! It's exactly like Maeterlinck!

The aesthetics of detritus, positing culture as refuse, offered the artist the entire rubbish heap of civilization—with its accumulated layers of discarded artifacts, styles of dress and manners, ideologies, and modes of imaginative representation—in which to pick and choose. Brought up in a flamboyantly stagy corner of the polyglot, multinational, and multicultural Austro-Hungarian Empire at its operatic finale, Witkacy had an eye for the makeshift and transitory, held together only by imposture. In the pseudoworld of his dramas and novels, inauthenticity is a spur to the theatricalization of life. Histrionics are the only reality, and they are, of course, false.

The dismantling and reassembling of others' imagined realities produces a fractured universe, pieced out of appropriations, exhumations, and quotations. Written at white heat during a period of less than ten years, Witkacy's more than forty plays are pictures whose images constantly disintegrate and then reconstitute themselves in new shapes.

Dedicated to his friend, the composer Karol Szymanowski, *The New Deliverance* unfolds in an enigmatic, disjointed world where time and place have lost cohesion and grown non-Euclidean, polyvalent, and interpenetrable. Incongruous historical epochs and realms of experience intersect as five-o'clock tea is served in a contemporary salon while masked assassins pin Richard III against a Gothic column. The title of the play alludes to Stanisław Wyspiański's *Deliverance*, a turn-of-the-century symbolist drama, and the young protagonist, Florestan, takes his name from the hero of Beethoven's opera, *Fidelio*.

Conjured up by the sound of a gong, as at a séance, Richard is a ghost haunted by ghosts, tormented by the spirits of those he has killed. Long an object of fascination to Witkacy, who at the time was himself "fighting with various ghosts" and dabbling in necromancy, the hunchbacked Shakespearean king (whose monstrosity accords well with the playwright's tenet of artistic deformation) has wandered out of the barbaric feudal past into a degenerate present. There he is forced to witness decadent bourgeois games of sexual initiation, courtship, and family intrigue and see exposed their inner mechanisms: Oedipal fantasies and nineteenth-century stage "secrets" concerning parentage.

With the surprising entry of the Unknown Someone and his six henchmen, the curtain suddenly comes down on the private wallowing in guilt and self-loathing—a revolting display of psychic sadomasochism—characteristic of the old regime. Privileged anguish is liquidated by the intrusion from outside of totalitarian terror, histrionically directed by a masked androgyne (combining the worst of the two genders, not the best—as the symbolists had hoped of bisexuality). In Witkacy's postindustrial vision, the old Marxist social classes have lost their functions and are being replaced by new nonclass formations, such as technology and bureaucracy. Recruited as secret policemen, security agents, and state thugs, the former proletarians have become anonymous technicians of torture. Although still dressed as working men, they have turned their tools from production to extermination and use pincers, hammers, and a blowtorch to eliminate socially undesirable victims.

The terrorism unleashed at the end of Witkacy's plays—including *The New Deliverance*, *They*, *The Water Hen*, and *The Anonymous Work* (dedicated to Malinowski)—comes as a nasty *coup de théâtre*, all the more menacing because arbitrary and unpredictable; its origins, ideology, and sources of power are not easily identifiable and cannot be reduced to any single political party or platform. All we know is that it is collective terror—less systematic than spontaneous—of the mass against the individual. Secrecy characterizes its organization, and brutish joy in destruction constitutes its strongest bonding element. The victims find in their very doom the only possible justification for ever having lived and readily accept their own suffering and extinction, even inventing pretexts to hasten the retribution.

A drama of social masks and hidden anxieties, *The New Deliverance* could take as its motto *Capricho* No. 6, "Nadie se conoce," by Goya (one of Witkacy's masters of the grotesque), for which the full text is: "The world is a masquerade. Face, dress, and voice, all are false. All wish to appear what they are not, all deceive and nobody knows anybody." In the world of Witkacy's plays things are never what they seem; behind the scenes there is always a more sinister reality to be apprehended. Equipped with paranoid vision, the Polish playwright was drawn to deceptive appearances and manipulations— as was his guide in the exploration of psychic depths, Sigmund Freud, who (according to Ernest Jones) took special interest in people not being what they seemed. The Witkacian dramatis personae live in constant dread of a masked power structure whose identity and operation are unknowable. THEY—ubiquitous and protean—have usurped authority and enforce the tyranny of society over the individual.

Although he had doubts, based on his own experience, about the therapeutic value of psychoanalysis, Witkacy admired Freud as a thinker whose ideas made possible his own sexual theories of creativity. Art, philosophy, and politics are all perceived by the Polish author in sexual imagery; the creative impulse itself is "a desire to violate the universe," and the interplay among social classes is an ill-disguised longing to rape. Having lived through the erotic revolution at the turn of the century and absorbed Schopenhauer and Otto Weininger's influential *Sex and Character* (1903), Witkacy in his novels and plays was able to dramatize the insecurities and tensions in the sexual relations of men and women as symptomatic of a larger irrational threat to order, on both a personal and social plane, suspending all norms and hurling mankind back to primordial chaos. A direct assault on individual consciousness, reducing one's inmost self to nothingness (in other words, to species-ness), sexuality is an absurd, alien force. Hence, the eternal war of the sexes, the abject male fear of the all-devouring woman, or "praying mantis." But in marked contrast to the deadly seriousness with which these demonic sexual themes were treated by Strindberg, Munch, Przybyszewski, and the other modernists, Witkacy speeded up the seductions and rendered hilarious the erotic stereotypes, which by the early twentieth century were already on a downward slide to boulevard farce and lurid thriller.

By politicizing sex and eroticizing politics, the Polish dramatist succeeded in transposing both of these essential realms of human experience into what he called "a sixth-dimensional continuum." In this respect *Janulka, Daughter of Fizdejko* is undoubtedly his most daring Pure Form experiment in creating a totally autonomous dramatic universe that refers to nothing outside itself; and yet at the same time its kaleidoscopic images—composed of bright colored fragments that are shaken out in ever-changing patterns—seem an eerie refraction of our own dislocated world.

For Witkacy's friend, the mathematician and artist Leon Chwistek (whose theory of the plurality of realities figures prominently in the play), *Janulka* dramatizes "the struggles of a brilliant thinker at the outermost limits of knowledge." In *Janulka* the playwright not only applies the principles of modern science—strangely congruent with mythic and oneiric thinking—to old-fashioned notions of plot and character but also makes this application the subject of dramatic discourse. The new physics, mathematics, and geometry, along with Schönberg's atonality and Picasso's cubism, shape the dramatis personae's perceptions of art and history and fashion their consciousness of self and its relations to the world. The second law of thermodynamics becomes the principal source of theatrical tension. The real dramatic issue in *Janulka* is the "overcoming of entropy"—the ceaseless struggle with encroaching nothingness, the unending task of erecting psychic superstructures.

In response to the optimistic utilitarianism of the Russian constructivists and their building of a new society and a new human nature, the Polish author opposes an entropic view of a postrevolutionary world of endless, meaningless change and deepening stagnation where all that remains is the fabrication of artificial selves and kingdoms. Creativity has turned in upon itself. Not only does the universe move increasingly toward disorder and death, but the very forms of creation are self-destructive. The central problem is how to live in a deteriorating universe. Life grows ever more gray, boring, and repetitious; everything has already been said and done. After having been predigested by previous centuries, culture is available to be consumed and reconsumed. Past dramas are constantly recycled.

Witkacy is a virtuoso at the rechewing of the past. The starting point for *Janulka* is a popular nineteenth-century historical romance, *Pojata, Daughter of Lezdejko; or, Lithuania in the Fourteenth Century* by Feliks Bernatowicz. Through the deformation of a few names, characters, and details of setting and costume pillaged from Bernatowicz, the playwright begins to construct his "artificial" realm. The parody grows voracious, and it is not Bernatowicz but Shakespeare's histories and tragedies that serve Witkacy as the model for the dynastic struggles in postcommunist Lithuania. The characters are ghosts at a séance. For the conjuring up of the spirits of the dead and the cycle of repeated killings, *Macbeth* is the parodied text, but *Macbeth* read in the light of Jarry's *Ubu Roi*, Einstein's theory of relativity, and Oswald Spengler's historiography. The dramatis personae (derived from an earlier writer's "creation") engage in "transformational exercises," assume new costumes and identities, play inventive games, and enact imaginary lives. *Janulka* may be read as a work about the pitfalls of creating Pure Form in life.

Witkacy's mythical Lithuania is a special workshop for exploring the future of entropic societies. Its rulers and subjects, intensely self-conscious and yet unsure of their own reality, devote themselves almost exclusively to the study of history—personal, national, and universal. They do not know whether they are living in the fourteenth or the twenty-third century. Civilizations have become freely displaced in time. *Janulka* is a revisionist history play about the nature of modern history, feeding upon and devouring its own subject matter.

"History has doubled back until its nose touches its backside and now it's eating its own tail," Janulka explains. Witkacy places his drama under the sign of the Ouroborus, the mythical tail-biting serpent that symbolizes both spatial and temporal infinity and the primordial self. Its ending is its beginning. The eternally closed circle contains the antinomic forces of life and death, energy and entropy, golden age and apocalypse. The circular shape of the tail-eating snake leads directly into the negatively curved Möbius universe, where one can wander forever and never get out. The Grand Master of the Neo-Teutonic Knights announces that "history is starting to flow backwards." The drama being enacted forever recoils upon itself. "This has all been a bad dream," Fizdejko explains. "We're starting everything all over again."

At the last minute a possible key to *Janulka* and its enigma suggests itself to the characters: perhaps they have all been dreaming the same dream. Of his friend and contemporary Bruno Schulz, Witkacy wrote that he "objectified the dream, made it intersubjective and intelligible for all in its 'auto-individuality.' " The same can be said of the dreaming mind that controls the hermetically sealed world of *Janulka*—it is intersubjective and has fashioned a deforming image of the senseless chaos and brutality of twentieth-century history; in the modern state the greatest barbarians are able to live in the highest form of technological civilization.

In plays like *Janulka*, Witkacy's accomplishment was to create a new autonomous theatrical language, based on linguistic playfulness, verbal games, and a variety of juxtaposed "performance" styles. Polish critics in the 1920s noticed the disjunction of action and dialogue in Witkacy's dramas and objected to the refusal of these two elements to run on the same track. The dramatis personae wander off into disquisitions on culture, philosophy, mathematics, and aesthetics, quote the author's own theories of Pure Form and the death of art, and then suddenly make fervid declarations of love or shoot one another.

The words themselves come from different provenances: the secret codes of the adolescent Witkacy and his friends Malinowski, Chwistek, and Szymanowski; philosophic and scientific jargon; the hyperbole of Polish modernism and its passion for capitalized abstractions: Nothingness, Death, Diabolical, Demonic. The playwright reveals the theatrical values—the acoustic and rhythmic dynamics—of garrulity, gibberish, and garbling. The flow of the discourse is never linear or univocal but sinuous in its constant revisions and reversals of course that establish the back and forth motion of free play.

The terrible intensity, the absolute feelings of modernist posturing are subverted, viewed as heightened performance, put in the context of theater. The same process of self-deflation transforms the author's ideas from ideological matter into elements of drama as soon as his own philosophical views become subject to the mutually deforming performances of his interlocutors.

"Please do not attribute any objective significance to the opinions expressed by the characters in these plays," the author cautions, denying that he ever used the stage to express his ideas.

"In art (and quite possibly in life too) everything depends exclusively on the connections," Witkacy asserts in *The Only Way Out*. His works in Pure Form break the single code of either realism or fantasy by destroying the familiar connections of traditional storytelling and psychology, and by severing the usual coordination of action and dialogue. Once these disconnections have been effected, entirely new sets of formal relations can be established, enabling author and audience to recapture their sense of wonder at the fact of existence and to experience metaphysical feelings. By his theory of Pure Form, Witkacy hoped to disconnect the mimetic links of cause and effect imposed by material reality—in other words, to defuse "real" life with all its accelerating pressures leading to the growth of an anthill society—for the sake of art and its eternal truths.

"The development of an artist is a battle with life as raw material for the purpose of creating formal constructions in which form will dominate content," Witkacy the theorist of Pure Form declared. Yet it soon became apparent that in the struggle of form with content Witkacy was backing a losing position. Already in the plays, even those designated as tending to Pure Form, such as *The New Deliverance*, the forces of social reality kept intruding, much as the masked figure and six thugs had burst into the drama uninvited. In the public arena, a growing desire to comment on social issues made Witkacy gradually abandon his role as a formalist instigator of metaphysical feelings. In the personal sphere, owing to desperate financial circumstances, the artist—forced by poverty to live in his mother's rooming house in Zakopane—could not afford the role of a detached creator. "Money nowhere to be found, hotel empty, again I have to work on those ugly mugs," the artist complained to his wife, Jadwiga Unrug (who lived apart from her husband in Warsaw), lamenting the necessity of earning his living by painting portraits.

4.

Although there was never any absolute break, 1924 constituted a major turning point in Witkacy's career. It was then that he definitively abandoned painting as an art and became a commercial portraitist. He began to formulate the rules of the S. I. Witkiewicz Portrait-Painting Firm, a complex intellectual and artistic ploy expressive of the artist's deepest impulses and in many ways comparable to Marcel Duchamp's renunciation of art for a program of irony and destruction at exactly the same time. Like a dadaist provocateur, Witkacy declared his career as an artist finished and created a mock-capitalist enterprise that gave exhibitions of its works and issued a brochure (published in 1928 and reissued in 1932) designed to attract bourgeois customers.

The firm's clientele fell into three groups: first, the paying customers—merchants, officials, and their wives and children—who preferred the most conventional likenesses; second, women with striking and unusual faces, whom Witkacy regarded as "mediums" offering inspiration and fit subjects for repeated sessions; and third, friends—doctors, philosophers, artists, and writers—for whom Witkacy, under the influence of drugs, did wildly distorted portraits for free. The deformed work he always signed as Witkacy; the straightforward portraits as Witkiewicz.

At the same time, Witkacy turned away from the writing of drama, where, because of the immediate sensuous impact in the theater, Pure Form was possible (as it also was in music and painting) and devoted himself to the composition of impure, mixed genres that directly addressed social and political issues and expressed the author's opinions—and from which he frankly hoped to make money. Theater, a pure and sacred domain, he would never so exploit. After having spent the six years since his return from Russia attempting to provide models for Pure Form in painting and theater, the author henceforth devoted all his energies to writing cultural and social criticism for newspapers and journals, popularizing his philosophical and aesthetic views, lecturing on his theories (he spoke too fast, too softly, and too indistinctly to be effective on the podium) and engaging in polemics with his many enemies and detractors.

Considering the fictional genre to be "a bag into which you can cram everything without paying any attention to Pure Form," Witkacy composed in rapid succession two long dystopian novels, *Farewell to Autumn* (written 1925–26, published 1927) and *Insatiability* (written 1927–28, published 1930). The Witkacian fictional "grab bag" eschews any conscious experimentation with narrative technique but stretches the traditional nineteenth-century novel completely out of shape through a monstrous infusion of erotic adventures, philosophical speculations, and apocalyptic predictions of coming disaster, which are sardonically presented by the author's alter ego serving as narrator.

Set sometime in the future during the last days of a disintegrating capitalist regime (unnamed but resembling Poland) menaced by totalitarian revolution, *Farewell to Autumn* portrays a social crisis that is at the same time an individual crisis of identity for each of the characters. Social and psychic breakdown coincide as anxious dread grips a dying breed of crazed artists, philosophers, and playboys struggling frantically to give meaning to life. "No one realized exactly who he was (not metaphysically now, but socially), given the complicated and transitory structures of society. . . . They all felt death within themselves more or less consciously."

Witkacy paints the collective state of mind of an entire class undergoing extinction. Sinister boredom and emptiness prevail. Everyone desires to change and start a new life, but the only transformation possible in the ersatz world of *Farewell to Autumn* is pseudomorphosis. Witkacy has taken the term from Spengler's *Decline of the West*. In mineralogy pseudomorphosis refers to the process by which new molten masses from volcanic outbursts, not free to find their own special forms, are forced to fill hollow molds in rock strata whose crystals have been washed out. Applied to the growth of civilizations, historical pseudomorphosis results when a new culture cannot develop its own forms but must twist and deform the established shapes.

As used by Witkacy, pseudomorphosis serves to characterize the process by which the new grows misshapen when trapped in old forms. The external shell remains unchanged while a radically different inner content attempts to grow within its confines. Pseudomorphosis is Witkacy's chief dramaturgical and novelistic method. Old character types and plots—the preexistent theatrical and fictional molds available to the author—are filled with new content and fresh sensibility but cannot produce new forms. Instead, the old forms are wrenched and distorted into incredibly grotesque shapes.

Philosophical discourse lies at the heart of *Farewell to Autumn*. Athanasius Bazakbal, the antihero of the novel, is a superfluous man, a pseudo-Hamlet, an artist manqué for whom "conversation is the most essential way of experiencing life." At first a series of colloquies between Athanasius and his friends and lovers about art, sex, and social revolution, *Farewell to Autumn* ultimately becomes a desperate dialogue of the hero with himself as he journeys through the mountains under the influence of cocaine. Up against the "metaphysical wall," the mind in extremis races wildly in its attempt to know the universe.

The eighth and final chapter of *Farewell to Autumn*, "The Mystery of an Autumn Morning," recounts Athanasius's return from India to his newly Communized homeland and his escape into the mountains, where he finds the self-destruction he has been seeking for so long. For Athanasius—and his creator—climbing mountain peaks was a sure way of rising above the terrible banality of everyday life, of fleeing the anthill society and leaving behind civilization, the world, and all its constraints.

Cocaine and snow-covered mountains are Athanasius's death-white companions in his final battle against the red of revolution. The sweeping view from the heights arouses metaphysical feelings and permits the dreamer to look to a future in which individualism can flourish on a mass scale. Mountain peaks are nature's eternal response to the false creed of the levelers. But although he makes a Nietzschean ascent into the mountains followed by a descent into the valley with a great message for mankind, Athanasius is no true prophet or Zarathustra. He is dependent on drugs for his vision of a transformed humanity. The mountains and cocaine are Athanasius's two interlocutors: the first a genuine source of metaphysical wonder, the second an artificial (and destructive) way of trying to regain the lost mystery. His encounter with the she-bear brings him back to earth. By throwing cocaine in her face, he escapes from the beast only to meet the Russian "bear," whom he cannot evade.

In his earlier confrontations with collectivity in the Bolshevized capital, Athanasius recoiled from the regimented work and play, compulsory sports and physical togetherness, thought control, and insect purposefulness. In these activities Witkacy forecast the totalitarian movements of the 1930s, but in his hero's final monologue the author looks far ahead to the possibility of reversing the course of history and undoing the fatal legacy of communism. Athanasius poses the question: can individual creativity be reinstated after the inert uniformity of an entropic regime? Athanasius's paradoxical solution (conceived on the "highs" of the mountains and cocaine) is to remetaphysicalize humankind—not by a return to mealymouthed democracy (meaning liberal capitalism) and its iniquities, but by using all the social mechanisms of the state to foster the individual. Athanasius's tragicomic attempt to set history flowing backward inevitably ends in personal disaster—as it also would for Witkacy on an autumn day near the Russian border twelve years later.

For Witkacy the issue remained a real one. How could the direction of socialization be changed so that it would promote, not destroy, human creativity? By seeking to reconcile metaphysical sentiments with the inevitable transformations of society toward greater progress, Witkacy, like Athanasius, hoped to safeguard continuity with past art and culture.

In Witkacy's novels content had clearly triumphed over form, but even along these "real-life" coordinates the Polish writer's primary concern still remained the problem of artistic creativity. The representative of a worn-out generation and a vanishing intelligentsia threatened by revolution, Witkacy produced cultural criticism in which he examined the position of the artist in a changing social order that rendered his own status (as a proponent of Pure Form) obsolete and untenable.

Thus Witkacy was obsessed by the fundamental questions posed by modernist literature during the interwar years concerning the results of historical change, manifested by war and revolution, for the inherited past of Europe and the fate of Western civilization. After the events of 1917 the Russian symbolist poet Aleksandr Blok proclaimed the end of humanism based on an elitist belief in the individual and welcomed the triumph of the barbarian masses. The religious thinker Nikolay Berdyayev, the historian Oswald Spengler, and the philosopher José Ortega y Gasset, among others, addressed these same issues, without, however, welcoming the approaching cataclysm. Even before the outbreak of war and revolution, seismographic sensibilities like Blok and Witkacy felt a deep sense of malaise, forecasting the catastrophe to come and signaling the end of civilization and art as hitherto known.

As a cultural critic, Witkacy was unsparing in his analysis of the failure of the intellectual strata to play a creative role in social change during the 1930s, when totalitarian ideologies on both the right and left were imposing rigid controls in the name of the masses. Witkacy's political stance shifted constantly but was ultimately ambivalent. Denying that he was a reactionary opposed to social progress and the general welfare, the Polish author acknowledged the inevitability of the leveling forces transforming society but pointed out the disastrous consequence of a happy, tranquilized society for the individual and the tragic sense of life upon which art, religion, and philosophy depend. Although he condemned the liberal capitalist regimes of the West as rotten, Witkacy had none of the illusions held by Western leftists about the new Soviet system, having witnessed at firsthand the revolution in the East.

By their failure to play any guiding role in the great cataclysmic events of revolution, artists and intellectuals had been rendered superfluous. In the utopia of the future—and all utopias are totalitarian—Witkacy feared that art would be either domesticated to serve the purposes of the state or totally nullified. In seeking to preserve cultural values and maintain tradition, while at the same time admitting the obsolescence and irrelevance of the intelligentsia, he attempted to resolve contradictory attitudes with a plea for historical continuity between old and new, past and future. At pains to preserve individual creativity within a mass society, the Polish artist protested against cultural repression in the USSR—believing above all in the value of free philosophical inquiry.

Several of Witkacy's later books—*Narcotics* (1932), *The Only Way Out* (1931–33), and *Unwashed Souls* (1936)—are indeterminate as to genre. These heterodox speculative works, mixing sociology, art theory, philosophy, and cultural criticism with personal observations and confessions, push to extremes one of Witkacy's favorite disconnective devices: digression. Of *Unwashed Souls*, the author declared, "I see that this book will consist only of digressions; it will simply be one long digression." The ardent proponent of Pure Form was also a grand master of digression. Abandoning the search for a transcendent form that would directly reflect the mystery of existence, Witkacy now approached the problem from an opposite, pragmatic point of view in "instructive" handbooks and treatises (containing advice on the treatment of hemorrhoids and suggesting shaving techniques) designed to be socially useful and written to make money. "Desperate financial situation," the writer avowed in 1928. "If it weren't for the novel [*Insatiability*], hunger would be unavoidable. I am writing the book on drugs in haste. I'll make some dough on it."

Often taking the shape of polemic attack or confessional revelation, Witkacy's essayistic excursions in the realm of self-help literature are demystifications that go behind the scenes of Pure Form and explain the effects discursively, that is, by entering into the reasons why certain phenomena produce metaphysical feelings, rather than by actually calling them forth. Digression, like Pure Form, derails normal connections. Witkacy wields his parenthetical weapons in dialogic battles with himself, interrupting the flow of argumentation in midstream and revising his ideas in the act of thinking them (a device made use of by Dostoyevsky in *Notes from the Underground* and later taken up by Kafka and Céline). In this way the Polish writer captures the process of thought, the workings of the brain under pressure, the creative act as it is performed.

In his last extensive philosophical work, *The Psycho-physical Problem* (1932–39, published posthumously in 1984), Witkacy abandoned the concept of metaphysical feelings, historiography, and the ontology of art and took up strictly philosophical issues dealing with the sources and limits of cognition and the structure and substance of nature. In this way the apocalyptic playwright was able in his last years to make a rather more optimistic prognosis about the fate of philosophy in the future.

5.

Drugs played a major role in Witkacy's life, both as a stimulant to creativity and as a metaphor for other essential modes of experience. The author of *Narcotics* was for most of his adult life addicted to nicotine, and he used—and abused—alcohol, cocaine, and other narcotics. He found drugs an indispensable means of disconnecting the usual real-life mental circuits that inhibited his creative powers. In his essay "The Psychology of the Creative Work," the Russian modernist Yevgeny Zamyatin (a writer often compared to Witkacy because of his antiutopian vision of the anthill future) asserted that writers use narcotics to put the conscious mind to sleep and free the imagination. Once again Witkacy's attitude was ambiguous; while warning against all forms of addiction, he indicated that nothing can equal the visions produced by certain drugs and confessed his own inability to stop taking them. In *The Only Way Out* (a novel he called his "double") he gave a detailed account of creating Pure Form in painting while taking large doses of cocaine. Like Antonin Artaud, Henri Michaux, and André Masson, the Polish artist was fascinated by the interplay between drugs and art.

In its Type C offerings, the Portrait-Painting Firm produced works under the influence of drugs and alcohol. These were usually noncommissioned portraits for friends, characterized by extreme distortion of a psychedelic nature, sometimes oneiric and mystical in character. Different drugs or combinations of drugs were used by the artist to produce widely varying effects. What Witkacy called the metaphysical or antisocial drugs—peyote and mescaline—evoked the strangeness of existence, as opposed to the "realistic" narcotics: "eucodal," ether, cocaine, nicotine, and alcohol. The portraits painted under the influence of peyote (obtained from Alexandre Rouhier, a French drug expert) utilize the colors red, violet, blue, and lemon yellow and contain geometric forms, reptiles, and monsters. These peyote heads, executed in detail, often hang suspended in the air, above mountain landscapes or surrounded by mediumistic nebulae. Hashish, on the other hand, produced doubles, of both people and things. The combination of peyote, cocaine, and alcohol led to strong deformation of the face and dark colors: black, brown, violet, and red with thick, heavy lines.

The uncanny self-portraits that Witkacy executed shortly before his suicide, in 1938–39, were called forth by small doses of beer and cocaine. Like Freud, the Polish artist was drawn to the "white fairy," even though he felt it to be the most pernicious of narcotics. In all cases, he indicated on the portrait in abbreviations the type of drug he had been using, and also the number of smoking or nonsmoking days, as well as the number of drinking or nondrinking days. For Witkacy, these artificial means were a final attempt to recapture, if only briefly, the metaphysical feelings that had been lost to social progress.

Nietzsche had repeatedly gone to the imagery of drugs for his assessment of human culture as a painkiller designed to counter the depression caused by the contemplation of existence. For Witkacy, the metaphoric use of narcotics is central to his cultural criticism. "Art is an escape, the noblest of drugs, that can transport us to another world without bad effects on the health or the intelligence," he asserted in the early 1920s. Only later did he begin to have doubts about the efficacy of the drug "Art." Eventually, he came to fear that the new mass totalitarian societies, by means of mental regimentation and social tranquilization, would do away with any need for narcotics, in either the literal or the figurative sense.

6.

Complaining that the sort of intellectual novel he would like to read did not exist, Witkacy decided that he must write such fiction himself, even though he would gain neither money nor recognition from his efforts. Witkacy denied that the novel can be a work of art, because fiction that claims to represent reality does not act directly through its form; content is the dominant element. Nonetheless, in 1934 when Witkacy first read Bruno Schulz (whose work he then helped to promote through articles and interviews), he was forced to admit that *Cinnamon Shops* produced a "staggering impression" and achieved Pure Form in many of its parts.

The Only Way Out (of which only the first part was ever written) is the least narrative of Witkacy's four novels; philosophical discussion and artistic activity have almost entirely replaced plot and character. Living under a repressive totalitarian regime some time in the future, three figures in a triangular configuration—Marcel, a painter, Isidore, a philosopher, and his wife, Rustalka, Marcel's former love—pass the time in "essential" conversations. The two protagonists are doubles into which the author has split; the schizoid theorist Isidore is a thinking, perceiving mind, whereas the pyknic artist Marcel—the creator as metaphysicalized beast—believes that the true artist destroys himself. Yet at the end of the novel (or as much of it as exists) it is the creative Marcel who cuts the throat of his philosophical alter ego, Isidore, in a form of artistic suicide whereby he murders an integral part of himself. "The only way out" indicated by the title is no longer art, or even philosophy (for Witkacy the most durable of man's quests for meaning), but a desperate act of self-annihilation. Stripped of its ontological mystery, existence is a gray reign of boredom, and the games played by the artist and philosopher as they await death can only postpone the grim end.

Striving to express the inexpressible, Witkacy often questioned the possibility of writing fiction and cast doubt on the nature and value of fictional representation. Confronted with the fact that all a writer can do is repeat things long since formulated and use a literary language already exhausted, he was driven to the invention of nonexistent words such as *kalamarpaxa*, explaining, "This expression is given as an ideal example of a newly coined word whose meaning remains undefined and primarily onomatopoetic, and which in a given context . . . can have . . . a purely artistic (= formal) meaning." In such a fashion, he strove to reintroduce formal values within the loose, baggy structure of the novel.

In his final years, Witkacy felt increasingly isolated and sensed the coming of the world disaster he had foreseen from afar. Suicide runs like a leitmotiv throughout the playwright's life and works, from the time of his fiancée's self-destruction in 1914 until his death by his own hand in 1939. "I often think about suicide," he wrote to a friend in 1937. "It's going to be necessary to bring my life to an end a bit earlier that way, out of a sense of honor, so as not to live to see my own total downfall. Even philosophy, unfortunately, won't see me to the very end." Although he always struggled against disintegration, first through art, then through philosophy, seeking totality in an overarching interpretation of existence, Witkacy now experienced the despondency of physical and psychic exhaustion. "I feel a nightmare that encircles me all around and soon will choke me," he confessed to the German philosopher Hans Cornelius in 1938. "I am absolutely *old*. . . . The old portrait prostitute (as I have called myself) has been doomed to annihilation."

Witkacy had consumed himself as an artist; his whole career was only a slow prelude to suicide. He who had so long resisted definition was finally "fixed" in a role that he abhorred: a decrepit whore plying a noncreative trade. After the Nazis invaded Poland on 1 September 1939, Witkacy fled to the east. He had reached the little village of Jeziory (now in the Ukraine) when word came on 17 September that the Soviets had attacked and the Red Army would soon arrive. There was no way out. During the night of 18 September 1939, Witkacy killed himself by slashing his wrists and cutting his throat. The void had triumphed—for the time being.

Witkacy showed uncanny skill in predicting his own resurrection some twenty years later. On a striking portrait all in dark red, done in 1931, there is the inscription: "For the posthumous exhibition in 1955." It was in 1956 that Tadeusz Kantor opened his theater Cricot II in Cracow with *The Cuttlefish*, the first postwar production of Witkacy's work. Bizarre contradictions continued to pursue the playwright as he slowly won fame and acceptance in the sort of leveling mass society he had said would mean the death of art. Like one of his own dramatic heroes, Witkacy rose from the dead to enjoy a triumphant second life in Communist Poland, where he successfully battled censors and commissars. The year 1985, the one hundredth anniversary of his birth, was declared the "Year of Witkacy" by UNESCO, and the Polish People's Republic issued commemorative postage stamps bearing his self-portraits. Was this recognition the long-awaited justification of his existence, or the ultimate realization of his fears?

An ironic answer to this question came in 1988 when the Polish Ministry of Culture finally decided to act on the long deferred plan (first initiated by the Writers' Union many years earlier) to bring Witkacy's "mortal remains" back to Zakopane. There, it was decreed, the playwright would be given a state funeral accorded only to Poland's greatest writers.

Witkacy had been hastily buried in Jeziory in the old Orthodox cemetery in a coffin made of simple planks of wood. A pine cross bore the writer's name carved with a penknife. Neglected for many years, the grave and marker had become effaced. In the 1970s a tombstone and plaque were clandestinely placed on the site by a former Polish resident of Jeziory whose parents had sheltered Witkacy for several days in that distant September and who returned illegally to pay tribute to the playwright. Before glasnost, the USSR would not permit Poles to travel to their former lands for any such purpose.

All that had radically changed by 11 April 1988, when the body of the revered author was publicly exhumed at Jeziory before the assembled Ukrainian and Polish party dignitaries. After the panegyrical speeches by the bureaucrats, the sealed coffin was officially handed over to the Polish delegation, along with an X-ray photograph of its contents. When a Witkacy scholar traveling with the Polish delegation took a look at the X ray, he immediately pointed out that the skull contained a full set of teeth, whereas the playwright had had many extractions. The photograph mysteriously disappeared, and the ceremonies proceeded as scheduled.

When the body of the "false Witkacy" arrived in Zakopane on 13 April, a week of festivities began at the Witkiewicz Theater (an outstanding private theater established in 1985). There were eulogies, lectures, concerts, films, and theatrical performances from throughout Poland. On 14 April "Witkacy's remains," draped in the national colors and decked with mounds of flowers, were displayed in the lobby of the theater. An honor guard composed of leading Zakopane citizens, actors, and relatives led the funeral procession. The coffin was transported to the cemetery on a local peasant wagon drawn by horses caparisoned in black, followed by a huge crowd of fifty thousand, including representatives of the central government, delegations from the Ukraine, and leaders in Polish arts and sciences. The minister of culture spoke at the grave site, as did the deputy minister of culture from the Ukraine. An orchestra of Tatras Mountain highlanders played on folk instruments, and a solemn funeral mass was celebrated. The body of the "false Witkacy" was placed in his mother's tomb, a few steps from where his wife is buried (his father's grave is at the other end of the cemetery). A large tombstone proclaims the return of the author to his native land.

The fraud was exposed almost immediately, and the ensuing scandal led to accusations and recriminations as to who was responsible for the grotesque farce. All true admirers of Witkacy rejoiced that the playwright— famous for his "risen corpses"—had succeeded in evading the authorities once again. Their author had staged yet another posthumous triumph. The Communist cultural hierarchy, which for years had suppressed his work, censored his books, and tried to keep his plays off the stage, could seize possession of neither his body nor his spirit. The officials and bureaucrats who "honored" the author of *Farewell to Autumn* by burying an unidentified skeleton in his mother's grave have now faded into oblivion. Witkacy's corpse enjoys its lonely freedom no one knows precisely where. Here is an author capable of appearing and disappearing unexpectedly. He will continue to surprise a world that has never understood him.

Fascinated by the strange fate of the poet and playwright Tadeusz Miciński, who had been killed in the Ukraine in 1918 without leaving behind a trace, Witkacy often said that he too would like to have no grave. How splendid, he exclaimed, that all the world knows a writer and finds him everywhere, even though there are no material remains. May that be his epitaph.

PART I: WITKIEWICZ FATHER AND SON:
YOUNG STAŚ'S UPBRINGING
1885-1914

The Witkiewiczes were a large upper-class family from Polish Lithuania, impoverished but with "good connections." They were related to Józef Piłsudski, Poland's political strongman in the interwar years, and to the Gielguds, of whom the British actor, Sir John, is the celebrated offspring. Russian tyranny over Poland shaped the family's destiny. The playwright's great uncle, Jan Witkiewicz (1806–39), after first being arrested for anti-tsarist activities, became a highly trusted Russian secret agent, prized for his mastery of Middle Eastern languages and impenetrable disguises and engaged in complex missions against the British in the struggle between the two empires for dominance over Persia and Afghanistan. The writer's father, Stanisław Witkiewicz (1851–1915), as an adolescent spent four years in Siberia with his father, who had been exiled and deprived of his property for taking part in the Uprising of 1863. After studying art in St. Petersburg and Munich, he came back to Warsaw in 1871 to make his name as a painter and cultural critic. Handsome and charismatic, Stanisław Witkiewicz achieved the status of a national sage, preaching a patriotic gospel of creative renewal through a return to native Polish arts and crafts.

Born in 1885 in Warsaw—and thus a Russian subject in his partitioned homeland—Witkacy grew up and spent most of his life in the picturesque mountain town of Zakopane (then a part of the Austro-Hungarian Empire), where in 1890 his father had moved for reasons of health. There Witkiewicz senior made his only son the object of an unusual educational experiment. "As your painting progresses, you're going to be a marvelous proof of the truth of my theories of art," the father explained to his son. The cornerstone of these theories was Witkiewicz senior's belief in the creative power of the untrammeled self developing in harmony with nature. As a proponent of extreme individuality, independence of character, and personal talent, the father was opposed to all formal education (he himself had no high school diploma), on the grounds that it enforced mediocrity and conformism. "In our times," Witkiewicz senior wrote, "school is completely at odds with the psychological makeup of human beings. . . . The methods of instruction and the goals of learning have nothing in common with the living person and with real life."

Accordingly, Staś was not sent to school with the local peasant boys and never had any formal education (although at his own insistence and over his father's objections he did take the secondary school examinations and earn the diploma). Instead, he was truly self-educated, allowed to study what he wanted, when he wanted—assisted by his father and various distinguished tutors—and to develop his talents freely and precociously. The family's home in Zakopane was an intellectual center visited by the best artists and writers of the time (including the young Yiddish writer Sholem Ash), and the boy came into daily contact with art through his father's painting and writing and his mother's piano playing and music lessons.

By the time he was three Staś was producing drawings, highly praised by his father, and he started painting in oils when he was only five. At the age of six, the young artist turned from painting to the piano and began improvising and composing. At the same time he became interested in various scientific ventures: collecting rocks and insects and constructing museums to house them.

Staś's next passion—one that was to stay with him throughout his life—was for the theater. "He is terribly interested in everything that's written in dialogue form," his father commented. "Perhaps that's due to the influence of Helena." The boy's godmother was Helena Modjeska, the famous Polish-American actress, with whom Witkiewicz senior had been in love. The child set up a small theater in the house and wrote a number short plays, some of which he then printed and published himself on his own hand-printing press. His father copied by hand many of these comedies and sent them to various relatives, noting that they contain "such authentic details taken from our life and such well observed typical traits."

A boyhood friend, Władysław Matlakowski (who appears in the *Comedies of Family Life* as Kiesio) describes how Staś came under Shakespeare's influence.

> From childhood on Staś had unlimited freedom in the choice of the books he wanted to read, and no interests were imposed on him either. His father considered that there should not be any restrictions on the independent development of the individual and consistently avoided being directive to such an extent that he did not even exert any pressure on his son to begin learning to read and write. Staś learned to read and

write without anyone's help and wrote for some time in big, printed letters. . . . Very early he began to read Shakespeare's works, which were lent to him by my father, who was then working on *Hamlet*. Under the influence of this reading he tried writing works for the stage.

Much later, in 1905 when Staś was twenty, his father wrote explaining other influences behind the childhood plays. "When you wrote your comedies and dramas, you were an exceptionally subtle observer of life. . . . And at the same time you were under the influence of Shakespeare, Fredro, Gogol (whom I translated for you), and Maeterlinck, consequently quite a varied influence, but principally childish observation (involuntary, like good observation) of life held it all together and gave it order and point, completely in earnest."

Prophetically, Witkiewicz senior recognized that the curious mixture of joking and seriousness in these childhood plays was an expression of his son's inmost nature and predicted that eventually under the right circumstances he would turn into a writer and transform parody into his most powerful creative weapon.

You wrote as a joke. . . . Now . . . it seems to you something not serious—a farce. And often it was a farce, but in making that farce, quite unawares you are following a serious need and you are putting into what you write entirely essential elements of your soul. . . . You constantly mix up those essential things with that inclination for parody, done with a perfect feeling for the nature of the things parodied, and because of that you are constantly in a nonserious relationship to your own need and talent for writing. . . . One day there will come some chance happening, some pressure from life, which will take those slighted and yet very valuable elements of creative strength and concentrate them, hammer them into their own appropriate form crystallized out of themselves—and there is the writer.

The eight-year-old Staś was surrounded by a variety of forms of artistic representation. Daddy painted pictures in his studio. Everyone posed and postured in front of the camera, which became a speaking character in the *Comedies of Family Life*. Playing, enactment, and capturing likenesses were favored activities in the Witkiewicz household. When the young playwright Staś set out to represent the world of his childhood, the fledgling artist placed himself at the center as the creator of the dramatic scenes. Family life assumed the shape of a series of "comedies" reflecting the artistic narcissism and self-reflexivity so fashionable in the fin de siècle Hapsburg Empire.

In urging his son to become whatever he wanted, the elder Witkiewicz considered himself to be a loving and permissive parent, but for the immature adolescent, homebound and deprived of schoolmates, his father's relentless commands to be creative proved a kind of cultural oppression more insidious than ordinary philistine browbeating by a crass bourgeois patriarch. Staś felt obliged to be an artist or nothing. Witkiewicz senior practiced coercion in the name of the highest moral and aesthetic ideals, and his unremitting supervision of his son's psychic development became an extension of his public role of teacher of the nation.

In more than five hundred letters of passionate instruction, often sounding like a blend of Zarathustra and Polonius, the elder Witkiewicz urged his son to be spiritually unfettered and to shun unworthy male and female companions. "We must go ever forward, my precious!" the father wrote in 1903. "In intellectual concepts reach to infinity, in social ideas, go to the ultimate extremes of boundless universal love." Instead of pursuing selfish pleasures, the boy was told to rise above his lower nature and create a new "I." This Nietzschean concept of self-transcendence and perpetual renewal, which would be the driving force behind expressionist art and drama, haunted Witkacy throughout his life, appearing in his mature works as a formula for disaster.

Attempts at self-construction and "starting a new life" inevitably failed. Instead of directing the boy's energies to outer goals, Witkiewicz senior's exhortations simply focused his son's attention on an experimental study of his own personality that led to brooding self-absorption. As a child Staś had been free to play at art and life, finding both a great game, but upon reaching maturity the young man suffered persistent difficulty in achieving personal definition and a sense of calling. Although he began exhibiting his paintings as early as 1901, the future playwright found it impossible to commit himself to any career, owing to inner doubts and a Nietzschean compulsion to live all the things that he had within him.

The adolescent Staś attempted to manipulate his own identity and that of others through artifice and disguise. A playmate from his childhood days, Maria Sienkiewicz (daughter of the Nobel Prize-winning author of *Quo Vadis*), wrote of the young Witkacy:

He used to lie. . . . And he was always playing some role or other. He was never himself. Most likely that is why his talent for painting, which at first seemed much more promising, grew warped and stunted. And he was singularly nasty to his father. The elder Witkiewicz suffered greatly on his account. Perhaps the father was simply too good and too gentle for such an unruly temperament. Staś himself later said when he was grown up that he blamed his father for not beating him.

At the beginning of the new century the elder Witkiewicz moved to the seaside resort of Lovranno, on the Istrian peninsula (now in Croatia), settling there permanently in 1908. The ostensible reason for the move was his declining health (he was fatally ill with tuberculosis), but the great man was accompanied by a female admirer who paid his bills, and he left behind in Zakopane a wife now compelled to keep a rooming house in order to support herself and her twenty-three-year-old son. Witkacy had already begun to oppose the imposition of his father's ideas, and in the growing estrangement between Stanisław Witkiewicz and his wife, the son took the side of his adored mother. Open hostilities between these two powerful individuals first broke out when Witkacy left home in 1905 to attend the Academy of Fine Arts in Cracow, where he was an off-and-on-again student for the next year and a half. The young man's decision to "conform" pained his father, who wrote: "What a peculiar mixture of contradictions life is, and must each new generation unfailingly be the antithesis and reaction to the previous one? Did we really battle against the servitude of the school and herd mentality in art so that you and your peers could actually feel at home in the school system?"

In Cracow Witkacy studied drawing, neglected in the elder Witkiewicz's pedagogic system, and became acquainted with modernist paintings and painters. He also frequented bohemian circles and visited the Green Balloon artistic cabaret famous for its parodies and mockery of all styles and conventions.

In his own artistic development Witkacy now moved away from an initial orientation to landscape, his father's preferred genre, and soon abandoned forever faithful reproductions of nature for bizarre pictures—called "monsters" by his admiring father—of demons, doubles, and other phantasms locked in libidinal duels and Oedipal family dramas. These charcoal drawings, bearing such titles as *The Prince of Darkness Tempts Saint Theresa with the Aid of a Waiter from Budapest, A Man with Dropsy Lies in Wait for*

His Wife's Lover, and *Suicide to Be Three Seconds Before Pulling the Trigger,* are miniature dramatic scenes in which the characters confront their fear of life and often succumb to the attractions of nothingness.

In the early 1900s Witkacy also began to create his own intimate "theater" on film, producing a long series of photographic portraits of himself and his many alter egos, as well as of his family, friends, and surroundings. While still a child he had learned the value of photography for his creative work from his father, who encouraged him to play in front of the camera. He served his apprenticeship as a photographer taking pictures of locomotives and the mountain scenery of Zakopane, but soon found his true subject in the human face, which often fills the entire frame of his pictures and becomes both the foreground and the background. These psychic studies are revelations of the inner man and his terror in the face of existence. Witkacy kept photographing himself throughout his life, catching the look of incipient madness in his own haunted eyes as well as the social masks and camouflage of his role-playing personas. He also photographed his own paintings and drawings (sending prints to his father in Lovranno), arranged his work in albums according to categories, and created a museum of his work.

Fin de siècle Zakopane, with its penchant for histrionic role-playing, artistic poses, and perverse eroticism, was a small stage that fostered the performance aspects of life and the wearing of masks. To the young Witkacy, captive to the theatricalized self, it seemed a place of seductive charms, productive of demonism, which he associated with female sexuality, proliferation of forms, and creativity itself.

Despite his father's repeated warnings that he would dissipate his creative energies, the handsome, brooding young man, who was prone to romantic intrigues, became involved in a tempestuous love affair that plunged him into what he called "the metaphysical monstrosity of sexuality." In the fall of 1908 the twenty-three-year-old Witkacy met the modernist actress Irena Solska, ten years his senior; by March of 1909 they had become lovers. Recently separated from her husband, the celebrated actor and theater manager Ludwik Solski, Irena was then at the height of her career. Her green eyes, abundant red hair, high forehead, sensuous lips, irregular features, graceful long neck, and sculptured hands gave her an ethereal art nouveau intensity that proved fascinating both on- and offstage. Painters and sculptors competed to create her likeness; dramatists sought to have her interpret their works and often conceived roles specifically for her. Irena spent the summer and autumn of 1910 in Zakopane with her five-year-old daughter. Always ready to turn life into art, Witkacy photographed mother and daughter, painted many portraits of Irena, and worked feverishly on *The 622 Downfalls of Bungo; or, The Demonic Woman*, his autobiographical account of the love affair, which he gave Solska to read in regular installments, unconcerned as to how she might react to his portrayal of her as a deceitful and lascivious femme fatale. Gossip in Cracow about their romance grew so intense that Witkiewicz senior felt obliged to discourage their plan to visit him together in Lovranno.

His father also dissuaded Witkacy from attempting to publish *Bungo*; its intimate revelations about real people and its frank treatment of sexuality made it morally unacceptable in conservative Catholic Poland. In this *roman à clef* Solska is the sexually insatiable, lying actress Acne (a passing but embarrassing ailment of youth), his friend Malinowski is Edgar, Duke of Nevermore, and Witkacy himself Bungo, an unfocused, introspective young man totally immersed in artistic self-creation and his own theories of art. The fact that Witkacy showed his father such an uncensored rendering of his own sexual life, both with Acne/Solska and Nevermore/Malinowski, says much about their closeness, even though the elder Wikiewicz judged both attachments to be harmful to his son's development. Ten years later Witkacy urged Solska to play the role of Tatiana, the aging demonic woman in his one-act drama *The New Deliverance*.

The affair with Irena came to an end in 1911. Compared with his successful friends Malinowski, Karol Szymanowski, and Leon Chwistek, who had already made names for themselves, Witkacy was without any direction in life. In his mid-twenties he underwent a severe mental crisis and was analyzed by a Freudian psychiatrist, Dr. Beaurain, who told the confused young man that he was suffering from an "embryo complex." In January 1913 Witkacy became engaged to Jadwiga Janczewska, whom he had decided he must marry in order to salvage his wasted life. Janczewska, who had come to Zakopane because of a lung ailment, was a boarder at the Witkiewicz rooming house. Then, on 21 February 1914 (four days before his twenty-ninth birthday), Witkacy's fiancée committed suicide, shooting herself at the foot of a cliff after placing a bouquet of flowers nearby in a modernist gesture linking Eros and Thanatos. Janczewska's death—probably the result of some intrigue or mystification involving Karol Szymanowski—plunged Witkacy into a state of suicidal despair. At this point, Malinowski came to the rescue with an invitation for his guilt-ridden friend to accompany him to Australia to attend the Congress of the British Association for the Advancement of Science.

COCKROACHES

■

A Comedy in One Act
1893

KING	COURTIERS
PRIEST	PETER
PEASANTS	JACOB
PUG DOG	PAUL

Scene One

[*Priest, Peter, Jacob. Peter is sleeping.*]

PRIEST   Do you see those gray things?

JACOB   Where?

PRIEST   Over there! [*Points with his finger.*]

JACOB   Oh, yes!

PRIEST   What is it?

JACOB   And it's moving.

PRIEST   Seriously, what can it be?

JACOB   It's coming closer.

PRIEST   It's strange.

JACOB   Wake up Peter.

PRIEST   What for?

34

JACOB   Why?

PRIEST   And then what?

JACOB   He's a naturalist!

PRIEST   So what if he's a naturalist?

JACOB   Maybe it's a cloud of insects.

PRIEST   So?

JACOB   He'll be able to tell what kind of insects they are . . .

PRIEST   All right.

JACOB   Peter! [*Peter gets up.*]

PETER   What's happening?

PRIEST   Do you see those gray things?

PETER   I think it's a cloud of COCKROACHES!

JACOB   Oh! Good God!

PRIEST   We've got to tell the King!

Scene Two

[*The above and a Courtier.*]

PRIEST, JACOB, PETER   [*Together.*] Is the King in?

COURTIER   Where?

JACOB   At home!

COURTIER   No, he's not in.

JACOB   Then where is he?

COURTIER   In the street.

JACOB   What street?

COURTIER   Gold Street.

PETER   Here you are talking and the gray thing is coming closer. It's a
        cloud of cockroaches!

PRIEST   How do you know?

PETER   I looked through my telescope.

PRIEST   Oh, so that's how! [*They all exit.*]

Scene Three

[*The above and the King.*]

KING   Now what?

PETER   The COCKROACHES are attacking people's houses! [*Paul
        enters.*]

PAUL   [*To Peter.*] What are all those cockroaches doing in town?

PETER   I was just about to send someone to tell you to be careful . . . It's
        a gang of COCKROACHES from Ameri . . .

PEASANTS   [*Offstage.*] Cockroaches! [*The Pug Dog can be heard barking.*]

Scene Four

[*The above, the Cockroaches, and the Pug Dog. The King chops up the
Cockroaches with his sword. The Pug Dog bites the ones left.*]

PRIEST   [*Enters, setting the Pug Dog on the Cockroaches.*] Sic'em! Sic'em!

PUG DOG   Bow! Wow!

THE END

COMEDIES OF FAMILY LIFE

■

[Volume One costs one penny.]

First Comedy

Act One, Scene One
[*The action takes place on the porch. Enter Mrs. Muckley.*]

MOTHER   Good morning, Mrs. Muckley.
MRS. MUCKLEY   What a storm!

[*Enter Daddy.*]

DADDY   Good morning.
MRS. MUCKLEY   Good morning. Well, I'm just going home now.
DADDY   Can we give you an umbrella?

[*Mother and Daddy go out to get the umbrella.*]

MRS. MUCKLEY   Oh, please don't go to any trouble.
MOTHER   I'm just getting it now.
DADDY   It's raining.

[*Exit Mrs. Muckley. Thunder and lightning.*]

Scene Two

[*Enter Mountaineer. Brings the umbrella.*]

MOUNTAINEER   Here's yer umbrelli.

DADDY   Mary dear, give that mountaineer a penny.

MOTHER   Which one?

DADDY   That one there who brought the umbrella.

MOTHER   Oh, of course!

[*Mother goes out to get a penny. Mother returns.*]

MOTHER   I don't have any change.

DADDY   Maybe Ursula has some change.

MOTHER   Very well. Ursula, do you have any change?

[*Ursula undoes the cloth in which she keeps her money and gives Mother ten cents.*]

URSULA   If it please ye, Ma'am, here's ten cents.

MOTHER   Here's ten cents for you.

MOUNTAINEER   God be with ye.

Act Two, Scene One

[*The action takes place in the kitchen.*]

MOTHER   Maybe you could make chicken soup for dinner, Ursula?

URSULA   All right.

[*Mother goes out for a walk. Enter Galica—Galica is the mountaineer who brings the meat. Mother comes back.*]

STAŚ   Oh, Mama, when are we going to go?

MOTHER   Stop pestering me!

[*Galica goes out carrying the meat on his shoulder.*]

MOTHER   Ursula, I'm going out now.

STAŚ   At last we're going!

Act Three, Scene One

MOTHER   Is dinner ready?

URSULA   Coming up.

[*Enter Daddy.*]

DADDY   Well, my little rabbit! Where have you been?

STAŚ   Ho! Ho! Ho!

DADDY   [*To Drill.*] Oh! It's you, Drill!

DRILL   Bow! Wow!

MOTHER   Chew on that!

[*Drill grabs the bone and sits down.*]

URSULA   If it please ye, dinner's on the table.

MOTHER   Staś, come to dinner.

STAŚ   Just a minute.

Scene Two

MOTHER   Ring for Ursula.

STAŚ   Just a minute.

MOTHER   Oh! If you're going to act that way! I'll ring myself!

[*The clanking of spoons on dishes. We eat dinner. Enter Mr. Staszel, the teacher from the public school.*]

DADDY   Oh! Good afternoon, Sir.

MR. STASZEL   Good afternoon.

DADDY   Mary dear, give Mr. Staszel a bite to eat.

MR. STASZEL   No, thanks. Good-bye.

Second Comedy

Act One, Scene Two

[*The action takes place in bed.*]

STAŚ   When are you going to get up, Mama?

MOTHER   Stop pestering me! Go back to sleep.

STAŚ   But what time is it?

MOTHER   Oh-hun . . . hun . . . huuun . . .

STAŚ   Are you going to get up, Mama?

MOTHER   Close the door to Daddy's room.

[*Staś puts on his slippers.*]

DADDY   Peakaboo!

STAŚ   Are you going to sleep more too, Daddy?

DADDY   No . . .

MOTHER   [*Stretching.*] Did he wake you up?

DADDY   No.

STAŚ   Mama, put my stockings on.

MOTHER Well, bring them here.

STAŚ They're lying on the bed.

MOTHER Come here, I'll put them on for you.

[*Staś hands her the stockings.*]

Act Two, Scene One

[*The action takes place where we were sleeping.*]

MOTHER Go wash your face and hands.

STAŚ Fix the basin for me, Mama.

MOTHER Can't you do it yourself?

STAŚ But I don't know where the soap is.

Scene Two

[*We eat breakfast.*]

STAŚ The milk's so good!

MOTHER That's right! You see, it's from Mrs. Obrochta's.

[*Daddy goes to pour the cocoa.*]

MOTHER Stanisław dear, give it to me, I'll pour.

Act Three, Scene One

[*We eat dinner.*]

MOTHER Staś, come to dinner.

STAŚ Just a minute.

MOTHER Hurry up!

[*Mother goes to get Staś.*]

STAŚ But I'm coming!

MOTHER Well, hurry up!

STAŚ But I'm not going to eat my meat.

MOTHER Well, sit down at the table anyhow.

Act Four, Scene One

MOTHER Ursula, serve the soup.

URSULA Right away.

DADDY I'm so hungry.

MOTHER Ursula's just about to serve dinner.

DADDY Bunny, pass the bread.

STAŚ   I'm going.

[*Staś brings the bread.*]

DADDY   Thank you.

[*Staś goes out to the kitchen.*]

STAŚ   [*Comes back shouting*] The roast! The roast!

URSULA   Get out of the way or I'll spill it all on ye.

MOTHER   Ursula, serve.

URSULA   Right away.

DADDY   Is it lemon soup?

MOTHER   Yes.

STAŚ   With rice?

MOTHER   That's right!

STAŚ   It's delicious!

DADDY   Oh! What a little charmer!

STAŚ   Hee! Hee! Hee!

[*Enter Mr. Potkański.*]

DADDY   Would you like a drop of vodka?

MR. POTKAŃSKI   No.

DADDY   Une toosh?

MR. POTKAŃSKI   Well, all right.

DADDY   Ursula, give Mr. Potkański a small plate.

URSULA   Right away.

DADDY   Why don't you help yourself to the butter . . .

MR. POTKAŃSKI   Very well.

Third Comedy

Act One, Scene One

[*The Jordanówka villa. Auntie Gielgud's room.*]

MOTHER   Good morning.

STAŚ   Good morning.

AUNTIE GIELGUD   Good morning.

MOTHER   Kiss her hand.

STAŚ   It's too late now.

MOTHER   Did you hear what he said?

AUNTIE GIELGUD   No, what did he say?

MOTHER   I told him to kiss your hand and he said it's too late now.

AUNTIE GIEŁGUD   Ha! Ha! Ha!

Scene Two

[*Enter Mr. Beetle.*]

MR. BEETLE   Good morning.

MOTHER   Good morning.

MR. BEETLE   May I take your picture?

MOTHER   Fine.

STAŚ   And mine too.

MOTHER   All right.

[*Mr. Beetle starts to take the picture.*]

MR. BEETLE   Sehr gut! Sehr gut! All right now, don't move.

MOTHER   All right.

MR. BEETLE   I've got it now!

CAMERA   Click! Click!

MR. BEETLE   It's all done.

MOTHER   So quickly?

MR. BEETLE   It's an instant camera.

[*Enter Mr. Akcentowicz.*]

MR. AKCENTOWICZ   Good morning.

MOTHER   Good morning.

MR. AKCENTOWICZ   Now I'll take a picture of Mrs. Giełgud.

[*Enter Popsio.*]

MR. AKCENTOWICZ   All right. Please sit down.

AUNTIE GIEŁGUD   Very well.

THE CAMERA   Click! Click!

MR. BEETLE   Oh, that'll be a wonderful picture with that jacket hanging
   there.

POPSIO   Regarday, Madam Witkiewicz, tray ban fotographee.

[*Mother bends over and looks at the camera. Enter Daddy.*]

Scene Three

DADDY   Ban jure.

POPSIO   Ban jure.

DADDY   Mary dear, allan.

MOTHER   Coming.

[*Exit Mother, Daddy, and Staś.*]

Scene Four

MOTHER   Good morning.

MRS. MATLAKOWSKI   Oh, my!

MOTHER   How's Kiesio?

MRS. MATLAKOWSKI   Better.

MR. MATLAKOWSKI   Much worse! Coughed all night.

MRS. MATLAKOWSKI   But, Władysław, how can you!

Fourth Comedy

Act One, Scene One

[*Enter Kiesio and Staś.*]

STAŚ   Mama bought me a pair of pliers!

KIESIO   But I've got a much better pair; if your finger gets caught, they
can cut it right off.

STAŚ   All pliers do that. [*Shows him his drill.*] That's a good drill, isn't it?

KIESIO   My drill drills much better.

STAŚ   You never drilled with my drill.

KIESIO   But I can see.

[*Both exit.*]

Scene Two

[*Staś is playing with his monkeys.*]

STAŚ   Fire! Fire! Hoist up the ladders! Help! Help! ! ! The pumps! The
pumps! ! ! Water! Water! ! ! Faster! ! ! Hey! Hey! ! ! Ladders!
Ladders! ! ! The fire hoses! The fire hoses! ! ! Faster! Faster! ! !

MOTHER   All right, maybe you could do your lessons now.

STAŚ   Just a minute.

MOTHER   Well, hurry up, Miss Jastrzębska will be here soon.

STAŚ   I'm coming.

[*Staś does his lesson. Enter Miss Jastrzębska. Miss Jastrzębska finishes
giving the lessons.*]

MOTHER   Have you seen Staś's comedies?

MISS JASTRZĘBSKA   No.

[*Mother shows her Staś's comedies.*]

MISS JASTRZĘBSKA   [*Reading.*] Mrs. Witkiewicz! It's exactly like
    Maeterlinck!

Scene Three
[*The action takes place on Krupówki Street. Staś is riding his bicycle.*]

MOTHER   Wait for me!

[*Mama goes into the post office. Staś waits. Mama comes out.*]

STAŚ   How's the cholera epidemic?
MAMA   It's decreasing.
STAŚ   Is it in Warsaw?
MOTHER   No.
STAŚ   I'm glad.
MOTHER   But it's in Cracow.
STAŚ   Maybe it'll come here.
MOTHER   Maybe.

[*Daddy makes faces through the window of his studio.*]

STAŚ   Mama, let's go see Daddy; he's making faces.
MOTHER   All right.

[*They leave.*]

Scene Four
[*The action takes place in Daddy's studio.*]

DADDY   Well, how do you like the picture?
MOTHER   It's wonderful.
DADDY   And what do you think of it?
STAŚ   It's pretty good.
DADDY   So the picture's pretty good?
STAŚ   Of course.

[*They leave.*]

Act Two, Scene One

[*Enter Mr. Zamoyski.*]

DADDY   Oh, Mr. Zamoyski! Mary Dear, could you give Mr. Zamoyski some tea?

MOTHER   I was just about to pour him some.

[*Mother brings the tea.*]

MR. ZAMOYSKI   Thank you very much! [*In French.*] Une fwa a commensay la bataille de sec . . . [*Mr. Zamoyski speaks too loudly and spills his tea on his pants.*] Oh! Excuse me!

DADDY   The worst of it is you've burned yourself.

MR. ZAMOYSKI   No. Good-bye!

STAŚ   Good-bye!

MOTHER   Good-bye!

[*They exit.*]

Act Three, Scene One

[*The action takes place on Krupówki Street.*]

MOTHER   What's that?

STAŚ   Dust.

MOTHER   No, it's smoke.

STAŚ   Oh! Is it a fire?

MOTHER   Maybe . . . Fire! ! Fire! !

STAŚ   You see, Mama?

MOTHER   That's right!

SMOKE   Shoo! Shoo! Shoo! Shoo!

[*A racket can be heard; the smoke bursts forth.*]

STAŚ   Oh! My!

MRS. GÓRSKA   My House!

STAŚ   Mother!

MOTHER   What?

STAŚ   Won't it get to us?

["*Help,*" *Mrs. Wal cries.*]

STAŚ   What's going to happen?

[*Enter Mr. Szukiewicz.*]

MR. SZUKIEWICZ   It looks bad.

[*Crackling of burning beams.*]

STAŚ   It's so stifling.

MOTHER   It certainly is.

STAŚ   This is the first fire I've ever seen.

MOTHER   Do you feel the heat?

STAŚ   Oh, yes, I do!

Scene Two

[*Staś gives Ursula a chemistry lesson.*]

STAŚ   What's left after coal's burned?

URSULA   Ashes.

STAŚ   No, ashes are the waste from the coal, but what's happened to the coal?

URSULA   I don't know.

STAŚ   I'll tell you. The coal combines with the oxygen in the air and forms a new substance that is called carbonic acid.

URSULA   Oh, really?

STAŚ   And what happens when you combine sulphur with iron?

URSULA   I don't know.

STAŚ   I told you before: it's iron sulphate! And do you know how to combine it?

URSULA   No.

STAŚ   You take iron particles and sulphuric acid, then you pour it all into an eggshell and add hot water.

URSULA   Oh, really!

[*Exit Ursula.*]

ON DUALISM

■

"Il n'y a conscience du déterminisme que par la liberté."
■ Maurice Blondel, *L'Action*

The question of psychological dualism has been with us constantly ever since Descartes set a new course for modern philosophy. The question is incapable of resolution, because we humans, unchanged throughout the entire course of evolution, have remained completely immersed in the mystery that surrounds us.

This is the danger spot, a sort of underwater reef barring access to the calm waters of universal knowledge, against which, over the centuries, have crashed steamships laden with logical systems and swift sailboats bearing reflective intuition. This trouble spot is difficult to locate precisely. It is the fine dividing line separating subject from object, mind from matter, the known from the knower, etc. Seemingly an insignificant little line, it has proved to be an invincible obstacle, holding back the greatest of human minds from even momentarily elucidating the mysterious "thing-in-itself."

And in our predicament it never can be known. It is like the asymptote of a hyperbola continually approaching but never meeting a curve.

Science has been unable to provide any valid assurance of truth, thus leaving only our sense perceptions as the sole sphere for making a synthesis. And yet here too this turns out to be impossible and it seems as though along with the perfecting of the means of reciprocal cognition, there has also arisen a sphere of sense perceptions and apprehensions that are as unknowable and mysterious as before. Dualism is constantly present in everyday life, in the simplest of its manifestations. In each person there exist, as it were, two tendencies: synthetic and analytic, centripetal and centrifugal, but always only within certain limits, beyond which the analytic component does not stop feeling, and the synthetic component does not stop thinking. The relation between these two opposing tendencies determines the nature of people and the differences among them. It could be likened to the interference between two sets of waves with precisely designated limits to their amplitudes.

The analytic or empirico-logical trend attempts to define the subject by all that lies outside it; it is centrifugal cognition. All materialistic systems belong to this category. The second tendency takes for its point of departure the conscious "self" as the only directly given entity, and everything that is external to it is conditioned by the cognitive mind.

Such duality is characteristic of all great philosophers. This holds true of Descartes with his mind and matter, God above mediating between the two; of Spinoza with his substance and its attributes of thought and extension, both of which are God; of Kant with his pure and practical reason; of Schopenhauer with his world as will and as idea, cherishing the illusion that by means of words he had explained the mystery of being, the unity of will and the plurality of individuals.

Every human being has moments when he feels his own nothingness in the face of the world surrounding him. What is the point of painting, playing roles, creating, or even living if we belong to the system of the "Milky Way," which is sixty-five light-years distant, while somewhere in the immeasurable distances there whirls the nebula of the constellation Andromeda, along with thousands of other illimitable worlds. Thousands multiplied by thousands, infinity times infinity equals infinity, and thus, wherever we stand, on either side there always gape bottomless abysses, above which we are forced to scale the rocky mountain ridge of life without ever stopping to rest. Conversely, contemplation of oneself and of others makes the pitiful inadequacy of all mental conceptions only too evident. What are time and space, and the causality reigning over the diabolic chaos of worlds, and the amoebas in a drop of water, and the nebulae in the infinite heavenly expanses compared with the life of the human soul? What is all that compared to the musings, fraught with forebodings, on one's own being, what is it compared to the terrible power and consciousness of the self when unfathomable silence fills all the empty spaces of the brain for a moment which becomes all eternity? And so these two tendencies continue to battle within man, and the result of their conflict is this life of ours, so miserable, shabby, and mean, and so inconceivable, magnificent, dazzling, and infinite.

■　■　■　■

The problem of what is called "free will" likewise belongs to these questions of dualism. Schopenhauer is right: we look at the world from one viewpoint but at ourselves from two. Hence the dualism and disproportionateness in our currents of thought. When, submitting to our centrifugal tendency, we attempt to explain our existence by what lies outside us, i.e., by motives from outside, i.e., by physical causes, we quite abstractly reach the conclusion that we are only links in a huge chain of something that reveals itself to us in time and space as unconditionally subject to the law of causality. But this marks the end of our knowledge. And although it can be infinitely expanded, nothing can advance our consciousness one iota, since it always remains a cipher compared to the infinitude of the mystery that surrounds us. "Free will" strikes us as a corollary of internal and external causes and nothing more than that. Discouraged at this point by the feeble results of our analytic reasoning, we turn to our center, to the inexhaustible depths of our feelings, and here alone, in the mysterious and inscrutable worlds of synthesis, we derive our strength and the consciousness that our existence is free and unique. And if on the one hand, on dualistic grounds, we cannot deny the existence of causality in external phenomena as well as in the motives directing our seemingly free actions, then, on the other hand, by submitting the same question to the judgment of our unmediated consciousness, we absolutely deny any predestination on the basis of our feeling of unconditional power. In both instances we are right. It is interesting to note that if a matter of truth touches both us and the world surrounding us, this question becomes twofold depending on the point of view from which a given phenomenon is observed. The question of free will also will remain unresolved, oscillating between absolute causality and absolute randomness, drawing infinitely close to the truth but never reaching it. Hence it follows that our predicament, from which we cannot escape no matter how hard we try, rests on a split into subject and object, whose real relationship we shall never clarify, since we are not indifferent spectators of the phenomena but one of the active parties.

DECEMBER 1902

LETTER TO MALINOWSKI

■

[1906]

Dear Bronio:

I'm answering you right away to explain that I wrote a letter to Zofia Dembowska saying I told you about the debauchery she and I engaged in (I wrote her everything so you can discuss whatever you want with her). Well, then I had such sharp pangs of conscience with regard to Z.D. that I wanted somehow to set things right, even if it meant playing a dirty trick on you, and I asked her to write you everything, since you know all about it. She is so fabulously magnanimous that she wrote you everything. I offer you my sincere apologies for doing that, but a person who has played as many diabolically dirty tricks as I have can somehow find reasons for just one more (at your expense), which he has done in order to conceal the previous ones. I can see your demonic smile as you read this. I'm sending you her letter, from which you will perhaps draw interesting conclusions. As for your reproach that I am "low," I forgive you thinking so with all my heart, since a person with whom someone plays a game is bound to consider as low the person who is toying with him or who plays games all the time. That is why my whole life may seem to you to be hopelessly low. But there's nothing we can do about it. Evidently you haven't worked on mathematics hard enough to find the equation for the curved line drawn by my artistic hand. I am making an attempt to idealize my life once again and perhaps then you'll be willing to talk things over with me.

My father is gravely ill. He has a fever and is spitting blood. The house is in a state of pandemonium and that's why I'm in no mood to write anything interesting.

I'm painting quite a lot and making constant progress.

Will you let me come to the defense of your thesis for the doctorate? Write when it will be. After the exam you can treat me to dinner at the Grand Hotel.

Many kisses.

Your Staś

I hope we won't bear each other any ill will. Forgive me, son. Farewell, Margaret. The Duke and Warwick force me to do it.

THE 622 DOWNFALLS OF BUNGO
OR
THE DEMONIC WOMAN

◼

(1910–11)

Part 1: Life and Dialectics

Chapter 1: Essential Conversations

At about four in the afternoon the Duke of Nevermore's huge black automobile pulled up in front of the garden gate. The Duke's chauffeur, a little old man with long gray hair whose face bore the marks of homosexual deviation, ran up to get Bungo, leaving the motor idling. A moment later, followed by the uneasy gaze of Bungo's mother, who without any justification regarded the Duke as her son's evil genius, they were racing along at a speed of sixty kilometers an hour in the direction of the great forests of Bukowina, which enclosed the distant horizons.

The Duke was not alone. His private physician, Doctor Riexenburg, known as the Instrument, was with him. He was a tall man, impeccably dressed all in black. His balding, egg-shaped skull was encircled by a crown of bright red hair that turned yellowish white at the temples. His nose was broken almost at a right angle, and his gold-rimmed glasses rested on a ridge parallel to the horizontal. Behind them were lurking the penetrating gray eyes of a notorious hypnotist. His sensual mouth, which seemed to be constantly savoring something exceedingly nasty, was concealed from above by a dark-hued fiery red mustache and protruded slightly over an almost completely atrophied lower jaw. This person resembled a tripod used to support some kind of surveying instrument; it seemed that his limbs could be unscrewed and the pieces put into one another. And moreover, he himself appeared to possess the elasticity of a certain part of a bull's anatomy. It was impossible to imagine a situation in which this strange character would be out of place. When Bungo entered the small, dirty room cluttered with an astonishing number of apparently unrelated objects, the two gentlemen were discussing the correct functioning of a gasoline motor recently invented by the Duke.

"Why, of course, listen, old boy (the Doctor had the privilege of addressing every one as "old boy"), if the pressure in cylinder A was greater than in the small tube we have called C_1, cylinder B_1 would blow up right away; obviously if . . . "

"How are you, Bungo," said the Duke interrupting him. "Doctor, come at nine, and have the reader come at ten."

After the Doctor left, the Duke changed his mask. A lascivious smile of complicity played around his lips, while his eyes retained a tinge of jealousy mixed with admiration and disdain: an expression he could not suppress whenever he talked with Bungo about the most real conquest of life.

"So you have had another letter, Bungy boy, show it to me," he whispered in a childish little voice. There was something demonic in the Duke's artificial sweetness. His lips, like a strange fruit freshly cut open, quivered slightly when Bungo nonchalantly threw him a letter covered with a woman's angular handwriting.

"Donna writes that she loves me again and longs for my lips. She also writes that your friendship cannot satisfy her entirely. The letter is, however, unmistakably in your style. The word 'essentially' is used at least ten times. So you obviously have an 'essential' influence on her," Bungo drawled slowly, playing with the Pravatz syringe lying next to some garters and Webster's tome, *The Dynamics of Particles*. "Evidently your perfect tutelage of her soul (Bungo accented this word in a special way) is not in her opinion the most essential thing in her life and she would like to fall a second time through my efforts, sinking lower this time so you could raise her even higher. You should establish a home for fallen women, and appoint me as inspector general of bedrooms," Bungo went on sarcastically. But by now the Duke had already gained complete control of himself.

"I received a letter identical as to the date, and only slightly different as to the contents; be good enough to look it over." So saying, he handed Bungo a letter seemingly identical to the other one. Bungo avidly set about reading it.

"So if you had physically been that woman who underwent a laparotomy on 3 September, she would not be able to love you, despite all of her pity, even if your soul remained absolutely unchanged," Bungo said after a moment. "I find myself hard hit by that." They were both convulsed by an attack of uncontrollable laughter and for a few moments rolled in the Duke's dirty bed linen until the latter finally cried out:

"*Carrajo!* I think my rupture has broken open," and unwinding his antirupture belt, he examined a huge wound on the right side of his stomach. "But read on."

Bungo read out loud. "I went to the theater yesterday. Dear, beloved Edgar, forgive me. There was an actor so like Bungo, who so reminded me of his lips, that I could not resist writing a letter to him. I know that it is not essential and that is why I am writing. Forgive me. Tomorrow I shall begin to concentrate anew and then I'll write to you again. It is two in the morning (I am writing in bed). Dear, beloved Edgar. I am already concentrated. Tomorrow I am going to paint a still life with fruit and I shall try to get control of myself, even in such trifling matters. I squeeze your hand very, very hard. Your friend, Querpia."

"That is enough for you now, Bungy boy," said the Duke and he tossed the letter into a drawer containing a suspicious looking syringe and a flask made of dark glass lying on top of several dirty collars, some tinsel decorations, and dried flowers. They remained seated for a while, thinking of the perversity of women in general, and a dull melancholy began to take possession of them. The Duke was the first to get hold of himself.

"Enough of such absurdities," he said harshly. "Donna Querpia is a nice, decent little girl who has a certain English chic, nothing more. Let us go discuss essential matters. In two hours I have a conversation scheduled with Riexenburg."

"Donna Querpia is a perfect example of the spiritual prostitute, the hysterical liar, and the fundamentally perverse woman. But let us go discuss essential things," Bungo replied with a certain air of exaggeration. The Duke smiled imperceptibly. "Fortunately Brummel cannot see me now," Bungo thought, and they went out into the meadow in front of the house.

The meadow sloped down toward the river, beyond which there rose a hill covered with a coniferous forest. The sun was about to set and a mass of rainbow-colored little flies, visible against the dark wall of the forest, floated in the gold-drenched air. To the right, in a shed, the perverse chauffeur was fixing the overtaxed automobile.

"Good evening, Howard. Please be ready at five in the morning. We shall go to the Great Lake for the whole day," the Duke sputtered.

"All right, Your Grace," the old man muttered without raising his head.

Every year Nevermore underwent treatment for his nerves. His sole luxuries in this wilderness were the automobile and the doctor, who lived at the other end of the village with his snakelike mistress, a first love of the Duke's. Blasé about salon perversions, for which he used to dress up in special black tights, and bored with fanatical work (he was an incomparable chemist and a dilettante in mechanics and mathematics), the Duke had given himself up to total rest and all kinds of country diversions. Once even, the peasants almost flailed him to death for having overindulged in simple country pleasures. Over and above that, he worked a little so as not to get out of practice, but always in moderation. He and Bungo had known each other for a long time, and they were even distant cousins on the side of Bungo's mother, née the Duchess Fitz-Patrick.

They went walking as in the old days, when they had given themselves up to typical childhood perversions, into which they had been initiated by Bungo's first cousin, the Duke Fitz-Patrick, head of the younger branch of that illustrious family. Bungo walked with the disjointed gait of a little boy (a pose for which many things were pardoned him in life), observing the insects' last erotic escapades before the onset of winter. Nevermore, taut as a bowstring, barefoot (he had feet like those of Greek statues), and in khaki pants and leggings, strode ahead with a sure, steady step and looked off into the distance, overcoming his astigmatism by cocking his head slightly, and his face, charged with frightful will power, expressed a longing to satisfy every appetite for life—a desire thwarted by the sickly Nevermore constitution progressively enfeebled over thirty-six generations. After a moment Bungo grew serious and hunched over. That meant he was ready. From time to time, beyond their shared erotic experiences, beyond their reciprocal outsmarting each other by means of plotting, gossip, and atrocious pranks, at which the Duke excelled, as well as by carrying on a rivalry in all possible and impossible fields, they felt the need to disclose their inmost thoughts on "essential" matters. Their friendship, strengthened by conflict, demanded more enduring, more perfect bonds. Nevermore, besides being the friend who complemented Bungo's nature the way the color red complements the corresponding green, had until now exerted a fundamental influence on his views about life, and Bungo, despite constant quarrels with Edgar, was *au fond* on better and better terms with him. He knew how to take from Edgar the best that was in him, because he truly loved him. In moments when he was depressed with life, the Duke served as his most essential "stimulant" and in Bungo's inner struggle symbolized the element working for unity in life.

"My dear Bungo," the Duke began, "I want you to grasp well what I am saying. All joking aside, you are undoubtedly quite an intelligent fellow. According to the criterion of 'higher consciousness'—my new theory—I place you, relatively speaking, rather high. *Mon cher*, your 'menu' of spiritual transformations is highly characteristic. That is just exactly *it*. If you do not have any spiritual underpinning, if you cannot forge within yourself a single steel axis around which the whole complex system of the life machine is able to turn, you will become an intellectual Harlequin, patched together out of old scraps. You see, no one will serve you life on a platter, on command. For that one has to have another kind of capital. Know and want: reflect on this, analyze it, and you will be convinced that it is not merely a hackneyed saying. Once you had Isis and the 'center.' You remember the center of the circle that graphically symbolized your inmost self. Now I no longer know what the center of your being is, because art alone cannot resolve those problems for you."

Under the impact of the Duke's harsh words, Bungo felt that the quintessence of his most secret being was consolidated and crystallized inside him, and that a strange, almost alien force within him was lying in wait, like a cat ready to pounce. At the same time he felt that this force was absolutely hostile to the contents of his soul from which flowed—or so it seemed to him—all his artistic work. "But what if it were only an inessential problem, a question of time, a matter of will power?" This indistinct thought flashed across his mind and it was as though he had glimpsed a far-off and unfamiliar horizon, illumined by distant lightning. "Then everything would become clear and all of a piece. Then perhaps I could truly rest," concluded a voice within him that was alien and yet so familiar. "The Satan of gravity tempts me in a new fashion," he continued thinking to himself. The Duke interrupted him.

"My dear boy," he resumed, hissing slightly in a hushed voice. "Life is either a masterpiece or a farce, which we create out of the raw material of our ego, starting, broadly speaking, with the subtlety of our conscience and ending with the elasticity of our ankles. Believe me, that is what life is. One has to enact it on a grand scale. Naturally, at present there is more life in perversities with Donna Querpia or in deflowering village broads than in variational calculus or a study of the construction of the human body. But, my dear boy, we must have the raw material, a kind of wild strength. Beyond that, it is necessary to understand what life amounts to. In this respect you must consider art the chief means. Art will give you the possibility of obtaining certain material needed for acquiring strength. Understand that life per se—to rot, screw, conquer, struggle, work, break, and be broken—is both the goal and the means. Read Cellini's memoirs. To be able to do everything with one's energy at the bursting point. To experience happiness, pain, love, rotting in jail. After months of suffering, of personal defeats and losses, that man emerged strong and joyous. Take Goethe. An incredibly strong and happy individual, who lived like no one else perhaps, and what is most interesting, in conditions not unlike our own."

The Duke fell silent and went on walking for a moment, crushing invisible obstacles between his jaws. Time after time his mouth assumed the shape of a frightful sucker and his whole being resembled a huge tapeworm attached to the stomach of the universe. Bungo looked at him with true artistic delight. His own personal experiences struck him as something vastly insignificant measured against the immensity of the tasks the Duke imposed on him. Although the concept of art as a means of acquiring strength in life was almost repulsive to him, he felt that the Duke's words had awakened his consciousness of the metaphysical strangeness of life—a feeling he so often lost in the chaos of events, in other words, those inessential experiences with various matrons and maidens, during vile orgies with notorious café dandies as his companions or often while communing with that immaculate Mistress Art. "Perhaps the fault lies in the very mechanism of creation itself," he thought unclearly.

"First of all, get that whole moronic harlequinade out of your head and toss it on the trash heap," Nevermore resumed. "You are expending too much intelligence trying to understand the subtleties of syphilis, the charm of Don Juan or of that pimp, Don Alphonse. Those seemingly trifling digressions may keep you from seeing the only essential thing: life for life's sake. I am a clever ape and I am sure you could do a thoroughly hilarious caricature of me. And undoubtedly you will make fun of me, surrounded by your aides-de-camp and the general staff of your artistic demimonde. But believe me, I treat these things more seriously. I live on intimate terms with all that and gradually make it a part of myself. You discovered the center of a little circle lost in a fog of artificial artistic experiences and you were satisfied that that would be enough for you. You won't find life that way, and above all you must understand that life and action are two different things."

Conversation with the Duke acted on Bungo the way a platinum sponge does on a mixture of oxygen and hydrogen—it served as a catalyst. He felt the uniqueness of his being, and at the same time that there was growing within him a mysterious force, undeniably his, yet sometimes alien to him. Then he was overcome with a desire to make monstrous sacrifices by which he could attain ultimate knowledge of life and its mysteries. At this moment they were passing through a beech forest with an undergrowth of wild raspberry bushes. It was almost dark. The first stars were twinkling between the trees. The chill of the autumn evening went through them both and imparted an especially pure character to their whole conversation.

"*Me cago en la barba de Dios!*" the Duke swore in Spanish, stumbling over a protruding stone. "Give me your hand, I cannot see anything at all."

The Duke suffered from a chronic eye ailment, one of the truly monstrous specters against which he had to battle. Bungo, who acutely felt the weight of Nevermore hanging on his arm, was reminded of a picture he had seen in some American magazine showing Washington coming back wounded from Great Meadows, and for an instant he had the impression he was the adjutant of a famous general who had done battle with all the nonessential powers in the world. After a while they came out of the woods. The road ran along the crest of a hill between fields of stubble. To the east, from behind the horizontal lines of delicate little clouds there slowly came into view the gigantic dull orange disk of the rising full moon. For Bungo, this sight brought back the most distant past when for the first time he had grasped the essence of life, and as he always related his experiences to changes taking place in nature, he felt himself suddenly "propelled" in a direction diametrically opposite the one imposed on him by the Duke.

"Just think, Edgar," he suddenly began in a powerful voice, surprised himself at its deep tones. "Your principles for the acquisition of strength and the conscious creation of life are good for people who have lost the capacity to live. Those who lived the way you were describing lived that way because they had to, because they had an excess of ungovernable strength that compelled them to reveal their whole being in every action, with all the strength of their stored-up energy. Not one of those of whom you were speaking analyzed his psychic states that way, or needed to produce a machine for creating artificial strength. For them, what you are searching for was an inborn need. They did not need to convince themselves, by having constant fits of depression and breakdowns, that life does indeed have its own charm, although one must find the strength to master it. For them, life had charm because the creative force, which you must forge by means of self-conquest and endless painstaking work on yourself, was theirs naturally in overabundance. When you finally decide to live, you won't have anything to experience or anything to create. That is precisely the error of the theory that proclaims that life is the goal itself and that life and action are two different things. Formulating the problem that way exposes one's physical and spiritual decadence and one's incapacity for life. For me you are like the miser who had hoarded money all his life, and after he had grown impotent and crippled with arthritis, developed a liking for wine and women. I cannot live in that fashion," Bungo continued to rebel, failing to notice that Nevermore, having lighted a thin English cigarette, was walking beside him with an assured step, his face a cold mask, like a man for whom that way of thinking was *ein überwundener Standpunkt*. "I have too spontaneous a desire to live to think of storing up capital for the future," he continued in the tone of someone who hopes to deceive himself as well as others. "Considered in that light, what for you is a worthless artistic experience, causing you to stray from your deliberately chosen path, for me can have the most essential value as, very indirectly of course, material for artistic creation."

"Very indirectly. On that point I am in complete agreement," the Duke observed coldly.

"And I do not understand how one can consider art as a means of acquiring strength. Certainly, artistic creation gives strength, but there has to be something to create from. This is not a problem in differential calculus or Swedish gymnastics. By means of science you merely treat the organic sickness of your body and your soul, as you would by taking a sunbath. Without either of these, you would be an utter zombie, incapable even of creating brilliant ideas about life," Bungo persisted, goaded by the Duke's cold attitude.

"You are being a bit brutal, Bungy Boy," Nevermore said, interrupting him, his voice full of frightful sweetness.

"Forgive me, Edgar, but to consider art a means of achieving anything extraneous is in my view a perversion quite unworthy of a person who has reached a certain level of inner development. Art has no direct connection to life. All work by its very nature has such a connection. Whether you stitch shoes or paint a brilliant composition, you have to carry it out. In every art there is the actual making. There is the execution. But one cannot transform such work, which must be closely connected to the creative process, into a mortification of the flesh for attaining spiritual perfection," Bungo ranted on. "When I talk with you and adopt your way of thinking, I have the feeling I am no longer an artist. I become a machine for assimilating technique—understand? Not the mystery of existence, but the technique of living, which any third-rate parvenu has at his fingertips."

"Now don't be irritated, Bungy Boy. Let us talk without resorting to personal allusions," the Duke replied calmly. "I wonder if your chaotic life has brought you one step closer to your goal in art, to the extent you have any clearly defined goal. You are not saying anything, which means I can go on. Your life is a series of accidents, from which you happily extricate yourself, quite by accident too. In your creative work you do not have what I would call a coherent conception of yourself, not even as an artist. Compare Beethoven with Chopin. Beethoven is hewn from unfamiliar matter not of this world. In all of his compositions there is a single unbroken structure. In my view, that is what you are lacking, *mon cher*, and you will acquire it solely by hard work and not by squandering yourself on minor happenings. I know that the anecdotal side of your life is seemingly rich, but your experiences do not constitute a whole bound together by a single will, just as your 'works' do not bear the mark of any single style. You must learn to be solitary, the way you must know how to draw. Now I am absolutely alone regardless of whether I am at a ball at the Duchess of Norfolk's or on the summit of Pic de Teyde."

"Precisely because art," Bungo replied, already much calmer, "is a world apart, the ultimate reflection of the unity of existence . . . "

"No metaphysical divagations, please, *mon cher* Bungo," Nevermore interrupted him. "Let us stick rigorously to life."

"Since there still is no better method for raising artists," Bungo said obstinately, "as, on the contrary, there is for raising bulls, each artist lives according to the dictates of his own artistic intuition."

"Is your intuition unerring?" the Duke interjected.

"That remains to be seen," Bungo went on in angry tones. "You are all of one piece, but why? Because you never had any inborn natural gift for diversity. *Sie sind eine 'lebensverarmende Natur,'* Durchlaucht. I must live out everything I have in me. And if some day I become all of one piece, it will mean that I have taken hold of all the flying sparks I consist of," Bungo continued, lying impudently. "Nietzsche said, 'To give birth to a dancing star, one must have chaos in one's heart.' "

"True enough, provided the star is not a Roman candle you can buy at any corner store," the Duke concluded.

They were now approaching the house. The moon had risen higher and higher, and long shadows were spreading over the meadows and stubble fields. Dew fell, and their heads, as they walked side by side in the darkness, seemed to be ringed by luminous halos.

"My dear Bungo," the Duke said in a firm voice, "the automobile is hardly dependable. I am keeping you for the night. I shall be free in two and a half hours. I must have a talk with the doctor, and then that half-wit, Spleeny, my new reader, will read Goursat aloud to me. Afterward we can still discuss things before going to bed. I am leaving at five." So saying, he disappeared into the depths of the house.

Bungo knew that at such moments all arguments were useless. He sat on the porch and vacantly smoked cigarette after cigarette. It was a splendid autumn night. In the distance, above the sinuous line of hills intersected by black clumps of forest, the mountains were transparently etched in the hazy moonlight. A few tiny white clouds drifted by almost imperceptibly in a straight line above the mountains. "The wind is lying in wait," he thought after a moment and lit yet another cigarette. "Two more hours. I must go to the woods." It was humid and somewhat misty in the forest. Drops of dew glistened on the pine needles, and the dead leaves of the beech trees shone like polished metal. An overpowering smell of mosses, worm-eaten wood, and mushrooms reminded him of his earliest childhood days and his first excursions into the forest. After an hour of aimless walking (he was tired from his talk with the Duke and felt a monstrous emptiness), he heard a noise. A large animal rushed directly at him through the glade flooded with moonlight. He pulled out his Browning and fired straight ahead without taking aim. The animal vanished without a trace. "What rotten luck! I have experiences even here, while Edgar, who constantly roams through the woods, has never once run into a single wolf. How preposterous!" He felt shaken by this insignificant fact and suddenly the Duke's theories struck him as being quite true. After all, Tymbeusz said the same thing. "And what if I hadn't had my Browning?" he thought, somewhat unnerved. He began walking back to the house quickly. The Duke was drinking buttermilk on the porch while a pimply-faced young man read one of Goursat's works on mathematics aloud to him in an atrocious French accent.

"I shall be done in half an hour," the Duke interrupted the reading. His eyes were dilated, almost black, and the look on his face was one of concentrated will power forcibly self-imposed. One could see that by making a supreme effort, he was thinking about parameters, and that the slightest relaxation would send him spinning from mathematics to heaven knows what. Finally they were alone.

"Let's go to bed. I am monstrously tired," Nevermore said in a flat voice.

They entered a dirty, stuffy little room. With simian agility the Duke gave himself a shot of arcicodile and, assuming a squatting position, he executed strange movements that were part of his bedtime ritual.

"You see, my Bungo, the difference is I can say of each moment of my life that I have created it myself. From the most to the least important things. Even including my relationship with Donna Querpia. I wanted to free her from your influence and I have succeeded in doing so. Her vacillations stem from a negligible instability of character and a lack of thorough self-analysis. That will pass. I wanted to take her soul in hand and I did not take her body, although I could have. She was never yours, but part of her life unconditionally belongs to me."

"No, I won't keep quiet! I'll be a perfect bastard," Bungo suddenly exclaimed and kicking the chair out of his way, he placed himself squarely in front of the Duke. "Remember this letter? The one I am holding?" he said right in the Duke's face. Nevermore still did not understand, but suddenly anxiety showed in the contractions of his facial muscles.

"What letter, *mon cher*?" he asked in an artificially calm voice.

"Her first letter to you, moron," Bungo shrieked. "The letter in which she begged you to get her away from my influence, in which she all but declared her sublime feelings for you. She wrote that letter at my dictation, Durchlaucht. I put it in the mailbox myself. I never possessed her because I never loved her even for a moment; her stupid perversities simply amused me. I grew bored with her and decided to make a fool of you, with her help. You were so ridiculous with your frenzied concentration after your return from Africa. You, the conscious creator of life, were as lovesick as a schoolboy for two whole months over a silly, perverse little girl, you are still in love with her now, because I wanted it that way, moron," Bungo roared in a voice that was no longer his. The Duke's face was frightful. It decomposed visibly under the impact of Bungo's words. His mask vanished. He sat there, helpless and pathetic, with tired eyes, like a scrofulous little boy. The impression created was that of a beautiful, robust body suddenly transformed into a mass of liquid putrescence. Bungo experienced a feeling of triumph not devoid of a kind of pity. Making a supreme effort, the Duke gained control of his mask.

"I tell this *du fond de mon coeur*: you are a swine," he articulated slowly, his voice hard as a diamond. He rolled over and a moment later began snoring gently.

Bungo could not fall asleep for a long time. He looked at the spot of moonlight on the floor and grew agitated by increasingly contradictory feelings.

Chapter 2: The Story of an Insignificant Downfall
(Bungo's Theory and Practice of Art)

A fundamental transformation started to take place in Bungo's artistic practice. If up until then he had painted only decorative canvases in which extrinsic elements functioned solely as pretexts, now, under the influence of recent experiences, more and more place in his creative work was given to the composing of certain psychic states—incapable of being precisely analyzed—in a form of composition, which qua composition (i.e, as an arrangement of lines and colors) was gradually becoming nothing more than a means of expression and not a self-contained entity. This gave rise to works that Bungo, while attributing a certain value to them, did not acknowledge as pure art. In his view, art was really pure decoration. The idea of a pure work of art, in his opinion, must remain foreign to any connection with real life and flow solely from the laws governing the colors and lines themselves, whose combinations and constructions were to present a world absolutely self-contained, which would be, according to his former theory, the direct reflection of the transcendental unity of being. "Everything that exists contradicts the principle by which it exists," i.e, the principle of transcendental unity. Art in such a system existed without contradiction, as a manifestation of the absolute unity of being in pure form. Then, under the influence of his reading of Mach and Cornelius, which Nevermore had prescribed for him as an antidote to metaphysical nonsense, Bungo modified his metaphysics, but he did not fundamentally change his theory of art. Now life had burst into his most essential creative work, and although he was somewhat uneasy on that score, he let himself be borne along by this inner current and waited to see what would result from it. . . .

He was unable to observe anything demented in his psychic states, and yet he sometimes felt that he was completely alienated from himself and he began to fear that he might end, imperceptibly and without realizing it himself, in madness. This thought actually increased his anxiety. He worked frantically, but his compositions, seemingly created by a strange kind of fluid without the participation of his will, became for him living symbols of the progressive decomposition of his healthy vital energy. Pure decoration ceased to exist for him.

Chapter 3: The Ball in Birnam Palace and Its Consequences

No longer able to tolerate grandes dames and pseudoartists, Edgar was frequenting, with Riexenburg and Spleeny as his constant companions, the highest circles of the impoverished intelligentsia. He had become involved in a complicated and abnormal affair with a former classmate of his at the university, Miss Saphir, who was a sadist at an embryonic stage of development. She confined herself to clipping the blasé Duke's nails till his fingertips bled, while he writhed in exquisite pain and used his tongue to lick her convex and, as he himself said, repulsive belly button. Only Riexenburg held back, although his mania for hypnotizing young ladies and forcing them into various autoerotic perversions was beginning to seem slightly paranoid. Under these circumstances even Spleeny got over his bad case of facial acne and took on the appearance of a stud bull. Bungo alone, free of all real desires, tagged after the Duke like his shadow, observing the degenerate faces of his friends and immortalizing them in his paintings and drawings, which, in contrast to the impotence afflicting him in real life, evolved more and more toward perverse pornography.

One night Bungo saw the Duke back to Birnam Palace. Edgar was so unnerved by the sadism of his girlfriend Saphir that he begged Bungo to come home with him because he felt that he could not stand to be alone but was ashamed to wake his footman. Bungo agreed, all the more readily since he hated his own room and regularly sought excuses to spend the night elsewhere. The Duke's laboratory was located in a large salon on the second floor. It also housed his bedroom in a little recess in the wall, in a kind of alcove. Above the bed there hung a dark cherry canopy with the curtains open, and it was all permeated with the scent of California Poppy, the Duke's favorite perfume. The salon was exceedingly strange to behold. The disorder that reigned in the Duke's chalet in Bukowina had been transferred to the Palace, but on a much larger scale. There were enormous tables covered with complicated instruments; glass cases gleaming with rows of jars containing chemical reagents or books in sumptuous bindings; a fine set of furniture in the Biedermeier style, a pile of red mattresses; a gasoline motor that powered a small dynamo; a collection of storage batteries and a model airplane hanging from the ceiling, not counting a vast number of the most disparate small objects. A striking characteristic of the salon was the total absence of any work of art.

"Dear Bungy Boy," said the Duke, lighting an arc lamp equipped with a green glass chimney. "I am exceedingly grateful to you. You would not believe how rotten I feel when I am alone. You can have my bed, and I'll sleep on the mattresses."

"It will be a pleasure for me to stay with you tonight," Bungo answered, having no desire to begin a discussion about "creating one's life." "I simply can't stand my own room." The Duke placed a mattress several feet from the alcove and began to undress slowly. Then he washed in the tub and suggested that Bungo do the same. It was terribly hot in the room. Edgar was now squatting on the mattress, absolutely naked, and smoking a cigarette. He suddenly tossed it aside and began to examine his injured hands. Then he gave a start as if he wanted to get up, but did not move.

He sat with his back slightly turned toward the alcove, but in such a way that Bungo could see his shortened profile. Bungo undressed quickly, hoping to fall asleep right away. However, Edgar's movements made a strange impression on him and he began to watch him closely. Edgar started again and this time got up, turning his back to Bungo as he did so. He remained standing that way for a moment, as though he wanted to overcome a strong urge; his arms were partly bent and his fists clenched.

Suddenly he turned around, stepped off the mattress and began to go over to the alcove.

"What are you thinking about that makes you so excited?" Bungo asked with a laugh, having noticed a certain fundamental change in the Duke. The latter did not respond, but suddenly switched off the lamp that lighted the alcove and looked at Bungo. The laughter froze on Bungo's lips. The Duke's face was frankly atrocious. His parched lips were half-open in an imbecilic smile, his eyes, without his glasses, were hazy and had a confused look of criminal desire, mute supplication, and repulsive sorrow. For a split second Bungo looked at him with artistic satisfaction. That face, almost alien to him at that moment, resembled the demonic figures in his drawings. But at almost the same moment he saw everything clearly and something so hideous gripped him that he was suddenly paralyzed with fear. At times he felt strongly tempted to commit acts that were contrary to his innermost essence and potentially ruinous. When traveling by rail, for example, he often had to restrain himself forcibly from reaching into his pocket and throwing all his money and identification papers out the window, or from blurting out some choice obscenity in the presence of proper matrons and staid elderly gentlemen. And there were other, more menacing temptations that concerned the most important questions of his life. At this moment, reacting to the Duke's penetrating gaze, he fell prey to a temptation of precisely that kind. But it was so powerful, so seductively criminal that he realized the futility of any resistance and at the same time knew that something that could ruin his entire life and decide his entire fate had to happen.

"Want to?" he asked in a voice he hardly recognized as his own.

The Duke gave a slight nod of assent. "Got those things?" Bungo asked again. "Otherwise, nothing doing," he added with a touch of disgust in his voice.

"I'll look," the Duke answered, feeling that he must act quickly before the moment passed. They both spoke softly, rapidly, and yet quite calmly and coldly, like people threatened by danger. Moving with the stealth of a hyena, Edgar ran over to the little stand and began searching. Bungo waited transfixed, in a terrible state of tension. So after all there was something that could shake him to his very depths. That thought was almost a source of satisfaction. The Duke came back.

"There aren't any," he said utterly at a loss, his voice filled with gloomy, hopeless desire. But now Bungo pursued his scheme.

"Then let it be perversion and I demand my turn later on," he said coldly, as though bargaining in a store.

"All right."

"Word of honor?"

"Word of honor."

"Put out the light," Bungo whispered. The Duke turned off the light and slipped under the canopy. The dim greenish rays of another lamp sifted down from above.

An hour later it was already dark in the Duke of Nevermore's workshop. The only light that filtered through the blinds on the large windows was the barely perceptible glimmer of the street lamps, which reached up to the second floor. The noise of urban life in the outlying factory districts could be heard in the distance and only from time to time was the relative silence interrupted by the sound of a train rushing by on a branch line or the plaintive whistling of a locomotive. Bungo was lying in bed by himself, his eyes open, totally unable to understand what had actually happened. A few minutes later he had a strange impression. He saw the city in three-dimensional space, but everything in his vision was flat, two-dimensional, and moved in only one direction. Automobiles, wagons, streetcars, and people went along on parallel lines, and between them there was the impassable void of the third dimension. Bungo felt that he too was flat and he moved ahead without knowing how, parallel to all the rest. Then he drifted off into a heavy sleep without dreams, and when he awoke, it was already bright daylight.

A tiny little beam of sunlight streamed through the only chink in the blind, opposite the alcove, marking out its path in the dusty air and making a bloody spot on the edge of the red mattresses, on which Edgar was sleeping on the floor. From the first Bungo felt that something bad had taken place, but he did not know what. It all came back to him in a flash and the pain of the loathsome act that once done could never be undone crushed him beneath its monstrous weight. He suddenly saw his whole life pass before his eyes, and Isis above all stood out with frightening clarity. And now he would have given anything in the world had the events of the night been only a dream. For a moment he tried to believe it had never happened and that he had been the victim of a repellent hallucination. But he looked to the right. The ray of sunlight had just reached the lower half of the sleeping Duke's face. Nevermore's mouth was half open and colored scarlet by the reflection from the sun, while his eyes and part of his nose remained engulfed in the shadows. The impression made was of an innocent little boy wearing a mask. With a speed that seemed frightful to Bungo, the ray of sunlight rapidly disclosed more and more of Edgar's face. Finally it touched his eyes. The Duke suddenly awakened and stretched on the bedding. His face, all squinted up because of the light, now resembled that of a prematurely born embryo. Bungo felt such frightful hatred for the Duke that for a moment he had to restrain himself from leaping out of bed and scratching the monstrous little face he saw in the light of the sun. He closed his eyes briefly and pretended to be asleep. The act once done confronted him as a reality that could not be revoked and Bungo had to look it straight in the eye. "All the same, it was a crime," he thought with childish satisfaction. His habit of drugging himself with whatever came his way reasserted itself even at this wretched moment and he felt a sense of relief. He heard Edgar washing in the tub and snorting loudly, and then as he dried himself, he moaned softly all the while. Bungo was seized with a sudden fury. He leapt out of bed and immediately cooled off. When the Duke turned toward him, he seemed a total stranger—and a rather likable one at that. They said not a word to each other except a formal "Good morning." Bungo hastily splashed cold water over his face and body and even felt that the events of the night had agreeably jolted his blasé mechanism for receiving external impressions. "I am curious what Brummel will have to say about this," he thought as he dried himself with a soft, thick towel. "No matter what, it was an experience."

Soon they went out together. The day was warm and beautiful. It reminded Bungo of the day he went with Querpia to the Great Lakes, and he thought the weather in the mountains must be just the same. One could feel spring in the air. They parted without saying a word about what had occurred. Bungo sensed that their friendship had been broken off, if not forever, at least for a very long time.

Shortly thereafter Nevermore left for England with his mother to take possession of the lordly estates inherited from the last scion—recently deceased—of the English dukes and he settled there permanently. Birnam Palace was sold and Bungo did not see the Duke again for almost a whole year.

Since that accursed night Bungo worked tirelessly and lived in total seclusion. At first that night even had a certain positive effect on him. He totally lost all desire for artificial situations, anomalous relations, and various perversions. From afar he perceived the abyss into which he could have fallen had he gone on living from day to day in his former style and permitted himself everything for the sake of purely artistic experiences. Once and for all the artistic justification of one's transgressions had to be crossed off the list of real-life theories. Bungo had come to understand the impossibility of exploiting every situation, even the most demonic, for the goals of art. Only now had he drawn back sufficiently to be able to go ahead at full speed. That conviction was the ultimate deception he practiced on himself. He lived a whole month in seclusion, avoiding all experiences and sometimes working madly to give his nerves a complete rest. He rose early, slept a good deal, and tried not to think or analyze anything. He sank into a state of absolute torpor that deadened all his feelings, and his passivity toward mere women and even ladies became absolute. He did not think of approaching any woman, knowing that at this point he would have embarked on one of those familiar byways that always led him to inner straying. Sometimes he went to call on Dunderhead, who now professed great friendship and played the piano for him by the hour. From time to time they spoke ill of the Duke, but rather circumspectly, afraid to touch on overly sensitive matters. From these conversations Bungo was able to deduce that the Duke had been corresponding with Fenixane and that he must have written her something about the memorable night in Birnam Palace. Hatred for the Duke and his system of conquering life grew still stronger in Bungo's heart, because, although he could not admit it to himself, the life he now led was somewhat similar to the Duke's in bygone days. However, events were going to happen that would radically change his life and take him into a world of experiences hitherto totally unknown to him.

Part 2: The Demonic Woman (Bungo's Views on Music)

"I believe that music is a world so closed, so separate, so devoid of all feelings that come from life—of course, I mean true, great music—that singing, which recalls man and his paltry emotions, is for me simply a profanation of true music. . . .

"Between singing and music there is something qualitatively different, something incommensurate. I am an opponent of all feeling in art, although not long ago I myself did drawings imbued with real-life content, but those were moments of deterioration in my own life, which I tried to justify artistically. Singing cannot be abstract, it is a cry of the body and therefore it speaks only of the emotions, without being able to give us a totally different dimension, which I would call metaphysical, for experiencing the self. . . . Take, for example, Beethoven's Sixth Symphony. During the first part am I necessarily obliged to have a vision of cows, tails in the air, gamboling across a green meadow, or later to hear thunder? No. There is only the music and I can interpret it any way I please. But its metaphysical content, the content of its sounds in and of themselves, is unique and all interpretations of the above kind are, in my opinion, a crime against art. It is the same with painting. Looking at paintings by Gauguin, I can either see heavy-set, cigar-colored women playing on a billiard cloth, as some Frenchman said, or grasp the eternal laws of Being expressed by the composition of the lines and the harmony of the colors." . . .

The young composer Anodion had just finished the second theme of his sonata and after repeating the entire section, he began the development of the first theme. Bungo opened his eyes. Anodion looked magnificent. His face grew monstrous and took on a fierce, cruel look. His whole body bent over, he seemed forcibly to tear the sounds out of the piano by a frightful effort. . . . Bungo closed his eyes again and only now began to listen in earnest. After a moment he completely stopped knowing where he was, and what he, or his life, or anything else was. He lost all feeling of real space and existence. It seemed to him there was nothing except the sounds filling the universe, but the medium in which there occurred the succession of phenomena that defied being grasped in any form was itself something that defied being defined and analyzed in any fashion. The combinations of sounds produced in him the sensation of a totally separate world incapable of being reduced to any simpler elements, and that sensation was for him the characteristic trait of pure art, free of all decidedly emotional coloration. Only music and pure painting gave him this kind of sensation.

Part 3: Too Late!

Chapter 1: In Search of a Mask

"Listen," Riexenburg began, "I don't suppose you've heard the news about Nevermore, have you?"

"No," Bungo answered, "except that in England they say he is leading a wildly dissipated life which has reached positively criminal dimensions. That is what Brummel told me, and he found out from an Englishman in Göttingen."

"That's right," Riexenburg said, smiling almost lasciviously. "But I ask you for absolute discretion. You can see Nevermore if you wish. He is here in an insane asylum." Bungo was absolutely astounded.

"What? Has Edgar gone mad?" he exclaimed, jumping out of bed.

"Wait, here is the situation," Riexenburg said with some satisfaction. "Nobody knows about it yet. It happened a few days ago. Nevermore came here a short while ago to take care of some financial matters. He came to see me and displayed only a slight nervous excitability. The following day he had an attack on the street and now is in solitary confinement. It is an uncommonly curious case. It appears to be acute paranoia, or perhaps creeping paralysis. But the diagnosis is far from certain. Even Professor Kreitz is of two minds. A friend of mine will be on duty tomorrow. Be at the Café Feigel at three o'clock, and we'll go together. But absolute discretion please." Bungo shuddered at the thought of seeing the Duke in such a state.

"Let me bring Tymbeusz and Brummel," he begged the doctor. "I mean, it's beyond belief. They have to see him." . . . Riexenburg finally agreed, having more faith in their discretion than in Bungo's.

The next day the four of them were silently heading in the direction of town where the hospital was located. Bungo quivered with nervous excitement. Tymbeusz had a look on his face that combined extreme distaste and uncontrollable curiosity. His eyes popping out of his head, Brummel was scarcely conscious, but he smiled perversely at the thought of the scene that awaited him. Only Riexenburg was cold and indifferent, although it was not without a certain satisfaction that he was bringing the three friends there to show them his enemy in a state of total collapse. It was a glorious autumn afternoon. The silhouettes of the trees were sharply etched against a bright, clear sky that seemed made of thin slices of transparent stone aquamarine in color. Some of the trees were already bare, others still had a few multicolored leaves which kept falling at every gust of the cold, piercing wind. Washed clean by the night rain, the town sparkled as the sunlight struck the colored walls of apartment buildings and mansions and the green, patina-coated roofs of the churches. Through a small swinging gate in the wall they entered a garden surrounding a huge red-brick pavilion. Then the young doctor on duty, beautiful as a seraph, with penetrating black eyes of burning intensity, whom Riexenburg introduced to his companions, led them down a long corridor, and then opened a small isolation cell for first class patients, where the deranged Duke had been temporarily confined. As he ushered them in, the doctor said to Riexenburg, "If he starts to sing, call me immediately. I'll be in the next room."

The barred window was covered by green gauze, and it was so dark in the cell that at first it was impossible to discern anything. Riexenburg went to the back of the room, but the others stayed close together near the door, not daring to go any farther.

"It's all right, there is nothing to be afraid of," Riexenburg said. Brummel approached first, followed by Bungo. Tymbeusz brought up the rear, tugging hard at his beard with his thin, nervous hands. The Duke was squatting on the bed. His head was closely shaved and without his glasses he kept blinking, all the while masticating something between his jaws and smacking his lips, as though he were eating chewy caramels. His brow grew furrowed from the frightful effort of will he was making, and his eyes squinted as though he were staring off into the infinite distance. Riexenburg touched him on the shoulder.

"Listen: I have brought you some guests. Don't you remember us?" Edgar raised his head and looked around. Evidently without glasses he did not see much of anything, since he did not react at all. At that point he resumed his former position. Then he muttered something under his breath in a hushed voice, hissing with suppressed energy, and squeezed together his powerful, aristocratic hands with polished nails resembling the claws of a predatory lizard. Bungo bent down over him.

"One more mask, just one more," the Duke whispered. "That is the one I cannot master. I see to the very depths of people's eyes. I must gain control over everything. I cannot master crime. I must learn how. I must have the strength. I am still too weak. Just one more mask, just one more . . . "

Bungo was overcome by a frightful surge of pity and he felt that despite everything he had never for a moment really stopped loving the Duke.

"Edgar," he appealed to him in an emotional voice full of scarcely repressed tears, "wake up, there is no such thing, no such thing whatsoever.

It is all in your imagination. Look at me." The Duke raised his head and looked him in the eyes with a dull and painfully obstinate look. He brought his face right up to Bungo's and stared at him. And it seemed to Bungo that a double living corpse was looking at him, so frightful was the Duke's mask in the greenish semiobscurity of the hospital room. He had the sensation he was hanging over a monstrous abyss that tempted him by its fatal, overpowering charm. One moment more and he felt he would lose control of his nerves. Quiet reigned behind him. They were all waiting in silence, and it seemed to Bungo that he was alone with the dreadful living corpse of his friend shut up forever in an eternity of torture. Suddenly a childlike smile played about the Duke's enormous yet exquisite lips, and the expression of pained tension that had furrowed his brows between the eyes entirely vanished.

"My little Bungy," he whispered in an innocent boyish voice, taking Bungo in his arms and kissing him on the lips. Totally overwhelmed by truly monstrous contradictory feelings, Bungo did not dare move a muscle. "I remember," the Duke whispered with a smile. "You are the one who wrote: 'And steely glints from the blade of my sword, with which I cut the flowers—I won't break eternity.' I won't break it," he repeated painfully. "What nonsense, what wretched nonsense," he said over and over again and suddenly jumping from the bed into the middle of the room and pushing away the terrified Bungo, he began to dance, taut as a bowstring, lifting only his legs, which he bent at the knees. At the same time, in a shrill voice quite unlike his own, he sang an absurd song, "Le plus beau des mirliflores, c'est le duc de Nevermore," and the expression on his face was one of mad glee and self-satisfaction.

"Come on, hurry up, hurry up," Riexenburg said, pushing his charges out the door. He rushed into the next room and gave the keys to the doctor, who hastily dashed into the Duke's isolation cell, from which there now came a desperate cry, "Help, mama! Help, mama!"

They quickly descended the stairs and came out into the hospital garden, which sparkled with gorgeous autumn colors and was flooded with afternoon sunlight.

Chapter 2: The Mask That Fell Too Late

Bungo and Brummel kept walking in silence through the damp, glistening streets that reflected the multicolored lights of the shop windows, the street lamps, and the streetcar headlights. Suddenly a silhouette very familiar to Bungo appeared from around a corner. Wearing a heavy fur coat and a derby on his head, the Duke of Nevermore came toward them with his usual self-assured and steady step. They both stopped dead in their tracks. Bungo saw only the Duke's eyes staring off into the distance with an expression of incredible tension from overexerting his will, then the light from a street lamp was reflected in his glasses, making him for a second resemble a frightful corpse with phosphorescent, glowing eye sockets. Nevermore passed close by, without noticing them at all.

"Edgar! Edgar! Stop!" Bungo screamed after him. But the Duke kept on going, and in his relentless manner of forging ahead he seemed to be a bullet hurtling blindly to destroy all possible obstacles in its trajectory. He rapidly disappeared into a side street. Bungo looked at Brummel. The Baron stood erect, tight-lipped and eyes bulging, staring in the infinite distance with a grim determination that was both boundless and inflexible.

"Well, there is someone who has mastered even his own madness," Bungo said to the Baron. "We must pardon him if from that height he cannot see ordinary mortals like us. Incidentally, I had the impression that someone passed close by us who was already on the other side of Tymbeusz's famous line; it seemed absolutely clear to me that Edgar's corpse had risen from the grave and that he gave off a cold breath that was not of this world." Brummel suddenly came to his senses. He quickly extended his hand to Bungo and without saying a word left in a great hurry, creating the impression of a man fleeing from himself.

Bungo slowly headed towards home and for a split second he experienced the monstrous metaphysical strangeness of existence, but quickly lost this feeling under the sway of the usual closed circle of thoughts in which he had been going round and round for so long without finding any way out. A few days later he learned from Riexenburg that Edgar had left the hospital fully cured and had departed for England the very next day, without wanting to see any of his former friends. The doctor held consultations on this exceedingly strange case that proved baffling to the best psychiatrists. Even Professor Kreitz racked his brains to no avail trying to figure out what had happened. With a strange feeling of jealousy, fear, and yet at the same time a certain joy, Bungo thought that the Duke of Nevermore's strength had exceeded the expectations of the local authorities in psychiatry, and he dreamed of acquiring similar power himself.

Epilogue

Bungo was not destined to enjoy for long his final metamorphosis. Approximately six months after the events described, as he was passing through a deep forest thinking about truly essential things (persevering for half a year in his resolutions guaranteed him a brilliant future), he suddenly felt a terrible blow to his right eye and a monstrous pain went right through his entire skull; lost in thought, he had, in the shadows, run into a sharp spruce branch and knocked out his right eye. Attracted by his bloodcurdling screams, local peasants from a nearby hut came to his aid and carried him, howling in pain, to the hospital. His head and eye wrapped in bandages, alone in a single room, Bungo used his remaining eye to cast melancholy glances at the world now drenched in sunlight, now veiled by sheets of rain, and he understood for the first time what the essential problems really were. . . .

After a few months Bungo grew accustomed to having only one eye. . . . Wearing a black patch, he even engineered a few erotic conquests. But soon what is called a sympathetic (indeed!) inflammation attacked his right eye and in a fit of despair Bungo cut his throat with a Gillette razor blade. . . .

Of the entire band that had once wandered in the enchanted land of the mountains discussing essential things, there remained only the Duke of Nevermore and Brummel. The Duke was deported to New Guinea for certain unheard-of crimes he committed in the byways of Whitechapel with a pair of lords and while he was there he wrote such a brilliant work about the perversions of those supposedly savage people contemptuously called Papuans that he returned to England as a Member of the British Association for the Advancement of Science and a Fellow of the Royal Society. The rest of his life was nothing but a series of wild and improbable triumphs.

PART 2: TROPICS AND REVOLUTION
1914-18

T he four years between 1914 and 1918 were decisive in the formation of Witkacy the artist. After the suicide of his fiancée, Witkacy left Poland for the journey to Australia a broken man, psychologically and morally. He returned almost exactly four years later, confident of his calling as a painter, playwright, and theoretician, ready to embark on the most creative period of his entire career. What he saw and experienced in Ceylon and in Australia and in Russia gave him the impetus to become an artist. The tropics and revolution were fundamental to his concept of the strangeness of existence.

In novels, plays, essays, and letters, Witkacy portrayed the experience of the tropics as a vision of mysterious power to which he would be a slave until the end of his days. What the future playwright saw during the two-week stopover in Ceylon inevitably influenced his ideas on art and theater. Witkacy and Malinowski stayed in the British colonial capital, Colombo, but traveled by train to the ancient city of Kandy, the cultural and religious center of the islands, in the central mountain range of Ceylon. The spectacular train ride over deep gorges introduced the young painter to the splendors of tropical vegetation, and to the intense, bright colors that would henceforth appear on his canvases. While in Kandy they certainly visited the Temple of the Tooth, with its holy relic of Buddha's tooth. Perahära, the largest and most important annual festival, usually takes place in Kandy in July and August. The processional pageant with its forty elephants starts at the new moon and concludes on the night of the full moon. Since Witkacy and Malinowski left Ceylon on 11 July, it is unlikely that they could have witnessed the entire festival itself, but they would at least have seen the renowned Kandyan dancers in rehearsal and learned of the magical animism of the Sinhalese myths and rituals. A British guidebook for tourists from this period, *The Book of Ceylon* (1908), describes the sort of spectacle presented at the festivals: "groups of masked devil-dancers in the most barbaric costumes, dancing frantically, exhibiting every possible contortion, and producing the most hideous noise by the beating of tom-toms, the blowing of conch-shells, the clanging of brass cymbals, the blowing of shrill pipes and other instruments devised to produce the most perfect devil-music that can be imagined." As has been said of Antonin Artaud's encounter with the Balinese actors and dancers at the Exposition Coloniale in Paris in 1931, Witkacy's direct exposure to the art and artists of Kandy helped him to shape his notions of a theater of physical language and metaphysical content and to develop more precisely his antimimetic aesthetics.

The two friends disagreed philosophically on the implications of what they saw during the trip. Witkacy placed the origins of religious feelings in an ontologically based metaphysical anxiety and accused Malinowski of reducing such feelings to real-life emotions of fear, hunger, and sex.

On a personal level, Witkacy always remembered the miraculous rescue that his friend performed by taking him to Ceylon and Australia, and the tropics seemed a "way out" whenever he grew particularly depressed. He even fantasized during the trip itself that the tropics could have spared him the tragedy of his fiancée's suicide, writing to the dead girl's parents from the Hotel Suisse in Kandy: "It's too bad that I didn't borrow 2,000 rubles from you and come here with Jadwiga. I could have made a fortune painting the fabulous things I'm seeing here—instead of being cooped up in that lousy Zakopane with all that riffraff."

The same motif recurs later in the playwright's letters to his wife. "I don't see the future clearly," he wrote in 1932. "Maybe go to the Tropics in some capacity or other and disappear there. If I could make it as a court painter. That scoundrel Malinowski might try to help arrange it."

In 1914 Malinowski was planning to stay two years in Australia to do field research in New Guinea, for which he had received several grants. The anthropologist, who wanted Witkacy to join him as a photographer and draftsman, arranged for his friend to become a member of the British Association for the Advancement of Science so that he could make the trip. The outbreak of hostilities in Europe shortly after their arrival in Australia brought an end to all these plans. As an Austrian subject, Malinowski was interned as an enemy alien but allowed to pursue his research.

The war at first became an occasion for further hysteria on Witkacy's part because of his separation from his family and homeland, but ultimately it offered him a chance to redeem himself and expiate his guilt for Janczewska's death. He was finally able to start "a new life" by re-creating himself as a man of strong will and iron purpose. Because he was born in Warsaw, Witkacy was a Russian subject, but as an only son he would have been exempt from military service. Nonetheless, he chose to volunteer in the Imperial Army. This decision was particularly painful to his anti-tsarist father, who as a Polish patriot longed to see the Russian Empire collapse. Witkiewicz senior died in Lovranno in 1915 without seeing his son again. Maria Witkiewicz, however, defended her son's decision.

In St. Petersburg Witkacy was admitted to officers training school thanks to the political connections and financial help of his aunt Aniela, Stanisław Witkiewicz's sister, who was married to a general in the Russian Army. He thrived on the military discipline, completed the accelerated training program in five months, and was sent to a reserve regiment of the elite Pavlovsky Guard in May 1915. His unit was moved to the Minsk area behind the lines in the autumn of 1915. After the Brusilov offensive against the Austrian forces along the two-hundred-mile eastern front in June 1916 produced heavy losses, the guard regiments, numbering 60,000, were brought in as reinforcements. Witkacy reached the front in July 1916 and was commissioned a second lieutenant. During an engagement in the eastern Ukraine on 17 July he was severely wounded, suffering a concussion and injuries over much of his body from an exploding shell. He was decorated with the Order of St. Anne, fourth class, and spent the rest of the war convalescing.

During the next two years Witkacy pursued his interests in the arts and painted extensively, producing perhaps as many as eight hundred compositions and portraits. He also had the time to travel to Kiev to see Karol Szymanowski, visit the Shchukin Gallery in Moscow with Tadeusz Miciński (where he became convinced of Picasso's genius), and write his first major treatise, *New Forms in Painting*, for which he had done drafts before 1914. At this time a Polish legion was being organized in Russia in anticipation of the granting of independence to Poland, and Witkacy thought seriously of joining but in the prevailing chaos was unable to offer his services.

After the February Revolution of 1917, when old titles of rank were abolished and soldiers gained the right to select their own officers, Witkacy was temporarily chosen by the men of his battalion as their commander. The October Revolution and the triumph of the Bolsheviks totally changed his privileged position. Many tsarist officers went into hiding for fear of being caught by the Red guards. Some were held prisoner in barracks and treated like convicts; others were slaughtered. Witkacy's situation grew precarious, even though he had been discharged from the army on 15 November and was already in civilian dress. Throughout this period of famine and hardship he survived by living with Polish residents of St. Petersburg. Like thousands of his fellow countrymen, he waited months for an exit pass and transportation out of Russia. It was not until June 1918 that the ex-officer was able to return to Poland by military convoy.

In later life Witkacy always avoided talking about his Russian adventures, thus giving rise to many rumors and speculations. For example, the Polish futurist poet Aleksander Wat claimed that Witkacy had been extremely popular with his soldiers, but that he seemed haunted by an act of cowardice or a drama of conscience in which fellow officers were betrayed and massacred. The one certainty is that Witkacy retained a deep fear of the Bolsheviks.

LETTERS, 1914-18

■

[BEFORE 21 FEBRUARY 1914]

Dear Bronio:

I'm in absolutely no condition to write a letter. Sometimes I don't write to my father for over two weeks despite pangs of conscience. It's a very painful condition because there were many things I wanted to write to you about, but I can't. When I sit down to write, I get into such a state of nerves that I start to fly into tiny pieces.

I'm working quite intensively, but by fits and starts. I'm not writing you anything about my new discoveries in the artistic realm because these things are intelligible only to someone who is doing the same thing himself. As for "erotica," my situation hasn't changed in the least.

I'd be very grateful to you for James and the pragmatists, and for the address of the bookstore from which I could get such things.

Please write at length about your experiences, situation, work, etc. What I can write you about my work isn't interesting for you. It is just the opposite with what I learn from you.

Maybe in a week I'll be able to face writing a letter. I wish that all the summer trivialities could be wiped out.

My basic attitude toward you is always one of the most profound
·friendship.

A fixed point in the universe. The end of my life will be horrible.

A posthumous exhibit would be interesting.

For the time being I can't write anything.

The state of my nerves is disastrous.

Karol Szymanowski is staying with us.

Miciński and Wielopolska are supposed to come. I'll write you further
about this.

I hug you.

Your Staś

Greetings to Mrs. Malinowski.

Mother sends you both warmest regards. She's very busy with the boardinghouse.

[CA. 28 FEBRUARY 1914]

Dear Bronio:

The most frightful misfortune imaginable has happened to me. Poor
Miss Jadwiga has committed suicide. Much that has taken place since the
beginning of the year is my fault. I was deeply troubled, she thought it was her
doing, and as a result things occurred that, given the fatal web of circumstances, led her to such a step. If it weren't for Mother, I would long since
have ceased to be among the living. Those who force me to live when life has
become completely impossible take a terrible responsibility on themselves.

I am completely broken as a human being. Only for her did I try to
accomplish something in art, conscious of my own worthlessness. Now I can't
help feeling that I am completely finished as an artist. But as long as Mother
is alive, I must go on living; it's my duty to stay with her and deal with this
period of my life and so I've decided to force myself to work as I'm forcing
myself to live. I could have kept her from the edge of the abyss and I failed to
do so. That reproach is killing me, and besides I'm all alone and feel abandoned by everything and everyone.

I am not going to describe to you what happened. I am afraid of life
without belief in anything, which forces me to make compromises. I am afraid
of life below the level of what I demand of myself as an artist and as a man,
but as long as Mother is alive, I cannot leave her. A person who has not

experienced something that frightful cannot know or understand anything. It is not weakness. It is a feeling that everything has come to an absolute dead end. And the superhuman strength by which I keep myself under control so as to go on living gives me no satisfaction whatsoever. On the contrary, it lowers me in my own eyes. Seeing you would be a great joy for me in this hideous desolation. No point thinking about it, since it's impossible.

I've no idea how long my strength will last enabling me to go on living like this. I fear madness most of all, because it would take away my power to deal with the issue of death.

A week has passed since the incident took place. At times I don't believe that it ever happened. Sometimes I think that it was years and years ago, and at other times it seems that it only just happened.

Each day is worse than the one before and my only thought is the desire to end it all.

I could vindicate my life by some kind of unprecedented creativity. But I don't see anything like that ahead of me. Nothing but the frightful emptiness of life after the death of everything important that makes life worth living.

For me you are the sole bright point in the world other than my parents. Remember me and don't accuse me of cowardice.

Many kisses.

Your Staś

I kiss Mrs. Malinowski's hand and ask to be remembered to her. The letter I wrote to her was returned to me.

Write to me about yourself without further delay. Maybe you'll be able to give me some advice. *Send a list of books without fail. I don't have anything to read at all.*

[MARCH 1914]

Dear Bronio:

My state gets more and more horrible with each passing day. I cannot get a grip on myself in Mother's presence; for her sake, I'm pretending to live, and I'm poisoning her life and destroying her health. Today again I had an attack of suicidal frenzy. I can't sleep at night, and during the day (I wake up between six and seven after fitful sleep) I try to work, which seems to me to be a hideous comedy and fills me with terrible disgust for life and for the remainder of this frightful existence which lacks all sense of purpose. Only the thought of traveling with you to some savage country offers any hope. A change so radical that everything would be turned upside down.

I suppose that on a trip like that I could still do something that would enable me to pay back the costs. But how can I get something for the start? This morning I wanted to set out for London immediately. But these are only ways of dulling the pain. Death is within me wherever I am, and it's not dependent any more on memories or on places. Only death can cure me.

There is nothing I long for so much as not to exist. Nothing more can I leave behind me than what I have so far accomplished. I don't have any belief in my creative endeavors. I am writing a theoretical work in which I hope to put all my views and ideas on questions of art, philosophy, and social issues. But even writing this seems to me to be a wretched farce in the face of the nothingness that I see ahead of me. Each day drags on like a nightmare. To be able to save oneself, a person must have at least a speck of belief. I have nothing—neither strength, nor belief, nor faith in anything.

A trace of concern for Mother holds me to life, but it is a weak feeling, considering the inner destruction of my being. Perhaps it is not worth trying to accomplish anything, because whatever I do it will all be over soon.

You are for me something immeasurably valuable and I love you very much, but I still cannot rely totally on thoughts of you. I don't think that there is anything that could save me.

Disgust for a life wasted through my own fault, too late to do anything, a collapse of every belief. What do all those years mean in the face of what has happened? And old age. I already feel I am old and cannot begin all over again.

Forgive me these letters. I can only repeat the same thing ceaselessly. There is nothing else and nothing can save me.

I hug you fondly.

I kiss Mrs. Malinowski's hand.

Your Staś

Mother sends you both warmest regards and expressions of gratitude.

[MARCH–APRIL 1914]

Dear Bronio:

Thank you very much for your frequent letters and friendship. My state grows worse every day. That means I have no right to go on living. I don't deserve to. I have to make a superhuman effort to get a grip on myself for

Mother's sake. But I'm afraid I'll go mad. My work has turned against me. That's the worst of all.

I feel a terrible disgust with myself except when I think about death. While I'm working, I have the impression I'm playing a part in a comedy so as to save my life. Now I've come to realize the very worst about myself. At first I thought I'd do away with myself once I saw that I couldn't accomplish anything anymore. But now I see that even if I did something truly wonderful, it would still fill me with the greatest revulsion for life.

I fall asleep late at night and wake up at 6 A.M. The mornings drag on in a nightmarish fashion. I'm writing a theoretical treatise (you might say a comic piece, it's my pessimistic philosophy of life). I do a lot of reading, but the days stretch out so hideously long and senseless.

Just thinking about the days to come makes me feel sick to my stomach. The only thing I'd like to do is to go on the trip with you.

Write and tell me how much money is necessary right away, and then how much more or less will be needed each month. Couldn't I serve as a photographer and draftsman? I draw fast and render likenesses well. Write and tell me what you think of the idea; in the frightful void that engulfs me, thinking about going on the trip with you is the only bright spot.

Don't think that I've given up. What's actually most dreadful is that I'm still fighting.

I give you a big hug.

I kiss Mrs. Malinowski's hand.

Make your plans about the trip of course without any special consideration for me.

My Mother sends warmest greetings to Mrs. Malinowski, and is deeply grateful to you for all your kindness to me.

[MARCH–APRIL 1914]

Dear Bronio:

I must admit that the postponement of your trip here has upset me a lot. I'm in just a terrible state. The wish to die does not desert me even for a moment. Awful pangs of conscience oppress me and I see absolutely no way out. Bearing such torment is beyond my strength and only death can bring it to an end. I don't know where I can find the strength to live through this and stay on here with Mother. Anyone who knows what inhuman torture life is for me wouldn't hesitate to put a bullet through my head.

I'd like to ask a favor of you, and I think that as my true friend *you won't refuse to do this for me.*

I want to have some potassium cyanide so that at every moment I can be the master of my own life. If I decide to end my life, I don't want to shoot myself, because it's unreliable and I might only wound myself and be saved. If I do it, it's got to be carefully planned and infallible, and I wouldn't want to come back to life again at any price. You won't have anything on your conscience, because if I don't want to live and can't go on any longer, I'll find a way to do it anyhow. But it will just be more unpleasant for me. My dear friend, don't refuse to do this for me. Rest assured that *I won't act irresponsibly.* Wasserberg carried it in the past. But with your contacts it will be easy for you to get (on account of the trip, being roasted alive by savages or something of the sort). If you love me even just a little, you'll be doing me a big favor.

All of you who are urging me to go on living have no idea of the state that I am in.

Each day pulled out of nothingness by a superhuman effort.

Don't write anything about this request of mine, so that Mother won't find out. Just bring it with you for me (from the laboratory in Leipzig), you must know people there. Enclose it in a glass tube.

Forgive me for giving you so much trouble.

I've been sketching a few compositions, I'm not getting anywhere with painting portraits. I won't ever amount to anything.

A hug and kisses.

Your Staś

I kiss Mrs. Malinowski's hand and send warmest greetings to both of you from Mother.

[BEFORE 15 MAY 1914]

Dear Bronio:

Thanks a lot for the card and the book. Maybe you'd be willing to bring me (but I insist on paying you back) a pair of black English shoes, approximately your size, maybe a little smaller. My condition is simply *frightful.*

Don't forget about my request. You can be sure that I won't act thoughtlessly out of consideration for Mother. Destroy that letter.

My suffering is so hideous that there's no way I can live, and yet live I must. For example, I cry all morning long like a small child.

I'm painting a composition, but I lack belief in continuing it.

I don't believe in anything. There's no possibility of my developing. I'm finished. I used to write before, but now I can't. I sketched a series of compositions, but now I can't do anything more and I see ahead of me no hope of doing any work. What's in store for us is destitution and then Mother will go begging, with me on display as a madman. I never believed in earning money before, and now the very thought of it makes me go cold all over. Since I'm so shattered morally I won't be able to do anything for Mother.

All of life for Mother is nothing but greater and greater suffering. Every day I make an effort and every day I crack up because of frightful self-reproaches for wasting her life and my own and I suffer in such a cruel fashion that no words can express it.

Since I'm going to tell you everything, maybe you'll understand why my life is so ghastly.

My dear friend, you wouldn't say anything now about states of deterioration if you knew what true suffering was and how it wrecks and destroys a person without any hope of recovery.

Gather your strength while there's still time.

For me it's already too late for anything.

All I wish for is death.

Free me from life, and you will be doing me a kindness.

If only Mother would stop believing in me and want it that way herself.

I hug you, my dear Bronio.

Staś

Helena is staying with us. She's very good to me. Everyone is good to me. And you are exceptional. Come quickly because maybe this is the last time that we will ever see one another. Not to console me or give me strength, for no one can do that.

Your Staś

[RMS *Orsova*]
[EARLY JUNE 1914]

Terrible pangs of conscience for coming on the trip and spending the money, all for nothing. But some of the responsibility also falls on the people who wouldn't let me do away with myself when the time was right.

That is why my end will be even uglier. Seeing the world's beauty is the cruelest suffering that can be imagined. What in other circumstances would be happiness (such a trip) is unbearable torture. I shall try to get hold of myself, but if I don't hold out, I beg for your forgiveness. Take pity on me and don't bear me any ill will for doing away with myself, because if you could really see me as I am, you would kill me yourself to take me out of my misery. I must force myself to live through each second with its frightful pain and with the consciousness that my suffering will go on endlessly until my death. I actually feel worse and worse with each passing moment. The first day of the ocean voyage already seems endless. What will it be like later? I don't know if I'll last until Colombo. It will be even more beautiful there and for just that reason, more dreadful. It is dreadful that just when I feel *better* on the whole, then it is the *worst*. Then the entire monstrosity of my unhappiness appears with terrifying force. I see everything that I have within me and that is condemned to annihilation. If I am depressed, I think of death and everything appears in a single tonality. In the moments when I feel the variety of life and want to go on living, it is most dreadful for me. That is why any rebirth is an impossibility. Take pity on me and forgive me and don't think ill of me. When she was alive, I wasn't able to appreciate her and I destroyed everything myself. But my "friends" Karol Szymanowski and Tadeusz Miciński abetted me in all of this. Karol is a born scoundrel, and I feel less resentment against him than against myself for believing him. But Miciński—what an obscene ham. In all of this he was the behind-the-scenes instigator of many things. It's all dreadful, but the worst guilt is mine. May remembrance of me when I'm gone not be poisoned by reproaches. I am too tormented now to be burdened with reproaches after my death.

[CA. 15 JUNE 1914]

For Bronisław Malinowski
Send it to my family

I am writing for the last time. The terrible wrongs for which I am to blame prevent my living any longer. Forgive me, dearest parents. I cannot go on. I am frightfully guilty. She was a saint for being able to stay with me as long as she did. Forgive me, Broneczek, for abandoning you, but you don't know how frightfully I'm suffering. I kiss you and bid you farewell. Don't be angry with me.

You alone know the entire ghastliness of my suffering.

Your Staś

Last Will and Testament

To Irena Solska: a composition (*Begging for Mercy*), a drawing and an oil portrait of her.

To Mr. and Mrs. Janczewski: her remaining drawings and my portraits (drawings) of her. Negatives of photographs of her.

To Mr. Langier: a painting with "The Dream Bird," two compositions: *An Ill-matched Couple* and *Melancholy*. A walking stick carved by me which belonged to her. All the negatives except those of her (including the reproduction rights for the compositions).

To Bronio Malinowski: My camera. If he returns from the expedition, he may choose any paintings he wants *à discretion*.

To Miss Jadwiga Zielińska: All the portraits of her and the albums containing reproductions of my works, which belonged to the late Jadwiga Janczewska.

To Miss Aniela Zagórska: Photo albums of my works, which were in my possession. All my literary works (the novel, poetry, etc.).

Bury all her letters and mementos with her under the stone which is to be erected for me at the spot where she took her own life.

God forbid that that ultra-ham Miciński should write a single word about me. This is my most ardent wish. I would rather be completely forgotten. Read this to him: *The Last Will of the Deceased.*

Once more I ask all of you for forgiveness. Don't judge me too harshly for choosing death. It is preferable to constant suffering without end and lack of creativity.

RMS *Orsova* between Tarent and the Suez Canal on 15 June 1914
Stanisław Ignacy Witkiewicz

P.S. *Important*

To Mrs. Eugenia Borkowska: a composition entitled *The Kiss of Death*, one of the last, on the understanding that she will never try to take her own life. I mention this because two years ago she talked about it several times. She must never do it.

HOTEL SUISSE
KANDY, CEYLON
MONDAY, 29 JUNE 1914

Dearest Father:

I'm in no state to describe the wonders I am seeing here. These things are absolutely monstrous in their beauty. We spent our last days at sea in frightful heat, apathy, and lethargy. The ocean was relatively calm and we weren't at all sick to our stomachs. On Saturday the second-class passengers were allowed to sleep on the first-class deck so they wouldn't get buried under the coal while they were refueling the ship at Colombo. Bronio preferred to choke in his cabin. I didn't sleep from the moment I saw the lighthouse at Colombo. From then I waited for us to land. At 2:30 A.M. we dropped anchor. Except for several nearby ships and different colored signal lights, I, of course, couldn't see anything. They woke me up at six and we packed, sweating profusely in the forty-degree centigrade heat in the cabin. My first impressions were unpleasant. Sweltering heat at nine in the morning. Red houses, streets red as the earth (*terra rossa*). Lush greenery. I went to look at the ocean (the color of the Baltic plus a beach). As soon as we passed by India, the sea changed from blue to green. There I chatted on a bench with a Sinhalese for the first time in my life. Bronio went to see some guy to whom he'd been given a letter of recommendation. Then we took rickshaws (each of us in a separate one) and went to Cinnamon Gardens.

I had thought a ride in a rickshaw would be something unpleasant because of having a guilty conscience. That's not the case at all. They give the impression of being animals. Wonderful people. In color ranging from red chocolate to black bronze. Some with long hair, others with a top knot and circular combs all around their heads; the ends of these combs sparkle in the sun like phlox roses. The diabolical impression a tropical garden makes. Trees with forms and colors that are beyond belief. Bamboos, lianas, eucalyptuses, flowers of every color with shapes out of fairy tales. Then a Buddhist temple 150 years old. New wall paintings and gigantic painted statues and frescoes. But everything gaudy and exaggerated. You could tell that everything was new. We were taken for Jews. Six little Sinhalese took our shoes off. After lunch we went out of the city. Little houses in the midst of palm forests. Wonderful costumes. Pieces of chocolate and black flesh amid purple violets. Clean-shaven priests in long yellow garments with fans. We're in tropical outfits with pith helmets covering our heads. Despite the sweltering heat and dirt, and garbage in the streets, almost no unpleasant smell whatsoever. Colombo isn't any city at all. Just little houses scattered among the palm forests. Every blade of grass, every stone has its own individual character and doesn't remind us of anything we know. Outside the city, scrubby brush amid swampland skirting a golf course where stodgy Englishmen play golf. If you half-shut your eyes, you might think that you were in Lithuania. We slept for a rupee a person in a Sinhalese hotel. Everything is so original down to the smallest details. Mysterious, bronze monkeys wait on us half-naked. The beds have mosquito nets. Terrific heat. The sweat pours off a naked person lying quietly. Colombo is full of ravens that croak hopelessly all day and night and give a dismal cadaverous atmosphere to everything. (We were late for the train to Kandy and thus had to spend the night in Colombo.) In the port, instead of seagulls, red-bronze vultures with jagged wings fly about.

In the morning we're on our way to Kandy. The capital of the independent state of the Sinhalese. A rich Sinhalese planter is going with us and he's explaining things to us. Diabolical vistas. Meadows flooded with water in the midst of forests. Strange olive-green calami. In little ponds, purple-violet water lilies. The vegetation madder and madder, and the people more and more gaudily but wonderfully dressed (violet, yellow and purple, sometimes emerald green), which along with the chocolate and bronze bodies, and the strange plants in the background, creates a diabolical effect.

The mountains begin halfway there. Angolla Peak. The mountains give the impression of something soft made of peat. Everything is choked by the frenzy of luxuriant vegetation. Trees with leaves in unheard-of shapes, from huge voluminous ones to different designs fringed with minute jagged edges. The mountains bigger and bigger. We're going over valleys hundreds of feet deep, in the midst of which rice fields lie drowned in water, cut out in strange patterns. The trees are covered with flowers going from purple and orange vermilion to violet and red and white. . . . [A page is missing.]

They cart around fruits resembling orange melons, full of sweet juice (a quart in each one) contained within thick, white walls. Green, yellow, and violet fruits. Gum trees, breadfruit trees. Coconut and banana palms. By the railroad-crossing gate, a group of children going to school. Further on you can see the school without any walls, full of children of many different colors. Mountains in fantastic shapes. Sheer cliffs fall off into the thick of the jungle.

We were in Kandy at eleven in the morning. All along the way bushes covered with flowers, orange bordering on vermilion.

The hotel where we're staying, on the slope of the mountains covered with palms, lianas, and the devil knows what, on the edge of a lake full of fish and turtles, is an enchanted palace. (Eight rupees including meals.) All this causes me the most frightful suffering and unbearable pain, since she's no longer alive with me. Only the worst despair and the senselessness of seeing this beauty. She won't see this—and I'm not an artist.

I wouldn't wish my worst enemy to go through what I've been living through mentally on the ship and what I'm suffering, looking at the inconceivable beauty of the world.

All this is too much for me mentally and spiritually. Everything is poison which brings close thoughts of death. Will this inhuman suffering ever come to an end! I kiss you, Dad, my dearest Dad.

I kiss Mrs. Dembowska's hand.

Stas

Bronio sends his respects.

2 July 1914

ANURASDHAPURA

Explications for the Authorities of Ceylon

Having lost my fiancée who committed suicide, I wanted to kill myself four months ago. My family counseled me to make a journey. My friend (one of my two best friends) was just about to go to New Guinea on a scientific expedition. He was kind enough to lend me fifty pounds to add to the sum I already had and has taken me with him in a very bad psychic state and on account of it has had many troubles. He was as good as the best brother and I am sorry that I must do him such an injustice and abandon him on his dangerous trip. But I see that traveling instead of improving my state causes me horrible pain. Because I see beautiful things that she never will see and this make me most unhappy. More than I was before.

I am writing this in the hope that my dearest friend Dr. Malinowski will have no troubles on account of my death and that he will be able to avoid any formalities or inquiries that might make him late for his ship. That is my last will: that he is not disturbed on account of me in his journey, because he must be in Australia for the Congress of the British Association for the Advancement of Science. It would be for me a very great pain if instead of expressing my gratitude to him I would cause him any trouble.

Excuse me for my horrible English.

Yours,

S. I. Witkiewicz

[Original letter in English, here slightly corrected for intelligibility; postscript in Polish.]

Dear Bronio:

You'll think this is ham acting.

I don't wish you ever to suffer even a part of what I've been through.

[Printed on the envelope:]

Clarke's Botanic Hotel
North Terrace
Adelaide
Telephone 665

[In Witkiewicz's hand:]

B. Malinowski
Open in case of my death

[On the reverse side of the envelope:]

H.M.
To the authorities or Police of Ceylon
St. Ignacy Witkiewicz
Explications
humorous [added later]

Freemasons Hotal   Albany, 3 August 1914
Stirling Terrace   Western Australia

Dearest Parents:

Today the terrible news about the war reached us in Albany. If it turns out to be true, then I'm coming back on the first steamer from Fremantle. This is the only way I can be useful and do something. Otherwise there's nothing left but the frightful prospect of going mad without being able to do creative work, the sole justification for my existence. Perhaps in this fashion I'll end my life more worthily than by suicide or painting landscapes in New Guinea or catching yellow fever.

This whole trip makes no sense at all. I worry about you, Mother. What's going on back there now?

There are unconfirmed reports about an Austrian-Russian and a French-German war. Personal matters must be put aside and in some way I must try to justify this miserable existence of mine.

The absurdity of this trip is dreadful. Bronio is increasingly distant from me. Looking at specimens of Australian flora while back home such terrible things are happening makes no sense whatsoever. In the face of such things life acquires a new meaning. I'm postponing any further description of Australia.

I'm too distraught to be able to go on writing.

I hug you both.

Staś

What can I write in the face of truly great events?

I shouldn't have come here at all, feeling as I did during those last days in Zakopane and London.

What strange bad luck that everything in my life happens at the wrong time.

Both my personal life and art have been totally wasted. Perhaps now there's a chance for something really to happen or at least to die.

RMS *Orvieto*
5 August 1914

The time has come to set aside personal matters, renounce suicidal thoughts, which are utterly trivial compared to what is. actually happening, and make something of one's life and of what is left of one's strength. Just think what frightful things are still happening to me. At such a frightful time, when you and the country are threatened by danger, I cannot reach you— many thousands of kilometers distant from you, reduced to inactivity and despair. Truly my fate is tragic. I had a premonition, which is why I felt so strongly against going. This trip was not something I willed. I played no part in the decision, since I didn't even want to live. Now the sole possibility of saving one's honor and at last accomplishing something by dying in the ranks of the combatants has been taken away from me. The most frightful suffering was not enough. The worst absurdity was still to come. I cannot write this, because I am crushed by despair more atrocious than anything I have ever known before. I'll try to get back to Poland, but if I do not succeed, what will I do? I won't survive such inaction.

The last opportunity is eluding my grasp and there remains the monstrous absurdity of life robbed of any possibility of action. When art came to an end, it was still possible to do that. But even that is gone.

For what am I being so frightfully punished?

What's happening now defies description.

Suffering without any possibility of ending it all beautifully in suicide.

I'd like to be there now and take part in the fighting, and at least end my life in a worthy cause.

But even that is denied me. Terrible remorse for having come.

But it wasn't solely my responsibility. Who will ever understand how frightful all this is. Not to be able to be there with everyone else when the fate of Poland hangs in the balance, and to travel through Australia sightseeing.

I can't write.

Horrible, beyond all endurance.

If I am not able to get back to Poland, I won't be able to go on living.

The absurdity is really too horrible.

The last possibility taken away from me.

Frightful suffering.

10 AUGUST 1914
BOTANIC HOTEL
ADELAIDE

It may seem foolish that crushed by a frightful personal misfortune and by the frightful news about the war and by my own enforced idleness, I concern myself with things of slight importance, with superstitions. But in my life fate is linked in such a strange fashion with the hour, twenty minutes before ten, that I cannot keep from describing the facts concerning this time of day.

My first impression connected with this time of day.

I was about ten years old. I'd gone to bed. Mother was playing the piano. Two dark rooms separated me from her. A candle was burning. I was afraid of something, but I didn't know of what. It was then that hour of the day. At least that is the earliest memory I have connected with that hour of the day. I call attention to the fact that when I was a child, I was especially taken with Australia. Evidence of this is the map of Australia in a small atlas which I received from Mrs. Dembowska, and which was heavily underlined. The city of Adelaide is specially marked, with its geographic latitude and longitude. A second dream of my childhood from the period of studying chemistry was potassium cyanide. I dreamed of having it in my collection of chemicals.

Whenever I saw that hour on a clock that was running (even if it wasn't right, say at five o'clock or at midnight), always in the course of three or four days something unpleasant happened to me.

The first time I saw a clock at that hour was in Lithuania in Syłgudyszki. I forgot my watch when I went out for a walk. In the evening when I returned to my room, I found my watch showing that time. The next day I came down with typhus, a rather dangerous attack. (The only serious illness I've had since I was seven years old.)

The second time was in Rome [in April 1905], I had to meet Miss T. [Ewa Tyszkiewicz] in Florence. I hoped to have a decisive talk with her about our future relations.

I had been in love with her since I was seventeen. I went to bed early about nine o'clock. Karol Szymanowski, with whom I had made the trip and who knew about my superstition, saw that my watch had stopped and *set it at that time.* In the morning I didn't wake him up and I left with the conviction that something bad would happen. Three days later I had a talk with Miss T. in Florence in the Borgello Museum; what emerged from this conversation was that there could be no kind of future for us together. Despite a subsequent exchange of letters, our correspondence came to an end less than a year later. In Florence for the first time I began to have suicidal thoughts.

In 1909 in December (or at the end of November) at the Śmiałowskis I set an antique clock—which hadn't ever been running—at that hour, hoping to overcome my superstition. By March I had met at Miss M.D.'s the late Jadwiga Janczewska, in March I had met Mrs. Irena Solska. After I had established a relationship with Solska, I had to go to Zakopane at the end of June. She was already there.'I was staying in Cracow on Grodzka Street. (The time of the occurrences was as follows. If the clock was running and I saw the fatal hour, a minor unpleasantness would take place in the course of the three days after my noticing it. If the clock had stopped, the time would be three months. Why there was exactly that time limit and when the ritual first arose I cannot recall any more than I can the very beginning of this superstition.) Whenever I went to the town square, I always went along the left side. On the day before my departure, when I left the house I noticed in front of the gate a wagon loaded with coal. I had to go around it. To do so, I automatically crossed to the other side and for the first time I noticed that there was a watchmaker there. A huge wall clock was pointing to that hour. (The minute hand had to be not past the eight, either VIII or 8. It didn't necessarily have to be at exactly the right point.)

In the course of a month I experienced things with Mrs. Solska that had a decisive influence on my whole future life. I tried to break off my relations with her, but I didn't have the strength, and this affair (as a result of which I was later judged very harshly) dragged on for a long time. (I have always said that I can see my life up to the age of thirty. There's no getting past thirty, and numbers like thirty-one, thirty-two, thirty-five, or forty have no meaning for me as numbers measuring the years of my life. Seventeen was my fatal number, I don't know why either.)

When I was to go to London from Brittany in 1911, my watch stopped at twenty to ten. In the evening it had stopped at twenty-five to ten, I must have pushed it aside and forgotten to wind it—in the morning it had stopped at that hour. Evidently it went those five minutes more because of being jolted.

In Cambridge from the bus I saw a large wall clock stopped at that hour in a store window. And at the dentist, glancing through the newspaper I noticed a watchmaker's advertisement with a clock at that hour. Within two months the breakup of my affair with Mrs. Solska began, which cost me a great deal of strength, and that whole period of my life was extremely painful.

We lived for seventeen years in the Ślimak house. After seventeen years we moved to Bystre to the villa Nosal. (We lived on Bystre the first time we were in Zakopane when I was two years old.) There was a painting hanging there with a clock in the middle. I had the habit of always looking at clocks in a new place. I was pleased to note that this clock was stopped at twenty minutes to eleven. Within two months, when we were completely settled in this house and when the late Jadwiga Janczewska had been living there for quite a while, I noticed that this clock had not stopped at twenty minutes to eleven, but at twenty minutes to ten. It was in the morning. I told her about this superstition and spoke about the clock. I went over to the clock and noticed (almost with terror) that the hour hand was slightly bent and the clock actually had stopped at twenty minutes to ten. As though the clock had been lying in wait and showing another hour for two months so that we wouldn't leave the house. That was when I realized that I would certainly meet with some terrible misfortune in that house. Because after living for seventeen years at Ślimak house, to move to another house and find the clock there stopped at that hour is perhaps more than a little uncanny.

On 17 January, a Friday (Friday is my bad day), I proposed to the late Jadwiga Janczewska. I didn't want her to go to Leszcze in June. The round clock that Mother got from Miss Tyszkiewicz had stopped at twenty to ten in April.

The best days of my life came to an end with that trip of hers. Our relationship deteriorated more and more (it was all my hideous fault. Failure to esteem either myself or her, for which I have been punished so frightfully). In January or February 1914 for a joke I set the clock in the sanatorium at that hour. It was when Rubinstein had his concert. The awful thing happened on 21 February. On 24 February I began the thirtieth year of my hopelessly wasted life. On Friday the twentieth there was a misunderstanding between us that was the cause of this terrible catastrophe.

When I received the letter from Bronisław Malinowski that decided everything about the whole trip, it was in the morning at Tadeusz Langier's. His alarm clock was pointing to that hour.

In London at Gani's when I was buying a tropical outfit for the first time, I saw a large wall clock pointing to that hour. That's not all, a few days later, also in London, when I left my watch to be repaired, I saw an alarm clock pointing to that hour.

Another evening instead of getting off at Gray's Inn Road, I got off at Southampton Row and going down Theobald Road I noticed the hands on an alarm clock in a store window pointing to that hour. Leaving the dentist's office in West Hampstead I had to go to King's Cross. *Without knowing why* I bought a ticket for Baker Street. Later going down Baker Street I noticed a small clock pointing to that hour.

Despite all these warnings I went on the voyage. This was *the seventeenth voyage of the* Orsova. In Ceylon at Domhilli and at Naalande I tried to kill myself. I sat with my Browning pressed against my temple. I could not do it, thoughts about my Parents kept me from it at the last minute.

This trip is unmitigated torture. Between death and thoughts about Mother. In Kolgoorlie (in Australia) I took a bit of sodium cyanide in a gold factory. I had finally got hold of cyanide, in Australia of all places. That's an odd coincidence too. (When we went aboard the *Orontes* in Colombo, it was twenty minutes to ten on the clock in the dining hall.) In Perth before our departure for Albany I had a terrible day. I wrote to Father that only marriage to Miss S. could save me (despite correspondence with Miss Z.). As I was leaving for the post office to mail the letter, I saw twenty minutes to ten on the clock in the hotel. When I came back, I wanted to kill myself by taking the cyanide. Once again I didn't have the strength. I held the crystal in my hand, I *even* licked it and didn't have the courage to put it in my mouth and bite into it. Isn't that dreadful? And at the same time monstrously funny.

Only thoughts about my Parents tie me to life, but what can I do for them in the state I'm in?

Earlier that day I went to look for Malinowski at the Museum. I *thought* that I would certainly see twenty to ten then. And coming back I didn't go as usual along the left side of Barrack Street, but along the right side (I don't know why) and I *noticed a small clock pointing to twenty to ten.* That evening we went to Albany and there I learned that war had broken out.

Frightful anxiety about my Parents and the complete hopelessness of my position. There in Europe truly great things are happening, for which one can give one's life, and I'm here looking at Australian flowers in the company of Englishmen and I am helpless. The monstrous nonsense of this situation. Suicide seemed to me to be something repulsive in comparison. I decided to return.

I intended to stay in Perth and wait for the boat. News about the detaining of the Australian steamships. I listened to Malinowski's advice and went to Adelaide (it was fate that I had to be in Adelaide). On the way we passed the *Orsova* returning to Europe. Perhaps it is the last steamer that will make it. Bronio's advice, seemingly good, always turns out to be bad. My helplessness here in the face of the war is something monstrous. As though there wasn't enough misfortune already. Now the most dreadful thing of all is coming true. The impossibility of rehabilitation and of carrying out the final and only act for which I'm qualified.

Today between an unsuccessful visit to the Russian consul and a visit to the Austrian consul (where I found out that there wasn't any hope of returning), I saw a clock *pointing to twenty to ten* in King William Street. At the Russian consulate it was the same story. No hope of returning and carrying out the final act. The ship by which I could have gone leaves Melbourne on Wednesday. Will I leave on it? What will happen? What will become of my Parents? Father will not get money from Russia. What will Mother do with that boarding house in such times? No one will send me money either. To travel further is monstrous nonsense. To return is almost ruled out. Despair because of her, because of my ruined life and creative work. Despair about my Parents and despair on account of the impossibility of joining the struggle in which I could still end my life in a worthy fashion. What a frightful thing my life has suddenly turned into. What will happen next?

On the day that Helena Czerwijowska left, when I stayed alone with the late Jadwiga Janczewska, I saw Mrs. Solska at Antałówka for the first time since our breaking up. That was the day on which everything that was destined to happen already seemed imminent. The fact that I continued social relations with Mrs. Solska and the presence of Helena Czerwijowska in Zakopane— these were the real reasons why it all ended so frightfully. Janczewska was progressively losing faith in me. As I was returning from Antałówka (when I went to get Helena Czerwijowska's wallet, which she had forgotten), I found a playing card in the mud on the way back. It was the nine of hearts, which in my way of fortune-telling stands for erotic feelings. I don't believe in fortune-telling. I don't believe in anything like that, not even in the superstition of the fatal hour. And yet the facts that I am setting forth are strange enough.

I kept that card. In May 1914 I found it by chance, tore it up, and threw it away. When I went to Olcza to see Miss Z. (why did I reject her deep love through an excess of honesty? I couldn't give her anything except despair over the Dead Woman. I shall again never be able to love anyone. Why did I come on this voyage which in the last moments of my life has turned into a futile, horrible torture and made it impossible for me to carry out the final act), I found that same card, the nine of hearts, on the way to Olcza. Apparently I had returned from Berlin at that point on account of Miss Z. Wasn't this a premonition and the last opportunity I would have in life? In London, making a superhuman effort, I resolved to go on the trip.

And what has been the outcome of it all? I am half deranged. My state is frightful. Each moment is frightful torment. And now there's the war and all that. I don't know how I'll endure it all.

This is the thirtieth year of my life, about which I've always said that I don't see it distinctly ahead of me. Only twenty-nine made sense as the number of years for my life. Ahead lies madness or death. To torture oneself so is not possible. There is only one chance, and I'm losing it.

I ask your forgiveness, whatever happens to me.

Bronio, don't laugh at what I'm writing. Someday you'll understand it all.

Dearest Parents, forgive me if I'm not able to endure all of this.

Staś

In 1913 I dreamed that I tried to commit suicide in my room at Nosal. *The clothes cabinet was standing there* as it has been ever since the spring of 1914 when I lived in that room with Mother. Helena Czerwijowska was sitting by the window. I shot myself in the temple with my Browning (the one with which she, poor thing, killed herself). The Browning misfired and I woke up.

In January or at the beginning of February 1914, I dreamed that I poisoned myself. I took poison and went along a winding path through the fields. Then I fell down and could not die. Now, when I was going to Albany, I dreamed that I was with Mother in a room (like a huge *coupé* in a train) and Mother said, "I saw Miss Jadwiga." I asked where. Mother pointed out to me the corner of the room where there was a sofa. Initially I didn't see anything, and then slowly there began to be outlined a transparent face at first. It was Her ghost. Then more and more clearly, but she was entirely transparent. She sat sideways to me, wearing a karakul fur coat (in which she always sat on the veranda) and looked off to the side with frightful sadness. She always had that expression when she said that she was in a suicidal state.

It's all so frightful.

Frightful and absurd like a dream that will never end.

On the way to Albany I had another dream: that I took cyanide. I drank the poison and couldn't die and suffered frightful torments.

For more than ten years I've had an ominous feeling all the time that I'd die accused of things I didn't do.

A poem about my death written in October.

In the diary that I burned I wrote in October, "I'll die in frightful torments."

HOTEL METROPOLE
SYDNEY, 2 SEPTEMBER 1914

Dear Bronio:

I wanted to let you know that I've received letters in answer to my letters sent from Kandy, so probably yours have got through as well. I'm staying in this hotel for three shillings sixpence.

Quite by chance I ran into Nechayev. On Saturday I'm resuming my trip.

I won't write on the question of our relations, since I don't have anything more to say on the subject at this time. You'll have lots of time in Papua to think it over and perhaps you'll come to understand many things when you look at them from a distance and in solitude. If it's not too late and if you truly care for me (which I haven't been able to detect so far), perhaps someday at Olcza we'll be able to talk about it quite differently. My greatest wish is for you to change before life teaches you various things in a much crueler fashion than up until now.

I feel deep gratitude to you for certain things. If there haven't been any results, that's because I'm a completely broken human being whom only death can cure. Half a year has passed and everything is exactly as it was, but even worse. May my death be something more than a foolish accident and I hope to end my life in a useful way. This is the only thing that you can wish me.

I have great faith that your expedition will be a success and that you'll come back safely.

Staś

P.S. When we left Toowoomba, photo albums with pictures of the Kingsland district were given out free. The clock on the tower in Toowoomba pointed to twenty minutes to ten (naturally that's in the picture). Lupton is a witness. Isn't that the height of bad luck?

SS *MOREA*
14 SEPTEMBER 1914

Dear Bronio:

Thanks for your letters, but even if I were in London I'd try to avoid taking advantage of your offer. Of course, Turner's help is now completely out of the question owing to the revelations on both sides. As it now stands, Nechayev and I are planning to leave from Port Said. It's possible that money from Russia will be waiting for me in Greece or Bulgaria. I have no idea how telegrams are faring in circumstances like these now.

Nechayev is traveling first-class so I see him only occasionally.

The Goldings are extremely kind and considerate to me. I like them very much. I wish you'd devote some thought to your character. Not for my sake, but for your own. You may have some very serious regrets later on.

A person can make mistakes and try to atone for them. But one cannot regard oneself cynically. Because that closes the door on any hopes of improvement.

I must confess that as it stands now I don't believe in you. Not because of your attitude toward me. It couldn't either harm me or help me. As you rightly observed, twenty pounds more or less is of no importance compared to the "horrors" that I'm going to experience. At any rate there's nothing that can help me or harm me. And I hold no grudge against you on my own account, only on *your* account.

I wish you good luck in your scientific work and in leading another life, above all another inner life. With a squeeze of your hand,

Staś

I'll write if anything important happens.

P. & O.S.N. Co.
SS *MOREA*
1 OCTOBER 1914

Dear Bronio:

I'm sorry that I wrote such disagreeable letters. Couldn't help it, you know, sir, damned if I could!

We'll probably never see one another again as long as we live, and not have any chance to discuss this question.

The *Morea* is very appealing, far better than the Orient liners. We stopped in Bombay. A marvelous city.

Tomorrow we're stopping at Aden, and then continue from Port Said to Alexandria, and from there to Salonika.

I'm running out of dough, if I can only hold out till we get to the border. My fate is to a high degree uncertain. Mrs. Golding is a marvelous woman. Too bad she's old.

I seduced a Portuguese whore from Brazil, but without any great pleasure. Two trepangs, afterward I lost the urge.

My life is frightful.

I've been flirting with various foreign broads. I hardly recognize myself. I've gone completely soft in the head. I'm sketching quite a few portraits. Social life quite diabolical.

In moments of clearsightedness it's hideous. I try to stupefy myself so as to endure this trip. Afterwards I'll take whatever comes my way.

I squeeze your hooked claws. Sometimes I'm fearful about your health.

I miss the tropics. But in the state I'm in the beauty of the world is torture.

[Excerpt from a letter written by an unknown British woman to Malinowski, sent from England to Papua in late 1914.]

Witkiewicz "came out" tremendously on the homeward voyage—did charcoal sketches of various passengers, fell in love temporarily with a professor's wife, and became quite an intimate chum of mine and my husband's and Mr. McLaren. He certainly has the most lurid personality of anyone I have ever met and we got very fond of him in spite of his peculiarities and difficult temperament. I expect you know that he and Prof. Niechieff (can't spell it) were arrested in Alexandria on suspicion of being Professors Penck and Maas and had rather a bad one and a half hours until they had established their identity. I have had three letters from him since he left us, the last being from Petrograd just when he was joining the army, but he gave me no address and I fear my attempt to reach him through the Russian consul has failed. I should be glad of news of him. He must be having very hard times if he is fighting.

[St. Petersburg]

[October 1914]

Dear Bronio:

I've been in "Petrograd" for two days and I'm trying to get accepted into the army, which given the fact that I don't have any papers is incredibly difficult. For quite some time now I've been acting according to the dictates of my own will. Other than that, my condition is identical to what it was and only the hope of taking an active part in the war now keeps me in a state of relative equilibrium.

The handful of riflemen fighting over a piece of Galicia as allies of the Germans, who in the most savage fashion laid waste to the greater part of the Kingdom of Poland and who prey like beasts on the Poles living there, constitutes a tragic and horrifying phenomenon. The soldiers' sense of honor, which ties them to Austria and tells them to fight on the side of the Germans, so beautiful in other circumstances, is in this case something appalling.

Thus it is that in our abnormal circumstances virtues become crimes against the soul of the nation. I stood alone in my thinking about Russia and the necessity of fighting with her against the Germans, and I underwent some frightful moments on this account. Now the skirmishing in Galicia has completely collapsed and every Pole can with a clean conscience go against our only true enemy, the Germans.

What frightful things are happening (not journalistic fabrications, but letters from eyewitnesses). Poor Mrs. Janczewska there in Leszcze, facing such a deluge. If I manage to go into the army, I won't even be able to read Miss Jadwiga's diaries before possibly getting killed. And you may die there in Australia of a tropical fever or something worse. No matter what, I have pangs of conscience that you stayed on there alone.

But the way you behaved toward me was not what I would have liked. I'm writing to your former spirit. Malinowski has ceased to exist for me and I must admit that I haven't once experienced any nostalgia for him. In your company I felt nostalgic for Bronio, and now I think about the good old days when the dialectic of the void and the spouting of quintessential lies concealed the poverty of our deeds.

At this moment every Pole has a heavy conscience. But there's only one course of action possible. What does it matter if Żeromski has been wounded fighting with the Austrian-backed sharpshooters. He's an artistic genius with a false ideology. What does it matter if Strug has been killed. Since it's impossible to agree with those ideas. A tragic error. There's only one course of action possible. I understand them, but I am consistent. I always considered that band of sharpshooters to be an attractive form of suicide. (Włodzio Tetmajer put a bullet through his head after the entry into Kielce. Apparently he saw the truth. That is acting in accord with honor.)

What a frightful liar you are when you say that I taught you cynicism. It was you who taught me to regard everything including myself with cynicism. Think that over for a moment. A convenient attitude: to have a total lack of faith in any noble impulses whatsoever and your cold ironic smile, and the conviction that at bottom human motives are always petty and mean. If one wishes to see life that way, it's quite easy. Flowers grow in the swamp. One can look at them, without sticking one's nose in the mud. I was alone and suffered frightfully. Now I see that everyone is like that. But many still don't believe in Russia and they keep snug without getting involved.

People are so prejudiced against me that my uncle Jałowiecki won't even shake my hand. The Janczewskis have so influenced opinion against me. I hope it will at least preserve her poor memory from gossip. May all the guilt fall on my head. I won't apologize to anyone.

Ada Żukowska is recommending me to people, perhaps something will come of it. She is the sole person who is on my side. I endured frightful attacks from Aunt Jałowiecka for everything. They keep imagining that I have some kind of responsibility to my Parents. It's either this course of action, or moral decay. I didn't come back from Australia to rot somewhere in a corner, once more failing to confront my destiny. It's all like some hideous dream.

Don't think that it was making the trip with Nechayev that changed my ideas. I came to this myself after frightful doubts and tortures. And now my conscience is no longer divided. I only want it not to be cheap, and I want to accomplish a deed that can confirm these ideas.

Quite unbelievable things can be read in the Russian newspapers now. What is written about Poland. What enthusiasm, sympathy, how much money is given for the Polish population of the Kingdom destroyed by German pillage. The sole moments in our history that we cannot let slip by unheeded.

The time on the *Morea* now seems an agreeable hallucination. Unusually pleasant memories of the Goldings. She is a marvelous woman. Too bad she's old and shaves. I'm left with a nasty aftertaste following my romance with that Portuguese woman, who turns out to be half-German. You see what a mélange that was. You have a right to smile cynically. There's a good deal of beastliness in my makeup. Sorry, sir, can't be helped. That's the frightful result of behaving inconsistently.

During the last three days of the trip, I fell madly in love with Mrs. Minchin, the wife of the crippled Puscoccus from Uganda, Nyanza, and London. A woman utterly plain but marvelous, stupid and full of charm. As the result of several conversations with me, she got sick and at the last minute I didn't see her. She said she had no taste for "gruesome things." What a frightful injustice!

See how horrible inconsistency is. And at bottom it's all the same. Despair caused by the death of the One and Only. You may consider all this "ham acting." Oh, how you've expanded the concept. The same goes for the concept of snobbery. These concepts are so broad that if they are pushed just a little bit further, there'll be room for all the manifestations of the human soul and the world will be thoroughly "Malinowski-ized."

Forgive me for writing this way. Don't think I hate you. It's just that

Malinowski has ceased to exist for me. I'm writing to Bronio about Malinowski and about the person who has stopped being Staś, but has not yet become anyone else.

I've asked the Minister of War to let me join the Izmailovsky Regiment of the Guards. I don't have my birth certificate or record of service in the reserves. But maybe I'll succeed.

I was at the Brzezińskis, but the fire on the side of Fontanka cut short the visit. When the war broke out, your mother was staying with the Staszewskis. That's all in German hands now and it's impossible to get any news.

I give you a hug.

I felt the need to write to you, and I couldn't do it less than frankly.

Staś Witkiewicz

[Excerpt from a letter in French, dated 30 January 1915, from Aniela Jałowiecka, a paternal aunt in Petrograd, to Witkacy's mother.]

I thought that you had heard a long time ago about your son's destiny. As we figured it, you should have received his letter in which he tells you what has happened during the past few months of his life while he made the irreversible decision to enter the Russian Army to defend Poland. He got here toward the end of September and after many difficulties he was accepted in officers training school, from which he will graduate in two months with the rank of an officer, ready to enter the army, perhaps the Polish legions, which are in the process of being formed. No argument, no influence has been able to make him change his mind. Before he never was the way he is now. Calm, almost joyful, he holds himself straight with his head raised high—he has completely shaken off the despairing state of apathy in which we first saw him when he arrived. He's preparing for his theoretical exams remarkably well, and he's holding up under the rigors of army life splendidly. His health is excellent. He looks very well in his uniform, neither the heavy boots, nor the thick coat, nor the saber bother him in the least.

ST. PETERSBURG
[OCTOBER 1916]

Dear Bronio:

I may be going to the Crimea for treatment of my nerves. Can you find out in which bank in Sydney the money for me is located and can it be sent here? Mother wrote that there was money deposited for me there, but she doesn't say in which bank. It should be easy to find out by telephone but it's impossible to send a telegram to every bank.

You have no conception of how horrible I feel. If it goes away, I'll return to the front. At this moment I don't even wish to die, but then I don't have any great desire to live either.

Write immediately without fail and find out about that money.

Kisses,

Staś

Write either to the regiment or to the Jałowieckis.

New Forms in Painting
and the Misunderstandings
Arising Therefrom

■

Part 1: Philosophical Introduction

Artistic creation . . . is an affirmation of Existence in its metaphysical horror, and not a justification of this horror through the creation of a system of soothing concepts, as is the case with religion, or a system of concepts showing rationally the necessity of this and not any other state of affairs for the Totality of Existence, as is the case with philosophy.

Part 3: Painting

Chapter 1: General Considerations

We live in a frightful epoch, the likes of which the history of humanity has never known until now, and which is so camouflaged by certain ideas that man nowadays has no knowledge of himself; he is born, lives, and dies in the midst of lying and does not know the depth of his degeneration. Nowadays art is the sole crack through which it is possible to get a glimpse of the horrible, painful, insane monstrosity that is passed off as being the evolution of social progress; finding the truth in philosophy is virtually impossible since it has become so entangled in lies in the shape of empirio-critics and pragmatists. In the forms of art of our age we find the atrociousness of our existence and a final, dying beauty which in all likelihood nothing will be able to bring back anymore.

Part 4: On the Disappearance of Metaphysical Feelings as a Result of the Evolution of Society

Chapter 1: The Evolution of Society

The views expressed here are not those of some "social reactionary," for in fact we believe in the inevitability and necessity of certain changes that have as their goal justice and the common good. We are concerned only with the secondary effects of these changes, as to whose consequences, in our opinion, certain delusions are much too prevalent. . . .

Starting with the most primitive community, the development of mankind moves in the direction of restricting the individual in favor of the group, while at the same time the individual, in exchange for certain sacrifices, obtains other advantages that he could not attain all by himself. Subordination of the interests of the single individual to the interests of the whole—this is the most general formulation of the process that we call social progress. . . .

It goes without saying that vain are the dreams of naive communists who want to resolve the problem by a return to certain primitive forms of social existence while retaining all the achievements of present-day civilization. . . . Mankind cannot deliberately retreat from the level of civilization it has already attained; it cannot even stop, for stopping amounts to the same thing as going backward. We cannot give up the increasing convenience and security of our lives, nor can we deliberately stop man's further domination of matter and the resultant organization of the working classes on the vast expanses of our planet. . . . We cannot say: that's enough civilization and comfort in our lives for the time being, now we'll set to work on the equal distribution of civilization throughout the entire world and bring happiness to all by means of what has already been accomplished. As long as there exists raw material that can be processed and as long as technology encounters no barriers of catastrophic proportions (which for a short period is quite doubtful given the ever-new discoveries of sources of energy), our demands will constantly grow in keeping with the dissemination of previous accomplishments, and halting civilization on a certain already attained level is an absolute impossibility. We cannot foretell what forms the life of society will assume with the passage of time—this is an equation with too large a number of unknowns—in any case on the basis of the already known segments of history we can say that the process of mankind's socialization is a phenomenon that is irreversible in the long run although in the short run it can undergo certain relatively minute fluctuations. . . .

The gray mob was only a pulpy mass on which grew monstrous and splendid flowers: rulers, true sons of powerful deities, and priests holding in their hands the frightful Mystery of Existence. Today, with the astonishment of true democrats, we cannot understand how this mob could have endured so much suffering and maltreatment of "the dignity of man" without protest and revolt, or why they did not establish some kind of communistic regime. But the traditions of such realms are still alive even in our own times in the form of the great nations that succeed in placing their own honor higher than the lives of millions of individuals. The present-day ruler is only a ghost, a wretched caricature when compared to his ancestors—he is only the embodiment of all the people's power and strength, which in the past was the privilege of a person or a small group but today is the property of whole nations. But we live in times in which, as the ghosts of nations depart into the past, there appears a shadow threatening everything that is beautiful, mysterious, and unique of its kind—the shadow of that gray mob kept down for centuries, and it is growing to frightening proportions embracing all of mankind. This ghost is still not strong enough yet, but like a spirit at a spiritualist séance it is materializing more and more; already its grazing touch and first contact can be felt which, transformed into hard blows, will avenge the torments of all those wretched beings out of which the mob took shape. Now terrified of this shadow, rulers humble themselves before the people, begging them for the power which in the past they derived from themselves, from the deities who gave birth to them. . . .

This frightful shadow makes the rulers of the world tremble, threatens to destroy all understanding of the Mystery of Existence by making philosophers the servants of its demands, and hurls artists into the depths of madness. It is cast by a mass of former slaves, whose gigantic stomach and desire to enjoy all that they have been deprived of until now becomes the law of existence on our planet now that they grow organized. . . .

Whereas for the former ruler the mob was only pulp that he shaped according to his own will and he alone accomplished great deeds following his own bizarre notions and using the mob as though it were an obedient tool devoid of a will of its own, now the powerful master of times to come will be (and perhaps already is, in an embryonic state) only a tool in the hands of the mass, which strives for material enjoyment and a sense of its own power. . . .

We turn our eyes from the past in shame and from the future in dread at the coming of boredom and grayness, or we create artificial narcotics with which we hope to awaken the long-since dead feeling and fervor of individual strength, we create artificial mystery and artificial beauty in art and in life. It's all in vain—beauty resides only in madness, truth lies at our feet torn to pieces by contemporary philosophers, and of this trinity of ideals, for us there remains only the good, that is, the happiness of all those who have not had the strength to create beauty, or enough courage to look the mystery in the eye. What awaits us is the monstrous boredom of mechanical soulless life in which the little people of the world will wallow in moments of leisure produced by reduced work loads. . . .

The people of the future will need neither truth nor beauty; they will be happy—isn't that enough? . . . The people of the future will not feel the mystery of existence, they will have no time for it, and besides they will never be lonely in the ideal future society.

What will they live for? They will work to eat, and eat to work. But why should this question upset us? Isn't the sight of ants, bees, or bumblebees, perfectly mechanized and organized, a reassuring one? Probably they are totally happy, all the more so that undoubtedly they never could think and experience what we have during the four or five thousand years we have endured with a consciousness of the mystery of being. . . .

The physical and spiritual forces of the individual are limited, whereas the strength of organized humanity can grow, at least for the time being, without limit. The numerical limit of this phenomenon can equal the sum total of all the people in the world, but the first step on the way to total leveling of differences is the standardization of civilization, which, given the perfection of the means of communication and interchange of information, grows, at least in Europe, at an absolutely frantic rate. Abstract inequality and individual differences are being wiped out by the specialization of work, and at the extremes the machinery of the whole system will iron them out perfectly. In comparison with present-day cultural interaction, former civilizations were totally isolated, and most significantly, they developed extremely slowly. Nowadays whatever any genius discovers instantly becomes the property of all, and even the most individual accomplishments, quite independent of the will of the person responsible for them, add to the growing power of the mob of gray workers fighting for their rights. Present-day "great men" and geniuses seem to be a tame version of once savage and dangerous beasts, who for reasons of safety have been declawed and defanged. They have a strength, cunning, and resourcefulness that can be used to good advantage, but they pose no threat whatsoever to mankind, whom they have rendered happy, and the forms that the great men of our times use to make available for the general welfare the values they have created are extremely agreeable and pleasant. . . .

In our period, wars—once a splendid manifestation of the wild strength of nations—are neither spontaneous outbursts of hatred caused by essential differences between nations and a direct desire for domination personified by powerful rulers, nor a battle over ideas whose concrete embodiment was not a matter of material utility, as, for example, the wars of religion. War nowadays is nothing but cold, mechanical, systematic murder of one's fellowman, devoid of spontaneous emotional motivation, and it has as its goal the acquisition of financial profits carefully calculated and contrived by diplomats, businessmen, and industrialists. Instead of picturesquely dressed knights fighting breast to breast over what to us are completely fantastic issues, we have reduplicated crawling wretches who murder one another from a distance and poison one another with hideous gases. . . . At the moment when the old world died, a world based on the monstrous torments of the greater part of mankind, but which nevertheless bore the most splendid flowers of creativity, and the new transitional regime of moderate democracy based on parliamentary principles failed to produce universal happiness and simply led to exploitation, in another guise, of the same lower strata of mankind without being able to bring forth anything that could be compared to the former creativity, it can only be wished that the process of mechanization and the leveling of individuality will be accomplished as quickly and as uncatastrophically as possible, out of regard for the cultural values already achieved. . . .

Since there is no doubt but that life tends to more and more social justice, to the elimination of exploitation, to an even distribution of burdens, to comfort and security—for every one, not only for exceptional individuals—it might be assumed that the whole mass of until now wasted energies will be turned in another, more important direction than mutual slaughter and torture, and that now for the first time there will appear, perhaps in the near future, a kind of golden age of mankind. . . .

This, it seems to us, is a delusion to which in our times men of good will succumb since they wish to see the future in every aspect through rose-colored glasses. . . . Today's liberals see the future of the broad masses through the prism of their own present psychology. . . . The mystery of existence, unless it appears in the horror of daily life, loses its true significance. . . . Nothing can be achieved without paying for it, and universal happiness is no exception to the rule. Creativity of a certain kind must be lost as the price of this happiness, creativity that has its source in the tragic sense of existence which future people will not be able to feel. . . . While we recognize the necessity of social change and the absolute impossibility of going back to former times when millions of the weak were flagrantly oppressed by a handful of the strong, we nevertheless cannot close our eyes to what we will lose through socialization, and perhaps this awareness will at least permit us (if we are no longer capable of adopting an artificial naïveté in our thinking) to experience in a significant fashion our contemporary artistic creativity, which, although it may pass over into the realm of madness, is all the same the sole beauty of our age.

Chapter 2: The Suicide of Philosophy

In our times the educational function of religion has come to an end once and for all, and religion itself is slowly taking a secondary position. In fact today the only religion that has any validity is the cult of society. Today anyone may worship whatever fetish he wants in his own home or celebrate black masses as long as he is a good member of society. . . . Religion exists for certain individuals from the higher classes, and it also exists for the masses, but in the form of automated rites that have little in common with an essential metaphysical moment. . . . With unparalleled ease the masses are discarding all the dead weight of religion in favor of doctrines that propose alluring solutions to problems of property and the general welfare. The progress of science and the dissemination of discursive philosophy contribute to the decline of religion. Science, especially for certain narrow minds who do not understand its essential value, is taken as the final explaining away of the Mystery of Being, on the basis of one theory or the other, or of some "synthesis" of these.

As society evolves, as life grows more and more comfortable, more certain in its outlines, more automatic and mechanical in its functions, there is less and less place in man's soul for metaphysical anxiety. Our life becomes so defined that man is brought up from the start to fulfill certain partial functions that do not allow him to grasp the whole shape of phenomena, functions that so consume his time with systematically organized work that thinking about ultimate matters which have no immediate utility ceases to be something important in the course of his everyday life. . . .

From a certain point of view, all philosophies, all systems are only ways of reassuring oneself in the face of the inexplicable Mystery.

Each epoch has the kind of philosophy that it deserves. In our present phase we do not deserve anything better than a narcotic of the most inferior sort which has as its goal lulling to sleep our antisocial metaphysical anxiety that hinders the process of automatization. We have this narcotic in excess in all the forms of philosophical literature found throughout the entire world. . . .

The loneliness of the individual in the infinity of Existence became unbearable for man in the as yet incompletely perfected conditions of societal life, and therefore he set out to create a new Fetish in place of the Great Mystery—the Fetish of society, by means of which he attempted to deny the most important law of Existence: the limitation and uniqueness of each Individual Being—so that he would not be alone among the menacing forces of nature. . . .

Metaphysical truths are pitiless and it is not possible to make compromises about them without laying oneself open to the worst inconsistencies. When the problem is posed that way, the only solution is to forbid people to search for the truth, as though that were a kind of fruitless unhealthy mania from which mankind has already suffered long enough throughout the centuries.

This is exactly the position that has been adopted by contemporary philosophy, which deserves the name "philosophy" even less than the most primitive or the most newfangled religious systems. Even a person possessed by an unhealthy religious mania could be considered incomparably higher than a true pragmatist, Bergsonite, or follower of Mach. . . .

Our blasé intellect is only able to take cognizance of certain things passively; we can absorb information, but we are no longer able to say or create anything new on the subject. We have a free choice of the masks we can wear in an hour of deadly boredom, but we cannot feel or experience anything as at least some of our ancestors did. . . .

The proof that the Great Mystery has stopped existing for us once and for all and that we have lost the ability to feel it in its entirety lies in the search for half-mysteries, which, it is hoped, will provide life with some new magic now that the old has been taken away by the exact sciences, social stability, and metaphysics itself in its debased form.

The creation of artificial petty mysteries is a symptom of the disappearance of metaphysical anxiety. The same thing applies to all those mystical beliefs that contemporary America abounds in, despite all its sober approach to life: they are tiny symptoms of an anxiety that something has disappeared which needs to be restored *deliberately*, because without it, for some people, the grayness of tomorrow which is bearing down on us is simply too monstrous. But even these tiny symptoms will soon disappear and from then on mankind will sleep a happy sleep without dreams, knowing nothing in truth about the beautiful and menacing reality that has been its past.

Chapter 3: The Decline of Art

In the closed cultures of antiquity the great artistic styles whose beginnings are lost in the mists of history developed extremely slowly; these styles consisted of two fundamental elements: ornamentation and the presentation of religious images under pressure from the menacing conditions of life and a profound and implacable faith. The religious content of the sculpture and painting that adorned the temples was directly connected to the form; there was no difference between Pure Form and external content because, being close to its primeval source, metaphysical feeling in its purest form, the directly expressed unity in plurality was not divided from its symbol: the image of a fantastic deity. At that time there were not, in our sense of the term, any separate artists forging a style of their own. Rather there was a throng of workers within the context of a style that evolved slowly as the result of a collective effort to which each of them contributed certain relatively minor alterations. . . .

As religion grew superficial and gods were likened to men and the intellect developed in pace with social democratization, there was an immediate effect on art. This process reached its height in Roman sculpture, and then there was a total decline of Art. . . . When Christian mysticism arose, there was fertilization of the human spirit with regard to art. . . .

But from our point of view the Renaissance was a defeat for true Art. . . . Painting declined rapidly, and its ideal became fidelity in copying the external world. . . . The true revival of Pure Form took place in the last decades of the nineteenth century in France starting with the Impressionists who, however, did not leave behind them works of great value besides a riotous outpouring of color, which had been previously killed off by classicism. Even though it stopped being a soulless and even sentimental imitation of nature, painting during this period was not connected with a generally valid metaphysics in the form of religion but was rather the expression of a private, secret, and more or less deliberate metaphysics on the part of individual artists. . . .

The value of a work of art does not depend on the real-life feelings contained in it or on the perfection achieved in copying the subject matter but is solely based upon the unity of a construction of pure formal elements. . . .

Today we have come to Pure Form by another road; it is, as it were, an act of despair against life, which is becoming grayer and grayer, and for that reason, although art is the sole value of our times—excluding of course the technology of living and universal happiness—present-day artistic forms are, in comparison with the old ones, crooked, bizarre, upsetting, and nightmarish. The new art stands in relation to the old as a feverish vision in relation to a calm, beautiful dream. . . .

Nowadays an overworked person has neither the time nor the nervous energy for any thoughtful absorption in works of art, the understanding of which demands leisurely contemplation and inner concentration proportionate to the slow maturation of the works themselves. For people nowadays, the forms of the Art of the past are too placid, they do not excite their deadened nerves to the point of vibration. They need something that will rapidly and powerfully shock their blasé nervous system and act as a stimulating shower after long hours of stupefying mechanical work. This can best be seen in the theater, which, as most dependent on an audience, has most rapidly reached a point of decline from which most probably nothing can ever rescue it, despite efforts at restoring certain old forms. Irrevocably past are the times of metaphysical experiences in the theater, as was the case at the beginnings of Greek tragedy, and all attempts at extricating oneself from mindless realism by means of a "revival" of old forms are an impoverishment of what is and not the natural simplicity that was an expression of strength and spiritual equilibrium.

Today's theater cannot satisfy the average spectator; only the dying breed of theatrical gourmets appreciate the revived delicacies, whereas cabaret on the one hand and cinema on the other are taking away most of the audience from the theater. . . . Cinema can do absolutely everything that the human spirit might desire, and so if we can have such frantic action and striking images instead, isn't it well worth giving up useless chatter on the stage which nobody needs anymore anyhow; is it worth taking the trouble to produce something as infernally difficult as a truly theatrical play when confronted by such a threatening rival as the all-powerful cinema? . . .

Today, like everyone else, the painter as artist is compelled to live in the same atmosphere as other people. He is born in it, from childhood he's been exposed to all the masterpieces ancient and modern in reproductions, something which previously was quite unknown; while still a youth, he grows literally blasé about all forms, he succumbs to the general acceleration of life through the necessity of experiencing it with the frantically gesticulating people all around him, he becomes caught up in the feverish tempo of it all, even if he were to live in the country, drink milk, and read only the Bible; and his nerves are so frayed that metaphysical anxiety in his works assumes forms at the sight of which the general public . . . without understanding their profound substance, roars with laughter and the critic talks about the decline of art. . . . Such an artist either dies of hunger, embittered by the world's failure to understand his tragedy, or one or more gentlemen appear to take him on as an enterprise and launch his career . . . and make a pile of money out of him; and then the same critic who previously had virtually wiped the floor with him . . . now will write about him with wild enthusiasm, while the artist himself, after having created his own style at the age of twenty-eight, will long since have been in the cemetery for suicides or in the hospital poisoned by some drug, or calmed down in a straitjacket on a bed, or, what is still worse, alive and well, but imitating himself in ever-cheaper editions for business purposes. . . . Nowadays painting is teeming with hyenas and clowns, and it is often very hard at first sight to distinguish between clever *saltimbanques* and the true geniuses of our rabid, insatiable form. . . .

We do not maintain, however, that to be a genius one has to drink oneself to death, be a morphine addict, a sexual degenerate, or a simple madman without the aid of any artificial stimulants. But it is frightful that in fact whatever great occurs in art in our agreeable epoch happens almost always on the very edge of madness. . . .

In our opinion, true artists—that is, those who would be absolutely incapable of living without creating, as opposed to other adventurers who make peace with themselves in a more compromising fashion—will be kept in special institutions for the incurably sick and, as vestigial specimens of former humanity, will be the subject of research by trained psychiatrists. Museums will be opened for the infrequent visitor, as well as specialists in the special branch of history: the history of art—specialists like those in Egyptology or Assyriology or other scholarly studies of extinct races: for the race of artists will die out, just as the ancient races have died out.

13 NOVEMBER 1918

PART 3: PURE FORM AND MARRIAGE
1918-24

W hen Witkacy returned to Zakopane on 11 June 1918, he was thirty-three years old, at the height of his creative powers, and ready to embark on a career as a painter and playwright. The former tsarist officer brought back with him a number of canvases that he had done in Russia and the completed manuscript of his first theoretical treatise, *New Forms in Painting*, in which he fully developed his fundamental ideas on the precarious place of art in a mass society.

The next six years were the most productive in Witkacy's life. In an extraordinary outburst of creative energy, he painted hundreds of compositions and portraits, wrote over thirty plays (ten of which were lost during World War II), and published books and essays on aesthetics. At last, after years of self-doubt, Witkacy achieved his goal and became an artist—or at least assumed the mask of an artist. For the first and only time in his life, he joined forces with a group of like-minded painters, the formists, and exhibited with them until the movement disbanded in 1922, thus escaping briefly from the feeling of isolation that usually oppressed him.

The Polish formists were a loose association of artists with futurist and expressionist backgrounds, united in their opposition to naturalism and their belief in the autonomy of art, but hardly very radical by Western European standards. The political and cultural temper of newly independent Poland (reborn in 1919 with the Treaty of Versailles) was conservative and openly hostile to innovation in the arts. Censorship and government repression (formerly used by the occupying powers to silence Polish nationalism) were now directed by the Polish government against anything suspected of being Bolshevik or anarchist, which included all forms of artistic experimentation. Writers were frequently harassed and arrested, magazines confiscated, and theaters raided.

Although by nature an eccentric loner, Witkacy clearly hoped to be a part of the new artistic life of Poland. He published his "Introduction to the Theory of Pure Form in the Theater" in the leading literary journal, *Skamander*. He even tried his hand at translating Conrad's *Almayer's Folly*, which attracted him as an evocation of the tropics. But it was as a playwright that Witkacy was most determined and prolific. In 1918 he wrote his first five act drama, *Maciej Korbowa and Bellatrix* (about the violent overthrow of a decadent ancien régime), in ten days. During 1920–21 he composed fifteen plays in a year and a half. He sent around copies of his works for the stage to professional theaters throughout Poland and dreamed of financial success. Anticipating foreign productions, he arranged for French translations and gave *The Water Hen* to Frau Eckert, a German director from Hamburg. And he planned to have Karol Szymanowski write an opera based on *The Madman and the Nun*.

In a short time, however, it became obvious that between Witkacy and the reigning artistic establishment in Poland there was an unbridgeable chasm. Rejected by the general public, the professional theater, and the literary establishment, the playwright adopted an aggressive stance, often seeking to provoke scandal with his persona "Witkacy." In a series of polemical lectures and articles, he went on the offensive and attacked the provincialism, anti-intellectual tone, and lack of broad theoretical horizons in Polish cultural life, as well as the low level of the prevailing literary and dramatic criticism.

Witkacy's first exposure on the stage came with the performance of *Tumor Brainiowicz* at the venerable Słowacki Theater in Cracow. It had taken almost a year to obtain permission from the local censor, who found the play and particularly the prologue unintelligible and therefore potentially subversive. Even after higher ranking censors in Lwów and Warsaw gave grudging approval, special precautions had to be taken when *Tumor* was finally staged on 30 June 1921, at the close of the regular season. The production was of a private and experimental nature, the number of performances limited to two, and admission only by special invitation or written request.

When it appeared as a book in 1923, his collection of essays *Theater* was hostilely reviewed by the most influential critics. Antagonistic to the theater of his time, which for the most part followed the tradition of Stanislavsky's psychological realism, Witkacy maintained that the wrong people were writing for the stage; it was not professional men of the theater, but children and painters who should become playwrights, he argued. Through the theory and practice of Pure Form, he hoped to restore to the overly rationalized realist stage the magical perceptions of childhood and the modern painter's sense of color and shape. The theater could thus become an autonomous art with a scenic language of its own, independent of referentiality and literary baggage. Performance should take priority over authorial intentions or ideology, Witkacy asserted. "In my view, the director should totally forget about life and any need of being consistent to it and keep in mind only the web of the actions and words which, on the basis of the minimal indications given by the author, he must formulate in a construction that will reflect his own conception of formal Beauty in Time, while leaving the maximum of individual invention to the actors, who likewise will not be subservient to life."

Witkacy shared the traditional Polish view that the theater was an expression of the life of a nation and a measure of the vitality of its culture, but instead of a patriotic, socially minded drama, he wanted one of aesthetic and metaphysical dimensions. He felt that the stage, the most backward of the arts, still had before it a final moment of formally creative glory. His attempt to transform the theater focused on discovering "a new acting style," and in 1923 he developed an interest in pantomime, which he saw as a possible basis for theatrical innovation.

Physiognomy and gesture provided Witkacy an essential key to the human drama. As a painter, photographer, and playwright he was obsessed with faces. He even required pictures of the philosophers he studied in order to understand better their speculative arguments. His own appearance expressed his intense theatricality. Witkacy was over six feet tall and singularly handsome. His head was well shaped, his eyes gray-green, and his gaze cold and penetrating. When sober, he seemed cool and calm; when drunk, he grew exuberant and playful. Angry, his face became immobile and sculpturesque. A natural actor, he could imitate others brilliantly, both with his voice and with his face, but he was a poor public speaker. He liked to dress flamboyantly, favoring colored scarves, bright ties, and sports outfits, and was usually seen in a large red beret as wide as an umbrella.

To the public Witkacy may have appeared the very image of the rebellious bohemian, but friends who knew him well commented on his shyness, sensitivity, dedication to work, punctuality, and exaggerated sense of responsibility. He himself noted that, despite the inner chaos of his life, he was magnificently well organized as a workman, right down to the laying out of his pencils and crayons.

In his private life, as revealed in his letters, Witkacy showed another "face"—that of a suffering martyr, victimized by society and fate, who felt creeping infirmity and old age while still in his thirties. Haunted by frightful dreams and constantly proclaiming, "The end is near for me," he saw himself single-handedly battling a philistine cultural establishment and a hostile universe. "I am expecting the worst," he wrote a friend in his chracteristically hyperbolic style, "i.e., physical pain, blindness, fire, and imbecility."

The playwright lived with his mother in Zakopane, where she ran a boardinghouse in a rented villa, changing locations several times over the years. He had a room to himself, nothing more. Never in his entire life would he own a house or even rent an apartment, but he did not complain of the arrangement. Witkacy adored his mother and read all his dramas aloud to her, eliciting delighted laughter. The world at large was not so amused.

Despite an enthusiastic response to his playwriting from the leading expressionist journal *Zdrój*, in Poznań, Witkacy grew despondent at the uncomprehending critical reception given his work. "I've had enough," he wrote to friends in 1921, "I'm going to paint. I've lost all hope of 'success.' I want peace and quiet. I'm an old man. I'm in my second childhood. . . . I'm in a state of despair. My life is finished and all that awaits me is suffering."

In December 1921 Witkacy's short play *The Pragmatists* was presented at the new experimental theater Elsinor in Warsaw. On the day of the opening, the author gave two readings at the theater of a lecture on Pure Form designed to prepare the audience for what they were about to see. Given only four performances, *The Pragmatists* was the first and last production at the Elsinor, which closed its doors in March 1922.

After the disbanding of the formists and his failure to achieve success in the theater, Witkacy wrote, "I have the feeling that I'm totally abandoned and that nothing will come of my plans for the theater. I'm giving up my ambitions and shutting myself up in the bogus ivory tower of Zakopane." With its "hothouse atmosphere" and "dark and unhealthy passions" (in the words of his friend, the pianist Arthur Rubinstein), Zakopane had a claustrophobic and ultimately destructive effect on Witkacy. Although he frequently visited Warsaw and traveled to other Polish cities on portrait-painting expeditions, the playwright never once left Poland after 1918.

Witkacy was a compulsive and unhappy womanizer. From his early twenties, he was often in love and constantly involved in philandering romances. "Lying in erotic matters was the curse of my existence," he later confessed. Surrounded by pretty and clever women known as his "metaphysical harem," the playwright felt from time to time the need for a simple tart. He paid a price, physically as well as emotionally. He contracted a venereal disease when he was an art student in Cracow, and in 1919 he underwent medical treatment for gonorrhea.

Marriage often seemed to Witkacy the only way out of his psychological dilemmas, and as a young man he was frequently engaged or about to be engaged. The suicide of his fiancée, Jadwiga Janczewska, brought an end to these dreams of matrimonial salvation. Then in September 1922, during a severe artistic crisis that blocked his usual flow of words, the playwright—who had just decided to propose to the "Princess of Chicory," a wealthy Jewish heiress named Eichenwald—met Jadwiga Unrug, a woman eight years his junior in whom he found an understanding friend and intelligent helper. Moreover, her aristocratic origins and society connections flattered his vanity. They were married in April 1923.

A month before the religious ceremony, Witkacy set out in a letter the conditions governing the practical side of their life together.

> 1. My hotel brings in almost no income and at times there's a real shortage of cash. As long as the hotel is in operation, which isn't completely certain, there'll always be room and board. 2. I have to make clear in advance that I cannot give up my essential work in order to raise our standard of living. I can do whatever I'm capable of in addition to the essential line, but if my paintings and plays do not prove successful, I won't exhibit inessential things for commercial purposes and I can only limit myself to portrait painting, to which I cannot give my whole being and reach eventual perfection. 3. I count on the success of *Hellcat*, which is to be premiered in the middle of April. . . . 4. I can hang a signpost on the street advertising my portrait painting—that's as far as I'll go. I could write articles for the papers, but the entire press has boycotted me so far. My book on the theater . . . will earn me a fantastic number of implacable enemies. I cannot count on any friends being won over by the book because of the incredible stupidity of the great majority of "theater professionals." 5. Any sign of dissatisfaction with me on your part given these difficult conditions might prove to be beyond my endurance. . . . I am writing this not to scare you away from me, but only so that you'll see clearly the whole danger of the situation. In certain matters I must be "firm as a rock" [in English] and that's where my whole value lies.

Witkacy repeatedly called his marriage with Jadwiga an "experiment" and "something wonderful and artificial." An ideal construct, or Pure Form of marriage, it was at least in theory a highly innovative and nonconventional relationship, assuring to each of the parties previously agreed-upon rights. Like everything Witkacy did, his marriage was worked out in advance according to a theory and set of general premises from which his practice constantly departed.

Their union founded on tolerance and friendship, the couple was to live in unconditional freedom. Witkacy insisted that he be accepted as he was, without any pretenses: "The wearing of a mask (which I adopted thirteen years ago) is torture to me." After a year together in Zakopane, Witkacy and Jadwiga (who did not like Maria Witkiewicz) chose a life apart, she in her apartment in Warsaw, he with his mother in the hotel. They visited back and forth frequently, but each pursued an independent existence. "Total freedom," Witkacy wrote his wife, "and the absence of that repulsive feeling of being the property of another human being must be based on faith."

In their prenuptial understanding, Jadwiga insisted that her husband forgo stimulants and engage in a practical money-making enterprise. Witkacy's own overwhelming needs made him extremely dependent on Jadwiga. During the sixteen years of their marriage, the playwright wrote to his wife three or four times a week, growing frantic when he did not hear from her in return. As a creator, he relied completely on his wife's opinion of his artistic work, which occupied a central position in their shared life. Jadwiga read all her husband wrote and acted as his editor, agent, and publicist. She was the one who had to organize the typing of his manuscripts, do the proofreading, call the publishers, and keep after the printers.

Unable to escape from traditional notions of the husband as provider, Witkacy felt humiliated that he could not supply all Jadwiga's financial needs and offer her everything her class of woman deserved. He objected to receiving money from his wife and always sought to pay her back for gifts of clothes.

During the early years of their marriage, Witkacy was jealous of Jadwiga's sexual freedom and resentful of the circle of titled playboys surrounding her. The most that he actually demanded of his wife, however, was that, when he came to Warsaw and stayed in her apartment, all signs of her lovers be carefully removed. But the playwright was as insistent in giving pedagogic counsel as his father had been. When, for example, Jadwiga went to the French Riviera with her fashionable friends for a vacation of several months, Witkacy, who remained in Warsaw to paint, wrote to his wife almost every day with detailed advice about where to go, what to see, and how to travel.

Witkacy's more than 1,600 letters to Jadwiga are devoted exclusively to the playwright's immediate concerns and anxieties. Although often displaying his linguistic inventiveness and playful humor, they were never intended for publication and contain no literary discussions or essayistic meditations. These are letters "without a mask," depicting the petty, real-life problems that overwhelmed Witkacy but that he hoped to exclude from the aesthetic realm. From the letters we learn of his state of health, mental and physical fatigue, debts and financial obligations; we discover who were his customers for portraits and what was his rate of production; and we hear of his relations with friends and enemies and his participation in social gatherings and mountain climbing expeditions. Running throughout the letters as a leitmotiv are the author's reports on the number of days he has been able to go without smoking or drinking, and his comments on the impossibility of giving up stimulants and at the same time remaining creative. Without cigarettes, alcohol, and drugs, Witkacy declared, "creativity dies out," and yet the artist had to fight against these harmful narcotics all his life.

After dreadful relapses during which he resumed smoking or engaged in alcoholic binges, Witkacy suffered terrible remorse and swore that on the following day he would start a New Life, sometimes even a New Life on a Grand Scale. But nothing ever changed. As early as 1923 the playwright bemoaned the approaching exhaustion of his creative energies: "I've pumped myself dry for thirty-eight years, I still have enough left to do a few more interesting things, but the era of basic growth is over."

When he married, Witkacy agreed to use his artistic talent in a practical way to support himself and his family, but he soon grew to hate portrait painting, which as his only permanent source of livelihood became a terrible drudgery. To fulfill commissions, he had to travel extensively, always by train third-class, and he never took taxis. Driving himself to work five to six hours at a stretch, he could sometimes produce two or three portraits a day, since they were invariably done in pastels and usually at a single sitting. For a while Witkacy's portraits were fashionable and in principle commanded high prices, from 100 to 350 zlotys. But of the more than 3,000 portraits he produced before his death in 1939, he gave away at least half to friends and acquaintances, and those he did sell often went for 50 zlotys after the crash of 1929.

By the time of his marriage, Witkacy's output in playwriting—for him an essential artistic practice—had considerably diminished, although his speed of composition was in no way reduced and in matters of craftsmanship and dramaturgical inventiveness he appeared stronger than ever. In the first six months of 1923 Witkacy wrote three of his finest works for the stage: *The Madman and the Nun*, *The Crazy Locomotive*, and *Janulka*. The year 1924 saw the creation of two more powerful dramas: *Persy Bestialskaya*, now lost, and *The Mother*, which Witkacy began on the train as he set out on a portrait painting expedition at the end of November and finished two weeks later.

In 1924 *The Madman and the Nun* was premiered in Toruń, but because of its subversive nature, the authorities took the following precautions: the title was changed to *The Madman and the Nurse*, only three performances were allowed, students and soldiers were not admitted, the balcony was closed, and the number of spectators severely limited. Accused by the critics of failing to integrate dialogue and action and of giving his characters only digressions to speak, based on whatever came into his mind on philosophy, culture, and aesthetics, Witkacy replied, "I do not use the stage as a means for propagating ideas, which I present in separate theoretical works in a purely conceptual, not symbolic, fashion. These ideas enter my plays involuntarily and never fully defined or exactly articulated."

THE NEW DELIVERANCE

◼

A Play in One Act

Dedicated to Karol Szymanowski

CHARACTERS

FLORESTAN SNAKESNOUT—Thirty years old. Tall, dark-blond hair.
Completely clean-shaven. Handsome. Dressed in a black jacket and white
flannel trousers. Straw hat. Quite elegant. Shirt with violet stripes. Violet
tie. Low yellow shoes.
KING RICHARD III—Hunchbacked. Completely clean-shaven. A small
round red cap on his head; his crown on top of it. Wears a breastplate,
over it a loose red doublet (or something of the sort) trimmed in black fur.
Brown hip boots with enormous spurs. A large two-handed sword by his
side.
TWO MURDERERS—Dressed in black tights. Black masks over their faces.
Huge daggers in their hands.
TATIANA—Graying blonde. About forty years old. Monstrous circles under
her eyes. Traces of great beauty and great success with males.
AMUSETTA—Young girl seventeen years old. Pretty brunette. Light gray
dress with a blue sash around the waist. Blue ribbons in her hair, fanning
out on both sides. Black stockings. Black shoes.
JOANNA SNAKESNOUT—Florestan's mother. Thin matron, dressed in black

with gray hair, but worn the way young women wear their hair; a kind of casque in the middle with the hair wound around. Rather florid face. Sixty-three years old.

HOUSEKEEPER—Forty-five years old. Ball of grease with rolled-up sleeves. Rapsberry red blouse. Brown skirt. Lemon yellow apron. Red, sweaty mug. Walks with a waddle.

UNKNOWN SOMEONE—Dressed like the murderers, but in violet tights and a violet mask.

SIX THUGS WITH INSTRUMENTS OF TORTURE—Five with beards; two with black beards have pincers; one with a red beard has a saw; two with blond beards have hammers. Dressed like workers, in gray-yellow colors. The one without a beard has a small black handlebar mustache and wears a worn-out black jacket; he has on a red tie and holds a blowtorch, out of which a blue flame can shoot forth with a roar as the need arises.

[*The stage represents a huge hall. Two gothic pillars in the middle. A door to the right in the back, another door also to the right, further downstage, a little behind a dark olive green sofa that stands to the front of the stage, facing the audience, in a line with the space between the pillars. In front of the sofa, a small yellow table. On either side, two wicker chairs like those used in cheap Italian restaurants. Two more pillars to the right and the left, by the footlights.*]

Prologue

Typhon, give me your fire:
My heart I broke on the black edge of the tower,
And out went the lamp
That gleams behind that cage of wire.
In the corner, masked, the murderers lour
Who guard the king
Spewing out his ire.'
I enter—daggers behind, windows flung wide,
And the Angel of Darkness flashed through the distant hall.
Enormous mirror, six candles burning by the wall.
PRESIDENT: Oh, poison—I am torturer.
SOUL: And I am your brother extortioner.
The candles are dimmed, the rain-soaked gutters sigh.

Am I here? In the hall?

No, it is fear that chokes me,

"To arms! To arms!" I hear my madness cry.

And I see, I see, most clearly see someone push the door ajar

And six thugs with pincers he before him drives . . .

And in the mirrored‘wall six thugs

Tear out my sleepless eyes.

When I awoke stillness was all around,

Only the rain-soaked gutters louder sigh.

On the windowpane I see, most clearly see

An ink black spider chase an autumn fly.

1906

Scene One

[*King Richard III stands to the left, his back up against the pillar, and every so often he makes a move as if he wanted to tear himself away from the pillar and get away. The masked Murderers prevent him from doing so, instantly turning the points of their daggers at him and at the same time producing a loud hiss, made by drawing out the letter: A-Aaaaa! Taking turns, they likewise point their daggers at anyone who tries to come near the King. Tatiana is sitting on the sofa in the left corner, nearer the King, and knitting. Amusetta is sitting to the right, that is, on Tatiana's left hand. A lamp is burning overhead. Another lights the half of the hall behind ‘the pillars.*]

TATIANA   [*Knitting, to Amusetta.*] Today I'm going to show you someone new. Florestan is his name. He should be here any minute. I won't tell you anything about him because I want you to guess for yourself what he's like and what his destiny will be. [*To the Murderers, turning her head slightly, but without looking at them.*] My worthy Murderers, pay attention to your work like ordinary, hired workmen and don't get distracted by listening to our conversation.

AMUSETTA   I'm so frightfully curious. I had the feeling back then that no one would ever come, that everything was finished and done for in that hideous convent school.

TATIANA   Don't be silly, Amusetta dear . . .

[*The King roars. Tatiana keeps on knitting. Amusetta remains seated, staring vacantly into space.*]

KING   Won't you let me rest for a single moment. Oh! Cursed torturers! ! [*The Murderers point their daggers at him.*] My back is growing into this infernal wall, my hump pains me like a gigantic abscess. When will the torment of being rooted to these rough stones finally end?

TATIANA   [*To the King, turning toward him and looking at him.*] Five o'clock tea will be coming soon, Richard. You can have a cup of tea with us.

KING   [*More calmly, with regret.*] Such strength, and it's all wasted. And yet, if I wanted, not one stone in this entire house of illusion would be left standing. [*Shrugs his shoulders.*] Who did they think would be taken in by all this? [*With sudden rage.*] Really, aren't there any more people left in this world? Have they all become nothing but the wheels of a clock? At least let me wind up the clock!

MURDERERS [*Pointing their daggers at him.*] Aaaa! Aaaa!

TATIANA   The clock winds itself. It's one of those self-winding clocks . . .

AMUSETTA   [*Interrupts her, not paying any attention to the King.*] If only he's not a common, ordinary party boy. Like all the ones I've been meeting at balls recently.

TATIANA   [*Knitting.*] Calm down. I'm not one to supply you with inferior goods. But you've got to get him in your clutches right away.

AMUSETTA   But how? I don't know any of the ways yet. They didn't teach us that at convent school.

TATIANA   Your feminine intuition will tell you. He's an extraordinary little rascal. And even if he's thirteen years older, he's still much more of a fool than you are. It's always easiest to get the best of extraordinary people. In daily life they're sheep you can lead by the nose, up and down, and around the barn . . .

[*From afar, as though from beyond the walls, the sound of three blows struck on a huge gong.*]

KING   [*Enraged.*] A new round of visits is about to begin. Every day to see these hideous dramas of yours, to view your disemboweled psychic guts—along with their contents—to look at your metaphysical navels, stuck on sticks and sold like candied fruits! [*With mounting fury.*] Oh! I'll get my hands on life some day! I tell you frankly, this won't last long. I'm not afraid of death, but I'd like to see one more transformation of my role—just once to take a walk through the streets of your town. To get out of this cursed hole, as I once used to get out of the Tower. [*The Murderers hiss, with their daggers aimed at him.*]

Scene Two

[*The same. Enter Florestan through the door to the rear; without taking off his hat, he approaches the sofa from behind. He comes up to the sofa and leans on the back with both hands. Neither Amusetta nor Tatiana turns around. Tatiana knits. Amusetta shows signs of nervousness.*]

FLORESTAN   Sorry I'm late. I won an important tennis match and I had to change. The contest dragged on too long.

TATIANA   [*Without stopping her work.*] This is Amusetta, about whom I've told you so much.

FLORESTAN   More of that vile procuring. But I can make her acquaintance. That won't cost me anything. [*He makes a move as if he wanted to go around the sofa to the right.*]

KING   You could greet me first! [*Florestan stops and for the first time notices the King.*]

FLORESTAN   Where have I seen that hunchbacked monkey before? [*He goes over to the King.*]

TATIANA   That's Richard III. He's been given an indefinite leave of absence and now he's doing penance. It's a little comedy that I've staged.

FLORESTAN   [*Going over to the King and taking off his hat, addressing him in an offhand manner.*] I'm very glad to meet your Majesty. [*He tries to draw near and holds out his hand.*]

FIRST MURDERER   [*Pointing his dagger at him.*] Aaaaaaaaa!!!

KING   [*To Florestan.*] There's absolutely no need for you to stick your paw out at me, Mr. What's-it, whom I wouldn't venture to call by your true name. You can talk to me from a distance. [*Amusetta looks at Florestan admiringly.*]

FLORESTAN   But I say, Madam Tatiana, that Richard of yours is ferocious! I never thought a king could be so coarse and crude. [*The King wants to hurl himself at him and takes a step forward. The*

Murderers restrain him with the points of their daggers.] If it weren't for those gentlemen, I'd most likely be lying on the floor split in half by that saber. [*He points to the King's sword.*]

AMUSETTA   [*To Florestan.*] Mr. Florestan, haven't you already spent enough time on that puppet? He's not a real person . . .

KING   [*Enraged, interrupts her.*] I'm more real than all those characters of yours I've had to watch here for the past five years. I'm like a barrel of nitroglycerine. When I finally deign to explode, not even the dust of these dungeons will remain. [*Florestan listens to him with a polite smile.*]

AMUSETTA   [*Not paying the slightest attention to the King.*] That doesn't matter. Mr. Florey, come over here this minute, please, next to me.

FLORESTAN   [*Looking at her for the first time.*] But what a lovely girl. [*Approaching her.*] I just finished a story today in which there's a character exactly like you.

TATIANA   [*Interrupting him.*] Mr. Florestan Snakesnout. [*Florestan greets Amusetta and sits down on the chair to the right, his left profile to the audience. He's just about to say something when the King interrupts him.*]

KING   [*In earnest.*] That is how I condense my strength. What a pleasure to crush people when one is young . . .

TATIANA   [*To the King.*] Richard, we've had quite enough of your effusions for now. Calm down and think about five o'clock tea, which is coming soon.

FLORESTAN   [*To Amusetta.*] Miss, I see that Madam Tatiana hasn't made any mistakes about my taste this time. As a matter of fact, I needed a new woman. You know, people think I'm a Don Juan. It's not true. I'm only concerned with certain fleeting states which I subsequently use for artistic purposes.

AMUSETTA   But you're not an artist, are you? That's so common now. Everyone's an artist nowadays.

FLORESTAN   I despise art, Miss. I use it the way I use all other amusements, which I also despise. The only plaything I don't despise is woman.

KING   [*Angrily.*] I can't stand much more of that scalawag's company!

FLORESTAN   [*To the King.*] Quiet, you old marionette! [*To Amusetta.*] Go on, I'm listening. What did you want to say?

AMUSETTA Then what are you really? You're starting to become exceedingly mysterious. [*Tatiana looks at Florestan with a smile.*]

FLORESTAN Even if I told you what my profession is, you wouldn't believe me anyhow. I'd rather not say. To the extent that I'm able— I am everything.

AMUSETTA I have the feeling you've got a frightful appetite. You impress me as being a land shark.

KING Just say: a simple swine. Can't you see he's an ordinary pragmatist?

AMUSETTA [*Turns to the King for the first time.*] And just what is a pragmatist? [*Florestan tries to interrupt her, but she motions him to be quiet with her hand and listens to what the King says.*]

KING A pragmatist is an ordinary beast with only this difference, that by making a theory out of his beastliness, he tries to convince others that it's the only possible philosophy.

FLORESTAN He's raving. First of all, I'm not a pragmatist, and second, pragmatism isn't what the King imagines it to be. As for philosophy, I'm the creator of a school of transfinite monadologists. We totally reject the idea of dead matter.

AMUSETTA Well, that's just fine—then this table can fall in love with me?

FLORESTAN Not the table. But the living beings that make it up can be in love with each other, the way we can—we're just another small particle of the universe like them. You have the eyes of a coral viper. I remember how once one of them slept with me, on my breast while I was asleep too, and when I woke up we looked into each other's eyes.

AMUSETTA Then what happened? Didn't it bite you?

FLORESTAN If it had, I wouldn't be here talking with you now. A second later it was breathing its last between my fingers, as its tail kept hitting me across the arm and even the face.

KING Served you right. The only thing to do with people like you is to hit them right in the snout. Oh! If I could let you have it just once! [*He makes a move forward. The Murderers restrain him with a hiss.*]

FLORESTAN [*To the King, coldly.*] I'd advise your Majesty to stop making light of my person. Quite a few others have long remembered making little sarcastic remarks like that.

AMUSETTA Are you strong? Do people often make fun of you?

FLORESTAN   [*Flexing the muscles in his right arm.*] Just feel my biceps.

AMUSETTA   But I'm ashamed to somehow. I have the impression it must hurt when it's so hard.

FLORESTAN   There's never been a man yet who dared make light of me. I'm not counting that madman. [*He points at the King.*]

KING   [*Laughs savagely.*] Ha, ha, ha! For the time being there's nothing else I can do but laugh. But we'll see yet. I believe that in the last analysis everything has to make some kind of sense in the general scheme of things. [*The gong sounds three times.*]

Scene Three

[*The same. Enter the Housekeeper carrying the tea things and some cakes on a tray. She goes over to the table and arranges everything on it.*]

FLORESTAN   Our conversation has been interrupted. I can't say that I've fallen in love with you. In any case you're not part of the background, but a distinct complex of very intricate combinations. As such you exist in my consciousness. That's a great deal, a very great deal.

AMUSETTA   Complex is a horrid word. It sounds like a mismatch between compress and perplex. In the old days women used to be told they were like flowers. I read about things like that in the convent after lights out. Just what is this background of yours? [*Florestan tries to answer. The King interrupts him.*]

KING   [*To Amusetta.*] Hideous swinishness undoubtedly. You shine like a wonderful black diamond encrusted in a piece of rotten headcheese. [*To the Housekeeper.*] And how are you, my love? Do you still believe in me, despite my monstrous lies and my no-less-revolting infidelities?

HOUSEKEEPER   [*Respectfully, finishing setting the tea things.*] I am your humble servant, Your Majesty.

FIRST MURDERER   [*To the Housekeeper in a rasping voice.*] What time is it?

HOUSEKEEPER   Ten at night.

SECOND MURDERER   [*In the same sort of voice as the First Murderer, lowering his dagger.*] We can go to sleep. [*They both lie down and fall asleep against the wall. In a moment they can be heard snoring.*]

KING   [*Straightens up with relief.*] At last! Bring on the tea! [*Stretching himself, he goes over to the table. Exit the Housekeeper.*]

TATIANA   [*Putting down her knitting.*] Mr. Richard York—Mr. Florestan Snakesnout. [*Florestan gets up. They shake hands. The King sits down in the chair to the left. He unbuckles his sword and leans it against the sofa.*]

KING   You'll forgive my remarks, Mr. Florestan. When I stand there against the wall, my nerves are always on edge. [*Tatiana pours the tea.*]

FLORESTAN   But exactly why do you stand there?

TATIANA   Don't be indiscreet, Mr. Florestan. Go on amusing Amusetta.

FLORESTAN   It never occurred to me that there was any kind of mystery concerned with it. We, men of action, men whose lives are all creativity, do not acknowledge that there are any mysteries. Existence in and of itself isn't any more mysterious than this cup of tea. I drink it and digest it. It acts agreeably on my nerves. What is there beyond that? Just tell me. Nonsense!

KING   Yes—but what is there beyond nonsense, Mr. Snake . . .

TATIANA   . . . snout.

KING   Oh, that's right, snout. Look, my paid murderers are asleep over there. They aim at my heart until the appointed time comes. Don't we all have our own murderers?

FLORESTAN   But the ones you have here are real. You're talking symbolically.

KING   Just try to wake them up. Go over there and see how real they are.

FLORESTAN   [*Getting up.*] No—that's impossible. [*He goes over to the Murderers and shakes them.*]

TATIANA   [*To the King.*] How can you make fun of that poor, unfortunate great man?

KING   Let that teach him, the scum. I went through a lot before acquiring the knowledge of life I have now.

AMUSETTA   [*To Tatiana.*] Then he is a great man?

TATIANA   [*To Amusetta.*] You'll find that out for yourself. [*Florestan comes back. He has an odd look on his face.*]

KING   Well, what have you got to say now, Mr. Snakesnout?

FLORESTAN   [*Controlling himself with difficulty.*] Nothing to it—those are little known symptoms of hypnotism or something like that.

KING   [*Ironically.*] Hypnotism! ! [*Emphatically.*] Those are corpses, my friend, corpses that snore. How do you know that I'm not a corpse too?

FLORESTAN   [*Disconcerted, tries to shrug the matter off.*] The most
courageous people have their little weaknesses. I knew a certain
cavalry officer who would charge artillery with a detachment of
horse, but who quaked at the sight of a rat or a mouse. I have
known cavaliers who were afraid of a white spot on the wall. Do you
know those nights in the south of France when everything white
shines phosphorescently and the darkness seems to be full of
phantoms? [*His voice betrays that he is on the verge of tears.*]

KING   [*Banging his fist down on the table so hard that all the cups jump.*]
That's enough of that rubbish! ! You are an utter coward! !

TATIANA   [*Gently.*] Calm down, Richard. Not everyone has your powers of
endurance in the face of the strangeness of life. [*To Florestan.*] We
live in dark corners and byways. Life in the grand manner, out there
in the fresh air, has been poisoned by the weakness of the debased
mob. We can do nothing, we're like those fish that burst when
they're pulled up out of the unfathomable depths . . .

AMUSETTA   [*To Florestan.*] Still you're not so strong as you said you were
a moment ago. I'd so like to believe in someone's strength, in
boundless courage, in the possibility of overcoming the pain or fear
caused by the mystery of the other world!

FLORESTAN   [*In an artificially calm voice.*] That is what we have minds
for. Animal reflexes exist in man. The tiger is courageous, but does
it deserve any credit for that? We are all socialized animals . . .

KING   Not all of us, Mr. Snakesnout.

FLORESTAN   [*Not paying any attention to his words.*] It's only by using our
minds that we can defend ourselves against certain primitive reflexes
which at any given moment can gain the upper hand. Not over us—
of course—only over our nerve tissue.

AMUSETTA   [*To Florestan.*] You're beautiful, that's something positive.
But when you talk, I have the impression I'm in a class at the
convent . . .

KING   [*To Amusetta.*] Yes, my child. Admit that if it weren't for my
advanced age, you'd prefer me to that decadent young
whippersnapper.

AMUSETTA   Your Majesty, I think you're right.

FLORESTAN   You'll forgive me, Miss: I'm quite enough of an old man. I
don't fool around with the various little tricks that people anxious to
believe in artificial mysteries use to deceive themselves. I am, first

and foremost, a contemporary man. Those old beliefs, those attempts at hypnotism—they're bugbears to scare children. We have two things the people in ancient times were lacking: thought and organization.

AMUSETTA   Yes, but that's not beautiful. You're not an artist so you don't understand that . . .

FLORESTAN   Miss, I can be everything. I'm going to tell you who I am—come what may. I am the vice president of the largest metallurgical works in the world, but when I want to, I paint so well that none of the cubists is in the same class with me. [*To the King.*] I know what you're going to say, Mr. York. I never studied drawing—that's true. But I paint better than any of them. I sit down at the piano and I play as well as they do, those great musicians of ours. And maybe even better. By pure chance I create such combinations of sounds that the most sophisticated connoisseurs of music are astonished. Everyone tells me: Why don't you exhibit? Why don't you publish? For the moment I don't want to. I write too. Oh, if you knew what I created today! All the creative writers will be green with envy. [*Proudly.*] There's just one thing: they take it seriously, but I am a vice president—that's my business, and all the rest of it is amusement: art, women . . . oh, excuse me, Miss, you alone are different.

AMUSETTA   Yes. You say the same thing to every girl you meet.

TATIANA   [*Pointedly.*] Believe me, he doesn't. I know him well.

KING   [*Gobbling up the petits fours.*] Well said. I'm glad to see that there's at least one scum who speaks the truth. In my time we slaughtered one another like butchers in the name of God. But that God meant something to us. For you—the pragmatists, because you are a pragmatist, Mr. Straightsnout—God is just nonsense in which you are able to believe when it brings in a decent rate of return.

AMUSETTA   [*To Florestan.*] Mr. Florestan, is that possible? Are you really what the King says you are?

FLORESTAN   But really, Miss! He has a primitive brain incapable of grasping things as complicated as our intricate ways of thinking. I say: our, our contemporary ways of thinking. That man has a head like a double bass and a hump that's even bigger. He was a degenerate in his own times all right, but he doesn't have the faintest idea about the precision of thought that we've reached.

That's the intellectual shorthand of the Papuans. [*To the King.*] Go
to New Guinea, Mr. York. You'll find worthy disciples there . . .

KING [*His mouth full of petits fours.*] Tatiana—let me—I can't stand it
anymore. Let me teach that young whippersnapper a lesson. In our
style. Like the Yorks and the Lancasters—damn it all—in our style.
[*He raises his hand. Tatiana grabs him by the arm.*]

TATIANA [*Confidentially.*] Don't bother, Richard. I'll take care of him
myself. It will all work out by itself. That silly little goose [*Points to
Amusetta.*] is the litmus paper by means of which we'll get know his
works—what do you call them—the fruits by which . . .

KING Oh, that's it, that's it, the fruits. Mr. Straightsnout, where are your
fruits?

AMUSETTA I see only dried prunes, candied papayas, the apple Eve gave
Adam in the form of glazed sweets, but I don't see any fruits . . .

[*Three blows on the gong.*]

TATIANA [*Anxiously.*] What's that? No one else was supposed to come
tonight.

[*Everyone waits expectantly.*]

Scene Four

[*The same. Enter Joanna Snakesnout through the far door; with a rapid
step she goes over to those present along the right side. They all look at one
another.*]

JOANNA Where is my son? Where is Florestan? I haven't seen him for ten
years. I've heard that he's fallen into bad company. Are you the
ones who are tempting his noble soul? He was always noble!

FLORESTAN [*Getting up.*] Mother! It's not true. This is a den of evil
spirits. Over there they're torturing some crazy old man who keeps
insulting everyone in the grossest terms.

JOANNA [*Bursting out.*] It's you! It's you! How big you've grown! Who are
you now? [*Runs around the sofa to the right and throws herself at
Florestan.*] Is it really you?!

FLORESTAN [*Controls himself.*] It's me. It really is. [*Impatiently.*] Mother!
Calm down. There are strangers here. I don't have anything to do
with them! *I* am a vice president. It's by pure chance . . .

JOANNA   [*In Florestan's arms.*] You're mine! My one and only! At last,
after so many years of torture . . . [*Notices Tatiana.*] You're here?
You whom I practically brought up? You dare drag my son into this
filthy cesspool?

TATIANA   Joanna! There are strangers present. Couldn't we put off settling
our personal accounts until later?

JOANNA   [*Ironically.*] Personal accounts! Don't you understand that he's
my son, my darling Florey? Who is he now? Has he finally become
someone? My dearest son! Tell me who you are! Tell me quickly! I
have a weak heart; I'm dying of anxiety. Have you been untrue to
yourself, you're keeping so terribly still and your eyes are wild like
some madman's from another world?

[*Florestan stands with his back to the audience. The King and Amusetta
watch this scene with genuine interest.*]

FLORESTAN   [*Insincerely, with feigned emotion.*] Mother! My dearest
mama! Everything will be cleared up. I'm the same as always. Save
me! They're desecrating my most sacred ideals!

JOANNA   You dare ask me to save you? You?! After ten years of
separation? You dare? That's horrible. I've gone astray myself. I
want to escape from my own thoughts too. [*Terribly disillusioned.*] I
expect to be saved by you, and you, you . . . Oh, you're as vile as
ever. You're a vampire who's lived off my heart all your life and
sucked this poor abandoned heart of mine like a hideous
bloodsucker! [*Breath fails her, she clutches at her heart. Amusetta
springs up and supports her. The King gets up and bangs his fist
down on the table.*]

KING   Shut up! Cackling geese! Now you're going to listen to me. [*To
Joanna.*] Don't you recognize me? [*A pause.*]

JOANNA   [*After a moment, leaning on Amusetta.*] Richard! Is it you?

KING   Yes—it's me. I didn't know that you had such a son. He's a
zombie, not a human being. He's a soulless automaton, not a man.
He's the poisonous spittle spewed out by your rotten society! He's—
I don't know what he is, words fail me. That seducer of silly giggling
geese, that zero, that double zero . . .

JOANNA   Shut up—I love him! !

KING   Fortunately he's not my son. At last I know your real name. He's
the son of that monstrous family of Snakesnouts whose sole

representative I see here before me. Thanks to him I now can
appreciate your total wretchedness at the time you became my
mistress, you thrice cursed, common stupid hen! He is a
Snakesnout! [*In disgust.*] It's that foul blood which now reveals to
me the secret in our relationship, the secret of why you were never
really mine . . .

TATIANA So that's how it was? So Richard was your lover? So you lied to
me? Very well, I'll have my revenge too. [*To Florestan.*] Florey! Do
you remember that night, that night when you abandoned me
forever? Can you ever forget those diabolical sensual pleasures that
have devoured you ever since, from which you are running away,
but which you can never escape. I've taken my vengeance for those
other women! That's why I gave you all those others, because I
knew that you'd deceive them the way you deceived me then.

KING Oh, I like that. That's in our style. That I understand. There's
strength there.

[*Joanna, half dead with pain, keeps leaning on Amusetta, who looks at
each one of them in turn without understanding a thing.*]

FLORESTAN [*To Tatiana in a broken voice.*] Don't talk like that. If what
you say is true, my whole life is worth absolutely nothing.

TATIANA [*To Florestan.*] You loved me, and you still love me and only
me. [*To Joanna.*] Look, you wretch! He loved you with the hideous,
selfish love of a spoiled megalomaniac. But his body belongs to me
alone, whenever I want it. And through his body I'll have his vile
soul, whenever I want it too. But I didn't want it, because he was too
disgusting for me in his degradation when he begged me for mercy
like a hideous worm. Now just look. [*To Florestan.*] Tonight I'll be
yours. There is nothing in you except this desire. There's nothing
ahead of you in life, because you're just one huge lie, and that lie is
me, me! I alone enslaved your vile soul. I used you the way people
use inanimate objects. You are nothing. You're my plaything and
that's all you'll ever be, even if I live to a hundred and twenty.

JOANNA [*Weakly.*] Florey, tell her it's a lie . . . [*A pause.*]

FLORESTAN [*In despair.*] No, I can't tell her that. I'm what Tatiana thinks
I am. I love her. Her and her alone, because she is a lie that
reaches to the height of my own lies. My lies are innumerable
because I'm a man. She unites them and sanctifies them in one

huge orgy of falsehood. I don't have a mother anymore and I never had one. Today I started to love that silly little goose [*Points to Amusetta.*] and what is that actually but one of my little lies from the past, the kind I used to deceive even you, mother dear! It was your own fault and you will be punished for it.

[*Joanna collapses to the floor with a scream. Amusetta puts her on the sofa. The King runs over to Joanna, examines her, and checks her pulse and breathing.*]

TATIANA   [*Joyfully.*] For the first time in years I really feel I'm living. Oh, no one will ever know how much I've suffered!

KING   [*To Florestan.*] You've killed your mother, young man. Even I wouldn't have been capable of that.

[*Amusetta cries and wipes her eyes and nose with a handkerchief.*]

TATIANA   That's not true, Richard! She killed herself. Remember your own youth.

KING   [*In a conciliatory tone.*] Oh, yes, that's right. No one is perfect. Of course . . .

TATIANA   [*Interrupts him.*] Florey! You're mine! Come, humble yourself before me in the presence of the King. [*The Murderers wake up and stretch, then sit down on the floor. Florestan falls on his face in front of Tatiana. She stands beside him and puts her foot on his head.*] Do you feel the new life entering you at the final moment of your destruction? The meaning of your life lay in destruction alone and you have built the foundation for your splendid edifices on a frightful quagmire that swallows up every living thing. Come and acknowledge the sole truth of your life.

KING   [*Slowly backing over to the pillar on the left.*] Can't you all see that none of this is what it seems? It's only make-believe. The only truth is that my hump is growing into this wall.

TATIANA   [*To Florestan.*] Get up and come with me. Perhaps when you've really destroyed your life, the truth will grow out of your hideous male lying.

KING   [*Leaning against the pillar. The Murderers stand close by him.*] Everything is sham. [*He is interrupted by three blows on the gong. The door to the right, nearer the audience, opens and the Unknown Someone in violet tights and a mask shoves a bunch of Thugs into the hall. The light in the other part of the hall goes out and the front*]

of the stage is thrown into much brighter relief against the
background of the dark interior.]

AMUSETTA   [*Frightened, to Tatiana.*] Who's that? What do those people
want?

TATIANA   [*Taking her foot off Florestan's head; uneasily.*] I don't know.
We'll find out in a minute.

KING   At last I see some of our kind. They'll give him a real working over.

[*The silent group of Thugs slowly emerges from the shadows, pushed*
forward by the Unknown Someone. Three blows on the gong. The door at
the back opens. The Housekeeper comes out of the darkness slowly. She
draws near and leans against the back of the sofa.]

HOUSEKEEPER   Well, now there'll really be something amusing.

[*Tatiana goes over to the group of Thugs, who slowly draw near from the*
right-hand side. Florestan remains lying on the floor, face down, without
moving. The Murderers stand in front of the King with their daggers aimed
at him.]

TATIANA   [*To the Thugs.*] Gentlemen, there's a dead woman present. You
can't do anything here today . . .

UNKNOWN SOMEONE   [*In a high-pitched, almost feminine voice.*] That's no
concern of ours! Don't meddle in other people's affairs! [*The Thugs*
move forward to the front of the stage and surround Florestan's
prone body.]

FLORESTAN   [*Without getting up off the floor, in a weak moan.*] Mama!
Save me! I didn't do it! They did it, those awful people . . .

KING   [*With sudden fury, trying to hurl himself headlong.*] Oh, that clown
is driving me over the brink! [*To the Murderers.*] Let me go for a
minute only, just one brief minute!! [*Tatiana stands to the right of*
the sofa, hugging Amusetta in her arms.]

HOUSEKEEPER   [*To the Murderers.*] Let him go! Let him have his fun for
once. [*The Murderers step aside and let the King pass; he goes over to*
the sofa and takes his sword, which he had forgotten to buckle on.]

AMUSETTA   [*Whimpering slightly.*] And what's going to happen now? Oh,
why did I ever come here! It's all so appalling. What's he lying there
for? Who are those people?

[*The Thugs kneel in a circle around Florestan, with the exception of the*
Unknown Someone. The clean-shaven Thug starts up the blowtorch, out of
which a violet flame shoots with a roar.]

TATIANA   I don't know myself. It's as much of a surprise to me . . .

KING   [*Standing on the left side of the Thugs, draws his sword out of its scabbard.*] Step aside right this minute! ! I'm going to settle the score with him for everything and for all of you too!

UNKNOWN SOMEONE   [*Who has been standing next to the Thugs, facing the audience.*] Your Majesty! [*Goes over to the King and speaks coldly.*] To your place this minute, if you please! Over there! [*He points to the pillar.*]

TATIANA   [*To the King.*] Richard! Defend him! I'll be yours till death, only let him live!

FLORESTAN   [*Stretched out on the floor.*] Hurry up! Just get this agony over with! [*The King retreats before the Unknown Someone and stands against the pillar once more, his drawn sword in his hand. The Murderers stand next to him.*]

AMUSETTA   [*To Tatiana.*] Why doesn't he defend him?

UNKNOWN SOMEONE   [*From the left side to Amusetta.*] Evidently he can't. [*Emphatically.*] Do you understand, Miss Amusetta, he can't. [*Suddenly to the Thugs in a shrill voice.*] Get him! Get him! [*The Thugs, kneeling, suddenly bend over Florestan and begin torturing him, each in his own way; with pincers, hammers, and the blowtorch. A terrible scream from Florestan is heard.*]

KING   [*Suddenly strikes one of the Murderers—on his left—in the teeth with the hilt of his sword, and hits another one—to his right—on the head with the blade, leaping into the place where the First Murderer had been and then dashing forward with a yell; the Thugs stop their torturing.*] Oh! Enough of that vile screeching! That degenerate doesn't even know how to suffer!! [*He finds himself eye to eye with the Unknown Someone in violet, who gently takes his sword out of his hand.*]

UNKNOWN SOMEONE   [*Pointing with the sword to the murky depths of the hall.*] There is the way for Your Majesty! [*The King retreats and goes to the left, circling the sofa, then heads for the door to the right in the rear. His heavy footsteps on the flagstones and the jangling of his spurs can be heard.*]

HOUSEKEEPER   [*Turns to watch him as he goes.*] Good-bye to Your Majesty!

AMUSETTA   [*Cuddling up to Tatiana.*] Why didn't he defend him? What's going on?

TATIANA   Quiet—quiet. This is the way it has to be—this is the way it ought to be—this is the way it will always be . . . [*The King leaves, slamming the door furiously.*]

UNKNOWN SOMEONE   [*To the Thugs.*] Get on with it, gentlemen! Do your duty!

[*The Thugs throw themselves at Florestan once more and start torturing him again. Florestan roars with pain.*]

CURTAIN

3 MAY 1920

LETTERS TO MALINOWSKI, 1921-23

■

Dear Bronio:

Thanks for your letter. I'm not writing much, because I'm not sure of your address. Send me your address right away and I'll immediately send you my *samtliche Werke*. My play *Tumor Brainiowicz* is now being printed and it will probably be produced in Cracow at the beginning of June. As for living conditions in Poland, I'm not able to tell you anything. One can live on a million a year, but as for the conditions of a professorship, talk it over with someone competent, after all, you have so many acquaintances here. I've made it up with Chwistek. He is a painter and we exhibit in the same group. Besides that there's logic. Tymbeusz married Zofia Ben and is in Paris. Nalepusz [Tadeusz Nalepiński] died of the Spanish flu. Miciński met his end in Russia. My Mother had a very serious operation. Now she feels fine. We've changed where we live. I'd have lots to tell you in person, but I have a terrible aversion to writing. I was at Olcza today, a marvelous May day, and I remembered the old times. Mardula and the Galarowskis always ask about you. Have you become completely Anglicized? Have you really changed religion? Ceylon and Australia are nothing compared to Olcza in the sunlight. Too bad that you can't come for the summer this year. Is the Jurek you're asking about Jurek Wasserberg? Wasserberg served in the army, and he's leaving his wife. I'd so like you to become Polish again. It's a pity to lose one's nationality that way. Remember how we considered Conrad a traitor. Answer immediately and include your address.

A heartfelt hug.

My regards to Mrs. Malinowski and Josephine. Mother sends you her very best to both you and Mrs. Malinowski.

Your Witkacy

Chramcówki St., Tatry Villa, Zakopane

[Postscripts on the margins:]

Żuławski died. Kazia is in Toruń. She moved recently. Many new acquaintances. Oh, oh. Zagóra [Aniela Zagórska] is in Warsaw. . . . She's earning her living working for Americans.

Janusz Tyszkiewicz died. . . .

I've magnified my individuality to gigantic proportions and I'm suffering from chronic but acute megalomania.

Last year I drank a lot. This year less. I'm working *like crazy*. . . .

Do you have a photo of me taken in Ceylon? Please send me the negative or a couple of prints.

20 JANUARY 1923

Dear Malinowski:

Thank you very much for your kind letter and for the postscriptum by Lady Elsie. My marriage is presently impossible on account of the complete absence of any feelings towards me on the part of the lady in question. I will wait a little longer (till March, I imagine) and meanwhile I will look around for something else and perhaps something better. For the first time I seemed to be in love without any reciprocation. What do you and (Lady Elsie also) think about the idea of marriage with a young *Jewish* lady, nineteen years old, horribly intelligent and very rich? Please write me immediately, because this is the most dangerous moment in my life. I'm going with the speed of an express train and there are no signals. The first lady is the daughter of the so-called "King of Chicory" (Polish) and is fair-headed and the daughter of my third love. But the damned beast (nineteen years old too) is in love with some bloody young rascal, and I cannot suffer rivals. You know I am quite paralyzed when I must fight for a girl. If it were not a question of marriage, I would overwhelm the damned scoundrel with my *Zakopaniacal* demonism without any difficulty—like some sporting assignment. But when I am seriously involved, I lose all my demonism and become an elderly stupid fool, completely without strength. She also has a little drop of Semitic blood inside, from her father, and is enormously rich. The other pure-blooded Jew is not so fair, but incomparably more intelligent. What to do? The first will come here in February and the thing must be decided. If not, advise me, please (both of you, do you hear? Eh!!) whether to throw myself at the Jewish girl, or not? Don't kill animals, unless you are very tormented by them, and you can't stop it any other way. How I envy you, Dearest Malinower, to have a good wife and a quiet life. Oh, oh! Most of my loves are simply vampires that are sucking my blood. My heart is sinking into my breeches when I think about my future life. I have stopped drinking and now I am taking the Karlsbad cure. But something horrible is happening with my painting. I cannot do a single thing. I have written two plays, one—*Jan Karol Maciej Hellcat*—about a village lord mayor (*wójt* in Polish) who has become President of the State and has become a wet noodle (*flak*) on account of that. The other is *The Madman and the Nun*. If I don't have any success with that thing, I am a damned fool. Write me if it is worthwhile for me to translate a play of mine in the way I am writing this letter and then to send it to you to improve it and get it to a theater in London. Write me quite "openly." I am not a megalomaniacal idiot and I shall not be offended. It is horrible that you cannot stay in Poland. Your plans frighten me. How dare you make plans for two years? When you accept the professorship in London, you will be lost forever. Keep alert! How tiring it is to write in English. Dear Bronio: I kiss you fondly on your cheeks. I shake hands very cordially with your Lady, and I grin amicably at both your daughters.

My Mother sends compliments (the best she can find) to the whole family.

Yours very truly and very unhappy friend,

Witkacy (*recte* Staś)

Don't be a fool and come back to Poland. We shall die at our posts in this fantastic land, which by mere, pure accident is our native country.

My play, *Kurka Wodna* [*The Water Hen*), has been translated into German and given to the Kammerspiel Theater in Hamburg. But I don't yet know if it has been accepted.

[Original in English, here slightly corrected for intelligibility.]

ZAKOPANE

10 MARCH 1923

Dear Bronio:

Thank you very much for your letter, which made a big impression on me. On that account I'm engaged to be married to Miss Jadwiga Unrug (first cousin of Aniela Zagórska). I want to have the wedding around 14 April. She wants to go somewhere even if it's only for two weeks. Write and tell me how much the fare would be to go second class to see you and how much it would cost to stay in a cheap hotel (pasta and a carafe of wine) for two people (without children), but two separate rooms. If I make some money in the theater, I could make the trip. Answer immediately by registered mail.

I am extremely upset by your illness. Maybe the doctors are alarming you needlessly. Write in detail about your state of health. Undoubtedly it's only *rechte Lungenspitzezatork*. Porter and lots of rest. I had it once—remember when I was screwing up a storm in Cracow.

My fiancée is not very pretty, but she's very likable. She doesn't love me at all, and I don't even appeal to her especially. But that's beside the point. She doesn't have any material possessions, but she understands the nature of the fantastic in life and beyond life. I don't have any idea what will result, but maybe this is the right premise to start from. I don't think I've gone over the deep end. I'm in complete possession of all my faculties, but I'm thinking of going to my wedding drunk, or under anesthesia.

I'm enjoying myself and making the best of life. But it is in preparation for the ultimate concentration and the defeat of all my hopes for life.

Please send me a quick answer.

Heartfelt kisses. To Lady Elsie and your daughters I send greetings. Mama sends both you and Mrs. Malinowski warmest regards.

Your Staś

If I don't get a letter in two weeks, I'll write again. I'd prefer that you answer me immediately.

I have the most dreadful forebodings in the whole world. But there's nothing to be done—you can't beat the wall against your head.

"Pure Form in the Theater"

■

(Lecture given on 29 December 1921,
at the Maƚy Theater in Warsaw)

Art is the expression of what I call *faute de mieux* metaphysical feeling, or in other words (please pay close attention) the expression *of the directly given unity of our individuality* in formal constructions of any elements (complex or simple), in such a way that these constructions affect us directly, and not through cognitive understanding.

Because the notion of Form is ambiguous and when used without making prior distinctions gives rise to hopeless misconceptions, I prefer instead the notion of Pure Form, which I define as a certain construction of any given elements, such as sounds, colors, words, or actions combined with utterances. Painting and music have simple elements, i.e., pure qualities, whereas poetry and theater have complex elements.

Every construction is a certain plurality of elements contained in a whole, in a unity. In contrast to utilitarian constructions (bridges, locomotives), whose external Form is the result of their practical use, works of Art have an autonomous construction, not dependent on anything else, and it is precisely their constructional aspect that I call Pure Form.

The notion of Pure Form is a boundary concept, i.e., no work can ever be a model of absolutely Pure Form, since it is the work of a particular real individual, and not the creation of some unimaginable, abstract spirit. Metaphysical feeling grows polarized in the psyche of a particular person and creates an individualized Form, with the result that the emotional and imaginative elements play a part in the way the Form arises and render it impure in the completed work. . . .

Artistic creation is not a rational combination of elements in a certain whole but the result of the directly given unity of our "I," which in the creative act, by means of real-life feelings and perceptions, directly produces a formal construction, likewise directly acting as such on the viewer or listener, evoking within him a heightened feeling of the unity of his individuality.

However, the essence of a completed work of art is to be found not in those "emotional elements," or in other words, those real-life feelings and perceptions that render impure Pure Form (which in a given work can be isolated in the abstract only), but rather in the formal construction that directly arouses metaphysical feeling, which by the way can likewise be awakened by powerful tensions in real-life feelings, philosophical reflections, views of nature, dreams, or any kind of phenomena that transcends everyday experience . . .

What alone matters is the proper division between real life and the purely artistic elements, which in each work of art must exist in different proportions. . . .

In my opinion, beyond certain limits set by aesthetic considerations, the material used should be of no concern at all to us, since for the immediate "betterment" of mankind we have special institutions: the churches and the schools. I think that the social significance of the theater could be infinitely enhanced if it ceased being a place for taking a fresh look at life, for teaching and for expounding "views," and instead became a true temple for experiencing pure metaphysical feelings. . . .

The concept of Pure Form is a boundary concept and no work of Art can be created without real-life elements. Some sort of beings will always act and speak on the stage, parts of the compositions in paintings will always be more or less analogous to actual objects in the visible world, and the reason is the impossibility of dispensing with dynamic and directional tensions. I must stress that the Theory of Art as formulated above in its general outlines can in no way be used to impose rules on creative artists. . . .

There is no theoretical necessity that would prescribe deformation and deviation from sense. If we disregard the inessential period of realism and look at the works of the old masters in painting and theater, we see that they were able to unite to perfection Pure Form and a total absence of glaring deformation and absurdity.

Theoretically we too could create in the same way. In practice, however, it turns out to be impossible. Because Art acts as a kind of narcotic whose effect is to evoke what I have called metaphysical feeling through a grasp of formal constructions, and because the effect of every narcotic weakens with time, necessitating increased doses, we have reached the point where the works of the old masters have stopped making an impression on us, and Art, given the waning of metaphysical feelings in the course of social evolution, starting with the Greeks and continuing through the Renaissance, has degenerated to an imitation of life and the world. Art's inessential elements assumed the first place, and the formal aspect became reduced to the role of intensifying qualitatively different elements: real-life feelings and the sphere of intellectual concepts.

The revival of Pure Form, which in a final desperate effort opposes the tide of grayness and mechanization flooding the world, cannot in our present circumstances dispense with the use of non-sense and of deformation of the world.

But this is not because of the impossibility of expressing in preexisting forms feelings unknown to our predecessors, but because it has become necessary to expand the compositional, purely formal possibilities and to intensify and render more complex the means of formal creation and of producing an effect on those receiving the impressions.

Just as artists cannot fully express themselves formally in preexisting forms, so likewise spectators and listeners cannot through contemplation of these forms be roused to true aesthetic satisfaction. . . .

We must keep in mind that the expansion of compositional possibilities can be achieved only by means of certain deviations from now-hackneyed forms that realism caused to degenerate.

Reared in realistic ideology, we always ask of each work of art, "Well all right, but what is it trying to say? What is it supposed to represent? What is the 'idea' behind this work?" As soon as we fail to get satisfactory answers to these questions, we turn away in disgust from the work under discussion, swearing more or less politely and repeating triumphantly, "*I don't understand.*" We do not want to grasp the simple truth that a work of Art does not express anything in the sense in which we have grown accustomed to use the word in real life. Thus it always has been and always will be until Art comes to an end, which probably (and fortunately) will not happen in the form of naturalistic stagnation, as our stormy and anguished times prove. We do not understand that a work of Art is what it is and nothing else, since we have grown accustomed to think that Art is the expression of some kind of real-life content, the representation of some real or fantastic worlds, something that has value only when compared to something else of which it is the reflection. Even if we actually experience something else, which was and is the deepest essence of our individuality—its directly given, irreducible unity—we pay no attention to this impression under the impact of an ideology falsified by realism. . . .

For those able to understand, Pure Form on the stage means that *like the significance of concepts in poetry, actions themselves in conjunction with utterances are the very elements of theatrical construction, as sounds and colors are in music and painting.* This is not the "musicalization" of painting and theater, it is the "paintification" of the former and the "theatricalization" of the latter—a reminder to artists and spectators of the true value of these Arts, due to which the works of the great masters speak to us down the ages, regardless of different "ways of looking at life and at things"—in other words, a reminder of their *formal value.* . . .

With regard to Art we must distinguish two forces: (1) the primal formal instinct of man, arising from the most profound principle of existence: unity in plurality, a principle of which we ourselves are the expression; and (2) the herd instinct, which finds expression in snobbery with regard both to the great works of the past and also to all kinds of novelty. Because of the first, what we call the great works of Art go down in history. Although the standard is relative, we can assert that it is the formal and not the real-life aspect of a work that determines its enduring quality. Of course, to this should be added the following determinants: the strength of the creative individual as a human being, the strength of his artistic intelligence, the strength of his talent, or in other words the strength of his purely sensuous skills (sense of color, imaginative power, sense of stage effect and of tempo and rhythm), plus what determines the value of Art and is no longer a matter of talent, but rather what we call artistic creativity in the strict sense of the term: the ability to compose, to construct certain formal wholes, the realization of which depends on the strength of talent. . . .

A work of Art does not consist of a single pleasing sensuous element— rather it is a composition or construction, which is made up of both pleasing and displeasing sensuous elements; it is directly perceived unity in plurality, giving a heightened feeling of the unity of one's individuality to the spectator and listener as well as to the artist at the moment of creation. The value of a work of Art does not depend on how faithfully it copies any reality, but on its constructional unity, which cannot be reduced to anything else. From this perspective the material used is of no importance, provided of course that it does not come to the fore in its own right and force the author to experience a variety of real-life emotions, whether uplifting or downright nasty.

A theatrical work in Pure Form is self-contained, autonomous, and in this sense absolute, despite the fact that there is not and cannot be any objective criterion for judging its value. The actors and actresses appearing in such a play, created by the director as a creative artist on a par with the author, do not impersonate more or less skillfully any sort of hypothetical people, but they create their roles within the overall totality of happenings on stage, consisting of formally joined actions, utterances, and images, capable of being put together, depending on compositional requirements, in the most fantastic way from the point of view of life and common sense.

In my opinion, the author is not at all the dominant figure, nor are the director and actors the renderers of his conception. He provides the kind of libretto that a writer gives a composer. Comparing musical performers to directors and actors is unfair to the latter.

Working together, the director and actors create the play on stage for the first time, naturally provided that they do not interpret it realistically, which can be done with any play. . . .

It is impossible to say whether we shall be able to attain the ideal of metaphysical beauty in the theater without perversity, "insatiable craving for form," and formal riotousness. Life is moving too fast and thus the rebirth of Pure Form is taking place in a way that may rather frighten the realistic ideologues who wish at least to doze undisturbed in the theater. But I think that even this is preferable to the senile torpor, spiritual tabes, and that mild feeblemindedness which is peering out at us from the gray, soulless atmosphere of a future full of socially disciplined automatons, unless we decide to blaze up and burn ourselves out in a splendid and menacing artistic cataclysm. . . .

What I am concerned with in a work of Art is formal ordering and composition, so that on stage a human being, or some other creature, could commit suicide because of the spilling of a glass of water, after having five minutes before danced with joy on account of his dearly beloved mother's death; so that a little five-year-old girl could give a lecture on Gauss's coordinates for apelike monsters beating gongs and constantly chanting the word *kalafar,* and then becoming a court of justice trying the case of the disappearance of a copper bell belonging to the director of private amusements for the Princess Chalatri, who after affectionately clapping her fiancé on the shoulder for tickling her favorite Doberman to death, then killed him with a cold smile for having accidentally brushed the dust off a withered geranium, the result being that the accused was sentenced to fifteen years of compulsory drinking of five liters daily of pineapple liqueur. Am I concerned with these or other similar facts as such? I have already said this many times—I will once again say no—three times over NO. (This is the concern at least in the theory of the futurists, some of whom, as true artists, despite their monstrous theory of realistic nonsense and childish dreams of "the futurization of life," are creating significant works in the sphere of Pure Form), but it is of no concern to me, either theoretically or practically. . . .

To pile up absurdities is one thing, and to create formal constructions, which have not been contrived in cold blood, is quite another. There is no specified degree of real-life truth or of fantastic psychology. Everything depends on in what formal construction a given effect is used and what is the formal relation of a given utterance or action to what went before and what comes after, quite independent of all relative truths and real-life experiences. What matters is that a play on stage should not be a copy of some "cosy little corner" or of a diabolical house of assignation; watching the action and listening to the dialogue, we should not need to be moved by the feelings per se, which we have more than enough of in life; we should not learn anything or resolve problems with the author, but watching the interwoven constructional stream of happenings, composed of actions, words, images, and musical impressions, we should find ourselves in the world of Formal Beauty, which has its own sense, its own logic, and its own TRUTH. Not the same truth as that of a realistic painting or of a "cosy little corner" on stage in relation to a real scene or a real event in life, but absolute Truth. Realistic art is always a more or less effective imitation of something, and the actors are better or worse imitators of beings assumed to be real. Art having a tendency toward Pure Form is something absolute, autonomous, something in which the acting creatures and their utterances exist only as parts of the whole, which occupies a given segment of time. Their past experiences can in no way concern us, unless they are formally linked with the present, and the same is even more true for their future.

Maria Witkiewicz, Zakopane, 1902. Photograph by Witkacy

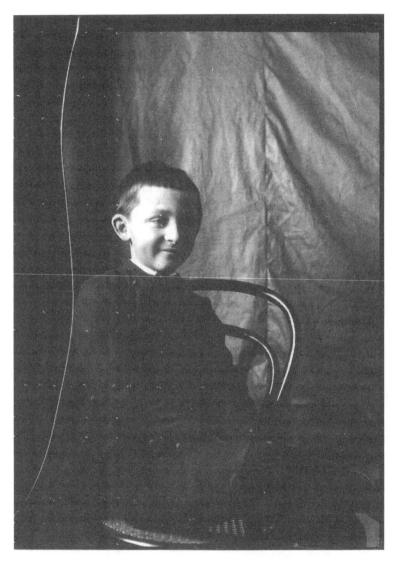

Me Sitting on a Chair, Zakopane, 1893. Photograpy by Witkiewicz senior

Me with Foka and Revolver, Zakopane, 1899. Photographer unknown

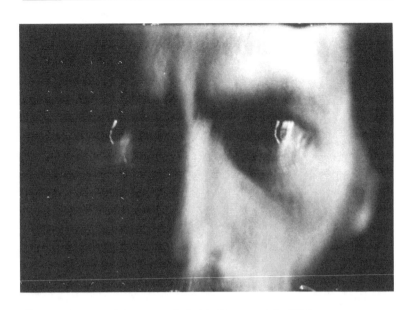

Tadeusz Langier, Zakopane, 1912–13. Photograph by Witkacy

The Fear of Life in Malinowski. Charcoal, 1912

Stanisław Witkiewicz, Lovranno, 1913. Photograph by Witkacy

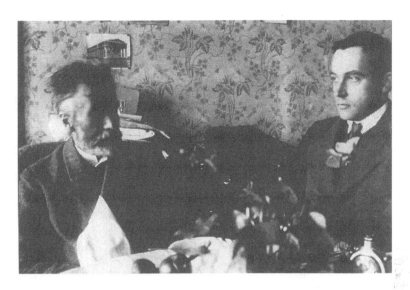

Father and son, Lovranno, 1913. Photograph by Witkacy

Jadwiga Janczewska, Zakopane, c. 1913. Photograph by Witkacy

Collapse by the Lamp, Zakopane, c. 1913. Photograph by Witkacy

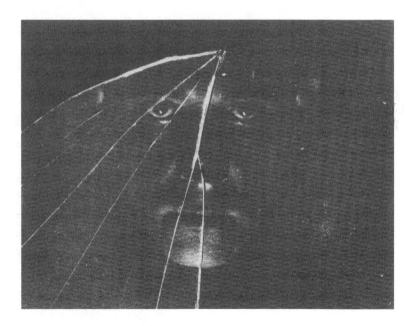

Self-portrait, Zakopane, before 1914

Bungo's Fall. Charcoal, 1913

The Prince of Darkness Tempts Saint Theresa with the Aid of a Waiter from Budapest. Charcoal, c. 1913

Suicide-to-be Three Seconds Before Pulling the Trigger. Charcoal, before 1913

Fearing Oneself. Charcoal, 1913

An Introduction to Cruel Perversions. Charcoal, before 1914

The Demonic Mrs. S., a Vulgar Demon (Reproaches). Charcoal, before 1914

Multiple Self-Portrait in Mirrors, St. Petersburg, 1915–17

Jadwiga Unrug, c. 1923, Zakopane. Photograph by Witkacy

Double Portrait of Winifred Cooper and Dr. X. Pastel, 1925. Museum of Art, Łódź

Studio portrait, Zakopane, 1927–28. Photograph by J. Kępińska

Self-portrait. Pastel, 1930

Self-portrait. Pastel, 1931

Czesława Korzeniowska, Zakopane, 1930s. Photograph by Witkacy

Witkiewicz, Zakopane, 1931. Photograph by Władysław Jan Grabski

Line drawing, 1933

Witkiewicz, *Madman's Fright*, Zakopane, 1931. Photograph by Józef
Głogowski

Studio portrait, Zakopane, late 1930s

SECOND RESPONSE TO THE REVIEWERS
OF *THE PRAGMATISTS*

■

(1922)

It is more difficult to prove something than to be ironical, although injecting a certain amount of vitriol into one's arguments is perhaps the best way of carrying on a discussion. . . .

In a work of art the important thing is the proportion of real-life and formal elements, and not the systematic elimination of the former for the sake of the latter. There is no denying that the judgments we make in evaluating these proportions will, within certain limits, be subjective. . . .

I have no wish to deprive words of their meaning, nor actions of theirs. Both these composite elements have a basic sensory and signifying component: the articulated sound and the conceptual significance of the word, and the visual image and the significance of the action. The novelty of my theory lies in treating the signifying components of words and actions as artistic elements, i.e., as elements capable of creating formal constructions, acting directly, as though they were simple elements, qualities, and their complexes. . . .

In general, I am pleased with the variety of opinion about my work. For some I am a "nihilistic bourgeois," for others (the critic Stanisław Pieńkowski) a kind of Bolshevik agitator. Quite a wide range of options! For some my art is "religious" (the director Wilam Horzyca interpreted my theory as an attempt to return to the mysteries), for still others it is absolute, even deliberate nonsense. We shall see how the future will judge. The one thing I could ask for is an understanding of my theory before criticizing it. Perhaps that will come with time. As of now I have lost faith in the value of carrying on any further polemics. I not only have not found any followers, but I cannot even discover a worthy opponent. My plays will certainly not be staged for a long time (and perhaps never).

Still, if any theater does decide on staging any of my plays, I would like to ask the director and actors for (a) as unemotional, straightforward, articulate delivery of the lines as possible, (b) as *mad* a pace of performance as possible, consistent with adherence to the preceding condition, (c) as strict an observance as possible of my "directorial" indications as to the placing of the characters, as well as about the settings according to my descriptions of them, (d) no attempts to make anything *stranger* than it already is in the text by means of setting-atmosphere-hit-them-in-the-guts gimmicks and an abnormal method of delivering the lines, (e) minimal cuts. . . .

As a formal construction, Pure Form acts directly, calling forth in us— at the moment when the plurality of elements is integrated into a unity— heightened "metaphysical feeling," or in other words it brings out the quality of unity per se against a "confused background," the unity of our individuality. That is why I have defined a work of Art as a kind of narcotic. Just as the visions are not contained in a dose of hashish preserves but rather are produced under its influence, so "metaphysical feeling" is not contained in the signification of the content of a work of art in Pure Form, which produces an immediate effect. The signifying content is given indirectly in signs—it is rendered intelligible in the context of the permanent associations of the sign with the signifying complex. The formal content of a work of Art (to the extent that we can so characterize a formal idea, given the actual unity of the plurality of elements), is directly given *without any symbolic function of the particular elements.*

JANULKA, DAUGHTER OF FIZDEJKO

∎

A Tragedy in Four Acts

Dedicated to my wife

Oder bin ich ein Genie,
oder ein Hanswurst,
Hanswurst oder Genie—
ich muss *leben*.
∎ Graf Friedrich Altdorf, *Bewegungsstudien*

CHARACTERS

EUGENIUS (GENE) PAPHNUTIUS FIZDEJKO—Prince of Lithuania and
Belorussia. Old man in his seventies. Very tall. Trimmed beard. Large gray
moustache and great gray head of hair. From time to time he puts on
round glasses.
ELSA FIZDEJKO—née Baroness von Plasewitz. Matron fifty-five years old.
Formidable and withered. Gray hair. Fizdejko's wife.
PRINCESS JANULKA FIZDEJKO—their daughter. Fifteen years old. Beast
blonde (not blonde beast), quite tall and thin. Pretty and rather ethereal,
but there's something monstrous about her face, although that
"something" is subtly accentuated. Perhaps her eyes are a bit too
protruding and fishlike; perhaps her eyebrows are overly slanting; her nose
is straight, not turned up, but perhaps pushed too flat; and maybe her lips
are too thin and her mouth overly crooked.

BERNARD BARON VON PLASEWITZ—Elsa's father. Old man eighty-five years old. Bald with a crown of gray hair around his head. Fat, stocky, and very good-hearted. Manufacturer of odorless and invisible gases that produce terrific psychological depression.

ALFRED PRINCE DE LA TREFOUILLE—young man about town. Blond, very elegant. Small moustache. Without a beard. French emigré.

PRINCESS AMALIA DE LA TREFOUILLE—his wife. Dark, Spanish-Rumanian-Hungarian type. Thirty years old. First-class demon. Not "née" anything.

JOEL KRANZ—international type of Semite. Small, dark. Short Vandyke beard. Roving eyes. Frantic nervousness in every gesture. Thirty-eight years old. Pilot, merchant in the grand manner, transcendental Zionist. He talks feverishly, so rapidly that he chokes and spits.

HABERBOAZ AND REDERHAGAZ—his assistants, Hasidic Jews. Between forty and fifty years old. One red-haired, the other dark-haired. With beards. Dressed in Jewish costumes with black-and-white stripes.

GOTTFRIED REICHSGRAFF VON UND ZU BERCHTOLDINGEN—Grand Master of the Neo-Teutonic Knights. Chivalric face, aquiline nose. Big, broad-shouldered, and wonderfully built.

TWO CHARACTERS WITHOUT LEGS—on stands which stretch as though made of flabby guts. Bird faces with short, hooked beaks like bullfinches. Covered with variegated plumage (red, green, and violet colors). One without a right arm, the other without a left.

DIRECTOR OF SEANCES—wizard out of a fairy tale. Known as Der Zipfel. Old man with a gray Vandyke beard. Black, seventeenth-century Dutch costume with a ruff around the neck. Pointed hat with a broad brim. A gold chain on his chest.

TWELVE LITHUANIAN BOYARS—wild peasants in sheepskin coats and caps. "Beards flowing, murly their custaches, hair long, and grimed begarments," and armed with huge clubs and hatchets.

SIMIUS GLISSANDER—dragged through every gutter, "a man for anything" (bon pour tout). Forty-five years old. Dirty-blond hair, unshaven, with a moustache. An improductive poet.

FOUR YOUNG LADIES FROM THE MASTER'S FRAUZIMMER—young and pretty. Black dresses, white pinafores.

[The action takes place in Lithuania with the chronology somewhat mixed up.]

Act One

[Huge hall, divided on the wall facing the audience and on the floor by a zigzag line with broad lightninglike jagged streaks (three on the wall, two on the floor). To the left, a small window with bars, located quite high; to the right, a large window with curtains. A door facing the audience, divided by a zigzag going from left to right. The left side is made out of a dilapidated, dank, moldy wall that has collapsed in various places. On the wall, gigantic, shiny Ceylonese cockroaches, executed in relief. They can even move. In the middle of the left half of the stage, placed at an angle from left to right, the foot to the audience, an ugly crooked wooden bed with monstrously dirty bedclothes. A quilt patched with red, brown and yellow scraps. On the bed under the quilt lies the dying Elsa Fizdejko, her unfastened gray hair streaming down to the floor. By the bed to the right, a bedside table, half falling to pieces, and enormous, disgusting, down-at-the-heel slippers. On the bedside table, a bright electric light without a shade, illuminating everything with a glaring light. In the left corner of the stage, a white stove, half caved in, in which a blazing fire is burning. To the right of the zigzag line, diabolical sumptuousness in the rococo style. The hangings on the wall are orange-red, as is the upholstery of the gilded white furniture. The rug is in russet hues. Rococo mirrors and old paintings are crammed together on the wall. Small tables of knickknacks. Miniatures in expensive frames and other exquisite eighteenth-century luxury items, which the author is unable to identify more exactly (perhaps he saw them in museums in his youth). At a small table, lighted by a candelabra with a dozen or more candles, sit the Prince and Princess de la Tréfouille dressed in eighteenth-century costumes, playing cards with Von Plasewitz, in a black frock coat and white vest, and Glissander, in a threadbare two-piece suit. De la Tréfouille sits directly facing the audience, with Glissander opposite him, Von Plasewitz on his right, and the Princess on his left. Fizdejko is dressed in a long snuff-colored frock coat from the 1830s, a Vater-Mörder and black Halstuch, checked gallifets, and high boots of reddish color. He paces back and forth across the entire length of the stage at the front, smoking a pipe a meter long. Quite frequently and without any apparent reason, he puts on and takes off his glasses; tends the fire in the stove, and now and then studies the cards held by the players. The latter indistinctly mutter various mysterious terms connected with the cards,

playing very fast (bridge, whist, or a commercial gambling game invented
by the author called Kumpol). This goes on for such a long time that the*
audience—to the extent that it has any character at all—should finally
begin to get impatient. At the slightest sign of anything of this sort, an
infernal peal of cannon fire is heard, and through the window on the left a
glaring blood red flash is seen. No one on stage bats an eyelash. They all
speak very loudly, until further notice.]

FIZDEJKO [*Calmly fixing the fire in the stove.*] So the Grand Master has
   been carousing with my boyars again today. I wonder what those
   slobs think about it all.

VON PLASEWITZ [*From behind his cards.*] I'd say just about as much as
   your bears do, Gene. Is Janulka going to join in the carousing
   again?

FIZDEJKO I don't know. She went there as usual, but whether she's going
   to stay I have no idea. Up to the last minute nothing had been
   decided. I've already lost all sense of time. I don't know how many
   days that orgy has been in progress.

[*The others keep on playing, still muttering about their cards. Fizdejko*
moves away from the stove and slowly approaches the cardplayers.]

ELSA The only thing that I worry about is whether Janulka hasn't been
   drinking too much lately. By the by, Gene, give me some vodka.

FIZDEJKO [*Coming over.*] You'd better look after yourself. Janulka can
   hold her liquor; she takes after me. I've been continuously drunk for
   fifty-five years. But is all that vodka the best thing for your stomach
   cancer—that's the real question.

[*He pulls a quart bottle out of the back pocket of his pants and hands it to*
his wife, who drinks ravenously and then puts the bottle on the floor by the
bed. Fizdejko goes over to the cardplayers.]

VON PLASEWITZ Would you take my place, Gene, and play a hand or two
   with the Prince and Princess? I'll have a little chat with my poor
   Elsa. [*Crosses to the left. Fizdejko sits down in his chair. The table is*
   placed slightly at an angle so that Fizdejko's face is turned three-
   quarters to the audience from the right side; Von Plasewitz sits down
   at the foot of his daughter's bed on the right side.] Elsa, I ask you

*Explanations as to this game can be supplied by the author or any other former officer in the
Imperial Guard of the Pavlovsky Regiment, First Battalion.

for the last time: tell me the secret cause of your poverty. After all, I am a multimillionaire, and Gene, a true aristocrat, lives like a king and probably will actually be one soon. What does it mean? After working like an ox for the past sixty years, can't I even provide for the happiness of my beloved daughter?

ELSA   This is the way it has to be. Whenever I've tried to live differently, everything's always turned against me. These are not penitential acts, nor fanaticism on my part. It's sheer necessity. I know if I once start to live comfortably, let alone luxuriously, I'll get fond of things I won't be able to keep. I tried it once already and . . .

VON PLASEWITZ   Was that when Gene was about to become king for the first time? Is that what you mean?

ELSA   Yes. Remember what happened then, Father? For days I wandered through the woods like a hungry she-wolf, clutching Janulka to my breast.

VON PLASEWITZ   But wasn't that exactly what you wanted yourself? You did everything you could to make it come out that way.

ELSA   Sssh! ! !—We bring on all our own misfortunes. There's no difference between what I did and what a person does when he deliberately chooses to stand under a brick that *by chance* falls on his head. Chance! Ha! ha! ha! Papa, do you know the theory of probability? The law of large numbers? Ha! ha!

VON PLASEWITZ   Don't laugh so wildly. There's no reason to. [*Loud din of voices offstage.*] That's quite some carousing. I think I hear Janulka's voice coming from the balcony.

[*A young girl's high-pitched squealing can be heard from the left side, about fifty meters from the barred window.*]

ELSA   Poor, poor Janulka! How much she still must suffer without even knowing it, and how happy she'll be when she realizes that her very happiness was the height of suffering! Isn't the worst suffering the suffering we're not aware of? Isn't that how the lower creatures suffer? That's why wicked people feel so much compassion for animals.

[*Again a frightful peal of cannon fire and cheers, amid which a young girl's voice can be heard.*]

FIZDEJKO   [*Throws down his cards furiously and gets up.*] Oh, damn! I've had enough of all these equivocations! Everything must be settled today . . .

ELSA   Remember, it's all just beginning today. In a moment, right here in this room, infinite perspectives of real-life creativity will be revealed to you. You must have absolute faith in the Master.

FIZDEJKO   From what I've heard, that dandy is so madly in love with Janulka as to raise serious doubts about his common sense. According to Glissander, he's just a tool in Janulka's hands.

VON PLASEWITZ   But the spirit of the age speaks through him. He's an indispensable person. Our first performance with the kingdom was a failure because we didn't have the appropriate mediums. Suggest someone else, Gene.

FIZDEJKO   There were others, there were others I've known . . .

VON PLASEWITZ   Like your first accomplices when you tried to seize the kingdom by a coup d'état? In those days we didn't have the Jews on the scene, and the problem of creating the artificial self wasn't as acute as it is now. An incalculable number of unknowns have entered into the equation since then. Our era . . .

FIZDEJKO   Stop talking about "our era," Papa. It's not an era, but an accumulation of anachronisms. I no longer know what century I'm living in: the fourteenth or twenty-third.

VON PLASEWITZ   That's right, our era is beyond time. Time has become relative even in history. In the past, changes took place slowly. Given the acceleration of our lives, we've got to accept Einstein's theory in history too. The nature of our era is that it has escaped from the cyclical laws of history. We're flying off at a tangent.

DE LA TREFOUILLE   [Getting up.] So this is the final era? Just how do you understand that, Baron?

VON PLASEWITZ   I don't understand it in the least. I'm simply speaking intuitively, like an art critic. You can understand it any way you like, according to your own intuition. There's a screw loose in the old bean, and I'm just talking rubbish. Which, in our times, is the height of philosophy. Beyond that there's only logical calculus. A sense of destiny cannot be expressed by concepts—it must be experienced— so said Spengler. Dadaism must be "experienced" too —so said Tristan Tzara or some other superclown. Duration can only be experienced too—so said Bergson.

DE LA TREFOUILLE   Oh . . .

FIZDEJKO   "Oh" me no "ohs"! Papa Plasewitz is dead right: I've finally grasped that. In our era, as a function of the speed of events, we

must accept time as becoming increasingly long and drawn-out. That
amounts to saying that the further we worm our way into history, the
more time seems to us long and drawn-out because of boredom.

ELSA   The only boring thing is asking such questions.

DE LA TREFOUILLE   That's not true, Princess. Let us consider Rousseau's
significance before the French Revolution. From such ideas future
events take their shape—they are already inherent in them . . .

ELSA   Idle fancies, Your Highness, idle fancies. In our times there are no
real events anymore. There is only one single interminable event—
the waking dream into which mankind has fallen.

[*Fizdejko goes over to Elsa and strokes her hair. They both drink vodka out
of the bottle.*]

VON PLASEWITZ   Mankind! Let's not use that disgusting word. Let me rave
on a little longer. Then I have the impression that something
actually exists.

ELSA   [*Suddenly ecstatic.*] You are all artists. In our times "artist" is
synonymous with the last remaining vestiges of individualism. You
don't paint, you don't write poetry: your lives are marvelous,
rainbow-colored embroiderings against the gray background of our
passage on earth, so sinister in its boredom.

FIZDEJKO   If only it were that way! Oh!—to awaken in oneself for just a
brief moment, even in a dream, a feeling of the charm of Existence,
and to die in such a dream, having seen life from afar as an
abstraction in Pure Form! Oh, dearest Elsie, why didn't we pay more
attention to that before! Within me there are still vast untapped
layers of the unknown. To grasp such possibilities consciously at
least once before dying and look at an image of the world in all its
potentiality!

DE LA TREFOUILLE   In a moment we'll all be looking in that direction.
None of you understands the Master. But I do him . . . and he does
me . . . but that's not what I meant to say—the new spiritual
discipline, which consists of creating a new "I" within ourselves,
begins with superfluous strength. But we've got to be able to bear it.

FIZDEJKO   Oh, come off it. You're just a young puppy. We've got more
than enough superfluous strength. We're all bursting with it. It just
comes down to one simple question: how to live? How to experience
one's life most essentially? I've been living for seventy years, and I

still don't know. That was Hyrcan's problem. And what happened?
Some wretched paint slinger shot him down like a dog and ruined
his whole Hyrcania.

DE LA TREFOUILLE   Hyrcan was a stupid conservative. In the old days
people didn't ask how to live. They simply lived as they had to,
and . . .

FIZDEJKO   Now look here, Mister . . . you're not going to teach me the
basic tenets of cattle braining. I've been through all that: from overintellectualized spontaneity to cattle-brained intellect pushed to its
ultimate limits.

DE LA TREFOUILLE   Yes, but purely techno-psychological questions . . .

FIZDEJKO   Don't interrupt, please. My Janulka is the fruit of that last
combination, and I'm sacrificing her for what is perhaps a sorry
farce. Artificial kingdoms—it's already come to that! I love my poor
Janulka, and she gets roaring drunk everyday with that cad in a
Grand Master's cloak. And yet all of you are holding me here in a
kind of prison!

[He collapses into a rococo chair and sobs quietly. Elsa drags herself out of
bed—she's in a patched multicolored bathrobe—goes over to Fizdejko, and
puts her arms around him.]

DE LA TREFOUILLE   Poor old Prince. All he needs is a tragic death to
become a much better knickknack than all that trinketry. [He points
to the knickknacks on the tables.]

VON PLASEWITZ   [Gets up off the bed and dances, singing to the tune of the
popular folk melody "Ojra, ojra."]

> Implication c'est relation
> Ram tararampam pam!
> Leibniz, Husserl and Bolzano
> Russell, Chwistek and Peano!
> Implication is relation
> And relation implication!

Comprenez-vous? The logic of ratios gives us wings—so said
Bertrand Russell. But Henri Poincaré reproached him for having
wings but never using them to fly. I—based on the fact that I am
I—prove that A = A. No one has found any other proofs for that

proposition. Long live psychologism and intuition! I shall keep on raving, and you, my son-in-law, translate it for me into terms intelligible to the rabble and even to me. Oh, Philosophy, what have they done to you! [*He sits down on Elsa's bed and bursts into bitter tears.*]

DE LA TREFOUILLE   Absolute inconcision in thinking. Devoid of homogeneous expression in every respect. Only the Master can save us from that, and you will all be able to create a great and glorious composition, [*With prophetic inspiration.*] a living picture that will eclipse Giotto, Botticelli, Matisse, and Picasso, and—God willing— if the whole thing once gets going, the resulting tragedy will surpass and simply beat hollow all theatrical works written since the world began, *y compris* Aeschylus and Shakespeare. Now the miracle is about to happen!

[*Offstage babble of voices and a deafening peal of cannon fire. The barred window to the left flies out and a terrific wind begins to blow through it, carrying in every so often clouds of snow. (This can easily be done by means of a bellows blowing on piles of shredded paper or cotton wisps, which can later be gathered up in the rug.) Princess Amalia and Glissander stand up.*]

GLISSANDER   God forbid that Seine Durchlaucht, the Grand Master of the Neo-Teutonic Knights von und zu Berchtoldingen, should find us in such a state. Get up and dry your tears at once.

[*The men get up blubbering and wipe their eyes and noses with their handkerchiefs. De la Tréfouille quickly removes all traces of the card game, notes down the various scores in a small notebook, cleans the cloth cover on the table with a brush. Elsa pins up her flowing hair. Meanwhile the following conversation takes place:*]

FIZDEJKO   What should I say to him? He claims he loves me and says I am the only person to whom he could become attached, because of Janulka and the cattle braining of my good people. All attempts to indoctrinate mankind by means of torture have come to nought. My encattled dignity fluffs like a wisp of unknown matter on the light coat of russet grime covering our programmatic contemporaneity. Oh, Great Switchman of Worlds, shunt our poor little spherical planet onto a track leading to the fourth-dimensional abyss!

DE LA TREFOUILLE That's metaphysics. The problem of the abyss does not exist in the physics of gravitational fields. We alone have abysses and directions. Minkowski's fourth-dimensional continuum is not a fourth dimension for ignoramuses and fatheads.

GLISSANDER [*In a frightful voice.*] Attention! ! ! Now the Great Switchman is on his way! Attention, I say! Dynamic tension in the highest degree.

[*The door opens noiselessly and the Director of Séances, Der Zipfel, enters.*]

DER ZIPFEL [*Speaks softly yet penetratingly.*] Is everything ready?

GLISSANDER Yes, Sir, Herr Director.

DER ZIPFEL [*With a courteous gesture pointing to Princess Elsa.*] That lady—Her Luminosity, ex-Princess of Lithuania and Belorussia, I presume—will be so kind as to climb back into bed. His Durchlaucht is not overly fond of unkempt, slovenly dressed women. [*Elsa crawls off to bed obediently.*] Lights out please, and those candles too. [*Elsa puts out the electric light, de la Tréfouille extinguishes the candles.*] There—very good. Now we can start the official presentation. [*Yells.*] You may come in! !

[*The door opens with a bang. Blue light can be seen in the space beyond. The stage is plunged in total darkness except for the blood red flames flickering in the stove. Enter the Grand Master von und zu Berchtoldingen. Black armor, helmet with a lowered visor. Black panache. A white cloak with a black cross draped over his shoulder. Glissander and the Princess quickly run out the door and bring in a luminous screen phosphorescently green (a shallow cardboard box with small lights inside), place it behind the Master and shut the door.*]

FIZDEJKO [*Breaking the silence.*] Where is Janulka?

GLISSANDER Silence! Your daughter is not feeling well, Prince. She drank too much last night and now is being sobered up by the young ladies from the Frauzimmer, in other words, from the Grand Master's harem. My lords, sole *lords* on this earth—and undoubtedly on the adjacent planets of Mars and Venus also—allow me.to unite you officially in order to carry out the final act of creation, no less worthy than the past deeds of our knights and great men in every realm. Prince Fizdejko—the Grand Master of the Neo-Teutonic Knights, Reichsgraf von und zu Berchtoldingen.

FIZDEJKO   I hope the Master won't think I'm a snob. At my age and with
my knowledge of life and human history . . .

GLISSANDER   Skip the introductions, Mr. Fizdejko.

FIZDEJKO   No hired flunky is going to tell me what to . . .

GLISSANDER   Get to the point, Gene, get to the point. The Master doesn't
like all that beating around the bush.

FIZDEJKO   Well, then, dear Master, I must confess that I don't understand
anything. Neither the what, nor the why, nor the how. A mystery.
The only thing that worries me is about Janulka. I love my little
daughter. All children born to parents in their later years are so out
of the ordinary. Don't you think so, Count?

MASTER   I must confess, Prince, that your daughter has captivated me
utterly with her simply fantastic charm, her openness and her
intelligence. An exceedingly shrewd young girl. [*Fizdejko makes a
vague gesture.*] Are you afraid that I've seduced her? No—I swear it
on this sword. The ladies of my Frauzimmer provide me with an
almost foolproof lightning rod, or rather—but that's enough about
that—for my desires, which surpass the average for a man of
my age . . .

VON PLASEWITZ   Master, my daughter is lying in bed over there.

MASTER   Oh, excuse me. In Princess Amalia's company I've grown
accustomed to feeling that anything goes. [*Goes over to Elsa and
kisses her hand for a prolonged time. Suddenly:*] But look here, Mr.
Fizdejko, why didn't you tell me your wife was Semitic?

FIZDEJKO   That was three generations ago, Count.

MASTER   No titles, please. Let's use first names without any further
ceremony. It will simplify the situation. I really enjoy telling people
off. Now to get back to the subject—enough of this cursed
blabber—the fact that I didn't know about that has ruined a number
of my supplementary plans. The entire anti-Semitic campaign will
have to be launched in a covert manner. But anyhow, we don't have
to fear the Jews, nor hate them either, just use them so they don't
even know they're being used.

PRINCESS AMALIA   That's a tricky business, Gottfried. You might get used
yourself, and yet be convinced that you were the one running the
show.

MASTER   Amalia, my dear, I know that myself. I like to pull off things that
can't be done . . .

FIZDEJKO   But Janulka, my little poor daughter . . .

MASTER   She'll throw up and come when she's through—didn't I tell you.
She has a strong constitution. Now I don't have anything against *un
tout petit brin de sang sémite*. There are two good combinations:
Prussian-Polish, that's what I am—my mother was née Princess
Zawratyńska—and Lithuanian-Semitic in the right proportions—
obviously, I'm not talking about half-breeds.

GLISSANDER   Oooh—I see that you gentlemen will never come to an
understanding. Master, cut it short, please.

MASTER   All right then, Eugenius, speaking straight from the shoulder: do
you want to be king or don't you? Unfortunately we must live out
our lives to the very end as an artistic transformation of coordinates,
or else blend in with the rabble. Truth in the usual sense is ruled out
here. Three hundred years ago that problem had already thwarted
all efforts to solve it. But I shall give—indirectly, of course, in the
form of new psychic creations—a totally new definition of the Truth:
*Truth is incompatibility with reality, being at the same time a
deformation of the latter.* Mutual concessions from those two
spheres create something different from anything that has previously
existed, just as a chemical compound differs from its elements. Our
coordinates are compound numbers. Something illusory has to be
added—there's no getting around that—it won't come about all by
itself. For many, *many* reasons *I* am powerless. I lack a certain
primitive quality which . . . But here's your beloved offspring.

[*Two young ladies from the Frauzimmer lead in Janulka, dressed in a white
ball-gown. Snow streams through the window in great gusts. Clouds of snow
reach Elsa's bed. The gale howls dolefully.*]

JANULKA   Mama! Vodka! I got chilled to the marrow out there in the snow.
I'd like to get whacked in the snout, impaled on a stake—how do I
know what. The Master is a fairy-tale prince.

[*She goes over to her Mother and drinks out of the bottle standing on the
floor. Delighted, Fizdejko looks all around, seeking approval.*]

FIZDEJKO   [*Beating his hands against his loins.*] Flesh of my flesh! Bone
of my bones! I swear to God! The Fizdejkos were always like that.

JANULKA   None of you has any idea of what a marvelous person the
Master is. He's a true knight of yore. Really and truly—history has
doubled back until its nose touches its backside and now it's eating

its own . . . tail. That is a true miracle. I could seduce him right on the spot, but I don't want to. I am an innocent little girl, while he is a frightful spirit looking at himself reflected in me as in a magic mirror that shows an object from all sides at once.

MASTER Yes, indeed, I have discovered depths within myself I didn't even suspect I had. Or rather lace trimmings on the foundations of my artificial self. But more about that later.

VON PLASEWITZ Have you thought that through to its logical conclusion, Count? I wouldn't advise it. I am an advocate of spontaneous insight, of pure conceptual nonsense.

MASTER I haven't thought it through, and I have no intention of doing so. Too many miraculous things have been happening here. It is fortunate that I met your daughter before I met you, my good Fizdejko. Glissander, our inestimable Glissander, created that essential protocol especially for us. [*Glissander bows.*] But a craving for strangeness predisposes me to worlds forgotten by present-day mankind . . . [*Covers his mouth with his iron-gloved hand.*] What did I just say? Mankind? In the presence of ladies? Oh, my God, what a faux pas. [*To Der Zipfel.*] *Also, mein lieber* Polish wizard, you can tell them to bring in your monsters. We'll feel better in their company. [*Exit Der Zipfel.*] Patience, patience. I warn you, I'm going to speak quite bluntly. That improductive poet, poor Simius [*Points at Glissander.*] has put my unbridled and giddy verbal fantasy into rigid forms. Assuming total freedom in the association of ideas, I dare assert . . .

[*The wind howls dismally.*]

FIZDEJKO Oh, just say what you have to say, Gottfried. Don't keep promising, just say it! My guts ache from waiting so long, and there's still so much ahead of us.

MASTER Right away—have them bring in the monsters first. Protocol must be observed. [*Two Boyars bring in a huge crate made of rough-hewn boards. Two other Boyars come in immediately after them, carrying a second crate. They place the crates on either side of the screen. Der Zipfel appears behind them.*] May I have a little light, Princess. Turn on the lamp, please. [*Elsa turns the knob. Light floods the stage.*] As a backdrop for my program, that squalor creates a sensational effect. Don't think I'm drunk. And now,

Princes of cattle-brained Lithuania, open the crates containing the monsters.

[*The Boyars start to open the crates, facing the audience. After they have unnailed the top and sides, they hold the covers in place, awaiting further orders.*]

JANULKA   This is the only thing I'm a bit afraid of.

FIZDEJKO   So am I. But since those are the Master's orders—it can't be helped. And I'm not even spared children's fairy tales in my old age. I've got to live through it all. Am I reverting to childhood? What in holy hell is going on here? I'm scared like a little boy in the dark.

MASTER   Have no fear. Here in our very midst we've got the noble Der Zipfel, Great Sorcerer and director of the most infernal séances in the whole world. He has tamed far worse monsters in his time.

DER ZIPFEL   Yes, Sir. [*To the Boyars.*] Take the covers off, old bears, and then clear out! !

[*The Boyars remove the covers, causing the nails underneath to creak, and with shrieks of diabolical fear they run away, bumping into one another in the doorway. Birdlike screeching is heard coming from the crates. The gale roars. Snow pours in through the window.*]

PRINCESS AMALIA   [*Approaching.*] Oh, what cute little monsters! Locked up inside them is the enchanted secret of our splendid future. They are our talismans, the mascots of our triumphant artificial constructs of the spirit.

MASTER   [*In a voice that trembles slightly.*] This is the first time I've ever seen them myself. The new state where the greatest barbarians enjoy the highest civilization is the basic axiom of future reality. There can be no civilization without barbarians to serve as a foil.

JANULKA   [*Goes down on her knees, wringing her hands.*] I'm so afraid, I'm so afraid!

[*The Monsters crawl out of the crates on their stands. They move like jars being pushed.*]

MASTER   If you're going to be afraid while you're with me, little girl, I'll really take offense. But without you we don't exist. Like some infernal glue, you alone bind us together in a new creation of life artificially reconstructed on the heights of a new metaphysical power.

VON PLASEWITZ   Even though that doesn't seem to mean anything at all, you put it very nicely.

JANULKA   [*Kneeling.*] I'm so afraid, I'm so afraid!

MONSTER I   [*Without a right arm; in a screeching voice.*] Put us nearer the stove. We're cold.

MASTER   [*To all those present.*] Get moving, you loafers! Help the monsters. Hurry up!

[*Fizdejko, de la Tréfouille, the Princess Amalia, and Glissander help the Monsters move closer to the stove. Der Zipfel goes over to the window on the left and puts it back in its frame. From the stove, which no one has shut tight, a red flame shoots forth so bright that it eclipses the electric lamp. All the chinks glow. As the Monsters pass by her bed, Elsa starts to moan quietly, "aa," "aaaa," then louder and louder until she finally dies emitting a wild cry.*]

ELSA   A! Aaa! Aaaaa! ! ! A! ! ! ! !

VON PLASEWITZ   [*Going over to her.*] Well, now at least we have one corpse. My daughter died of fright.

FIZDEJKO   There'll be more corpses soon. My heart has stopped beating I'm so afraid, even though I know it's all some kind of trick.

[*The stove blazes more and more intensely through all the chinks.*]

JANULKA   [*Cries out wildly, springing up off her knees.*] Take pity on me! ! ! !

[*The Master runs over and covers her mouth with his iron glove; he holds her around her waist with his other hand.*]

MASTER   [*In a hard voice.*] The mystery has made its appearance amongst us. Once again, like the people of yore, we are surrounded by the eternal, inscrutable depths of universal being.

VON PLASEWITZ   Hence the relativity of everything? Barbarians as a contrastive backdrop and artificial monsters? The deformation of life! Now I understand. So that's the price you pay for conquering life? And it's the same with art: New Forms, but at the price of deformation and dissonance? Am I right?

MASTER   No. Those were the daydreams of the kings of Hyrcania. No, decidedly not; barbarians are necessary not as a backdrop but as raw material. Out of the barbarians there will grow the marvelous flower of the Mystery renewed, the possibility of a new religion—not an artificial religion, but one as true as the mystery of my own existence. But for that we must be transformed.

VON PLASEWITZ   And what if you run out of barbarians?

MASTER   Socialism carried to its ultimate extremes will produce artificial barbarians. That's already happened here in our country, and sooner or later it will happen elsewhere too.

VON PLASEWITZ   You won't be able to get along without the Semites. They—or actually we—are the indispensable frame for every picture of the future.

MASTER   I have Semites to spare. I let them loose everywhere. We'll suck them like ticks.

[*Silence.*]

MONSTER II   We feel good here. It's warm.

VON PLASEWITZ   [*To the Monsters.*] Are you really signs of otherworldly powers?

MONSTER I   We're not symbolic characters—far from it. We really exist, we're alive, we're warm, we're hungry.

MASTER   They are as real as the Mystery of Existence, which nothing can crack: no system of ideas, no society, no . . .

JANULKA   [*Breaking away from him.*] Not even you, Grand Master. I love my monsters, my poor, dear little monsters. I'm not at all afraid of you anymore. You'll get something to eat right away.

[*She runs over to them and strokes their feathers. Birdlike screeches emanate from the Monsters.*]

FIZDEJKO   So it's at the price of her love for me and her mental stability that I am to acquire real power—I, a broken old man in his declining years.

MASTER AND DER ZIPFEL   [*Pointing to the screen on which there slowly appears a picture of Fizdejko's gigantic head wearing a fantastic crown, projected by a magic lantern.*] Look at that! ! !

FIZDEJKO   A magic lantern! Even that hasn't been spared me. I'm reverting to childhood all the way. I'm afraid, I'm terribly afraid, even though I know you've got a projector hidden there somewhere. [*Gets up off his knees.*] But I've got to have some supper too. This way, ladies and gentlemen.

MASTER   I'll stay here with Janulka and inject into her psychic skeleton the poison of the vilest mysteries. A certain dose of evil, of ordinary low-down evil, is not to be avoided even in our dimensions.

[*He goes to the left toward Janulka and the Monsters. Der Zipfel follows him. Fizdejko heads for the door with a heavy step. The Prince and Princess de la Tréfouille, Von Plasewitz, and Glissander follow him. The lamp goes out.*]

FIZDEJKO [*Leaving.*] A short circuit. That's all we needed! Oh, I'm going to be so afraid tonight by candlelight!

[*They go out. Der Zipfel is outlined against the blazing stove, which slowly dies out.*]

MASTER [*In a thundering voice.*] And now artificial mysteries avaunt! You Janulka, in my psycho-physical clutches, will become a medium for realizing the deepest desire to experience one's life in the most concentrated manner. I shall probably burst from sensual delight! You won't be able to stand it yourself: a psychic current powerful as a herd of elephants will pass right through you.

JANULKA Yes, but first I'll just bring my monsters something to eat.

[*She runs out.*]

MASTER [*Raising his visor and throwing himself on his knees in front of the bed on which Elsa's corpse lies; in a tearful voice.*] What's this corpse doing here? I'm an ordinary, decent person! What do you all want from me? Did *I* kill her? I don't want anything! Just to get a little rest, a little rest!

[*He breaks into hysterical sobbing. Birdlike screeching from the Monsters. Der Zipfel makes a downward motion with his hand.*]

CURTAIN

End of the First Act

Act Two

[*Autumn gloom; night is falling. The interior of a virgin spruce forest. Here and there, mountain ash, which has turned rĕd, shines through the dark green underbrush. Gigantic trees. Monstrous mosses and mushrooms in white, yellow, and red. To the left near the footlights facing the audience, a fantastic log cabin. The broad door is wide open. A fire is burning inside. From time to time smoke belches forth and pours out through the roof. The Director of Séances, Der Zipfel, sits on the high threshold in the doorway. Fizdejko, dressed like the Old Man of the Woods, sits to the right on a felled*] *tree trunk. A crown made of branches on his head. Long gray beard. White robe trimmed in pale green.*

Near him, Janulka, dressed like the Nymph of the Forest, sorts berries in a sieve. The Two Monsters are on their stands to the right. (The stands can be constructed like crinoline skirts, making it possible for the actors to get up and sit down by pressing the hoops together.)]

FIZDEJKO   Thus have I succeeded in staving off disaster for a short while. It's hard for an old man in his second childhood—I'll put it bluntly—for an almost feebleminded old man suddenly to cross such frontiers and behold such perspectives.

JANULKA   But *I* think that *they* deliberately planned this flight of ours on the eve of the coronation as part of their scheme. It was Der Zipfel's suggestion.

FIZDEJKO   I don't know. My mind is in a fog. I haven't had a drink for a week. All I want is peace and quiet. And yet I have a presentiment that someone will pay us a visit here today: it may be a person, or a whole gang, or some animal or spirit—it's not important who—but someone will come and everything else depends on this evening.

DER ZIPFEL   The hell with all that transforming life into a studied composition! Right, venerable old Prince? Better to eke out one's existence in a remote little cottage.

FIZDEJKO   Oh, yes! It's strange how the wildest things befall those who most long for peace and quiet. And yet, and yet I am constantly troubled by the feeling that I still have something left to accomplish. But perhaps I am only imagining it—simply from force of habit.

JANULKA   You know, Papa, on that memorable evening I found the Master crying like a child by my mother's deathbed. After that he was impervious to everything except certain erotic insinuations of mine by which I ensnared him in cold blood, fully conscious of what I was doing. I dragged it all out of him and brought it up to the surface. He told me such strange things that I had the sensation I was falling into a tiny little bottomless hole and staring into the totally expressionless eyes of Nothingness itself.

MONSTER I   He has moments of frightful sentimentality, as does—for that matter—every true comedian and athlete of the mind. But those are not what are called "real" feelings.

MONSTER II   You must help him at such moments, Janulka, and not be distant or alienated from him. Love him in cold blood for that spark of the unconscious which winds the springs in his brain—a brain possessed by itself, a monster of simply superhuman perspicacity about the history of this world.

JANULKA   [*Sadly.*] Is it possible I'll never see him again? I wouldn't forgive you for that, Papa dear. The one and only knight-errant left on the entire world horizon!

MONSTER I   You'll see him, you'll see him for certain—but in the concave mirror of your own emptiness, as a projection referring to Der Zipfel's make-believe coordinates—or rather as the make-believe system of reference itself.

FIZDEJKO   Here at least you could stop pestering us. I'm literally worried sick by the mystery of our arrival at this forester's lodge. Now as never before, I want to believe in historical materialism, and yet I can't make any headway.

MONSTER I   Remember the last crown in the world, the last closed civilization, the last thought on the edge of the abyss from which mankind—oh, excuse me: whatever you call it—will come hurtling down under its own carriage, descending, brakes on, from the vast mountain of nonbeing.

MONSTER II   Remember, for the sake of all the erotic myths incarnated in poor Janulka's soul. You and Janulka are unique, and so is he, so is the Master. Through Der Zipfel, he will reach you both even in death's embraces.

FIZDEJKO   I do not even have the strength to commit suicide, and I'm so tired of being myself I could curl up and die. Yet, curiously enough, I feel like a young man quite capable of falling in love.

[*The far-off sound of a horn.*]

MONSTER I   There he is. He has found us.

DER ZIPFEL   [*Getting up.*] At last the séance is about to begin. You all are spirits. Keep that firmly in mind.

[*Sound of the horn drawing near.*]

FIZDEJKO   So I'm not even spared that! I, Fizdejko, who all my life have loathed spiritualism—I, Fizdejko, who without believing in spirits have created the world's most idiotic biological theory of astral bodies—*I* have to be a spirit at a séance! [*Covers his face with his hands.*] How humiliating!

JANULKA   It is only now that we shall find out who we really are. I know very little about life, but I think it is possible to live it through to the end without ever knowing oneself in the least. Unless something happens to cause a revelation. If the Master finds us even here, our destiny will become clear. We must hurtle all the way down to the very bottom, like a stone which when dropped from the summit rolls down to the valley.

[*The sounds of the horn just behind the door to the right and the snapping of tree branches. The Master rushes in, dressed as for hunting. He has a white cloak thrown over his shoulders, as in Act 1. He is followed by Von Plasewitz, the Prince and Princess de la Tréfouille and Glissander, all in hunting costumes—then the twelve Boyars, in sheepskin coats. They all run across to the left without seeing anyone, and assemble by the door to the hut.*]

MASTER   [*To Der Zipfel.*] Ready, Director?

DER ZIPFEL   At your orders, Count. They are all certainly dead. We can begin the séance immediately.

[*They all crowd into the hut and sit down around the fire. The Master can be seen* en face *upstage, lighted by the flames from below. Der Zipfel, standing inside by the door, leans out and summons the spirits.*]

DER ZIPFEL   [*Solemnly.*] Spirit of Prince Fizdejko, appear!

[*Fizdejko gets up like an automaton and, walking as though hypnotized, goes toward the door of the hut. His silhouette stands out darkly against the fiery, blood red interior.*]

FIZDEJKO   Here I am. This is the height of humiliation. I wouldn't swear that I am not just pretending to be a spirit at a séance. But I shall say what I have to say. Insatiation with myself torments me hideously. I'd like to be everything: embrace the entire universe, acquire all possible knowledge completely on my own—for the first time ever. The curse of consumed civilizations stifles me like a frightful nightmare. I would like to be an artist too in all the branches of art and on my own create everything that already has been or ever could be created in those arts through all eternity. I'd like to be both the beggar and the rich man who, because he has a superabundance of riches, throws him a paltry gold piece. I'd like to live on my own entrails and eat myself up, bones and all, and then have my spirit blaze in all the nebulae and suns of infinite, amorphous space.

MASTER Through the highest complication to achieve an almost animal simplicity and strength—that is our first principle. You will be satiated, spirit of Eugenius Fizdejko.

[*Birdlike laughter from the Monsters. Fizdejko disappears, that is, he falls through the trap by the door of the hut.*]

DER ZIPFEL Now Janulka. Hurry. The fluid is running out.

[*Like an automaton, Janulka goes over and takes Fizdejko's place, discarding her sieve on the way.*]

MASTER What do you want, my one and only, beloved Janulka?

JANULKA I am the living image of my father incarnated in a woman. I want to be a saint, inviolable for everyone, even myself, and at the same time I want to be torn to pieces by the repulsive embraces of a million unknown males ready to slit one another's throats over my body. I want to be impaled on a stake and lashed with whips by human beasts monsterized by desires and at the same time I want an angel's sky blue kiss to fall, like an inaccessible flower, into the tranquil vale at the depths of my girlish soul. I want to rule the world through a frightful tyrant who would be but the breath of my own glistening blue-black lust embodied in his shape, stored in the bloody meat of his muscles bursting with power, and who at the same time would be the shadow of an insubstantial dream, never disclosed and dissipated into Nothingness within the petrified universal ether of Existence extinct for all eternity. Enough, or I'll burst!

DER ZIPFEL Go! I'm even sorry I am not your lover.

[*Janulka disappears into the trap by the door of the hut.*]

MASTER [*Gets up and goes over to the door.*] How frightfully demanding they've become now they're spirits! Will I be able to satisfy them— given my total skepticism in all questions of satiation?

DER ZIPFEL Become a spirit too, Count. I have a proven method of becoming one.

MASTER [*Coming out of the hut.*] How does it work?

DER ZIPFEL [*Coming out after him.*] Like this. [*Shoots the Master in the chest with a small revolver. To the Boyars.*] Could one of you Princes carry the Master's corpse off behind the hut? He must be transformed in solitude.

[*The Boyars carry the Master behind the hut and then return.*]

VON PLASEWITZ   See, intuition *is* a marvelous thing; whatever pops into
your head—just do it immediately. There's only one way to deal
with intuition: the police! Fortunately, here in our country the police
aren't sufficiently organized yet. Of course, I'm talking about life,
and not about philosophy. In that realm, the role of the police has
been taken over by that cursed system of formal logic that allows no
contradictions. [*Stabbing Der Zipfel in the chest with a short hunting
knife.*] Take that for all your tricks, you old prestidigitator! I'll free
your pseudospirits once and for all from the influence of those sham
fluids of yours. Just be thankful that before you died I didn't give
you a whiff of those depressing gases of which I am the inventor and
manufacturer. [*It is only at this moment that Der Zipfel falls without
a groan and immediately disappears into the trap in front of the
hut.*] Well, what do you know about that? He's disappeared into thin
air. [*Simultaneously the Master comes out from behind the hut, and
from the right among the trees Fizdejko emerges, leaning on
Janulka.*] Never mind about him. At least they are alive and healthy.

[*He wipes off the knife and puts it back in its scabbard.*]

MASTER   [*To Fizdejko and Janulka.*] Listen, you over there, why did you
run away from me?

FIZDEJKO   Forgive us, Gottfried! I'm afraid what you're asking of me may
be beyond my strength, and Janulka's too. It's still not too late to
give up the whole idea.

[*The Prince and Princess de la Tréfouille and Glissander come out of the
hut, followed by the twelve Boyars.*]

MASTER   Shame on you, Eugenius—how could we back out now that the
machine is all cranked up and ready to go? Our bridges are burned.
We have no place on earth except this cattle-brained Lithuania of
yours. Encircled by a ring of socialist republics, we must perish
unless we can create something diametrically opposed. Cattle
braining hasn't reached as high a level out there as it has here in
our country. Out there, the masses still believe in the future.
Here—before our very eyes—history is starting to flow backwards.
I've even stopped taking for granted the irreversibility of
socialization, and you want to run away? But where? And besides,
I've got the Semites in reserve. Nothing bad can happen to us.

FIZDEJKO I don't even believe in your strength. That is appalling. I'm missing some tiny little something—some atom of belief.

JANULKA [*Pointing to the Master.*] He's missing something too. He cried like a baby beside my mother's corpse. The Monsters told me all about it.

MASTER I am going to tell you the truth: I'm just an ordinary, decent kind of guy. And you're all just the same. None of those great things we've been talking about apply to us. I have a mother somewhere whom I love, and who suffers because she imagines I'm worse than I actually am. I have a little sister like her [*Points to Janulka.*] and I've got all I need to make me happy. I'm not even a seducer. I'm simply a great big nothing: I like to grow flowers, read a good novel every so often, drop in on friends, play a little tennis or chess . . .

FIZDEJKO God Almighty, Gottfried, I'm exactly the same! Everything we're doing is pure embellishment to hide our own nothingness.

MASTER No—my principle of deforming life inverts all traditional values and their criteria. It's all superstructure. The monstrous skeleton of my ship glides through the void. Don't look for flesh or guts there. Out of a hard substance I have constructed a base which hangs a few inches above my head. That is where I live. The artificial psyche. We haven't existed for a long time—not for centuries. But we're not soulless puppets decked out in rags. But it still has to be developed in you. And the base will be provided by mankind rebarbarized under socialism . . . Pooh . . . Mankind, damn it, that hideous word again.

FIZDEJKO My God! What am I to make a new artificial soul out of?!

MASTER That's for you to learn! I intended to lie to you, but I see it's not the right way. I'll teach you the true technique of illusory living. Listen to me: go down into the depths of your own nothingness, convince yourself that you are a perfect idiot, blockhead, and bungler, that you don't have a shred of honor, faith, or talent, that you are the most despicable parasite, pimp, and spy preying on your own self—and then on that basis, create a single steel beam, place it out in this nothingness, and know—I implore you, don't believe, but *know*—that it will hold fast like a planet in boundless space. In a perfect vacuum create that germ of the gravitational field which by expanding will hold unsupported the gigantic edifice of your new "I."

FIZDEJKO   All right, all right—but that first step . . .

VON PLASEWITZ   You've got to grasp it intuitively, Gene. No one can deal
with it conceptually. *I* did it a long time ago, intuitively,
subconsciously, and then I built a factory for producing depressing
gases. But somehow I was never able to inspire you with any
enthusiasm for it.

MASTER   That's a somewhat different matter. Joel Kranz and de la
Tréfouille did the same thing I did, but with *my* help. The results
depend on what one starts with. You have incredible potentialities,
Eugenius, but a poor education has kept you from realizing them.
Look here, old boy, just try and get started.

FIZDEJKO   All right—I'll make an effort. But you know what terrifies me?
All those tiresome little details: industry, trade, finances, et cetera,
et cetera . . . the hideous boredom of real life at the zenith of
power, the constant signing of endless papers . . .

MASTER   That's what Kranz and Plasewitz are for. We won't even lift a
finger in that department. Look here, old man, this is the last
chance. Hurry up.

FIZDEJKO   Ouf . . . I'm so afraid! I feel like a virgin who's been raped by a
battalion of rampaging soldiers, or a June bug that's been given an
enema meant for a horse. Just one more question: why precisely me?

MASTER   Because you have a daughter like Janulka, because you are a
blue-blooded prince of sorts, and because postcommunistic cattle
braining first began in your country. Everything else is pure chance.
Within certain limits, setting aside the physical viewpoint, there is no
absolute necessity why precisely one thing happens to exist rather
than something else. That is the final psychological solution to the
problems faced by Korbowa, Wahazar, and the King of Hyrcania.
Their errors were obvious: Korbowa got mired in compromise,
Hyrcan didn't have any heirs, and good old Gyubal wanted to be a
complete recluse. Without mutual trust, without total frankness on
the part of psychic potentates absolutely equal in strength—there
can be no question of a true deformation of life. I don't need to
explain that, because everyone knows about those unsuccessful
attempts to surmount the problems of mankind in the abstract—oh,
why can't we get along without that cursed word?

FIZDEJKO   [*In despair.*] I can't do it! I can't drag anything out of myself.
Senile stagnation. Why precisely me?

MASTER [*Passionately.*] Because you are unique, like your becrudded
Janulka. Where could I find better mediums? On the Trobriand
Islands? Or in New Guinea? Oh, damn it all to hell, I'm beginning to
lose my patience. Such endless loneliness in the diabolical edifice of
my artificial self, where I am abandoned like Charles V, or a sailor
marooned by pirates on a desert island. I need people who are my
equals and a woman who is my peer. My throat is parched from
yakking! Are you going to do what I tell you or aren't you? [*To the
Boyars.*] Light the torches there! Everyone look!

FIZDEJKO [*Huffing and puffing.*] I can't! I can't lay the cornerstone. I feel
a sense of emptiness and nausea. I know—I'm nothing. Oh! All this
will make me burst. Have pity.

[*The torches in the Boyars' hands have suddenly become lighted.*]

JANULKA Papa! Papa! Just a little more! Just a tiny bit more!

DE LA TREFOUILLE A little more! A little more! We've all gone through it,
only not so consciously. But then, too, we're lesser spirits in the
hierarchy of beings.

PRINCESS AMALIA Only now do we see the mechanism of future events.
It's marvelous! The Master has thrown his last card down on the
table. That takes terrific strength. Sincerity from the greatest of
artificial human beings! And we've been given the chance to watch!

[*Fizdejko bends over double and at the same time squeezes hard on the
balloon that he has hidden on his stomach under the costume of the Old
Man of the Woods. A dull thud.*]

FIZDEJKO I've outdòne myself. [*Falls over.*]

MASTER He's exploded like a bomb! Now you have proof it's possible.
That's artificial strength of mind. Physically he's healthy as a
stallion. He'll burst another forty times, but he'll create himself in a
different psychic geometry. [*To Fizdejko.*] But now you won't run
away anymore, will you? Do you feel the savage thrill of self-
creation out of nothingness?

FIZDEJKO [*In a tired voice, repeats "Ya" like a duck.*] Ya, ya, ya. Ya, ya,
ya. But I'm quite reduced. I've finally grasped the whole value of
your company, Gottfried. Now I see the necessity of our partnership.
Overcoming nihilism in life! Simply magnificent! [*He faints.*]

MASTER Well, how about that, Janulka? Isn't it all a magnificent proof of
the existence of the hidden depths in man—oh, what an

obscenity!—in an Individual Being? It's a stupendous piece of work: being absolutely no one, to drag out of oneself a new creation. I know what you are going to say: a deformed creation. And just what are the paintings by the cubists? or Schönberg's music, if not a caricature of human feelings? But we're not concerned with feelings—but with new forms in life, now that art has already come to an end. My theory is equivalent to Arrhenius's theory in cosmogony: the overcoming of entropy. Barbarians, the pulp on which we're growing, are being created for us by socialism—and only against this background can the reinforced-concrete, artificially constructional ghosts of our new selves mount up, story by story.

JANULKA [*Ruefully.*] So you won't ever love me, Gottfried?

MASTER You can be my mistress tonight without any further delay, but we won't ever love each other. Feelings are only a pretext for Pure Form in life.

JANULKA [*Cheerfully.*] Oh, if that's what you mean, it's a wonderful idea. I was only afraid we had to practice abstinence. Because I have a body too, and a very pretty one at that.

[*She rubs up against him.*]

MASTER Only not right now. We still have time for all that.

[*He blows his whistle. The sound of a motor can be heard and something heavy falling in the woods.*]

JANULKA [*In ecstasy.*] Now I feel my ultimate desire being satiated in this new void. Once, a long time ago, perhaps in a dream, I wanted to have everything. But that's only possible in the artificial psyche. Gottfried, you're giving me the world in the form of a concentrated pill and I'm satiating myself, satiating myself and filling myself with every bit of it.

MASTER I am extremely glad I've finally convinced you.

[*He embraces her and kisses her on the head.*]

JANULKA Listen, in this second self we can create new feelings—such as have never existed before—an amalgam of the greatest contradictions.

MASTER Only for form's sake, only for form's sake, my child. The Princess de la Tréfouille was my mistress. She'll show you the proper way to go at it. I believe in due time you'll give me moments of true self-astonishment.

PRINCESS AMALIA   I hope you'll be an apt pupil, Janulka dear.

[*She goes over to Janulka and embraces her.*]

GLISSANDER   And *I'll* create something stranger still: a new art springing from the artificially deformed self. Pure Form raised to the second power, or something of that sort.

MASTER   Daydreams of an improductive poet! But we'll need even the likes of him to plug up certain holes . . . [*Enter Joel Kranz with Rederhagaz and Haberboaz.*] Joel, starting tomorrow you and Mr. Von Plasewitz will organize our trade, industry, and other such horribly boring things.

JOEL   At your orders, Master, the schools, the courts, the prisons, the insane asylums, and a new religion for the rebarbarized masses. We're starting all over again from the very beginning. I invite you all to come aboard my aeroplane. Sorry to say so—but we are, whether we like it or not, the products of civilization.

[*From behind the hut there appears the Director of Séances, Der Zipfel.*]

DER ZIPFEL   [*Yells in a booming voice.*] The séance is over!!!

[*Fizdejko springs to his feet. The Monsters screech.*]

VON PLASEWITZ   And now on to the coronation of Fizdejko! Now we'll see what this new reality looks like—the fifth reality, according to Leon Chwistek's terminology.

[*The torchlit procession moves off to the right.*]

THE MONSTERS   But don't forget about us!

CURTAIN
End of the Second Act

Act Three

[*The left side of the stage represents the throne room in Fizdejko's palace in a fantastic angular style. To the left in the corner sits the throne, on a diagonal, facing the entire stage. The yellow left wall gradually changes into dark yellow and orange as it gets nearer to the black door, also in the angular style. Black designs made of intersecting triangles. The right half*] *of the stage is occupied by a café in a fantastic circular style. Many tables and chairs. Upstage, a window for passing dishes. Black circular designs begin at the door, and the color gradually changes from red through purple into an intensely pure violet on the right wall. The throne side is dim, the café side lighted. The black throne with yellow designs has two tiers. Fizdejko sits on the lower one. His moustache has been shaved off; his complexion is a frightful, cadaverous pale green. He is wearing a purple coat over what he was wearing in Act 1. The two Monsters sit on the upper tier. Glissander in a frock coat stands to the right of the throne, the Director of Séances, Der Zipfel, to the left. There are no windows except for the small service window. The Master dressed as in Act 1, with his visor up, accompanied by Janulka in a mourning costume and huge black hat, enters at the head of the twelve Boyars. They stand between the throne section and the café section. De la Tréfouille, as a waiter, and Princess Amalia, as a waitress, bustle about the tables.*]

FIZDEJKO [*Gloomily.*] I have the feeling I've been put in a glass jar and I'll never get out. My life has turned into an atrocious phantasmagoria. I'm creating new inner worlds with the facility of a notorious magician.

JANULKA [*Coming over to the throne.*] Papa, I may be creating something even more—artificial feelings such as could never exist in real life. I've infected Gottfried with them. I'm his perverse mistress and I think I'll even become his wife. He is heir to the throne, isn't he?

FIZDEJKO You talk about it as if the idea of being heir to the throne didn't imply the idea of your father's death. That reproach—to the extent it can be called a reproach—I'm making against you automatically, from this side of freshly attained frontiers. In fact, I'm alone—with him and you [*Points to the Master and Janulka.*] in this diabolical world of artificial psychic construction. A marvelous world! But it exists only potentially. I don't know what the reality will look like.

MASTER In any case, it will be the fifth reality. Chwistek has completely exhausted the first four. In a moment we'll have a run-through. Lights!

[*De la Tréfouille turns the knob for the arc lamp and numerous light bulbs. Enter Joel Kranz with his Hasidic Jews. Without paying any attention to anyone, they occupy places at a table in the café.*]

DE LA TREFOUILLE   Three black coffees for the gentlemen.

[*He runs to the service window. The Princess serves pastries.*]

FIZDEJKO   Why has that clown become a waiter?

MASTER   That's a totally inconsequential problem. "Transformational exercises" for spirits of the lower class.

FIZDEJKO   Well, then, what the hell, let's get on with this infernal comedy. I'm conceding—mark my words—more than the emperor Augustus Caesar ever did. He admitted it was all a farce only at the very end of his reign, while I'm doing so at the beginning of mine. And besides, the dimensions and coefficients are different; he started the decline of Rome, while we're stuck like ancient mushrooms in the depths of the Bolshevized wilderness—I mean, what was I about to say? Mankind? Down with mankind! The primitive barbarians are all around us.

MASTER   Oh, now, that's more like it. What will your first step as ruler be? I don't want to impose my ideas on you like this all at once.

FIZDEJKO   Bring in my vassals—I repeat, my vassals—and you'll see that they are totally indistinguishable from bears. They're cattle—a bona fide cattle-ocracy going meekly to the slaughter. Well—and what else? My artificial construction is going up story by story, ever higher. Higher and higher—until there's no more highness left. *I* am highness itself: His Highness, Prince of Lithuania, Eugenius I-don't-know-which-number Fizdejko! The name alone can give you a pain in the guts. Oh, I'll burst for the umpteenth time today—I'm all puffed up with pure nothingness. [*Yells.*] Joel! Joel! You otherworldly polyp from a different system of geometry! Have you already created all those institutions unspeakable in their immeasurable boredom?

MASTER   Calm down, calm down. Calmness is the greatest luxury that people of our stamp can afford. Speak, Joel. Don't be frightened by our sovereign's insatiability. Like a dry sponge in its boundless thirstings. Gulping down everything like a St. Anthony's pig.

KRANZ   [*Gets up impetuously from the table, spilling his coffee; the Hasidic Jews remain seated without moving.*] Gentlemen, *I* cannot be calm. I've tried to control myself, but I can't. I'm trembling all over in a wild frenzy. I don't have time. Life is so short—oh, so very short! And I have to do all the things I've been created for. The framework and the brilliant concepts are there already, but just who'll manage to carry them out?! You're all enjoying yourselves—I know, you're enjoying yourselves immensely—but I have to carry it all out—*I don't have time—I'm* asking you for orders!

FIZDEJKO   Cut all their throats! I don't want anyone. I want to be completely alone.

MASTER   If that's the case, don't occupy the throne, Eugenius. As a ruler you must always be in company that doesn't suit you—with the exception of one or two close associates, of course. The notion of holding power implies the notion of pulp. Charles V's well-known problem. But he solved it by becoming a watchmaker in a monastery.

FIZDEJKO   All right—I want pulp, but real pulp. As a last resort, you can stay on as heir to the throne, you and Janulka. But nothing else— just a sea of pulp! I want to be a solitary ruler!

KRANZ   Monsieur de la Tréfouille! Another coffee! There's going to be rough sledding with that gent. His artificial self has broken loose from its chain like a mad dog. Mr. Fizdejko, you're not treating seriously the fact that I, as it is, have already taken on burdens beyond my strength: the school system, the courts, trade—

FIZDEJKO   I know, I know: industry, finance, et cetera, et cetera. I'm bored to death just thinking about it.

[*De la Tréfouille serves Kranz coffee, which he drinks standing up.*]

KRANZ   Even though those branches of government are quite primitive in our newly formed state, still, for one lone Semite, I'm up to my ears in work . . .

FIZDEJKO   Better tell me, someone: why do I constantly feel the need to make normal connections between ideas?

MASTER   Here's the reason why: you're not sufficiently solitary in your relation to yourself. I advise you to concentrate your powers of distortion to the highest pitch and just for once be a caricature of your own will and destiny. *I* only liberate—I don't create. As heir to the throne, my activities can only be catalytic, nothing more.

FIZDEJKO   Catalyze to your heart's content, but why precisely me? Why can't the principal object of your designs be Kranz, or de la Tréfouille, or my late wife? [*Enter Princess Elsa dressed as in Act 1; she lies down slowly at the foot of the throne.*] Oh, as soon as I said that I wished I hadn't. May the Lord have mercy on her soul—it's no concern of mine any more. Only why me? [*Enter Von Plasewitz.*] Look—why not him? [*Points at Von Plasewitz.*]

MASTER   You took the words right out of my mouth. I'm not speaking about myself, but why not him? [*Points at Von Plasewitz.*] I'll tell you why. Because he's not the one. That's *why*. The immediate feeling of causality has created that devilish little word: "why." Its meaning is purely negative. One thing happens just because something else *doesn't happen*. We don't have an infinite series of causes going all the way back to the first cause—we have only the necessary segments. I mean, you don't want to be reduced to the role of a segment, Eugenius. Living matter: a grasshopper, a cow, I myself, and even you—we all refute that law absolutely. Get rid of those prejudices, or else the coronation will never take place.

FIZDEJKO   What a terrible threat! And besides, even pure chance is something I can understand, as long as it's outside of me. Still, I'll try to take a look at myself from the sidelines, entirely objectively. [*Twists to one side of the throne.*] Oh, there—there, I've done it. I already see myself on the throne, the only throne left on this earth.

MASTER   If you weren't under the influence of creeping democratization, you wouldn't raise any questions about it, Eugenius. You'd accept your destiny for what it is. [*Fizdejko wriggles frantically.*] But be that as it may, a miracle has taken place: through the concept of absolute causal or functional dependence, he has arrived at the concept of absolute freedom—contrary to Maurice Blondel, who maintained that only through freedom do we have a sense of determinism. All this may seem boring to you, but nonetheless, these are the first principles of Pure Form in social life . . . social . . . ugh, blast it, what a hideous word!

VON PLASEWITZ   I like the way you conceptualize it. Even the greatest pleasure isn't worth anything at all without the proper theoretical formulation. Let's start the ceremony.

KRANZ   [*Hurriedly.*] Right you are, let's start. The entire block of socialist republics next to us is starting to grow cattle-brained, and a mass of countries are waiting to be conquered. But first, let's create an army. We've got to sign decrees as fast as possible.

FIZDEJKO   But what astounds me is that you, Joel, such an ordinary little Jew, are now going against all the Jews in the world.

KRANZ   There are Jews and Jews. For you Aryans, we all look the same,
like deceased Chinese. But there are Jews and JEWS, with all four
letters capitalized. The last nation on this planet. But now that's
almost metaphysics. Hurry, hurry—without me you might at best
have managed to go on the stage. I fill old shells with new stuffing.
But what is the best stuffing without the shells—and conversely: the
forms without the filling are nothing. We've got to work together, but
above all, fast, fast, fast!

MASTER   We're starting. Kranz, got the crown?

KRANZ   Sure have—but no ceremonies. You don't have to feel
constrained in my company, gentlemen. [*Pulls out a gold crown
from under his overcoat and puts it on Fizdejko's head.*] I, Joel
Kranz, almighty prime minister, crown you, Fizdejko, King of
Neobarbarian Lithuania and Belorussia. And that's it—not another
word. I hope our entire state won't prove to be just another opening
night! Sign the papers, Sire, and I'm off. Not a moment to lose.

[*He gives Fizdejko a stack of papers and a fountain pen. Fizdejko signs
feverishly.*]

MASTER   The functioning of our state machinery is incredibly efficient.
Right, Boyars?

[*Muttering and bowing among the Boyars.*]

FIZDEJKO   Ready, Excellency Kranz. I'm making you a Count, Joel dear.
The first of so many, many dreams to be realized! [*He tries to hug
Kranz.*]

KRANZ   [*Pulling away.*] Don't have time. I've got the state on my mind,
not nonsensical titles.

[*He flies out through the door at high speed. The Hasidic Jews, who have
abruptly sprung up from the table, run out after him, mumbling
unintelligible phrases.*]

MASTER   Well—finally we've been left alone. We can take up the
fantastic side of the problem. I've had it up to here [*Draws his finger
across his throat.*] with those real-life affairs of state.

FIZDEJKO   Then let's enjoy ourselves. All the Boyars, my vassals and
rivals, I do hereby condemn to death by this oral decree. I won't
sign it because I'm already exhausted by my administrative duties.
Line up according to height.

[*The Boyars line up in a row in front of the throne.*]

MASTER   This is only the introduction. [*To the Boyars.*] Right face!

[*The Boyars execute a right face.*]

FIZDEJKO   And now each of you: take your ax and kill the man in front of
you. [*The First Boyar bashes in the head of his* occiputnik, *who is
standing with his back toward him. The Second Boyar falls.*] Well—
keep going!

BOYAR II   [*Expiring.*] I don't have anyone to bash. Oh, God—what
torture! Princess, we're dying because of you. We've been in love
with you for ages—almost since you were in diapers.

FIZDEJKO   Well—keep going, keep going: Number Three strikes Number
Four—Number Five hits Number Six—Number Seven whacks
Number Eight, and so on.

BOYAR III   Aha—I understand. Curses on you, Janulka.

[*He bashes in the fourth Boyar's head. The others do the same.*]

JANULKA   Oh, now I understand everything. How I love you both: Papa
and you, Master!

MASTER   What?

JANULKA   [*Hurriedly.*] No—I don't love either of you—that's an old habit:
what I admire about you both is the inversion of your natures, as
reflected in the crooked mirror of my deformed heart—but you,
Gottfried, differently than Papa.

[*There remain the first, third, fifth, seventh, ninth, and eleventh Boyars.
The corpses fall to the right.*]

FIZDEJKO   [*In a thundering voice.*] Close ranks! And then *Schlüss!* Oh,
what a marvelous game!

[*The Boyars stand in closed ranks.*]

MASTER   You're fighting your own vassals, Sire, like the German
emperors of old. But your task is much simpler. They're sheep, not
human beings, and what's more, the descendants of sovereign
princes. Keep going!

FIZDEJKO   Same as before! Faster! My power keeps swelling like a huge
ulcer full of pus! It has to burst!

[*The First Boyar hits No. 3, No. 5 strikes No. 7, No. 9 whacks No. 11.*]

BOYAR I   Seems I'll be the only one left.

FIZDEJKO Could be—I'm no good at mathematics. Close ranks and same as before! [*No. 1, No. 5, and No. 9 close ranks. No. 1 bashes No. 5.*] Number Nine—about face and fight it out man to man. [*The two Boyars fight.*] Just like gladiators. Gives me the feeling I'm a Roman emperor!

[*The Ninth Boyar fells No. 1, and stands proudly with his hands on his hips.*]

BOYAR IX Well, now what do you say to that, Mister Fizdejko? Am I less worthy of being King than you? Eh? As a member of the intelligentsia cattle brained by socialism, and what's more, a noble descended from nobles in a long unbroken line?

MASTER [*Shooting him through the ear with his Browning.*] Sure—you're worthy. But first swallow this caramel without choking on it.

[*The Ninth Boyar drops dead.*]

FIZDEJKO With that one shot, Gottfried, you've resolved the problem of power for me. You are worthy of my daughter. Take her, and go straight to the devil, both of you. I'm bored. [*Comes down from the throne, goes to the café, and sits down at a table.*] True enough, people of a certain psychological makeup can't live without cafés.

[*de la Tréfouille serves him coffee.*]

JANULKA Gottfried, forgive me. I'm already in the realm of illusory feelings. If you knew the perversity of my thoughts, you'd go crazy from regret mixed with sensuality, from disgust and pride, from indulgence, humiliation, tenderness, and from ordinary erotic stimulation. And yet I *am* a woman. It's all playacting by masquerading cattle, not exempting even Papa. Love me with an artificial love, Gottfried, like a wild little beastie. I can't take it anymore. That pistol shot did me in. My desire is so hopeless I'll go stark raving mad.

MASTER [*Coldly and categorically.*] Come have a cup of coffee, Janulka. You still don't understand me fully. It's not a question of complicating known feelings, but of something new and unfathomable. Your artificial self is still insufficiently developed. Before I lose my patience and beat you in a thoroughly vulgar fashion, I implore you: take my adjutant, Prince de la Tréfouille, as your lover. It's only after knowing him that you'll be able to appreciate my psychic charms, and not just my physical attractions. Some slight relief from purely erotic misunderstandings.

[*He sits down at Fizdejko's table. Pouting, Janulka goes over to Alfred and flirts with him by the service window. Princess Elsa gets up and takes a separate table. She is joined by Von Plasewitz and Glissander. The Director of Séances, Der Zipfel, sits down on the throne. The Master gets up respectfully.*]

FIZDEJKO   Two coffees and a cask of liqueur. Make it Strega. [*The Princess Amalia rolls in a cask with a rubber tube. Fizdejko and the Master offer one another the tube during the pauses in the conversation.*] Sit down, metaphysical son-in-law and heir apparent of mine. We worked ourselves dry with bookkeeping in the artificial upper stories of the self. My God! The fifth reality! So that's all there is? So we won't even be able to create a tolerably amusing dream? And besides, it would only be the most forthright of fourth realities, and Chwistek himself would burst from his inability to add even the one-hundredth part of a new coefficient. Did I really intensify my nothingness to the bursting point for this: to drop in at a café for a coffee? Now I understand why Glissander arranged the room this way. Symbolism! ! I'd rather end up as the Old Man of the Woods, or as forest inspector on your lands, Gottfried. Financially I'm totally ruined. Now I know why that ordinary prince-turned-waiter is seducing my daughter.

MASTER   [*Sitting down next to him.*] More coffee, Princess! Preferably the whole pot! The night is long—who knows if it will ever end. [*A bluish glow becomes perceptible in the room, despite the lack of windows, and the lights slowly go out.*] King, you want to accomplish something in an orderly, premeditated fashion, against our very natures, against our artificial selves, and even against our intuition of the moment. Look, I've just given your daughter, and my fiancée, to a flunky in a café. Out there the cattle-brained masses are agitated like the waters of an enormous puddle. We can either swim in it or amuse ourselves on the shore like children, setting loose our little boats. But first, in what remains of your lifetime, we'll play out the game of state between the two of us.

FIZDEJKO   For heaven's sake, in what way? Won't you give me a moment's peace?

MASTER   No—I'll reveal the ultimate truth to you: I want to be good, but
I keep playing the dirtiest tricks despite myself. I want to purify
myself today, at least by an honorable death. I'd like to fight, but
with a power worthy of me. My past victories were too easy. Let's
end the night with a duel.

FIZDEJKO   [*While Princess Amalia pours him coffee.*] Fight with Plasewitz,
fight with Glissander, fight with Kranz even—but not with me.
Respect your King and father-in-law. My daughter has let herself go
with a waiter—I don't claim any rights—I know it was an
experiment.

MASTER   Yes—that was my greatest comedown. I wanted to test her love
because I'd fallen in love with her in the most ordinary way in the
world. The experiment didn't work. It was vengeance for my lying to
her so many times, making her believe in make-believe.

FIZDEJKO   That's another story. But who is this rival of yours? A waiter
with a coronet in his pocket. We don't know anything more about
him. But, then, do we know much more about ourselves?

MASTER   [*Uncertainly.*] Well—maybe just a little something . . .

FIZDEJKO   No, nothing—sometimes something bizarre happens and gives
us a glimpse of what lies beneath the mask. But we can't even be
sure whether it's a face or something quite different. Who am I
really? I feel a diabolical horror at the thought of myself, and
nothing can ever bring back my peace of mind again.

MASTER   Please don't put ideas into my head. I don't want to be afraid of
myself. That's insanity. The greater the artificiality, the less the fear.
I haven't been afraid of anything until now.

FIZDEJKO   That's not true—you've only been hiding it from yourself like
a madman who won't admit his own madness. It breaks out all the
more violently later.

MASTER   Ha! This clairvoyant old man will drive me berserk. Save me.

[*Everyone in the room laughs. The laughter suddenly stops as soon as
Fizdejko starts to speak.*]

FIZDEJKO   Yes, yes—the more artificial the psyche, the greater one's fear
of oneself. You have dragged me up to the heights, and there I'll
croak from sheer fright, without ever being able to get down again.
And don't count on me any more, Gottfried. I won't get out of this
either, but so what—I'm old. I'm just sorry for you, my boy.

MASTER   [*Getting up.*] This is simply not to be tolerated. Instead of being my medium, he's transformed me like a sorcerer.

FIZDEJKO   Yes—we all have the impression we know who we are. I tell you: we know as much about ourselves as one-day mayflies and microbes know about themselves. We pass away as they do and no more of us remains than of them. My Boyars were wiped out—they were unworthy of being my vassals. We are alone, wretched orphans, and the world, frightful and unknown, confronts us. And nothing can delude us any longer: neither our profession, nor position, nor philosophy, nor religion. We know too much to know anything truly. And we have no desire to rule, and most of all—we have no one to rule over. Nothingness is winning out . . . [*Turns around and calls.*] Clean up the corpses back there! ! !

DER ZIPFEL   [*From the throne.*] Get up! ! [*The Boyars all get up at once in perfect unison.*] Keep in step! ! Now march out through the door!

[*The Boyars go out row by row, waving their axes.*]

MASTER   Look, there's discipline for you! Even corpses obey us. That idea has given me new life. Isn't it bizarre enough to make even our defeat seem justifiable?

FIZDEJKO   Bizarreness isn't an absolute. It depends on the individual who makes possible its materialization. For me, that clown Der Zipfel is triteness personified. Whatever he does is for me personally just a cheap trick. [*Gloomily.*] I too have some limits to my artificial, reinforced-concrete, contemporary par excellence self.

DE LA TREFOUILLE   Contemporary—but with what?

FIZDEJKO   [*Gets up, laughing.*] With the explosion of the one-hundred and fifty-sixth star in the nebula of Andromeda. In physics, contemporaneousness is pure fiction. Not to mention the question of the free displacement of civilizations in historical time!

DE LA TREFOUILLE   With that observation you've knocked the ground out from under me.

[*He sits down and wipes the sweat off his forehead with the tablecloth.*]

JANULKA   [*Running over to de la Tréfouille.*] I'll save you, my Prince. I know: you're the only one who'll fight with Gottfried—and over me. [*To Fizdejko.*] The Master gave me to *him* to complete my erotic education. And he did it out of true love! Ha! ha! ha! Now let him answer for what has happened.

FIZDEJKO   Oh, do whatever you like, all of you—I've got to get a little
sleep.

[*He takes off his crown and lies down on the floor between the tables,
wrapping himself up in his purple coat.*]

PRINCESS AMALIA   But on the condition that Mademoiselle Fizdejko give
me back my husband. France too will undoubtedly become cattle-
brained in our lifetime, and then who will make a better French
Fizdejko than the Prince?

MASTER   Today I agree to everything. If you're successful, perhaps
there'll even be a Lithuanian de la Tréfouille one day. Here's the
only thing that bothers me: to create a situation like the one today,
we didn't need an entire state complete with trade, industry, et
cetera, and all the infernal work that Joel Kranz has put into it. A
small room in some third-class hotel would have been quite enough.
Isn't the setting beginning to outshine what was supposed to appear
in it?

DE LA TREFOUILLE   That's the height of luxury: to create the setting for its
own sake and not to have anything appear in it. The inner life, with
its peaks and its precipices, exists independently of the degree of
one's power, wealth, or success . . .

MASTER   Consolations of that sort are good for pimps like you, Monsieur
Alfred. For that view to become a reality, one needs to be a saint.
But neither you nor I are saints. I'm taking the blow very much to
heart: I'm afraid of myself as I've never been afraid of any ghost, or
even of death until now. I'm perfectly terrified.

DE LA TREFOUILLE   All right, Master: let's have a staring match! [*To
Janulka.*] I assure you this duel is far more dangerous for him than
if we fought with swords, pistols, or even with Plasewitz's depressing
gases. [*To the Master.*] Look into my eyes, my good little
contemporary chap—remember the conversations we had five years
ago, when I was hardly more than a child . . .

[*The dawn grows brighter and brighter. The Master staggers back and looks
for something to hold onto. He grabs a chair.*]

MASTER   [*In a broken voice.*] I am unable to resist. I have the feeling that
you are the only one I love in this horrible, empty world. I am a
poor, weak mortal full of the most contradictory and yet totally
ordinary feelings.

DE LA TREFOUILLE   Amalia, take the Master off to your bedroom, and
  come right back for Janulka—the time will come for her too.

[*Exit the Master lifelessly, led off by Princess Amalia.*]

MONSTER I   All right—and now it's our turn.

[*He crawls down from the throne. The second Monster follows him. Der
Zipfel remains seated on the throne. The Monsters' stands hang on them
like skirts, revealing their torn, ragged, and a bit-too-short long pants and
their bare feet. They go over to the tables.*]

MONSTER II   Coffee, coffee and liqueurs. We don't know the brands, just
  make sure they're expensive.

JANULKA   So you *are* what I took you for! You are simply symbols of the
  utter poverty of our predawn delusions.

MONSTER I   We're not symbols. No one knows, not even us, which of us
  is a woman. We're awaiting a new sin. In and of ourselves we
  constitute a closed world of absolute but monstrous ideas. The fifth
  reality is an inherent absurdity, it's only the last mask worn by dying
  aristocrats of the spirit. Coffee! Coffee!

[*They both sit down at Princess Elsa's table.*]

JANULKA   So I can't even count on you anymore? Your bare legs and torn
  trousers are disgusting. I took you for living demigods, for beings
  not of this world. And now what's left of those hopes?

[*de la Tréfouille serves the Monsters coffee.*]

MONSTER I   [*Pouring his coffee.*] Our top halves are still pretty bizarre,
  I'd say.

JANULKA   And later on it will turn out that the tops aren't what they were
  supposed to be either. Oh, how disillusioning! Mama, I'm coming
  back to share in your utter misery! I want to start all over again
  from the very beginning.

ELSA   [*Calmly.*] Too late, my child. My father told me the whole story.
  Without benefit of marriage you gave yourself up to the Master's
  perverse desires. You can enroll in his Frauzimmer.

[*She drinks coffee.*]

JANULKA   That's not true! I'm just a demivirgin. And besides that's a
  minor detail. [*To Prince Alfred.*] So perhaps you're the only one who
  will have the courage. Fight with anyone you want, but no staring
  matches. Show that you're somebody. In the bottomless void I am

haunted by the figure of an unknown knight, without armor—he may wear a frock coat, he may even be a pimp or a thief, as long as he shows some courage, ordinary, human courage, and not that cowardly, suicidal waiting around for a lucky chance that masquerades as the artificial self.

[*Enter the Princess Amalia.*]

DE LA TREFOUILLE   Those are not problems worthy of my past. I never believed in any of that double talk of Gottfried's, but given the chance, I created a little world of my own too, not as fantastic perhaps, but all the more real. And I won't let anyone come in, not even my future wife—oh, Janulka, you didn't know I wanted to ask for your hand in marriage . . . [*To the Princess.*] Is everything ready?

PRINCESS AMALIA   Yes. And now go get some sleep, Janulka, and don't believe anything Alfred tells you. I'll initiate you into the subtleties practiced by these gentlemen. The word sounds loathsome, but there's no avoiding it. You'll finally stop considering life a feverish hallucination.

FIZDEJKO   [*Suddenly springs up and throws off his purple coat. He's wearing a snuff-colored frock coat.*] I am still here—I—the King! Down on your knees in front of me, all of you!

DE LA TREFOUILLE   [*Coldly.*] You don't have your stage manager, monsieur le directeur Fizdejko. The Grand Master is mine, and no one will pry him out of my clutches.

FIZDEJKO   [*Puts a bullet through de la Tréfouille's head with his Browning.*] He's sounding off like the hero of a murder mystery. Shut up, shut up for all eternity, you cursed symbol of my infamy. [*The four young ladies from the Master's Frauzimmer rush in and carry de la Tréfouille out through the door.*] All right—Von Plasewitz, time to spray your depressing gases. We're all in too good a humor, my friends.

VON PLASEWITZ   [*Pulling a strange tube out of his pocket and untwisting a screw; a loud hiss is heard.*] Want me to? All right, here goes.

FIZDEJKO   Janulka, it's all been a bad dream. We're starting everything all over again. You are avenged. I'll take on Princess Amalia as your governess.

JANULKA   [*Pointing to the Monsters.*] But what about those two? What will we do with them, Papa? Even the Monsters have been unmasked.

FIZDEJKO [*Going over to the Monsters.*] Those two—why, they're ordinary
back-alley cutthroats. [*The Monsters with birdlike shrieks sit down on
the ground in their former poses, on the stands in the form of
crinoline skirts.*] Those two . . . [*Nonplussed.*] Those two are
symbols, pure and simple.

JANULKA But symbols of what? Of the artificial self, or of the most
common of commonplaces? I can't take any more—*I'll* burst too! *I*
want to exist eternally, without end, but it's all running through my
fingers because it's too slippery, too petty . . . [*Birdlike laughter
from the Monsters; it is beginning to get almost light, but reddish in
color; the lights go out.*] This isn't an attack of hysteria, as those
Monsters undoubtedly think. I really do want to eat someone up,
and you're the only one I have an appetite for, Papa.

FIZDEJKO Come get me—your poor, unhappy father. Eat him up with
your reproaches. That's all that was lacking. I didn't succeed in
providing you with a suitable husband. [*To Der Zipfel.*] Free us at
last, cruel turnkey of otherworldly prisons. Do some new trick. For
once in my life *I* simply want to sleep like the ordinary little
nonentity that I am.

DER ZIPFEL [*Getting up from the throne.*] No—the séance is not over yet.
So you all wanted to jot down eternity on the little page of life, did
you? Now it's all yours. Dawn is breaking and you must begin the
new day without getting a moment's sleep.

FIZDEJKO Eternity! Janulka, did you hear that? *I* want no more
kingdoms, no artificial self, no eternity compressed into pills
moment-by-moment. To fall asleep and forget—those are my sole
dreams. Oh, and if only while asleep, a quiet, painless death could
finally come!

ELSA Didn't I always say so, Gene, didn't I tell you over and over again
that sleep is the supreme happiness for the weak in both spirit and
flesh? But there was no need to drink up all the coffee and liqueurs.

JANULKA And I'm so young, and beautiful, and strange—that's what they
all say—and yet such an ordinary little girl; I must admit that all of
you are in the right. The ones to blame are those cursed men who
proved unworthy of me.

VON PLASEWITZ Yes—even the wildest fantasy is incapable of creating
any psychic superstructure. We'll end our days as ordinary,
flightless swamp birds. Masks without jobs, corpses on vacation,

keys without locks, nuts without bolts, monkey tails without the
monkeys, we won't even play out our roles to the end.

DER ZIPFEL [*In a frightful voice.*] Out! Out of my sight, false spirits. I
have been deceived, betrayed!

[*Very loud screeching from the Monsters. Except for the Monsters and de la
Tréfouille's corpse they all run off suddenly in a wild panic, jostling at the
door.*]

CURTAIN

End of the Third Act

Act Four

[*To the left, the stage is the same as in Act 1. To the right, instead of the
salon, there is a garden. Flowering bushes surround a small square
sprinkled with red soil. Blossoming wisteria winds around the end of the
wall to the left, which is broken off along the zigzag line. Above the bushes
can be seen pines and deciduous trees in autumn colors. Morning sunlight
floods the stage from the left side. Birds singing, cows lowing in the
distance. Elsa comes out from behind the wall in rags, as in Act 1, turns off
the electric light which is burning on the nightstand, and crawls under the
quilt. Facing the audience, two rococo chairs from Act 1.*]

ELSA At last the storm has passed and I can return to my poverty with a
clear conscience, without worrying about royal dignity.

[*The Master comes out from the bushes, in full armor, his visor raised. He
is followed by Fizdejko, now with a moustache, dressed as a fantastic
forester: small hat with feathers, green facing on the uniform, gold
decorations. A Winchester rifle is slung over his shoulder.*]

FIZDEJKO So it's all settled! I've become a forester on the Master's estate!
Just think, Elsa, we're going to live in a little cottage—hollyhocks,
geraniums, nasturtiums, fresh rolls, honey straight from the woods,
without a care in the world. Sometimes on the eve of a holiday I'll
kill a poor hare or small deer, and that will be our greatest luxury.
Oh—milk, lots of goat's milk straight from the goat, and the only
thing we'll ever read is the calendar.

MASTER How I envy you!

ELSA And what about Janulka?

FIZDEJKO   I don't know what will become of her. She'll decide her own
fate. The Master won't have her, not for all the gold in the world,
and she doesn't want him either. Now she and the Princess have
gone mushroom gathering in the woods. The mushrooms have been
wonderful this year among the dwarf pines up on Wolf Heights.
They'll make nice hors d'oeuvres with vodka at lunch.

[*He sits down in a chair.*]

ELSA   Can't you forget about those mushrooms? [*To the Master.*] No,
that's no little woman for a person with your nerves, Count. She
needs someone really evil.

MASTER   You are insulting me, Madam. The evil in me is buried very
deep. Not just anyone can see it. Here we're dealing with a
completely different problem.

FIZDEJKO   Practically speaking, it all comes down to the same thing.
Gottfried, you're incapable of putting your evil to any use. But,
but—just what are you going to do with yourself?

MASTER   I'm in a state of utter despair. We've got to admit to ourselves
once and for all that our era cannot produce certain types of rulers.
We, the last people, the survivors, wanted to lead the masses by the
nose once they had been cattle-brained by socialism—we wanted to
be the masters at the initial phase of history—and it all came to
nothing! Still we did achieve one thing: here in the very depths of
our purely personal despair we now have faith in the possibility of a
cyclical order in history occurring at very great intervals. The
irreversibility of social transformations has been all but surmounted.

[*He takes off his helmet and armor and puts them on the ground in the
small square. He is wearing violet pyjamas and a violet nightcap with a
little tassel.*]

FIZDEJKO   As for us: it's good-bye forever.

MASTER   [*Sitting down in the other armchair and lighting a cigarette.*]
That's right, Eugenius. Perhaps at this very moment somewhere in a
little hut belonging to a contemporary cattle-brained mass man,
there is being born the counterpart of your ancestor from the twelfth
century, Prince Fizdo, famous for his cruelties. It might even be that
illegitimate son you've longed for so . . .

ELSA   Fi donc, Count. He was never unfaithful to me.

MASTER   Please, don't interrupt—these are very important ideas. Now if that son of yours knew he was your son, he'd never be able to establish a new dynasty. He has to be a true primeval conqueror—only then will everything start all over again from the very beginning.

FIZDEJKO   Still, isn't it marvelous that we can watch the whole thing as spectators? Let's be satisfied with contemplation. We're much too complicated to reign over cattle.

MASTER   The only thing that's been proved is this: even with railroads, telephones, battleships, water closets, and newspapers, human beings may well be the same breed of cattle as were your ancestors' subjects in the wilds of the twelfth century—that's the amazing truth. In other words, despite the irreversibility of all of civilization's attainments, the cyclical nature of history remains an absolute law, holding true until the total extinction of a given species.

FIZDEJKO   Knowing that truth I can die in peace. The experiment was necessary to convince us we'd been beating our heads against the wall. Even the second tier of the self, built on absolute nothingness, cannot equal the power of former rulers.

MASTER   You're old, Eugenius. But it's likely that I'll have to commit suicide. I learned just a moment ago that my mother has died. But that's a purely negative reason.

FIZDEJKO   Oh—do what you want, Gottfried. I wouldn't think of talking you out of it. I understand you perfectly. With regard to the creator of the new dynasty, it's a good thing all those Boyars were bumped off down to the very last man.

MASTER   It didn't occur to me when I shot the last one that I was working for the new ruler. All right—but time is pressing. [*The Monsters crawl in from behind the bushes to the right. A delicate little cloud covers the sun.*] Good-bye, Princess; good-bye, Eugenius. [*He and Fizdejko shake hands. The Master turns to the Monsters.*] Oh, it's you? And where's Det Zipfel?

MONSTER I   He's drinking his morning coffee. He'll be here any minute.

MASTER   Once more good-bye. And as for Janulka, what's discouraged me the most is the fact that when I fell in love with her, it was the commonest variety of, quote, "Great Love." That was the last straw. Yesterday, as an experiment, I was unfaithful to her with the Princess Amalia and with somebody else too, and it didn't help in the least. I'm far from being such an ordinary modern aristocrat. In the old days, we tried to live up to our names, which we inherited from truly great people. Nowadays most of us use these names to hide our own pettiness, and our often totally ordinary swinishness. No—I'm not that sort and never will be. Well, for the last time, good-bye.

[*He goes and sits down on the ground between the Monsters; then he puts a bullet through his head with his Browning and falls over backward. The noise of an airplane is heard.*]

FIZDEJKO   Marvelous, marvelous! I'd been dreaming of such a carefree morning for a long, long time.

ELSA   Our might-have-been son-in-law rambled on a bit too long before dying. I'm falling asleep. Wake me up if anything interesting happens.

[*She dozes off. The noise of an engine is heard very close by. An airplane crashes into the tree to the right of the wall, in such a way that one wing hangs down at an angle to the wall. From the trees along the wall there quickly come down Joel Kranz, dressed as a pilot, followed by the two Hasidic Jews in their former costumes, but with dark glasses, and Von Plasewitz and Glissander, in overcoats and caps. The sun starts to shine again, full blaze.*]

KRANZ   [*Not seeing the Master's corpse or the Monsters.*] Well—we're working like horses. Mr. Plasewitz is spraying his depressing gases at those who resist. It was a strenuous morning; from six to half-past six I created the judicial system. From half-past six to seven I set industry in motion. The new locomotives are magnificent. Coffee, please. In a quarter of an hour we're moving on and we'll be looking into higher education. But what are you up to, Mr. Fizdejko? Going hunting to get a little fresh air after such an eventful night? The wedding night consummating royal power. You amused yourselves like typical rulers while we were working for you like a single huge dynamo. I'm not making any reproaches—it's a completely normal state of affairs.

FIZDEJKO   No, really, the Semites have totally lost their gift of scenting what's to come. Can't you see, Mr. Kranz, we're not able to play the role of rulers? We're doomed people, period, the end.

KRANZ   But what about the artificial constructional self? Isn't it working
anymore? Yesterday it was all going splendidly.

FIZDEJKO   The artificial self is no fiction, but it's not suitable for the herd
society, not even one with a model school system, which only
produces cattle-brained specialists. Telephones and telegrams won't
help either; overspecialized, mechanized cattle can keep telephoning
one another and still remain cattle, but no one will be able to put in
a call to us, to our artificial selves, nor we to anyone else. We've
been cut off.

KRANZ   Mr. Fizdejko, stop joking. You're King. You're tired, Sire. Get a
little rest, Sire, go duck hunting, and then we'll talk it over.

FIZDEJKO   Look over there. The Master already got a little rest—for good
and all. Lord, may his soul rest in eternal peace!

KRANZ   Oh, mein Herr Jehovah! ! He's killed himself! And here you've
been telling me a lot of nonsense without saying anything about it.
But this is a real disaster. Where will we ever find another heir to
the throne and husband for Janulka?

FIZDEJKO   We don't need any heir to the throne if there's no king. I've
become a forester on Gottfried's estate, which he forgot to sign over
to me before he died. I'm totally ruined.

KRANZ   That's sheer madness, Mr. Fizdejko. I'll raise your salary. Now
that everything's boiling and bubbling, so to speak, in the pot, now
that I'm already half-cooked in the scalding water, you're
backing out!

FIZDEJKO   Become King yourself, Mr. Kranz. Joel For-Want-Of-Someone-
Better the First. That's an impressive-sounding title.

KRANZ   You know, that's a terrific idea! What do you think, Plasewitz?

FIZDEJKO   I was joking; at this very moment my heir is about to be born
in some shack. That's what the Master said. Cattle-brained society is
just the same as primitive society—it needs a strong ruling power
issuing from the midst of the cattle clan itself and not from us:
overcivilized manikins with psychic superstructures.

VON PLASEWITZ   But I don't think so. Perhaps you might not be able to
hold onto the reins, Gene, but don't forget that Kranz is a Jew. We
Semites have such a wide range of potentialities that in this cycle of
history we'll maintain our line in perpetuity. Kranz, it's a terrific
intuitive idea!

FIZDEJKO   I'm not convinced the Kranz dynasty will last long.

KRANZ   I've been getting telegrams from all over. In France, they're joining the herd; in England, they're getting cattle-brained; in America it's the same story. The whole world has taken off like a shot into the new era. In Norway they've already got something similar to what we have. By the way, Mr. Fizdejko, how about giving me Janulka as a wife?

FIZDEJKO   If she's willing, by all means. Let her reign a little while. There's only one slight drawback—they'll cut your throats in short order. Hear that, Elsa?

ELSA   I agree—with pleasure. Let the Semites unite among themselves. Racial purity is our greatest strength.

KRANZ   Thanks. But where is Janulka?

FIZDEJKO   She'll be back from mushroom gathering at any moment. I've had more than enough of these discussions and problems. I'm really exhausted. I'm falling asleep.

[*He sits down and dozes off. Princess Amalia comes out from behind the bushes; she is wearing a dressing gown and is accompanied by Janulka, in a pink dress.*]

JANULKA   Oho—my premonitions weren't wrong. The Master finally burst for good and all. May the Lord have mercy on his soul.

KRANZ   Miss Janulka, your father agrees—you're marrying me. I've been King of Lithuania and Belorussia for a full five minutes now.

JANULKA   Not a chance—I've had it up to here with all those kingdoms and artificial selves. I'm a pretty young lady of mixed blood, an ordinary demivirgin. Yesterday evening I got a glimpse of the total futility of our endeavors. Father has given up; so has the Master, although in quite a different way. *I* want to get married normally, to some unassuming young man, and have healthy animals as children. I want to be a member of the herd society. I'm exhausted too.

KRANZ   Oh, damn! ! To let such a beautiful young lady slip out of my hands. But it doesn't matter. The chief thing is power. I'm a bit too clever to be King, but if I once start drinking, maybe I'll go soft in the head like Fizdejko!

[*Enter de la Tréfouille, dressed as in Act I. His head is bandaged with a blood-stained scarf.*]

DE LA TREFOUILLE   I'm going back home where I'll be a King too. According to the latest reports, France has also become cattle-brained.

PRINCESS AMALIA   I'll go with you, Alfred. I have something coming to me too.

DE LA TREFOUILLE   Oh, no! Amalia, you've been my mistress during a transitional phase. I publicly declare: until now, none of the de la Tréfouilles has ever made such a misalliance. Mademoiselle Janulka, I ask for your hand and promise you the kingdom of cattle-brained France.

JANULKA   Oh, no, my Prince: I just turned down a similar proposal from—ha ! ha !—Mr. Kranz, who has become King of Lithuania. The experiment didn't work. The Master is lying there dead, and Papa is sleeping like a log.

DE LA TREFOUILLE   In that case, Amalia—

PRINCESS AMALIA   [*Putting a bullet through his head with her Browning.*] Too late, Alfred. In your family there must have been quite a few misalliances you never suspected. I can't stand genuine boorishness masquerading as false refinement. But Kranz has been in love with me for a long time, and now he simply doesn't dare confess it to me. Right, Joel my dear?

[*de la Tréfouille dies.*]

KRANZ   Yes—I readily admit it. For dynastic reasons I'd have preferred Miss Fizdejko, but I love only you. You are Queen, Amalia. Let's go. Now I've got to take up the question of fishing and cattle breeding—but this time the animals are real, not human. After six in the evening, I'm yours. Where is the crown?

ELSA   [*Pulling the crown from under the quilt.*] Here, my good Joel. I hid it just to be on the safe side. I'm only sorry you didn't become my son-in-law.

[*Kratz takes the crown and puts it on top of his pilot's cap. Enter Der Zipfel.*]

KRANZ   Plasewitz, today you'll issue a manifesto announcing my policies. Der Zipfel, I need all the Boyars today. See that they're alive and healthy. They are the core of my army.

DER ZIPFEL   At your orders, Your Royal Highness.

[*He runs out behind the wall and returns immediately.*]

KRANZ   Now I'll show you what can be expected from the Jews in their rightful places. A genius without a place is a zero. All right, Amalia, let's go.

[*He goes out behind the wall with Princess Amalia and Von Plasewitz, passing by Der Zipfel, who is returning. The Hasidic Jews also leave, speaking in unison.*]

HASIDIC JEWS   Hamalab, Abgach, Zaruzabel. At last we have our Messiah!

[*Exit.*]

DER ZIPFEL   You see, the Jewish question has been settled for the time being. In a minute there'll be an eclipse of the sun. A dark unidentifiable heavenly body is hurtling by us at unimaginable speed.

JANULKA   Oh, what do I care about the Jews or any eclipses? I am a Jewess who's been eclipsed herself. I don't have anyone really common on the horizon any more. I'm so fed up with those extraordinary people that it makes me sick to my stomach. I'd so like to have an ordinary, rosy-cheeked man-about-town for a husband: a nice little puppet, freshly scrubbed and neatly dressed, with nothing in his head. Couldn't you wake the Master up, Mr. Der Zipfel? You've already brought so many corpses back to life. I'd like to talk with him about the future.

DER ZIPFEL   No, Janulka. I have no power over suicides. But look at that little Monster on the left. Watch what's happening to him.

[*The sun is suddenly blacked out. The stage is plunged into almost total darkness. The Monster on the left gets up and suddenly throws off his entire mask and costume. He turns out to be an ordinary, good-looking man-about-town, exactly the sort that Janulka has been dreaming of. He is dressed in a gray suit and low shoes with spats. He goes over to Janulka.*]

MONSTER-ABOUT-TOWN II   Janulka, I love you.

JANULKA   I love you too.

[*She throws her arms around his neck.*]

MONSTER-ABOUT-TOWN II   We won't say another word on the subject because we know—and so does everybody else—what love is like from all those realistic plays: in French, German, Dutch, Polish, and

even Lithuanian and Romanian—and from novels too in all the
same languages.

JANULKA   Oh, why bother to mention it! That goes without saying. The
only thing is—I don't have a heart: I love rationally. The Grand
Master gnawed my heart out with his dialectics.

MONSTER-ABOUT-TOWN II   And I don't have a brain. I was just a monster:
a feathered cripple without legs.

JANULKA   [Intrigued.] Really? And what about that companion of yours? Is
he a man-about-town too, like you?

[Embarrassed, the Monster-about-Town remains silent. The shadows turn
reddish gray.]

DER ZIPFEL   I don't advise you to unmask him, you might get a bad
scare.

JANULKA   I'm going to try anyhow.

[She and the Monster-about-Town go over to Monster I.]

DER ZIPFEL   [Feeling the pulse of the sleeping Fizdejko.] A corpse. [Goes
over to Elsa and feels her pulse too.] Another corpse. The air in this
castle is unhealthy. I'm a corpse too.

JANULKA   [Standing in front of Monster I and not daring to touch him.]
So I'm a total orphan.

MONSTER-ABOUT-TOWN II   I'll be everything to you.

DER ZIPFEL   Go ahead, touch him, my child. For once in your life, make
contact with the ultimate mystery. Afterwards, you can join the herd
and become one of the cattle.

[Janulka touches Monster I, who disappears instantly, that is, he falls
through the trap.]

JANULKA   That's frightful! For the first time in my life, I'm horribly afraid.
I'm more afraid of myself than I am of all of that. Something
unfathomable does exist, after all. But you won't disappear, will you,
my pretty little man-about-town?

MAN-ABOUT-TOWN II   Never, never. I'm yours for all eternity.

[The Grand Master suddenly turns over from one side to the other, and
speaks as though he were praying, mumbling indistinctly at first.]

MASTER   Bihubaambobambagohamba—I'm journeying into the infinity of
boundary ideas, equal almost to zero. I am conquering new lands of
mysteries and colonizing them with my thoughts. The worst is the

penal colony of unexpressed ideas. I am crossing the divide between sense and nonsense! I'm already on the other side, where no one can reach anyone else, not even I the me within myself. And God, a lonely broken man, his heart rent by the ghastly aftertaste of his bungled work, invites the chosen to a final ball—a ball of mutual forgiveness. I see all of us there and many, many others. Finish me off! I don't want to go on existing in eternity. I forgive God for the monstrousness of that invention of his, but even He was incapable of creating any other Existence.

JANULKA   Let's get out of here! It's frightening here!

[She and the Monster-about-Town run off into the bushes.]

DER ZIPFEL   [In a frightful voice.] Corpses! ! Arise! !

[Elsa, Fizdejko, and de la Tréfouille spring up. Elsa jumps out of bed. A sudden blaze of sunlight lights up the stage.]

ELSA   [As though awakened from a deep sleep.] What's going on? ! !
FIZDEJKO   Where am I? ! ! Some strange place from one of my former incarnations! !

[He smashes his pipe against the back of the chair. He still has his rifle over his shoulder. The Master crawls toward him across the heap of his armor lying on the ground.]

MASTER   [Crawling like a somnambulant crab.] Finish me off. . . . That vision of the final ball is torturing me. . . . I don't have the strength to keep God company any longer. He's too good, too polite, and there's contempt hidden in every word and gesture. I don't want to have any more fundamental conversations. I was so happy with nonbeing, and once again, something exists. And even though I don't recognize who I am anymore, I go on talking about myself out of habit: I, I, I . . . [Almost groans.] Kill my second self. But what if it's immortal? Oh—what torture! Finish me off! Mercy!!
DER ZIPFEL   Fizdejko, give it to that crawling reptile out of both barrels. Finish him off like a squashed bug. Don't let him go on suffering.

[Fizdejko in rapid order takes the Winchester off his shoulder, aims quickly, and fires from both barrels at the crawling Master. The Master goes stiff, arms and legs outstretched.]

DER ZIPFEL   I think I've gone too far! A spirit kills a spirit with a real Winchester! ! Or perhaps, all of this is only something I'm dreaming?

FIZDEJKO   Well, maybe so, but exactly the same thing is happening to me.

DE LA TREFOUILLE   And to me, too.

ELSA   Don't I count? Aren't you forgetting about me? I may be the only woman in the group, but I'm dreaming the same thing as the rest of you.

DER ZIPFEL   [*In ecstasy.*] In the infinity of all conceivable possibilities, even such a coincidence is possible: the convergence of four identical dreams. That's sometimes called a miracle.

[*From behind the wall the band of Boyars brandishing axes rushes in. At their head, Glissander in a frock coat. Following them the four ladies from the Master's Frauzimmer, who kneel on both sides of the Master's corpse. There now begins the brutal massacre of the five characters onstage: Elsa, Fizdejko, de la Tréfouille, Der Zipfel, and the Master.*]

DER ZIPFEL   The miracle has ceased! The intersecting point of all possible coincidences in the entire world has simply gone mad! ! ! Ohhh! ! !

[*He falls under the blow of an ax. Blood spurts (small balloons filled with water colored with magenta which they all had under their clothes are burst). They all fall. Meanwhile, from behind the bushes, Joel Kranz appears in a purple coat with the crown on his head, accompanied by Amalia dressed in the same way. They watch the massacre with a smile.*]

CURTAIN
End of the Fourth and Final Act

27 JUNE 1923

PART 4: PORTRAIT-PAINTING FIRM, DRUGS, AND NOVELS
1925-31

The year 1924 marked a turning point in Witkacy's career. Having spent more than six years attempting to provide models for Pure Form in painting and theater without achieving any positive impact on the artistic community, the author declared that he had fulfilled his purely aesthetic program, which in no way depended on public acceptance. He now turned to impure genres and activities in which he could express ideas directly and incorporate his own experiences. Witkacy's interests in character analysis, psychology, philosophy, cultural and social criticism, and national issues were no longer circumscribed by the "insatiable craving for form," which he had said characterized the modern age. His shift to the practical and utilitarian can also be explained by a difficult financial situation that forced him to earn a living by his pen and brush.

By the end of 1924 Witkacy renounced forever painting as a pure art of formal constructions on plane surfaces in favor of the applied art of portraits. In 1925 he established the Witkiewicz Portrait-Painting Firm, held the first exhibit of the Firm's products, and formulated its Rules (which he would publish in 1928). By setting up an ironic business enterprise, the artist created an imaginary construct to distance himself from the demeaning hackwork of painting on command for money.

It was a troubling time for Witkacy. His wife had an abortion, but he was not responsible for the pregnancy. They never had a child. His letters are unusually gloomy, full of talk about suicide and material squalor. "My state is deplorable," he wrote to Jadwiga in 1925. "I live in a psychic superstructure in which it is difficult to hold on, so rarified is the air." Unable to forget the suicide of his fiancée, he attended spiritualistic séances conducted by the celebrated mediums Jan Guzik and Franek Kluski, then fashionable in Warsaw, at which he saw "the ghost of Jadwiga Janczewska and other wonders." The playwright even conducted his own séances, until he was eventually caught pulling the strings that produced the spirit rappings. These adventures with the supernatural provide an analogue to Witkacy's most striking dramaturgical device, the resurrected corpse that nonchalantly reappears and resumes life as if nothing had happened. Plays like *The New Deliverance* and *Janulka, Daughter of Fizdejko* actually take the form of dramatic séances.

Just at the time he was abandoning playwriting for the novel, Witkacy enjoyed his greatest success in the professional theater and became actively involved with his own amateur group. Whereas his other dramas had been performed, if at all, only two or three times under special circumstances, *Jan Maciej Karol Hellcat* (written in 1922) was a genuine hit in 1925 at the Fredro Theater in Warsaw, where it played thirty-four times. It then went on tour for another thirty-four performances and won a prize from the Artists Union. *Hellcat* owed its popularity to topical appeal; this "drama without corpses," in which a country bumpkin rises to be president of the republic, seemed to be a satire on the peasant politician Wincenty Witos, who had recently enjoyed a similar career. The critics, praising the author's mastery of dramatic technique, argued that Witkacy could write excellent plays if only he would abandon his absurd theory of Pure Form. Witkacy replied that he was willing to compromise in the painting of commercial portraits, but that he was not such a cynic as to write plays for money. Even though there was something disingenuous in this claim, given his earlier ambitions for *Hellcat*, drama remained for Witkacy a supreme art above market considerations.

After first attempting to create a new type of play, Witkacy then turned his attention for several years to the formation of an alternate theater that would present innovative drama. To realize the theory of Pure Form on the stage, the author and a circle of friends established the Formist Theater as part of the Theater Society in Zakopane. Its star was Winifred Cooper, an English painter who had come to Zakopane to be married but whose fiancé died of tuberculosis before the ceremony could take place; Zakopane so fascinated her that she never left. Her odd-shaped face ("like that of an American Indian") and her foreign accent had the effect of strangeness that Witkacy particularly desired in the theater. The playwright praised her performance as Sister Anna in *The Madman and the Nun* and as Tatiana in *The New Deliverance*, which he himself directed as a double bill for the opening of the Formist Theater in March 1925. Also at the Formist Theater in the same year Witkacy designed the scenery and costumes for his plays *The Pragmatists* and *In a Small Country House*. After directing the latter work at a professional theater in Lwów in 1926, Witkacy concluded that practical work in the theater was not his calling. The Formist Theater came to an end in 1927 because of aesthetic disagreements among its members, one faction wishing to do realistic productions of plays successful in the commercial theater.

Witkacy's only surviving play from this period, *The Beelzebub Sonata*, is his farewell to Pure Form in the theater. A contemporary version of the Faust story anticipating Mann's *Dr. Faustus* by some twenty years, *The Beelzebub Sonata* tells the story of a modern artist driven to self-destruction by his own calling. Creatively exhausted and superfluous once his sonata has been composed, the lonely musician hero hangs himself. Previously Witkacy had hoped to "blaze up and burn himself up in a splendid artistic cataclysm," but now the danger seemed to be that he would simply drag out his existence as a living corpse.

Constantly "taking a posthumous look at himself," the playwright saw his own demise as it appeared from the other side. He even reported that Winifred Cooper, struck by his expression as he lay peacefully in bed, once exclaimed, "You look like an angel. How beautiful you will be dead."

In August 1925 Witkacy embarked on a new career when he began writing his first novel since the youthful *roman à clef*, *Bungo*, fifteen years earlier. Fiction was for Witkacy an imaginative projection of the hidden self as well as a hoped-for source of money. While working on the new book, the author explained to Jadwiga, "I'm hacking my way through the dense underbrush of my own psychophysiology." *Farewell to Autumn* appeared two years later, for which he was to receive 1,500 zlotys if 2,000 copies were sold, but despite its sensational subject and many erotic scenes, the novel did not attract many readers and was unfavorably reviewed. Immediately thereafter the author started work on *Insatiability*, a huge dystopian novel in which Russia is overrun by Chinese Communists, while the West, whose bulwark is Poland, becomes softened up for collectivism by the Murti Bing pill of universal contentment. On its completion in 1930, Witkacy was paid the large sum of 8,000 zlotys, which enabled him to cover debts connected with the hotel.

In the later 1920s narcotics played a more and more important role in both Witkacy's life and his art. He had experimented with drugs in Russia, where he began painting under their influence. He would record the exact nature of the stimulants on the canvas by means of special symbols. Drugs were an impetus for new creative experiences. In 1928 Witkacy obtained peyote, which he regarded as a superior metaphysical drug, from Alexandre Rouhier, a French researcher and author of *Peyotl, la plante qui fait les yeux émerveillés*, who did a mail-order business in narcotics. The precise, heightened visions induced by peyote represented for Witkacy the very workings of the imagination and the basis of art and fantastic theater. Although he regarded its false euphoria as inevitably leading to suicide, the author of *Farewell to Autumn* also took cocaine, which he could never completely renounce. Dr. Białynicki-Birula, in whose house Witkacy lived for several years, was usually present at the evening "orgies" when the artist carried out his experiments with drugs, thus reducing the risk of an overdose.

Witkacy's career in the theater was virtually over. A production of a double bill of *The Madman and the Nun* and *The New Deliverance* had fifteen performances in Warsaw in 1926. *Persy Bestialskaya* was presented twice in Łódź in 1927. The last professional production of any of his plays during the author's lifetime was *The Metaphysics of a Two-Headed Calf*, given five times in Poznań in 1928. When in 1927 he was asked to do a screen test for the role of a professor in *The Grave of the Unknown Soldier*, Witkacy thought briefly of a career as a film actor. Someone else was cast for the part.

As an artist, however, Witkacy continued to exhibit frequently. The Firm sometimes showed as many as a hundred portraits at a time. Reviewers commented that his works engaged the attention of gallerygoers and made them actively participate in the creation. In 1928 eleven paintings by Witkacy were shown in Paris as part of an exhibit of Polish artists.

Nonetheless, the exhaustion of his creative forces, which had first threatened him in 1923, seemed to have become a permanent reality. By the late 1920s Witkacy constantly lamented that he was not an artist. "I miss 'creative' creativity to which I grew addicted as one does to drugs. I'm going to have to sit down and write a novel." Only by creativity could he justify his existence and resolve the dilemma posed by Janczewska's suicide. For these reasons he began a new novel, *The Only Way Out*, his most speculative and confessional, and started work on a new play, *The Shoemakers*, his most social and political, while at the same time writing a popular treatise on drugs, based on his own experiences, in the hope of making money.

The last major event in the playwright's erotic life came in 1929 when he met Czesława Korzeniewska, seventeen years his junior. His passionate attachment to Czesława had the same intensity that characterized all his obsessions, and as usual he was unable to keep from disclosing his inner turmoil to all who would listen. Jadwiga was required to share the details of his unhappy love affair and to commiserate with her husband when Czesława frequently severed relations with Witkacy because of his unwillingness to leave his wife.

Swearing that he would never abandon her spiritually, Witkacy begged

Jadwiga not to keep him on a leash but to allow him freedom. He attempted to justify his infidelities as "those cursed sexual episodes" and pointed out that his former psychiatrist "old Beaurain always claimed that a man must have many women and that intercourse with only one is simply a form of onanism." At the same time that he denied any attraction to his wife, he confessed his utter dependence on her. "Since you are not sufficiently appealing to me," he explained, "I must have other women, and that makes you not want to go on living. You make a criminal out of me, but I know that living that way I would grow to hate you, go mad, be nothing and ultimately, at the very best, end my life by suicide. I cannot live in a prison. Life without you is frightful for me. The thought that you might not be fills me with terror."

FAREWELL TO AUTUMN

∎

Chapter 4: Marriages and the First Pronunciamento

The time of normal events had come to an end. What followed made wide circles at first and then began to gravitate toward that nucleus of strangeness, that abyss in the open field, which half a generation earlier was used to frighten ultraliberal statesmen of the ancien régime as they sat around the fire on long winter nights. Some felt that it would engulf every last vestige of individualistic culture, as the maelstrom swallows a fisherman's boat. For each the abyss presented itself differently, depending on whether or not the person in question had experienced the Russian Revolution, and of course according to the social class to which he belonged. And in any case the first of these factors sometimes modified the second in rather significant ways. For the moment there was nothing clearly defined despite historical examples, both past and present. Everyone had his own individualized dangers, his own private little abysses. But every so often these seemed to run together, like the separate pimples of a skin disease, creating blotches ("plaques musqueuses") over wider areas. Of course this afflicted the so-called higher classes, not to mention the leaders of the lower classes who by their style of life belonged to the former category. On the other side of the partially torn down fences, the half-demolished dikes and sluice gates, the mob—singularly foul smelling for some noses—was seething, like the turbid, foaming waters of spring: everyone said the revolution was coming. Everything had become so boring, so stodgy, so sexless and futureless that even the dullest old fogies rejoiced in the depths of their petrified nerve centers that something unexpected was about to happen. That is why war, revolution, and earthquakes are always a cause of rejoicing for people who don't have the courage to blow their own brains out even though they know it's the right thing to do. It will all take care of itself, they tell themselves, keeping death at more and more of a distance. But when it finally comes, they're ready to lick the executioners' hands, begging for just one minute more—to keep it from happening now. The only ones who did not rejoice were the people who had something to lose, and those included the following special categories: (*a*) sportsmen—the revolution might divert public attention from the fantastic records they were setting; (*b*) ballroom dancers—naturally for their gyrations the revolution meant an interruption of several months; (*c*) businessmen— cessation of their profitable labors could prove lengthy and eventually end in a transfer to actual infinity (whether infinitely short or infinitely long hardly matters), i.e., to Absolute Nothingness; and (*d*) another species of Individual Beings on their way to extinction—but enough said about that for now.

You can look at revolution, as at everything else for that matter, from two viewpoints: from the normal, sociopsychological viewpoint and its derivatives in the particular sciences; or from the metaphysical viewpoint, i.e., considering revolution as the consequence of absolute laws governing every possible grouping of beings. As Bronisław Malinowski correctly points out in his work entitled *Primitive Beliefs*, certain events seem more predisposed than others to induce that specific mental state increasingly rare in present times: the immediate perception of the strangeness of life and of existence in general. But it is far from accurate to assert that any powerful state of emotional tension whatsoever is capable of being transformed into a completely new feeling, a religious feeling: as though it could be created out of nothing. The pseudoscientific nature of this view, which claims to posit nothing beyond a description of indubitably extant states (hunger, sexual desire, fear, etc.), essentially falsifies the whole situation, preventing us from getting to the crux of the matter by ruling out in advance the possibility of the existence of specific states that are not necessarily derivative of other ordinary feelings.

"For people who exist marginally on the fringes of life, for characters like Lohoyski, Baehrenklotz, Prepoudrech, and me, revolution might be exactly what is needed to give the dormant mechanism of strangeness a powerful jolt. Although the final result and the very course of the revolution must be antireligious, the first explosion could momentarily awaken metaphysical feelings about life and even create new forms in art," so thought Athanasius as he was getting ready to attend Hela's christening. Nothing energizing could emerge from the recently concluded war with its mechanization and its absence of any ideology, or rather with its aim of fostering mealymouthed democracy, which unbeknownst to anyone had started to smolder during the hostilities. Only nationalism in the extreme form, following the course of its own natural evolution, came to an end during the war, without the forces opposing it even coming into play—in Russia even before the ultimate development, while the fighting was still in progress. If only it would all happen faster. Athanasius had the impression he contained highly combustible material that would never go off if everything around him kept plodding on so insipidly. He experienced the flow of time almost physically: he felt everything had stopped, and onrushing time seemed to be immersing him in its caressing currents. As in a dream he was unable to move or to precipitate the inner rhythm of becoming: the tempo had grown dependent on events that were floundering in the general atmosphere of swampy rot. People grew accustomed to the state of crisis, it became the normal atmosphere for them. "It's an abscess that has to burst," Athanasius repeated over and over again in his thoughts, and he imagined the bursting as an incredible sexual paroxysm in Hela's company, with political revolution as a backdrop. The events everyone awaited were made to serve as a pretext for breaking all the ordinary rules of daily life. For the time being the equilibrium of his feelings was at least perfect. Like two oppositely directed vectors, the contradictions held at rest the point of application of forces. The dual system of life began to please Athanasius; it had only one drawback—it wouldn't last. The end of this whole story was clearly delineated in moments of "listening to eternity," somewhere in that dark cloud floating above the revolutionary volcano, which was showing stronger and stronger signs of life. In the center of something that might be called a general life platform, Athanasius's tiny little conscience—covered with scarcely perceptible spots of remorse—was being broiled over a low flame. Winter was slowly drawing near. The city had become dark and dirty, blanketed at times by a blindingly white, powdery snow that dissolved in one's eyes. Then everything turned into an even slushier slush.

Finally the bearded Bertz appeared, disgorged from some Nord-Express, and without even bothering to go home first, he telephoned from the station and fixed the day of the christening for the following morning: that is, for 14 December. Both marriages were scheduled for the afternoon of the same day. The nuptial orgy was to take place in the Bertz palace: it was a result of the friendship that had sprung up between Miss Zofia Osłabędzka and Hela Bertz as an outgrowth of their religious experiences. Those claiming expertise in revolution predicted frightful things. Not long before, the abominable Sajetan Tempe had returned from abroad, and he dropped in on Athanasius as the latter was waiting for Lohoyski—they were to go to the christening together. Now almost a stranger, this friend whom he had not seen for years did not make a very favorable impression on Athanasius. He was dressed in a short grayish green padded jacket and a huge black jockey cap. Things had obviously changed a bit since "the good old days."

"Hi, Tazio, old buddy," Tempe said in an artificially sugary tone, trying to disguise the hardness and domineering impatience in his voice. "I hear you're rolling in clover: they say you're marrying a wealthy heiress. But your newfound wealth won't last long. On our side things are already stirring. It'll all go like clockwork—in the opposing camp they haven't got forces with great enough tension, they haven't got the weight. Once the avalanche breaks loose, it has to go down to the bottom—whether anyone likes it or not."

"Look here, Sajetan," Athanasius began, shuddering with disgust, "just don't carry on like that, please. I'm going through some fundamental changes in my thinking, but your way of treating these matters is enough to make anyone sick to his stomach."

Tempe was visibly disconcerted. "You haven't read my latest poetry, have you?" he asked. "Little meat dumplings with a social conscience, stuffed with explosive material. In my opinion, poetry has value only if its juices are made to do the work of agitprop. Economy of means . . . "

"I don't read poetry anymore. What disgusts me about poetry nowadays is that total lack of genuine inventiveness and the contrivance of utterly useless artistic devices unrelated to the aims of the work, that dredging up of subject matter out of random combinations halfway through the writing, and that technique of versification concealing a hopeless creative void! But I read your little volume, trembling with rage all the while. Art in the service of primitive stomachs—sure, the poetry is good—but what lèse-majesté and sacrilege!"

Tempe smiled a broad, easygoing smile. He reeked of tumultuous streets and steamed with all the heat of tight-packed human masses. He was truly self-satisfied.

"I expected as much; a typical petit bourgeois nihilist like you—and an aesthete on top of that—couldn't react in any other way. There's poetry and poetry: withered leaf or bomb. I'd like to sweep our poetry clean of all that stinking rubbish—it's shameful—fancy labels on fragrance bottles and condom wrappers . . . The content, the content is what counts and the content of my poems makes you indignant."

"You're mistaken," Athanasius retorted angrily, studying Tempe's face with unconcealed distaste. He now could not abide that man's fiery, restless dark eyes, his curly reddish hair, his baby-veal pink skin studded with tiny pimples, and above all his exasperating strength hidden no one knew where. "What matters to me is form, not content. The fact you depict martyred Communists and police spies leading debauched lives, and hard-hearted judges and nationalistic drivel doesn't in the least upset me in and of itself—it's raw material taken from real life like any other subject. But what I can't stand is that, without believing in its artistic worth, you deliberately stuff this new material into the decaying forms of traditional poetry, at most using a few threadbare futuristic tricks—that's why I feel such disgust, disgust for the detailed contents of your poetry: the stink of basements, the sweat, the poverty, the hopeless mechanical work, the prisons and the police agents glutting themselves on asparagus—disgust for the basic material itself which has not been transformed into artistic elements. That material does not arouse any of the intended feelings—as in undigested food, you can see the peas and carrots separately, and the green beans too; in your poetry the form floats separately, and so does the content, which is repulsive in and of itself. I don't even mention any more-general ideas, because I see few enough of them, but what annoys me is that I can't find any fault with the form as such."

"Yes, you'd like to watch the revolution from the best seat in the orchestra as though it were a show—better still, to have it all staged by those new, self-proclaimed social artists who try to make a pseudoartistic performance out of everything: a mass meeting, a rally, a shooting on the street, even work. Anyone can see what an idiotic idea that is, but there are still some serious people who think it's a real possibility. Oh, I'm revolted by our artists, whether socially conscious or just serious—they're vile worms in a rotting carcass. Only now that they've realized they may croak from hunger in their bogus ivory towers, because society has finally judged them at their worth, have they graciously consented to come down to society's level, offering the people their constructivist skills. Phoey, I don't belong to their ranks. Art must be put in the service of an ideal, in the menial service of an ideal. That is the most important role art can have: to express humbly the content assigned to it, like a docile beast of burden."

"But to what ranks do you belong?" Athanasius countered. "For me you are a typical instance of pseudomorphosis, to use Spengler's concept, which he took from mineralogy: if the forms preceding any given phenomena are sufficiently defined, and the new content does not produce them itself, then this new content flows into the old molds and hardens into shapes like those of the no-longer-extant formations of a past epoch that have rotted, crumbled, and dissolved into thin air. Your poetry is an example of such pseudomorphosis. And that is a proof of weakness. Perhaps a few Russians, thanks to their revolution, have created something almost new; over there, in Russia, the material stopped being the content of a versified propaganda pamphlet—it blended with the form, which like a fresh shoot broke through the layers of successive accretions. But even that is pitifully little. The social classes who are now finding their own voices have not created any totally new artistic form, nor will they ever. They have too much to say about the stomach and its rights. And time is fleeting . . . "

"Happiness depends solely on a full stomach," Sajetan replied. "All your problems are sham. Only by wholesale cattle braining, carried out rigorously and systematically, will mankind reach its true and desired resting point: not to know anything about anything, not to be conscious of anything, simply to vegetate agreeably. All civilization has turned out to be a fraud; the view along the way was beautiful, but now it's over: there is no further goal to strive for, there is no 'way,' except our 'way'; truth does not exist, science produces nothing on its own and has been taken over by technology. Art is really just a serious plaything for ineffectual aesthetic eunuchs—verily, whoever once sees what I have seen will never go back to that old pseudohuman world. It was fine while it lasted—now it's over and the positive achievements must be used for our purposes. Dancing and sport are important elements of mass stupefaction—with the ground so well prepared, the process of cattle braining mankind will be child's play. The closing of the dance halls by the Fascists, the world's biggest clowns, is an argument in favor of my thesis. But this revolution of programmed beasts of burden is only the first step! I'm of the opinion that until now the materialism in Marxism has been too carefully disguised. But who I am you'll find out soon enough, my little Tazio. My strength won't fail me, I know that."

He flexed his terrible muscles, making his pea green jersey ripple. Someone, let in by the cleaning woman, was taking off his overcoat in the hall.

"And what have your poems got to do with all this?" asked Athanasius, a bit put off by Tempe's frankness in formulating his views and for the moment unable to counter his arguments. "Are they the results of programmatic cattle braining?"

"Quit joking, beneath that popular term there's concealed truly profound content. And as for my poems, they are neither products of your asinine Pure Form nor artistic solutions to social problems or whatever you call them—I never could really understand your universalists. Eradicate lying— our civilization is lying itself to death. My poems are pure propaganda for truth—art is crudely and openly made to serve as a beast of burden."

(Athanasius succumbed to the spell of Tempe's simplicity and sincerity: he envied him the strength of his belief.)

"But your poetry's not programmed yet," said Lohoyski jovially, coming in without knocking. It was the first time he had allowed himself to take cocaine in the morning and he was in the best of humors. He did not know that he had just signed his own death warrant—if not physically, at least spiritually. Henceforth not for a single second of the day or night would he be free of the frightful poison or of his craving for it.

"Greetings, monsieur le Comte!" replied Sajetan with deliberate, ironic, and tasteless self-abasement.

"None of your stupid jokes, Mr. Tempe," Lohoyski snarled angrily, suddenly glum and on the defensive. He decided to start calling Tempe "Mr.," continuing the joke about forms of address. He couldn't stand being reminded he was only a count.

"So why don't you give away your title to your lackeys? I remember my visit last May . . . "

"All right, all right, let's drop the matter," Lohoyski muttered, blushing siightly. "I didn't know you'd already managed to get acquainted with my servants."

"Monsieur le Comte has changed his way of life: the member of the Social Democratic party now has a palace for himself, but they say it was his going over to the left that caused the old gent to kick the bucket from chagrin."

"Mr. Tempe, or should I say comrade Sajetan, let me remind you I don't like familiarities not specifically authorized by me."

"You didn't defend yourself so spiritedly against familiarities in the old days, comrade Jędrek," Tempe said impudently, winking his left eye.

Now Athanasius understood: Tempe had been one of Lohoyski's passing victims in his forays into inversion. Besides, Tempe was what is called "ambidextrous." At present he used inversion only to ensnare and dominate the men he had need of. "Well, after all he served as a lieutenant in the notorious Cadets Corps, so there's nothing to be surprised at," Athanasius recalled.

Lohoyski: "What's past is past, let's keep our distance now."

Tempe: "Who knows what kind of distance we're going to keep, comrade Count. I see you haven't been reading the newspapers lately. It's all hanging by a thread, that's obvious, at least for those who can read. And once things get started, we won't miss the opportunity. All those moderate reformers are working for us. Moderation and socialism are almost logical contradictions."

Lohoyski: "You, a naval reserve officer, dare say something like that? Listen, Tazio, we could simply turn him . . . " Tempe went somewhat pale at this little joke.

Tempe: "I didn't know Tazio was working as an informer." Lohoyski realized he had pushed his outrageousness a bit too far.

Lohoyski: "Let's stop trying to outsmart each other. I overheard your theory from out there before I came in. And I must admit you almost had me convinced. Perhaps I was even angry that someone else managed to formulate it before I did."

Tempe: "The honor's all mine. But you can't do it like that, all at once and at no cost at all. The road leading to happiness is long and difficult. And to start with, all the previous attainments of culture must be used to the highest degree: the intellect, monsieur le Comte, the intellect above all. But you've seriously neglected your cerebral hemispheres for the sake of other hemispheres, especially other people's hemispheres. I abandoned that path a long time ago."

Lohoyski: "That Tempe has become impossible, Tazio. I don't know how to talk to him. (Menacingly.) Comrade, Sajetan, let's talk seriously—I share your opinion that being excessively conscious of what we're doing takes away our enjoyment of the immediate experience. But I'm in favor of individual cattle-braining. Society will automatically turn into cattle if all its members willingly join the herd."

Tempe: "None of your stupid jokes, Mr. Lohoyski. I take my ideas seriously: they are not simply functions of my family's position and my financial standing. For you to be cattle-brained, cocaine is enough. I know a thing or two myself."

Lohoyski wanted to say something in response, but Athanasius interrupted him.

Athanasius (to Tempe): "In my mouth the word communism is a pale idea from the realm of abstract utopias—in yours it is a bloody bomb compounded of dynamite and shreds of quivering flesh. Let's stop our bickering. Coming with us to Hela Bertz's christening, Tempe? We're watching the final death throes of Jewish Catholicism. Soon they'll find another little self-propulsion device from which they can draw strength openly and on a grander scale. Mankind now needs a new type of prophet, something different from those bearded nineteenth-century socialists. Systematic cattle-braining has to be metaphysicalized a bit to make it appealing, its transcendental necessity has to be shown. No known religion can do the job—something totally new must be devised."

Lohoyski: "Mr. Tempe, if you're destined to be the model for the prophet of the future, I don't much envy mankind. Every idea you touch becomes odious."

Tempe: "Your malice toward me simply springs from the fact that you envy me the strength you lack. I had the strength to believe, but that belief has given me twice as much energy, if not more. (The other two fell into a lugubrious silence.) I have a diabolic talent for organization. I didn't even know it myself. The new order will have to make use of my services—and in the highest positions. You'll see."

They went out into the city smelling of frost and rabble. Something strange was in the air. One constantly felt there was a kind of shadow cast by something unseen—nor was the light visible that produced that shadow—making the impression all the stranger. But everyone felt something coming that hadn't yet been mentioned in the newspapers. The attitude of the moderate socialist press was alarming: they advocated the greatest possible moderation and appealed for quiet—evidently they were afraid themselves. Tempe bought a special edition and glanced at it as they walked along.

"I'll tell you quite frankly," Tempe explained. "Tomorrow General Bruizor is opening the first breach, working for us, of course, quite unwittingly—I've been getting secret information. We're waiting for the opportune moment. But keep it to yourselves."

Athanasius was stunned for a moment. So it would be tomorrow? Suddenly the whole world began to spin around in a dancing light: he felt exactly as he had back then, before the duel. But he immediately understood it was coming a bit too soon for him—he wasn't ready—marriage, Hela, unresolved problems. Both Athanasius and Lohoyski felt sick at heart there in the street with comrade Tempe: it was as though they were walking side by side with a bomb—the slightest inattention and boom! It was all well and good in theory—but in practice it frightened them. Lacking any positive antidotes within themselves, they saw the ground slip from under their feet—the abyss seemed to open right before them, on the sidewalk, in the entrance ways of the gloomy houses, on the faces of the people they passed by. Only the blue sky at the zenith, with wisps of fog floating across it, was indifferent and joyous—how they envied it its carefree, impersonal existence. What would they do with that abominable Tempe?

Tempe: "We've had our fill of those Promethean figures with their oil lamps—nowadays replaced by electric lights—who pay visits to the rabble in its dirty holes and then go back to their everyday heights, or rather their everyday depths of the soul. The masses will take everything for themselves without any mediation—at times quite profitable—by those enlighteners, and they'll let their own chosen people loose on the world."

Lohoyski: "You really don't know anything, comrade Tempe: Russia is backtracking—no one in the entire world takes communism seriously."

Tempe: "But then communism doesn't take anyone seriously either, except itself. And anyhow, this is only the beginning. Communism is a transitory phase, and ups and downs are inevitable—it depends on the point of departure. Remember where Russia was at the start. The nucleus of forces from which the universal wave issued may even be temporarily extinguished, but the wave has gone forth and done its work. And anyhow, where are your concepts, putrid democrats? How could you, microscopic observers at short range, understand the greatness of our ideas? You're screaming for ideas you don't have and can never have, because those ideas are now being spontaneously created in the masses and are finding individuals who'll be their spokesmen. An idea takes root and grows in life, it's not devised behind a desk, but first of all it has to be *true*: it must arise from historical necessity, and not merely be a brake designed to keep mankind at the miserable level of mankind-in-appearance only by maintaining all the privileges—not for the former type of rulers but for the new "operators," the various self-made men, the business sharks and hyenas sinking their teeth into commerce . . . "

Athanasius: "Stop it, Tempe, you're a bore—we know all that. When I'm alone and think about all that and about who I am, it seems to me something great, and all my individualism makes me feel petty and superfluous in comparison, and not just me, but those at the very top as well. But all it takes is for me to hear someone of your ilk mouthing those platitudes and all that greatness suddenly dissolves into boredom: then I no longer see superfluous people, but rather superfluous mankind, which will never create anything ever again—and that's the worst of all."

Lohoyski: "I believed in the Social Democrats because I thought that their goal was a true liberation of the spirit, freedom and glorious creativity for everyone—but now . . . "

Tempe: "Those are precisely the sort of high-sounding phrases that we've eliminated and in that lies *our* greatness. You both have pseudopromethean little souls. You'd like to give magnanimously, but you've got nothing to offer, and when the people take for themselves, you're deeply offended. Mechanization, or to put it more bluntly, deliberate and conscious cattle-braining—that's truth of the future, and the rest is superstructure, ornamentation, which has become so rampant that it's started to devour what it was supposed to adorn. We've reached the end point of bourgeois civilization, which never gave us anything except doubt about everything."

Athanasius: "That depends on what has been asked of it—the fact that philosophy has been confined to giving a purely negative definition of the limits of knowledge sets free reserves of energy that would otherwise have gone into a fruitless struggle with the impossible. ("Is that me talking?" he wondered.) The universal grayness that will result from socialization does not necessarily have to be equivalent to cattle-braining—it's possible to become mechanized while preserving the achievements of civilization. And that's where mankind is heading, but it won't get there by apocalyptic catastrophes that aim at the immediate implementation of state socialism."

Athanasius said all that without any conviction solely to avoid thinking about the problem of taking communion, which Father Hieronymus, of the Order of Parallelists, wanted to force on him that very day. The close proximity of the catastrophe had indeed changed his immediate state of mind—it was all just fine, but only when seen from a distance.

Tempe: "I know what you suspect me of, Athanasius: you think in bringing about the revolution I'm really . . . "

Lohoyski: "You're not bringing about anything, Mr. Tempe, you're just a pawn."

Tempe: "That remains to be seen. The fact is that in my work for the revolution I'm realizing myself as junk or debris from a disintegrating civilization I detest, I'm rising above myself in a dimension hostile to my own ideal. I know—perhaps you're even right as far as the present moment is concerned.

But now really, can we become different people without first going through all the intermediate phases? What you were saying about pseudomorphosis may apply more to me than to my poetry, but this is a transitional period. We must pass through all the stages with our teeth clenched, tearing ourselves loose bit by bit from the inert mass that we form along with the rest of the world. And at the end, instead of unconscious brutification, imperceptibly drawing near under the guise of supposedly great but actually false ideas, there will be a fully conscious descent into the abyss of happiness—an abyss that's dark and dim, I'll grant it, but doesn't greatness lie in precisely that, if you will: in realizing that too bright a light creates darkness, blinds and destroys the very possibility of seeing. We've already reached that stage. Now on that subject—and for you people this is beyond comprehension—I can't sleep soundly knowing I'm surrounded by an unfathomable sea of suffering that could be alleviated at the cost of certain slight unpleasantnesses done to characters like you. Forgive me, but how is one to have any hesitations?"

The conversation had grown simply unbearable for Lohoyski, who was furious at Tempe for spoiling his morning visit to Athanasius, the last such before his marriage. He no longer knew who was arguing for what against whom, all the more so since he had recently begun to seriously suspect Athanasius of cryptocommunism.

"Stop splitting hairs!" he screamed. "You're both self-proclaimed communists. I want to go on living a little longer. Don't poison my last moments. There's no telling what tomorrow will bring."

They had just reached the cathedral on the Old Town Square, where the christening and the two marriages were to take place. Prepoudrech, pale, without a cap, wrapped in a black sealskin coat, stood in front of the church.

"Hela wouldn't let me go get her. I'm half-dead with anxiety. She could kill herself at any moment. She's always like that—a bundle of the most extreme contradictions. Oh, Tazio, if you knew how I'm suffering!" exclaimed Prepoudrech, not paying any attention to Tempe, who was watching the three of them with undisguised contempt.

"I'm leaving," he said suddenly in a very loud voice, "I don't care for these farces. Death throes: you're right, Tazio. See you on the barricades, if you've got the glands for it. If not, come join us. We'll be able to make use of you. We need lost souls, but ones with glands, not wet noodles who don't even know how to amuse themselves in their final moments on earth."

He saluted, bringing his icy red paw up to his black jockey cap, and then went off whistling.

"That Swedish nobility is something pretty *minderwärtig*," Lohoyski sneered at Tempe as he watched him depart.

The revolution announced for the next day had upset Lohoyski's plans to some extent; there was no telling what would happen to the illicit cocaine trade after the coup d'état, and then too he had just arranged a little rendez-vous for tomorrow: to lessen the pain caused by his love for Athanasius, whose conquest, because of his marriage, would have to be deferred until a much later date.

Meanwhile the sky had brightened, and a promising early winter after-noon—sparkling with frost, merry, full of hope—gradually began to take shape. The warm sun penetrated the slowly rising mist; from the cornices of buildings and the dark trees melting caps of white powdery snow started to fall, splashing in puddles on the sidewalks. In his imagination Athanasius was transported high up into the mountains. How marvelous it must have been up there: the vast, glistening highlands, the deep blue sky, a pair of skis and an icy downhill course, and the indescribable charm of a little restaurant at the foot of the mountains where after an entire day spent in the snow you can drink tea and red wine. It had been a long, long time since he had been able to treat himself to a trip to the mountains.

Chapter 8: The Mystery of a September Morning

The moment of otherworldly ecstasy, causing his chest to burst with unbounded grandeur, seemed to endure for an eternity. "I've finally ceased to endure in duration," Athanasius said out loud in a voice not his own, as though someone else were speaking, and that phrase, like something absurd in a dream, seemed to have an incredibly profound meaning—and he took another stiff dose of cocaine. How is it possible to express what he saw when even in a normal state the beauty of the world is sometimes an unbearable pain—and now that pain was heightened to infinity and suddenly trans-formed into a new form of pleasure, cold, pure, transparent, and as intense as the pain . . . And on top of that he had the feeling that it was the last time, that never again . . . Before him were ranged the familiar and well-beloved peaks in unearthly glory, jutting over the valley, but in another dimension, in an ideal mode of being that in its perfection bordered on nonbeing—for is there anything more perfect than Nothingness?

And while he "was thus enduring without duration," Athanasius was suddenly startled by cracking and snapping sounds: from the tangled rowans and willows there emerged a dark brown, hairy mass that headed straight for him across a small meadow amidst rocks, where dried umbellets and fading autumn gentians could still be seen. The beast was followed by two smaller versions of the same creature: a she-bear with her young, which meant certain death—the female always attacks first. But under the influence of the coco Athanasius had lost all sense of danger. The she-bear had the wind behind her (a gentle fresh breeze was blowing from the shadows in the valley toward the sunbathed peaks of Jawor), she didn't smell anything—or see beyond the rocks. Then suddenly she came out into the open and saw Athanasius. She stopped. He saw her eyes full of fear and astonishment. The cubs stopped too and whined. "Now I'm in a real fix," Athanasius said without a trace of fear. "That bear is going to spoil my last moments." But both the new vision and what he had just said were linked to the preceding moment; they did not shatter the frame of its extraordinary dimensions, nor did they destroy its charm. A brief roar and then the she-bear, standing up on her hind legs, picked up a rock the size of two heads with her forepaws and threw it at Athanasius, and then began to run toward him on her two back legs. The stone flew past his head and smashed into pieces on the boulder he was leaning against. The would-be suicide sprang to his feet and looked around. The instinct for self-preservation went into effect mechanically, as the repro-ductive instinct does in the sphex when it perforates the caterpillar. "That's pure Bergson—can one really 'transform that into knowledge?' What hum-bug!" he thought just as automatically in a split second. He didn't have a gun. He grabbed a whole handful of the white powder he had put in a little pile on a piece of paper beside him and threw it into the bear's jaws, which were open-ing to attack him, and then he jumped up on a boulder. He remembered that Lohoyski used to feed cocaine to his cat and he suddenly burst out laugh-ing—it was priceless.

The she-bear, sprinkled with a powder that had an unfamiliar and re-pulsive smell, her black muzzle all whitened, dropped down on her front paws and began to snort and grunt, wiping her nose first with one paw, then with the other, and in this fashion breathing in what were for her enormous quanti-ties of the lethal poison. The effect was visibly devastating; she went positively berserk, forgetting about Athanasius. She rolled on the ground with a roar that began on a note of disgust—but soon turned into a grunt of sensual pleasure. The small cubs watched the frenzied behavior of their mother in astonishment. The she-bear lay there for a moment without moving, looking at the sky in ecstasy, and then she rushed over to her cubs and began to pet them and play with them in a seemingly odd and demented fashion. Instead of fleeing, Athanasius only gathered up his things (the rest of the powder, some ten grams, he carefully wrapped in the piece of paper) and watched the show, quite amused at first. "Getting a bear high on cocaine is no small feat. That's my great exploit before dying. One last ordeal before leaving the world." He glanced up. (There, amidst the grasses a relative calm had descended: the she-bear was licking and caressing her cubs, grunting with intense, inscrutable feelings. Everything was beautiful as it was before, but somehow different . . .

Suddenly the frightful lightning of consciousness rent Athanasius's brain: it was a thunderbolt of madness, but in his state of mind it seemed to him to be a revelation: "Is it possible? Could I be no better off than that miserable animal? And then is all my ecstasy and everything I'm thinking only a similar cheap swindle? And how do I know whether these thoughts of mine have any value if I can't even grasp them?" He didn't realize that what he was thinking at that moment was governed by the same principle: a narcotic state—a vicious circle—he was suffocating with shame and indignation. He quickly packed up his things and hurried back down to the foot of the Valley of the Fallen Boulders. He had already forgotten about the bear. Everything was dancing before his eyes. He staggered among the rocks and the hollows made by fallen trees, drunk and drugged to the breaking point. His heart still held out, but it might stop at any moment. He did not think about death—he wanted to live, but he didn't know how. He reached for the paper again. His mad frenzy gained strength. He didn't realize that at any instant he could drop dead from an overdose, and that that would hardly count as a suicide—he was bursting with demented, unutterable ideas—Hela, Zosia (she certainly was alive), Tempe, society, the nation, the levelers and the mystic Lohoyski, the mountains, the sun, the colors—it all was like mush, a magma of swirling images devoid of sense, but it contained a diabolic force and a desire for life and for duration throughout all eternity. Out of this chaos there gradually began to emerge a single thought that had permanence: a new transcendental law of evolution for the various aggregations of thinking beings—but what law? He still did not have any idea.

He stopped now and then and looked first at the ground, then at the forest, silent and calm, as though it were astonished by the chaotic frenzy of the poor man. And at these moments the chaos of the red whortleberries, gentians, and dried grasses suddenly took on the shape of a perfectly geometrical design, of a diabolical puzzle. He finally came out of the forest on the other slope of the Valley of Fallen Boulders, the one that he had gone down yesterday. His heart was pounding like a steam hammer, rapid, anxious to the point of madness. . . . But a certain order became established in his thoughts. He took stock quite coolly, and without fear, of his mortal danger. He felt his pulse—it was 186. He sat down to rest and drank a mugful of vodka without anything to go with it. His crazy idea became clearer and clearer, without becoming any the less crazy. "To reverse the mechanization of humanity in such a way that by utilizing the organization already achieved one could organize the collective consciousness against that apparently inexorable process. It is manifestly clear as the sun here before me that if instead of propagating socialist materialism, everyone, but absolutely everyone, from imbecile to genius, would become conscious of the fact that this system of concepts and of social action, which we are practicing at present, must lead to total stupefaction and automatization, to brutish happiness and to the disappearance of all forms of creativity, of religion, art, and philosophy (that trinity is inevitable), if that becomes clear to *everyone*, then by reacting against it through collective consciousness and action, we shall be able to reverse this process. Otherwise in five hundred years the people of the future will regard us as madmen, much as we, with slight contempt, look back at those splendid civilizations that are now extinct, because they seem to us naive in their conceptions. Instead of deceiving ourselves that everything will be all right and rejoicing in the supposed revival of religion, heralded by the appearance of various third-class mystical absurdities that serve only to lower the intellectual level already attained, let us use that intellect to gain awareness of the full monstrosity of the cattle-braining to come. Instead of drowning in the shallow optimism of cowards, we must look the terrible truth in the face, bravely, without burying our heads in the sands of delusion if we are to live through these last wretched days. Courage and cruelty toward oneself are what is needed, not narcotics. How does all that chatter by cowards trying to reconcile contemporary petty ideas, the Mystery of Being and a full stomach for the masses, differ from cocaine? It's utter rubbish either way. The worst of all are those petty optimists—the ones who block the only true way by their adaptations to the machine that's grinding them down. We should poison the whole s.o.b. tribe of semireligious intellectual self-indulgers. But just the opposite's happening—oh, my God! How can I convince the world I'm right? How can I battle against that pitiful, shallow belief in a spiritual revival? Only at the cost of momentary despair and desperate struggle—say for two hundred years—can we achieve true optimism, not narcotic euphoria, but optimism that creates a new unknown reality undreamt of even by Chwistek . . . "

Athanasius was thinking in circles, it made about as much sense as "duration without duration," and there was a certain lack of clarity and incoherence in his thoughts, but still something intelligible kept forcing its way into his brain with a relentlessness not to be denied. The next installment followed. "If everyone, but absolutely everyone made a 180-degree aboutface in ideology and stopped believing that the present road will lead to the heights of happiness, this would create a totally new collective atmosphere. What they'll get that other way will be the ultimate in materialism but the price to be paid is automation; they won't even know it, and actually will be happy, but we, whose heads still rise above that level, must *know it for them*—perhaps that is what *our greatness consists of*! It must be demonstrated that that road leads only to mindless mechanization instead of to the ideal humanity of our dreams, that it's not worth living, that it's better not to live at all than like that—oh, is it possible? All of human history says the contrary, but it would be necessary to dematerialize socialism—a diabolically difficult assignment. But then, in a collectivity rendered conscious of the task, a totally unknown social atmosphere could arise, but such a combination has never existed before, that is, the combination of a maximal social organization, not exceeding certain limits, with the universal individualization of everyone. But doesn't that require setting civilization back? Perhaps at the beginning, but later the possibilities are incalculable—at any rate instead of the boredom of certain automatism there's something unknown. Only through the intellect can we accomplish this, and not through a deliberate retreat into nonsense, into a once great creative religion that has degenerated. Then, only then, can new sources of creativity burst forth, and not now, in this state of semimystical cowardice. Perhaps then new religions will arise of which we now can have no idea. Something unimaginable is hidden beyond all this, the possibilities are unlimited—but we must have courage, courage! Physical revivals offer only palliatives in the fight against degeneration—they must succumb to the superior force of degeneration, even if nonparticipation in sports were punished by the death sentence. Social adhesiveness, which creates degenerative conditions, is infinite—the strength of the individual is limited. For what purpose do we possess the intellect, which at present is only a symptom of our decadence? Do we have it only for systematically besotting ourselves with pragmatism, Bergsonism, pluralism, and for systematically cattle-braining ourselves in a society ideally arranged from a technical point of view? No—use it as an antidote to mechanization. Change the course of civilization without changing its momentum. At any rate no one will stop it now any other way—that monster will keep growing until it devours itself and then it will be happy. And then it will digest itself and then . . . And what will be left? A little pile of . . . And what of it, if the automated people of the future are happy and fail to realize how far they have fallen? We know it for them now and are obliged to protect them from it. In such a general atmosphere there could arise new species of people, of problems, of creativity, about which at present we know nothing and can form no idea."

His "opuscule" on the necessity of mechanization, regarded as metaphysical and transcendental à la Cornelius (he repeated this aloud for himself and for the astonished fir trees surrounding him), now seemed to him clever, but one-sided and incomplete. "That was an interpretation of the known facts that followed necessarily from the old premises, but this idea is totally new and it also has an element of the transcendental: the possibility of absolute necessity. Absolute? No, perhaps not—because my idea is a diabolical case of pure chance, it does not result in any necessary way from the social situation—although a comparable idea must always arise in times of decadence, but that's not the point now—the idea exists, and that's all that counts."

He took another swig of vodka followed by another pinch of cocaine and now for the first time he realized that he must return to the valley with his new idea, make Tempe understand it and use him to create an organization for raising the public consciousness, utilizing for that purpose the already existing organization of the new state. His problems with Hela, Zosia, and that whole pitiful mess of personal experiences shriveled and turned to ashes in the artificial bonfire of his madness. And he owed it all to the she-bear—and of course to his much loved and hated coco. "Ha, ha! That's hilarious," he laughed a demented laugh, going slowly up the sunlit slope toward the cliffs of Bydlisko—it was shorter that way than through Bystry Przechód. He had the impression that it wasn't yesterday that he had passed by there, but many years ago—he had lived through so much since he had parted with his peasant guide, Jasiek. And yet what a splendid composition those last few days made! The former "artist of life" (a type known from third-class literary salons) reawakened within him. He walked slowly because he had to spare his heart, indispensable to all mankind—now if it burst, no one would know his great idea, and there was no telling if it would ever take shape again in someone else's mind. Now he no longer feared the guards on either side of the border—just as had happened during the duel when he was shielded by his love for Zosia. He was going alone toward them all with his "great" idea, which would finally justify his wretched existence. When he reached the first pass, a magnificent view unfolded before him. Athanasius was plunged into unbounded ecstasy. Dissolved in the afternoon mist, the mountains, drunk on their own beauty, seemed to be a dream of themselves. And at the same time their seemingly objective beauty was unrelated to the fact that it was he who was looking at them. They were beautiful in and of themselves. In their beauty he now was truly joined to Zosia's spirit, and even—oh, the wretchedness of his delusions!—he felt a certain superiority to it. Her ghost did not oppress him—on the contrary, he talked with it (somewhat condescendingly) on an equal to equal basis. He found the spot where Hela had twisted her ankle the previous winter. He stopped there for a moment, looking at the same stones. Yes—the stones were the same, eternally young, but he was someone entirely different. He had the impression that everything about India in the past was a huge balloon fastened to that leg, which no longer even existed.

The sun was setting when Athanasius, still not having met anyone, started down into the valley. On the way he took several strong doses of coco—to fortify his nervous system, as he said to himself—going down he could indulge himself that much. His iron heart, which only a bullet could destroy, withstood even that. He felt himself in harmony with the entire world and an otherwordly voluptuousness made his whole being expand. He was mentally lucid with the kind of lucidity typical of a bad case of poisoning by that infernal drug; for other people—if there had been any and if they had been able to see his thoughts, he would have been an out-and-out madman. The immensity of the world engulfed him, the purple reflections on the cliffs seemed to emanate from his own innards—he felt them inside him, he was everything, he actually dissolved into actual infinity with as much freedom as had Georg Cantor on paper with the aid of his innocent and unassuming little signs. The sky seemed to be a kind of Sardanapalus's baldachin (from some painting or other) of his glory, a monstrous metaphysical luxury created exclusively for him—by whom? The idea of a personal God loomed, as it had before, in an infinite but spaceless abyss (when was that, dear God!). "If you exist and if you see me, forgive me. Never, never, never again," he whispered in the highest ecstasy, in a euphoria bordering on nonbeing, or rather bordering on being turned upside down—it was heaven, heaven was it, really and truly.

He smiled at the world, as a small child smiles at marvelous, incredibly lovely toys—he was in heaven at that moment—and everything was related for him to the vision of a wonderful, unimaginable humanity created by his great idea. He was proud, but with the noble pride of a sage, and at the same time he humbled himself before the great anonymous force that had given him such a gift—perhaps it actually was God. What his life would be like, he did not know nor did he want to know. (One thing was strange: for two days he had not once thought of his dead mother—as though she had never existed at all.) Everything would come out all right, once the idea he had just discovered took concrete shape. Others would look after the technical realization and the detailed, nondilettantish implementation. That did not concern him. Just to put the whole machine in motion—that was the crucial task.

It was already growing dark when he reached the little mountain restaurant which the previous winter had been the starting point for all their expeditions—it was where they brought Hela with her supposedly sprained ankle. The stars shone mysteriously—they sparkled against the black void of the sky like visible symbols of the eternal mystery. That night Athanasius did not sense any disharmony between the northern sky and the southern sky—the entire universe belonged to him, abandoned itself to him, transfixed him, fused with him in Absolute Unity. Lights gleamed down below. Suddenly Athanasius realized that he had to cross the frontier at the border checkpoint and he pulled himself together a bit, or so he thought—he was actually stoned out of his mind on cocaine. He had the necessary documents (identity papers for a junior grade functionary), he was the friend of the all-powerful Tempe—but was he still? He had seduced Tempe's girlfriend Gina—well, somehow it would work out all right. As he went along, he kept looking at the stars, hoping that his previous thoughts would come back to him. "Dear Vega—she's racing toward us at seventy-five kilometers a second, maybe someday she'll enter our system and begin to rotate with our sun around a common center of gravity. What a wonderful thing that would be to see two suns . . . "

A dark silhouette sprang up before him in the shadows, as though it had crept out of the ground.

"Halt! Who goes there?! Give the password!" croaked a hoarse voice, and Athanasius had a precise vision of the face out of whose mouth those words issued.

The whole situation was etched with diabolical, hypernatural clarity. There was nothing for him to be afraid of: he had a relatively clean conscience and his papers were in order.

"I don't know the password. Friend. Lost in the mountains. Friend, friend," he repeated once more, hearing a click familiar to him from the war.

"What the hell you doin' here?" the voice said again, and Athanasius heard the rifle being reloaded. "Wasn't ready to fire, jeez, I could have made a run for it," he thought.

"Take me to your commander," he said brusquely.

"You gonna order me what to do? When I put a bullet through your gut that's the end of you. We got orders to shoot on sight," said the dark mass, already a little less sure of itself.

"Do what I tell you, comrade. You don't know who you're talking to: I'm a friend of comrade Commissar Tempe."

"Damn right I don't know. Step forward."

Menaced by the gun barrel, Athanasius stepped forward, and the guard followed after him, rifle at the ready, almost hitting him in his slightly arthritic shoulder blades with the bayonet. In the distance the waters of the raging streams could be heard and a cool breeze came down from the mountains. "As ever," thought Athanasius. There was such unfathomable magic in those words that absolutely nothing could possibly express it.

"Comrade Commander! A prisoner of war!" the guard yelled in front of the door to a little hut in which a light was shining.

Someone came out, followed by three big hulks with bayonets fixed on the barrels of their rifles.

"Vot ees up?" asked the "someone" with a slight Russian accent. "How you dare leave post, you low dog shit? Know vot ees for that punishment? Eh? Why you no right away shoot?"

"How come they're speaking that bastard Russian dialect here?" Athanasius wondered and at the same moment remembered that a large number of his Russified compatriots and even some native Russians had come to his country to help in the local revolution.

"He came from the Luptov side. Says he's a friend of comrade Commissar Tempe. Lost his way." The guard spoke in obvious terror.

Athanasius sensed unpleasant tension in the space all around them.

"Don't care who is he, what says he. I got orders. Shoot them both on spot," he said to the other three guards, accenting his words in a sinister fashion.

More troops came out of the hut.

"But I . . . ," the guard began.

"Shut trap! Either I shoot you or they shoot me and so on up line," the chief interrupted him.

Athanasius had kept quiet until then, convinced that things would take a favorable turn. He was sure he would go on living with his great idea in his head, cocaine in his blood, and the documents in his pocket. Now he was able to form an idea of how Sajetan Tempe's demonic power extended his magnetic field to the furthest frontiers of his realm, organizing the distant points into new nuclei of potentials. The hulks hadn't budged.

"Comrade, I . . . ," the guard began again in a voice quivering with boundless fear, almost with the certainty of death.

"I'm a junior grade functionary," Athanasius interrupted him and handed his papers to the individual who spoke with the Russian accent.

Meanwhile the hulks disarmed the guard, who was moaning softly. Someone else took his place. The one without a rifle read or rather glanced through his papers (by the light of an electric lantern).

"So what you doing on Luptov side? And how you get there? Eh?"

"I got lost," Athanasius said in a slightly trembling voice.

He wasn't afraid of anything, but he was sorry to have been caught doing something illegal and to be forced to lie. And why did he have to lie? Lying was exactly what sealed his fate—or perhaps what saved him. Who can tell anything until the last second? Perhaps it would have been better to say he had come there on purpose—or perhaps it would have been worse. In any case it was now clear the reign of terror was in full swing.

"So you come to spy on us for Luptov counterrevolutionaries? Spying, eh? Put him up against vall with Maciej! At stake my head and your heads too."

It was obvious that this was the first incident of the kind to happen there.

"Comrade, I have certain very important information for the Commissar of Internal Affairs. I'm his childhood friend."

Now, as he heard his own voice, Athanasius felt that it wasn't going to work, that he had played all his trumps. But he wasn't afraid—he was beyond such categories: where? He had no idea. He was looking on from outside as though he were not there, but someone else was, someone alien and indifferent and frightful because of that indifference. He felt his own suppressed power like a volcano that cannot erupt. He was suffocating, but he told himself that those were his last words to living beings—from then on he would only be silent—he would not even wince, no matter what happened. He was already in another world, the one he had dreamed of since childhood, the world beyond life and now even beyond cocaine. But he realized that he had managed to hoist himself up there only by means of that accursed fine-grained powder. "At that price alone can the end of life be beautiful," he thought. And coming already from the other world here on earth, he heard a voice that was no longer the voice of a Russified leveler, but the voice of fate itself, which meant something other than it said.

"Shut trap! Against vall!" said the voice from the world beyond, but *in reverse*. "Platoon, fall in!"

The bodily parts of the individual beings started clinking and clanking. Athanasius reached for a final dose. He had all the rest of that filthy stuff in the pocket of his jacket. He thought that even if he didn't have it (that last dose), he'd be no different. "Yes—it's beautiful—it's more beautiful than that view of the amphitheater of peaks in the Valley of Fallen Boulders. In any case I'm sure I'd be above all that anyhow." He did not even know very well himself what he was actually thinking. The truth of the final moment—who will weigh it and assess its true value? Drugs or no drugs, these are ultimate matters not subject to verification. The absolute condensed in a pill, yes, but who will there be to grasp it? Who? Might it be that a man lies the most when he has his back up against the "metaphysical wall"? Unfortunately Athanasius had no one to pretend in front of. Others have died differently, but *in point of fact* no one living knows how. The "I"—this "I" and not any other, identical to itself once in all eternity—can die only that one way, and not any other. Zosia's ghost clasped Athanasius in a passionate earthly embrace. At last! A moment more, and he might have been too late. There was no one near him except her. They took their places. He saw distinctly in front of him only the blinding glare of the electric lantern and the murky pack of thugs with their rifles aimed. Above them loomed the black mass of the mountains, out of whose midst a torrent murmured something unintelligible—a cold breeze bore this voice. The stars shone almost without twinkling in the luminous heavens. The sky was indifferent as though congealed. Athanasius tried in vain to reach an understanding with the stars. To no avail. The sound of rifles. "All right—it's now. I'm ready." Beside him stood that alien being because of whom Athanasius was dying. He could almost feel the man's body trembling.

"Aim! Fire!!!" (If only it's not where Prepoudrech shot him in the duel!) Detonation and frightful pain in the stomach, a pain to which he had been psychically insensitive for a long time (for a few minutes), the first intense physical pain in his life—the first and the last. "Must be the liver." And at the same time the voluptuous feeling that he had no heart and that it would never, never beat again. One of the bullets, the wisest of all, went straight through his heart. With a feeling of unearthly voluptuousness, drowning in black non-being, imbued with the essence of life, with what is not only an illusion of irreconcilable contradictions but *actually the thing itself,* unique and yet forever inaccessible, even at the moment of death, but only in the tiny infinity of time just after death . . . What does that mean? In any case it wasn't Athanasius anymore (but this time really, no joking) who heard the reloading, the order to shoot, and then the scream of the guard—Maciej screamed, evidently painfully wounded too, his howling growing feebler and feebler. Athanasius no longer knew that these were his final impressions. *He died listening to the howling of another human being*—it was only in his ears that the sound grew fainter and fainter . . . Maciej howled more and more abjectly—they had to shoot him a second time. Coming back to the previous subject: Doesn't an amoeba in a glass of water feel the same thing? It feels it but is incapable of expressing it. And are we able to? No, we aren't able to either. Athanasius had finally stopped living. . . .

Of course for Athanasius it was better that they killed him that night. You can imagine what a hangover he would have had the next day when, once sobered up, he discovered that his great idea was total rubbish, and what's worse, when he experienced the hideous aftereffects of an overdose of coco, "the white fairy." Ugh!

"Well, so there's one less superfluous man in the world—two actually . . . although . . . ," said someone (probably the most intelligent of the lot) in the group that did the shooting as they were entering the hut. Soon they were all snoring, with the exception of the new sentry, who undoubtedly was guarding Tempe's realm more diligently than his predecessor—making an example is a useful thing from time to time. In the background the mountains grew darker and darker and the quiet stars just barely twinkled; in the silence there could sometimes be heard the murmuring of the torrent, carried by the cold breeze. But who saw or heard it? No one could say with regret: "as ever." . . .

Yes, it was better that some people had died, particularly Athanasius. To live without being capable of either life or death, with the consciousness of the pettiness and wretchedness of one's own great ideas, without loving anyone or being loved by anyone, to be completely alone in the infinite, absurd (meaning here something subjective) cosmos—is something downright horrible.

Everyone knows what the subsequent destiny of the country was under the regime of Sajetan Tempe, who was always right—so there's no need to say anything more about it.

"Do some useful work," as Athanasius's old aunt used to say (it's time his name was forgotten). Those among the remnants of the old days who survived everything did settle down to work—but there weren't many of them. A new breed of people arose, different than before. . . . But *what kind* no one could imagine, or even have the vaguest idea.

And all the same everything is fine, everything is just fine. What? That's not true? It's fine, dammit, and whoever says the contrary will get smacked in the mug!

24 AUGUST 1926

LETTERS TO MALINOWSKI, 1927-29

■

[ZAKOPANE]
26 AUGUST 1927

Dear Bronio:

I haven't written to you but to your wife, since I consider that after a year of silence writing letters in the style you used was *somehow* unseemly. I showed your letter to Chwiston (with whom I'm on rather distant terms again) and he was indignant. But that's not really the issue. Your last letter, although a bit gloomy, gave me pleasure precisely on account of the absence of male bluster in the whorehouse style. I'm sorry that all those things that various people dream of as the height of happiness fail to satisfy you in any essential way. What can be done about it? Perhaps you should come back to Olcza. I'd gladly have long talks with you, but writing letters is an impossibility for me. I'd like to keep in touch with you so that when we do meet we won't be total strangers to each other. My inner state is pretty bad, and my external situation is hardly very encouraging. Maybe I'll become a film actor. (Quite seriously—I've had an offer.) It would be very interesting if you wrote, no matter how briefly, why you don't like my novel *Farewell to Autumn*. I'm dreaming about taking a trip, even to Spain would do. Write before too long, and maybe some kind of correspondence will get started. A heartfelt hug from me. I'd like you to feel my presence in the infinite absurdity of Existence. I send warm greetings to Mrs. Malinowski and your two daughters. Mother sends her regards to you and your wife.

Your Witkacy

11 MAY 1929

Dear Malinowski:

How can I explain the total lack of your letters and your not coming to see me the last time you were in Zakopane, when you spent time with that bloody and damned Chwistek and called me a Don Juan (as he told me with pleasure). Write at once or "taste not the Pierian Spring."

Yours Truly
Witkacy

Rules of the S. I. Witkiewicz Portrait-Painting Firm

■

Motto:

The customer must be satisfied.

Misunderstandings are ruled out.

The rules are published so as to spare the firm the necessity of repeating the same thing over and over again.

#1. The firm produces portraits of the following types:

1. Type A—Comparatively speaking, the most as it were, "spruced up" type. Suitable rather for women's faces than for men's. "Slick" execution, with a certain loss of character in the interests of beautification, or accentuation of "prettiness."

2. Type B—More emphasis on character but without any trace of caricature. Work making greater use of sharp line than type A, with a certain touch of character traits, which does not preclude "prettiness" in women's portraits. Objective attitude to the model.

3. Type B + s (supplement)—Intensification of character, bordering on the caricatural. The head larger than natural size. The possibility of preserving "prettiness" in women's portraits, and even of intensifying it in the direction of the "demonic."

4. Type C, C + Co, E, C + H, C + Co + E, etc.—These types, executed with the aid of C_2H_5OH and narcotics of a superior grade, are at

present ruled out. Subjective characterization of the model, caricatural intensification both formal and psychological are not ruled out. Approaches abstract composition, otherwise known as "Pure Form."

5. Type D—The same results without recourse to any artificial means.

6. Type E—Combinations of D with the preceding types. Spontaneous psychological interpretation at the discretion of the firm. The effect achieved may be the exact equivalent of that produced by types A and B—the manner by which it is attained is different, as is the method of execution, which may take various forms but never exceeds the limit(s). A combination of E + s is likewise available upon request.

Type E is not always possible to execute.

7. Children's type—(B + E)—Because children can never sit still, the purer type B is in most instances impossible—the execution rather takes the form of a sketch.

In general, the firm does not pay much attention to the rendering of clothing and accessories. The question of the background concerns only the firm—demands in this regard are not considered. Depending on the disposition of the firm and the difficulties of rendering a particular face, the portrait may be executed in one, two, three, and even up to five sittings. For large portraits showing the upper body or full figure, the number of sittings may even reach twenty.

The number of sittings does not determine the excellence of the product.

#2. The basic novelty offered by the firm as compared to the usual practice is the customer's option of rejecting a portrait if it does not suit him either because of the execution or because of the degree of likeness. *In such cases the customer pays one-third of the price, and the portrait becomes the property of the firm.* The customer does not have the right to demand that the portrait be destroyed. This clause, naturally, applies only to the pure types: A, B, and E, *without supplement (s)*—that is, without any supplement of exaggerated characteristics, or in other words the types that appear in series. This clause was introduced because it is impossible to tell what will satisfy the client. An exact agreement is desirable, based upon a firm and definite decision by the model as to the type requested. An album of samples (but by no means ones "of no value") is available for inspection at the premises of the firm. The customer receives a guarantee in that the firm in its own self-interest does not issue works that could damage its trademark. A situation could occur in which the firm itself would not sign its own product.

#3. Any sort of criticism on the part of the customer is absolutely ruled out. The customer may not like the portrait, but the firm cannot permit even the most discreet comments without giving its special authorization. If the firm had allowed itself the luxury of listening to customers' opinions, it would have gone mad a long time ago. *We place special emphasis on this rule, since the most difficult thing is to restrain the customer from making remarks that are entirely uncalled-for.* The portrait is either accepted or rejected—yes or no, without any explanations whatsoever as to why. Inadmissible criticism likewise includes remarks about whether or not it is a good likeness, observations concerning the background, covering part of the face in the portrait with one's hand so as to imply that this part really isn't the way it should be, comments such as, "I am too pretty," "Do I look that sad?" "That's not me," and all other opinions of that sort, whether favorable or unfavorable. After due consideration, and possibly consultation with third parties, the customer says yes (or no) and that's all there is to it—then he goes (or does not go) up to what is called the "cashier's window," that is, he simply hands over the agreed-upon sum to the firm. Given the incredible difficulty of the profession, the firm's nerves must be spared.

#4. Asking the firm for its opinion of a finished portrait is not permissible, nor is any discussion about a work in progress.

#5. The firm reserves the right to paint without any witnesses, if that is possible.

#6. Portraits of women with bare necks and shoulders cost one-third more. Each arm costs one-third of the total price. For portraits showing the upper body or full figure, special agreements must be drawn up.

#7. The portrait may not be viewed until finished.

#8. The technique used is a combination of charcoal, crayon, pencil, and pastel. All remarks with regard to technical matters are ruled out, as are likewise demands for alterations.

#9. The firm undertakes the painting of portraits outside the firm's premises only in exceptional circumstances (sickness, advanced age, etc.), in which case the firm must be guaranteed a secret receptacle in which the unfinished portrait may be kept under lock and key.

#10. Customers are obliged to appear punctually for the sittings, since waiting has a bad effect on the firm's mood and may have an adverse effect on the execution of the product.

#11. The firm offers advice on the framing and packing of portraits but does not provide these services. Further discussion about types of frames is ruled out.

#12. The firm allows total freedom as to the model's clothing and *quite definitely does not voice any opinion in this regard.*

#13. The firm urges a careful perusal of the rules. Lacking any powers of enforcement, the firm counts on the tact and good will of its customers to meet the terms. Reading through and concurring with the rules is taken as equivalent to *concluding an agreement.* Discussion about the rules is inadmissible.

#14. An agreement on the installment plan or by bank draft is not ruled out. Given the low prices the firm charges, requests for reductions are not advisable. Before the portrait is begun, the customer pays one-third of the price as a down payment.

#15. A customer who obtains portrait commissions for the firm—that is to say, who acts as "an agent of the firm"—upon providing orders for the sum of 100 złotys receives as a premium his own portrait or that of any person he wishes in the type of his choice.

#16. Notices sent by the firm to former customers announcing its presence at a given location are not intended to force them to have new portraits painted, but rather to assist friends of these customers in placing orders, since having seen the firm's work they may wish something similar themselves.

WARSAW, **1928**
THE "S. I. WITKIEWICZ" FIRM

Price List

Type A = 350

Type B = 250

Type B + s = 150

Type E = 150–250

Type C = without price

Type D = 100

Children's type = 150–250

NARCOTICS: NICOTINE, ALCOHOL, COCAINE, PEYOTE, MORPHINE, AND ETHER

In this book everything is indeed strangely mixed up.
■ Henryk Sienkiewicz, *With Fire and Sword*

Preface

Since by means of "free artistic creativity," i.e., "a little birdie singing on a branch," I have been unable to do anything for society or for the nation, I have decided, after a series of experiments, to share with the public my views on narcotics, starting with the most commonplace, tobacco, and ending with what is surely the strangest, peyote (for which I reserve a special place); in so doing, I hope to offer at least some small help to the powers of good in the battle against these most frightful enemies of mankind (after war, poverty, and disease). Perhaps this work too (owing to the tone in which bitter truths are formulated) will be taken facetiously or negatively, as was the case with my aesthetics, philosophy, plays, essential portraits, early compositions in oils, and other "free productions." I officially declare that I am writing seriously and that I finally wish to do something directly useful, but there is no way of dealing with idiots and dishonest people, as I have had occasion to become convinced during the course of my rather sorry career. If you say to someone, "You are stupid, learn, and perhaps you will grow wise," it won't help at all, because a stupid person is also conceited and even if he could

243

grow wise through hard work, his presumption would prevent him from getting out of the vicious circle he's in. To say to a scoundrel, "It's not nice to be such a stinker, stop and think, try to improve," is wasted breath: we fail to understand that the majority of rascals are quite consciously scummish—they know what they are and do not wish to be otherwise as long as they can effectively mask their swinishness. "Can we *pardon* a stick for being a stick," as Tadeusz Szymberski used to say—and he was right.

Once I was a "fighting man," a combatant par excellence; I had my ideas and I was ready to fight for them—wherever I could and with whomever I could. I have in no way abandoned my ideas (Pure Form in painting and theater and reform of criticism in the arts), I have simply come to the conclusion that in any case my ideas are at present untimely and that perhaps their time has definitely passed. What I maintained even before the war and discussed in the fourth part of my book *New Forms in Painting*, namely, that art is dying, is now taking place before our eyes, and accordingly, whether there will be art criticism in my sense of the term, i.e., formal criticism, and what it will be like are questions without any meaning. It is another matter if we are talking about literature with no pretensions of being art—there is still something to be said on the subject and perhaps I will eventually speak out. At present I am a relatively unperturbed middle-aged individual who no longer dreams of any "exploits" in the grand manner and who desires to bring to a tolerable end this life, about which so far at least, despite the defeats and setbacks, I have no regrets. Come what may. I must stress only that the present "opuscule" will have a highly personal character, and thus will be to some degree posthumous in nature. This is not megalomania or the desire to make myself (until now of no use to anyone) the center of interest for people occupied with something else far more agreeable. But in writing about my personal experiences I cannot omit myself. At any rate, what will appear on these pages in an accessible manner is a part of the truth about my life, a part that will be directly useful to the general public.

But what effect can this have in face of the outrageous gossip that is being circulated about me? In this respect, I appear to have been singled out, even in this exceptionally scandalmongering society of ours where everyone enjoys backbiting. Despite my complete lack of megalomania, which I stress in all honesty, I have the impression that not every Pole, taken on the average, can boast of the wide range of lies and absurdities that have been and that continue to be told about me. This is not the place to enter into the causes of this phenomenon, but I believe that a certain role in generating widespread hostility toward me has been played by the difficulty in squashing me intellectually that has been experienced by people not suitably qualified for the task, and, second, by a certain indifference on my part to public opinion, as a result of which many actions, which if done by someone else would have passed without notice (such as drinking three vodkas in a bar), have in my case aroused indignation harmful to me and out of proportion to their significance. Enough said on the subject.

So I am starting today (6 Feb. 1930) to write this book "in S," which means a state of smoking. Tomorrow, as usual, I shall stop smoking—I think that this time it will be definitively, or for a very long time—and I shall write the chapter on nicotine while trying to give up cigarettes, although there is the possibility that in the course of the writing I shall start smoking again and I "shall not fail to admit" this fact to my eventual readers. It has happened so many times! I have been fighting against smoking for the past twenty-eight years, and despite frequent periods of abstinence (lasting up to several weeks), I have not managed to conquer it entirely. The same result is possible now too, despite my undertaking the present work. However, the moment is coming when it will be a necessity unless I am to give up all my higher aspirations for myself. Details on the subject will come later. I believe that this method of notation—i.e., in NS_1,* or in a state of nonsmoking—will prove quite significant, since while craving a narcotic, both loved and hated, from what is surely the lowest category (cursed be the Indians and those who brought us the filthy stuff), I will be better able to analyze the temptations that assail the habitual smoker and to suggest the means of resisting them by remembering the hideous sensation (often hidden from oneself and from others) that one experiences on going back to that filthy, useless, and stupefying poison. In fact, I recently stopped smoking for four days (everyone knows that the second day is the worst and that on the third a change for the better begins), until "bang" I started smoking again (I shall analyze the mechanism of this phenomenon later) and "plump" it was all to do over again. Of course, I have not held out and I smoked a cigarette this morning—just to see what it all looks like over in S. Not that I could not last "any longer," but for one simple reason: to observe the world once more from "the other side" (from the perspective of deterioration, stupefaction, despondency, etc.), and then it will definitely be *Schluss*. That is how I justify the whole thing to myself. No—

---

*The numbers following NS indicate the number of days. I use this same notation on my drawings. [In Polish, NP for *Nie-Palenie*.—Trans.]

the worst of it is the weakness—*durchhalten*—just how awful I shall discuss in the chapter on nicotine. I've lighted up a cigarette—that is the sad fact (that really is of no concern to anyone, but what does matter are all the others, the thousands and millions of the asphyxiated, the besotted, and the enfeebled)—and I am writing the rest of this preface in a total fog. I actually wanted to continue working on my philosophical treatise (a very risky business and I still do not know what will come of it), but this turned out to be absolutely impossible: owing to obtuseness, lack of what Stefan Glass, doctor of mathematics, calls *igrivost' uma* [liveliness of mind], lack of ability to concentrate adequately. These are only preliminary admissions—it will all be described "in full detail" later on. I began to write this preface in despair at not being able, because of nicotine poisoning, to get to work on anything worthwhile, hoping at least to start this "opuscule" and justify my own existence to myself. Does not all "creative" work spring from such sources?

Coming back to public opinion: I have been and still am an inveterate smoker who has been fighting heroically with the frightful habit for the past twenty-eight years. To some extent I could be considered at *certain periods* an inveterate drunkard, if we can regard as such (the standards—the criteria—vary) someone who gets sozzled on the average once a week then does not drink much for a month, or even longer, and who only once in his life went on a five-day binge (on the occasion of a theatrical premiere—a highly extenuating circumstance) and no more than ten times on three-day binges, and who never swigged down vodka in the morning while shaving. But I have never been a cocaine addict—that I emphatically deny, although for many perverse morons even my declaration may actually be taken as proof of what I am denying. If I can be called an occasional drunkard, a *Wochensäufer*, for a span of ten years, I would suggest giving me the name of *Quartelkokainist* for a period of three years, and even that would be a great exaggeration. Twice in my life I took cocaine when sober and immediately tried to wash away the filthy stuff with booze. The other instances of my using that drug (which I have never hidden, signing the drawings done in this state with the appropriate symbol Co) were always connected with wild *popoiki* [Russian, "sprees"] *à la manière russe*. I was never a morphine addict, having an allergic reaction to that panacea (once in my life I had a tiny injection and almost died of it) or an ether sniffer, because of a lack of faith in ether, although I have taken it several times in my life: with vodka and by inhalation. The drawings, to be sure, were quite interesting and when one inhales it, the sensation of the world and the body fading out, followed by a "metaphysical loneliness in a spatial desert," is amusing, but somehow it never made a convert of me. Dr. Dezydery Prokopowicz, who has compiled the section on ether in this "opuscule," is of another opinion. Bohdan Filipowski, an occultist and inveterate morphine addict for many years, will deal with his favorite drug, the very thought of which makes me go cold all over—so frightful were the things I went through back then in St. Petersburg when for four hours I battled death, in the midst of vomiting and suspended heartbeats. So I emphatically refute all charges as to my habitual use of the previously mentioned drugs, while admitting to the sporadic use of peyote and mescaline, the first manufactured by Dr. Rouhier, the second a product of the splendid firm Merck. I likewise deny, while I am at it, that I am given to homosexuality, for which I feel the deepest repugnance; or that I have been having sexual relations with my Siamese cat, Schyzia (also known as Schizophrenia, Isotta, Sabina, whom I like a lot, but nothing beyond that), and that the kittens—not even purebred, anyhow—which she gave birth to looked like me; or that I had a portrait booth at the Poznań Exposition where I did ten-minute portraits for two złotys each (what won't those bastards think of!); or that I am a fast talker and a womanizer who never misses an opportunity to chase skirts; or that I seduce other men's wives, go about in a frock coat on Giewont (I never had a frock coat in my life), write plays as a joke, trick everyone and laugh at everything, and do not know how to draw. That is all malicious gossip invented by ugly harpies, morons, and idiots, and most of all by bastards who want to ruin my reputation. I refute all the calumnies that I know of and I reject in advance all those that will be circulated about me in Zakopane and its environs. *Schluss.*

One more thing: someone may think I am writing this book for self-promotion. Far from it: it will include revelations that will not bring me any honor, but its principal goal is to protect future generations from the two most atrocious "stupefiers" (*stupéfiants*): tobacco and alcohol, all the more dangerous because they are legal and their harmfulness is insufficiently recognized. Today the elite of mankind takes up the "white" narcotics of a superior brand, and these are not as dangerous—being the aristocracy of drug addiction. Most dangerous are the gray, everyday, democratic poisons that everyone can indulge in with impunity.

My method is purely psychological. I am concerned with drawing attention to the psychic consequences of these poisons, consequences that anyone, even a beginner, can notice in himself on a small scale long before he becomes completely dominated by them. I will not break eggs (hen's) before your eyes and toss them into 200 proof alcohol to show you how the whites harden on contact with "the purest of liquids" (as, if I remember correctly, Prince Giedroyć did); nor will I show you X-rays of a smoker's blackened lungs and swollen heart or a drunkard's degenerated liver or a cocaine addict's stomach shrunken to the size of a fist—"I shall not play you a sad song. Oh, shade, but my triumph will be proud and cruel . . . ," etc.—I want to present to you the slight *psychic* alterations that in their ultimate development reveal a picture of a completely different personality than existed at the point of departure, a personality spiritually deformed, devoid of any *Geist* (the Polish word for "soul" does not convey the same thing as the German *Geist* or the French *esprit*—knack, dash, push, spark, drive, etc.), of any creative force and of all that impetus toward the Unknown, for which one needs the daring and nonchalance that are systematically killed by such hideous addiction. What has saved me from the effects of nicotine, from which until now I have not been able to free myself entirely, is the fact that frequently and sometimes for rather long intervals (several weeks) I've stopped smoking so that on the whole I've actually not been smoking for a half or a third of the year. Of course, the effect of such abstinence par intermittence could not be as beneficial as prolonged and uninterrupted periods of total renunciation— but it still has accomplished something. But those who smoke constantly, and who in 90% of the cases must smoke more and more, are systematically committing spiritual suicide on the installment plan, imperceptibly, without even knowing it themselves, rendering every experience colorless and insipid and destroying the most precious thing, the intellect, for the sake of a virtually nonexistent pleasure. Because does the inveterate smoker really experience any kind of pleasure? Only a negative pleasure—the assuagement of a repulsive and unnatural need. The same thing holds true of all narcotics if the person in question reaches a sufficiently high level of addiction.

If you show an adolescent of sixteen the liver of an alcoholic of forty, hypertrophied and degenerate, will he stop drinking at the sight? No—the age of forty is too far off for a sixteen year old, it is something unimaginable—I know that from my own experience. And besides, everyone says: "Oh! Whether I live a few years more or less is *ganz wurst und pomade*—what counts is the present moment." And then, when those last five years come, which the poor wretch relinquished so heedlessly and which may in fact be taken away from him, he does his utmost to prolong a life that in most cases *is not worth prolonging*. At that point a person like that lives on after his own death, rendered internally imbecilic and externally decrepit too, incapable of doing constructive work, transformed into a hypochondriac, checking his pulse every five minutes and resorting to medicines, which cannot rejuvenate degenerate cells. It is imperative to show the psychic side effects, whose gradual encroachments (*schleichender Vorgang*—ugh! What horror!) are not visible to everyone and particularly not to someone who takes a given narcotic regularly without ever stopping. Superior narcotics produce violent reactions—their harmfulness is immediately apparent. The desire to overcome these reactions, and not a craving for the direct effects of the drugs, is often the reason why people become addicted. Nicotine does not produce a distinct "hangover" (*Katzenjammer*) and therefore is dangerous for the general public. In most cases only individuals somehow predisposed in that direction, who are degenerate and not worth much anyhow, can unreservedly grow habituated to cocaine or morphine. Tobacco asphyxiates, and in time alcohol gradually consumes the best brains. There are people who say, "I smoke and drink, it doesn't do me any harm and I feel wonderful"—of course, until the day of reckoning comes. A whole host of slight psychosomatic indispositions slowly keep accumulating, only to break out suddenly in the form of a clearly defined psychic or physical disorder. But just think, my wretched friend, how marvelous you would feel if you stopped entirely, since your organism is so strong that even being constantly poisoned it still is capable of functioning tolerably well. How will you ever find out what you would be if you stopped? It is impossible to measure and to assess the harm being done. Only those who have stopped and then started again know a little something about it. What wouldn't I give to have back the twenty-eight years during which I've been smoking, and that was with numerous breaks. And now when it is one hundred times more harmful for me than when I was eighteen years old, it is also a hundred times more difficult for me to give up the repulsive habit than in "the good old days." And it is frightful to think of what it must be like for confirmed alcoholics and cocaine addicts, among whom I cannot rank myself no matter how much my "enemies" might wish it were so.

So here is the plan: the ball is tomorrow, I get plastered and the day after I shall go on the wagon. It is much easier to get the best of nicotine with just the trace of a postalcoholic "hangover."

7 FEBRUARY 1930

Nicotine

Lev Tolstoy claimed, I am told, that a person who has never in his life smoked a cigarette is incapable of committing a true crime in the fullest sense of the word. There is a certain amount of exaggeration in that view, since we know that, in Europe for example, long before tobacco was introduced people cut one another's throats no less enthusiastically. Perhaps alcohol helped them do it—who knows, it is not my intention to write a history of narcotics throughout the entire world. Besides, once there was no alcohol either. But however far back one goes in human history, one can always come across some "narcotic phantasm." Evidently when human consciousness reached a certain level of acuteness, it simply could not live with itself in the midst of the metaphysical dread of Existence and had somehow to assuage its own perspicacity. The use of narcotics was always tied to religious rites and constituted an integral part of the various cults. Religion and art, after all, were once veils over the Eternal Mystery that shone with too hideous a glare from the black chasm of Being. Only starting with Greece does the conceptual battle with this mystery begin—a battle that must, of course, end in defeat. We are living in a period of violent transition. In our times all the elements of the past and of the emerging future are intermingled. Given the state of social tranquilization toward which we are heading, I think the time is drawing near for the end of all illusions, which means the end of narcotics as well. Today's scourge of drug addiction also marks their death throes at the point where the past and the future intersect. Since it is preferable for something gangrened and unfit for life to wither away as quickly as possible, the present work is intended to help speed up the process. What once had a function and served as something creative, now may prove to be an obstacle hindering the consolidation of mankind's future regime. Undoubtedly narcotics belong to that class of obstacles, although the role of a few (nicotine and alcohol) may still appear to some people as being socially beneficial. . . .

There is in man a certain insatiability caused by existence itself, a primordial insatiability, associated with the very fact of the unavoidable existence of individuality, an insatiability that I call metaphysical and that, if it is not eradicated by excessive satiation of real-life feelings, by work, by the exercise of power, by creativity, etc., can be appeased solely with the aid of narcotics. *"Für elende Mussigänger ist Opium geschaffen"* is what someone said on the subject. The apparent contradiction between this assertion and the arguments that follow about the "socializing nature" of nicotine and alcohol (to the extent that they are taken in moderate doses) in relation to social mechanization will be explained in due course. My practice is to divide narcotics into the seemingly social and the markedly asocial, but more about that later. In any case, this insatiability, to which reference was made above and which arises from the limitation of each individual in Time and Space, and from his opposition to the infinite totality of Existence, is what in the past I called metaphysical feeling. It is found in the most varied combinations with other states and feelings, thereby creating different amalgams, and is based on the directly given unity of our "I," of our individuality. It can be a motive force for different actions, and it can confer a special coloration on activities that are not its direct manifestations. If it is dominant in the psyche of a given individual, it becomes the cause of religious, artistic, or philosophical activity. If it is only a secondary element in the totality of a given psyche, it can be an impetus for the metaphysicalizing of any of that person's spheres of activity, or it may only confer a specific character to his inner experiences. . . .

In any case, I maintain that all narcotics—both the "social," taken at the beginning in small doses, and the asocial—lessen to some degree the feelings of insatiability and longing that result from the very essence of Being, in other words, from the limitation of the individual, and that their effect in the long run is to deaden those states and finally to eradicate them completely. Such is also the effect of religion, art, and philosophy, which initially express, in diverse ways, metaphysical anxiety, mitigating the horror of the individual's loneliness in the non-sense of Being with veils provided by the construction and orderly arrangement of metaphysical feelings in cults, and the construction of artistic forms in art and of conceptual systems in philosophy, and which, finally, as social tranquilization increases, degenerate and fade away, as does the anxiety itself that had produced them in the first place. . . .

In the sphere of art the creators of old devoured their material at a leisurely pace, digested it for a long time, and the fruits of their work ripened slowly. Artists found fulfillment in the creation of forms that were great and serene, and spectators and listeners could experience powerful artistic emotions from simple works devoid of the element of perversion, i.e., of the creation of a harmonious whole out of parts in themselves unpleasant in their effect. Nowadays, when the feelings fundamental for art, connected to the perception of the unity and uniqueness of the "I," are disappearing, the artist, in order to tear out of himself a moment of metaphysical ecstasy, must amass far more powerful means of expression. The spectator or listener, with a dwindling supply of these feelings to be experienced, can vent them only under the influence of works that attack his nerves with sufficient force. Besides, there is the question of the overuse and exhaustion of artistic means, which grows more acute as art evolves and now constitutes a problem clearly looming before us. In the past, the artist was ahead of his own time by only a half-step, and in comparison to the present, he differed from his predecessors in the minimal changes he made in the general conception and related deformations of reality and feelings.

As the socialization of mankind and the progressive mechanization and acceleration of life increase, it is precisely the artist who, as an individual specialized in the direct expression of metaphysical feelings, has been compelled, with regard to their form of expression, to distance himself from the social base, of which he is the function with regard to life. Hence there arises the growing discrepancy between *true* artists and society as it becomes organized in forms of the future, as well as the restriction of genuine understanding of their works to small groups of obsolete individuals in the process of extinction. I think it is clear why the disappearance of metaphysical feelings leads to riotous proliferation of artistic forms, which amounts to the end of art on our planet. But that's enough of that—let's not get bogged down in long forgotten and perfectly useless artistic theories. So if for a small band of individuals narcotics initially take the place of art, religion, and philosophy (I am of course talking about confirmed addicts taking poisons of a superior category), these drugs eventually render them totally sterile with regard to the heightened experience of their own individuality and finally destroy them completely in every respect, by cutting them off from society, by enclosing them in their impenetrable world of deranged experiences, and by deforming their perceptions of reality to an extreme point beyond which they become incomprehensible to normal people. The situation is different with nicotine and with alcohol taken in small doses.

These poisons slowly stupefy anxiety-ridden contemporary man, likewise destroying whatever individuality he has but without ruining him so completely as to render him incapable of fulfilling his mechanical functions in today's society. . . .

At present I am writing in S after several days of NS and that is why I see so clearly the horror of this phenomenon: positively, it gives me absolutely nothing—as is true for the majority of smokers—except for purely external pleasure: the appeasement of those miserable little appetites of touch, taste, and smell. Other than the deceptive speed of execution, the objective value of work done under the influence of tobacco will always be vastly inferior, if we take into account the effort that must be put into it for its definitive realization. Because work done by a smoker is never perfect at one stroke; subsequently he must spend long hours laboriously "doctoring" and improving his oeuvres instead of spewing them out all at once in an ideal form corresponding to his original conception. . . .

The stultification and besotting grow with each puff of lethal smoke, at the same time that one's anxiety intensifies. The contradictory feelings are the worst—tobacco actually entails the most disastrous of such pairs: superficial excitation and the inability to make use of it because of paralysis of the higher centers. I feel this to perfection as I write these words and as long as I continue to write systematically in NS every day, all of my readers will sense the change. And if not? That would be terrible—it would prove that I have been smoking for too long and that breaking the habit is not possible without extremely negative effects when one first attempts to stop. . . .

Every smoker is the ruin of what he could have been if he did not smoke. Of course, the personal example I am giving is an extreme case based on certain phenomena which I have observed in myself, and which as a result of my frequent attempts at giving up smoking did not develop to their ultimate consequences. . . .

Now I am going to describe to you the experiences of a person who stopped smoking overnight—but unfortunately only starting tomorrow, because I am writing these words with a lousy "weed" stuck in my filthy mug, thoroughly poisoned, having difficulty keeping up with as relatively easy a task as writing this "opuscule," which all the same should be read by everyone and translated into all languages. Yes, starting tomorrow, starting tomorrow—what else can I say? But we shall see if in actual fact starting tomorrow, it won't be the truth and if I, Grand Master of the Temporary NS, won't show you some real class and, starting tomorrow, won't stop smoking forever. And anyone who sees me with a cigarette between my lips will be entitled to think that I have given up all hope of ending my days on the highest level I am capable of and that I have totally given up on myself. . . .

Alcohol (C_2H_5OH)

I am in favor of total prohibition, but I must admit that sometimes, although it would be possible to get along without it entirely, alcohol resolves a myriad of difficulties, internal as well as external. In my opinion it should only be authorized, during a limited period, for consumption by artists and men of letters who know with absolute certainty that they can quickly "play themselves out" and that they would undoubtedly create nothing of value without the aid of alcohol. But given the inessentiality of literature, whose demise is beginning in our lifetime (this will be discussed more extensively elsewhere) and the end of art, which, its seems, is ceasing to be a myth even for the greatest superoptimists, this problem is also losing its—largely illu-sory—virulence. Who cares and why should even artists bother to poison themselves with narcotics if their final formal death throes are of no use to anyone? . . .

A question posed in moderate terms is condemned to failure a priori. The world moves forward (or, in certain areas, backward, relatively speaking) by leaps and bounds, and without revolution, taken in the broadest sense of the word, we would still be in the age of totemism, magic, and cannibalism. Perhaps we would be happier—who knows? But once society has begun to crush the individual, it should totally demolish him as quickly as possible. The mendacious period of democratic pseudofreedoms is drawing to an end. The concept of democracy was the final mask for the dying values of the past, now in a state of decomposition. . . .

The artistic sphere is characterized in its psychology by the fantastic, the unpredictable, and the nervous—the element known as "inspiration" enters into play. I say this quite simply without raising my eyes to the heav-ens: inspiration is a fact, and in certain respects it is a fact as commonplace as eating and drinking. Only we have no way of knowing exactly what conditions will call it forth—sometimes even a single small glass of vodka may be the cause of the creation of truly great works as a *point de déclenchement* (there is no word for it—more's the pity). . . .

As for me, until I reached thirty I drank almost nothing. Subsequently I sometimes made use of alcohol when I was writing the first draft of my works for the stage. In any case I never wrote them when I was drunk—it was only a result of my desire to outline rapidly the play in its totality that I had to fortify myself with several vodkas, simply to gain strength. Contrary to the view held by some, my novels are completely *Narkotik- und Alkoholfrei*. I admit that I used to draw when I was drunk, and not only when I was drunk, but I experi-mented with all known narcotics and although I do not favor drug-induced states for their own sake, in the portraits I painted in just such states I accom-plished on a very small scale what I never would have been able to do without that stimulus. I simply point out that I do not consider these compositions finished works of art but as belonging to a completely distinct genre. The portrait per se is a psychological pastime that makes use of artistic means, but it is not a work of art—of course, it could be under certain circumstances, just as three apples on a tablecloth or a bullfight can be. But that is enough on that subject—it is dull as ditch water—I am not planning to spend any more time on either art or theory. . . .

Alcohol stimulates the imagination, but only up to a certain point, and it apparently creates new conceptual combinations; it emits a fluid promoting understanding between actually incompatible human types and it facilitates emotional harmony, sometimes intensifying certain conversations and experiences to the limit of ecstasy at the moment of its impact. Always upon coming back to one's senses after the elation, and especially at the moment when the inevitable "hangover" makes its presence felt, one sees the worthlessness of the states experienced and the words pronounced—unfortunately it is often too late to turn back, and then one starts drinking again in order to recapture the "artificial Paradise," where the feeling of the absurdity of the universe disappears and everything seems necessary in its perfection, like the elements of a true work of art which are joined together by a formal conception of the whole. Alcohol, that lying consoler, often lends this illusory form to the formless pulp of life.

Cocaine

The danger of cocaine lies not so much in the pleasures it affords as in the disproportionately more disagreeable reaction that sets in after taking it. I maintain that people who become addicts are not trying, in their subsequent use of that hideous poison, to "recapture" the ecstasy, which in any case is no longer obtainable in its initial form, but that they want desperately to get rid of the "hangover" that is oppressing them. Cocaine is capable of producing a depression so real that there is no way to explain its origins and thereby to neutralize it. That is still possible to a certain degree with an alcoholic hangover. One can distinguish the actual disagreeable sensations, which are then considerably magnified, from the backdrop of despair and general pessimism resulting from the side effects of overindulgence. With cocaine this distinction is not possible; one stands at the very center of the horror of the world and of existence in general. Nothing can convince the poor "hungover" wretch that ultimately only in exceptional circumstances is life one long series of agonies. The slightest setbacks assume the dimensions of insurmountable calamities, small vexations turn into true misfortunes, and the shadow of the present thus deformed and rendered odious falls upon the entire past, transforming it into a series of monstrous errors and senseless torments, while the very thought of the future, seen in this light, or rather dark, becomes a torture not to be endured. It is an eminently suicidal state of mind. The devaluation of things which formerly constituted the sole aim of life, the disfigurement of even the most noble occupations and entertainments, the putrefaction of the human being to his innermost core—that is the usual cluster of sensations making up a cocaine "hangover." To the extent that, while the effects of the poison last, as a result of its lessening all negative sensations, everything seems easy to accomplish, and every impression no matter how slight (ranging from a knot in the wall to works of art) is bathed in a kind of unearthly perfection, which under ordinary circumstances is encountered only in exceptionally successful artistic or real-life structures, so afterwards there occurs (as often happens while increasing the doses of the poison during the same period of intoxication) a sudden inversion of all values from positive to negative, but in a wildly magnified ratio. This state of affairs asserts itself with such frightful force that there is no question of explaining it as something temporary; this is an authentic worldview with such structural coherence, because of its attack on absolutely all realms of the psyche, all feelings and interests, that to struggle against it would be something beyond human strength and logically absurd, given the sheer metaphysical density of this moment of horror. Either bite the dust or take a new dose of the poison—these are the only possible ways out. One can avoid it by taking a colossal dose of bromide or something similar and awake in a state far from spiritual serenity and joy of life, but bearable at any rate: a state of gray ordinariness—something like the atmosphere in the waiting room of a government office or railway station: one is at least waiting for something, and that is a lot. A cocaine "hangover" precludes even waiting: the basic motive of that state is a desire to terminate as quickly as possible the monstrous nonsense called life. Now if we can imagine such a state raised to the highest power, let us say after several months spent in the company of the "white fairy," then we can imagine, on the basis of the data furnished by such onetime poisonings, what takes place in the soul of an inveterate cocaine addict trying to free himself from the infamous habit.

Beyond this hypothetical picture, I am not in a position to give any additional data, since, as I have already mentioned, I allowed myself only twice as an experiment to go on a "two-day binge" and I would never dare do that again, not even a onetime use of "snow" for that matter, although I must admit that in the drawings done under the influence of cocaine in small doses, which from the point of view of an inveterate drug addict were truly infantile—and always in combination with relatively large doses of alcohol—I accomplished certain things I could never have done in a normal state. If, however, we take into consideration the terrible mental ravages caused by cocaine addiction, the whole thing is simply not worth the risk. Unless a person believes that a certain kind of line in a drawing or a certain deformation of the human face, unattainable by any other means, or a special harmony of colors or arrangement of the whole is really the most important thing for him, without which his life is utterly worthless. But I believe that, even among artists, there are fewer and fewer individuals who follow that line of thinking. Even I, who to some extent was ideally predisposed in that way, have overcome the worldview that advocates "sacrificing one's life for the sake of art," and this should be a warning to young people who might be tempted by this sort of "justification" for "white manias." It is better not to execute a certain number of deformed blobs than to lose what in contemporary man is still most valuable, i.e., a properly functioning mind. In this regard cocaine is an even greater delusion than alcohol. It does not create anything new, nor does it even elicit any valuable combinations of essentially already familiar elements. On the contrary, under the guise of revelations, cocaine presents the naively enthusiastic "daredevil" with things done long ago and laid to rest, but which have been rouged and refurbished, decked out in old rags and frippery pieced together to give the illusion of being new garments created specially for the occasion. Because the diabolical "fée blanche" is not even capable of creating new clothes. Destroying all self-restraint, yet not providing any really new psychic states or metaphysical formulations, it only compels the intoxicated victim to marvel at the most stupid and commonplace reality as though it were an incredible miracle. In so saying, I am not denying the unique value of our reality, the reality of the world, its creatures, objects, and of us ourselves. But it is a matter of selection—there are, after all, certain criteria for making valuations when one is in a normal state. Cocaine takes away our ability to make valuations: it destroys all criteria. It leaves us helpless and naive like idiots (not like children) and for hours on end we admire a spot on the tablecloth as the highest beauty on earth, only a few minutes later to fall prey to the most frightful doubts about the very essence of Existence and the most beautiful and noble of lives. From afar in hopeless rage we hear only the diabolical laughter of the "white fairy," sneering at us and luring us on to still worse orgies in her infernal company. Not to yield to it—even at the price of a thorough poisoning with bromide or some other such nasty antitoxin—not to yield and forget forever—and above all not to let oneself be tempted for the first time. One may pay too dearly for it.

Peyote

I shall relate only my own personal experiences with peyote, which I consider absolutely harmless when taken occasionally, and which offers, besides unbelievable visual images, such penetrating insight into the hidden recesses of the psyche and inspires such distaste for all other narcotics, especially for alcohol, that given the almost absolute impossibility of becoming addicted to it, peyote should be used in all sanatoriums where addicts of all kinds are treated. I only note, as proof of the impossibility of being addicted to peyote, that the Indians of Mexico who use this plant, honored by them as the Deity of Light, have been taking it for more than a thousand years only at the time of their religious ceremonies, which do not last a full two months including the harvesting of the cactus in the desert—the expedition sometimes lasts up to several weeks—after which it is impossible to discover that it has had any harmful effects on its devotees, as is the case for example with the Peruvian devotees of coca leaves, the chewing of which leads inevitably to full-scale cocaine addiction and both physical and moral degeneration.

Of course, since first hearing about peyote and the visions it produces, my dream was to try the marvelous drug. Unfortunately, in Europe it was considered such a great rarity that I despaired of ever having the opportunity. Naturally I considered what was said about the visions an exaggeration, as does everyone who, knowing nothing about peyote, hears the personal experiences of someone who has had the incomparable good fortune of seeing with his own eyes another world incommensurate with our reality, greeting such accounts with disbelief, tinged with suspicion that at bottom there is not only some exaggeration but even an outright hoax. I should add that I knew nothing about the "edifying" effect of the "holy" plant (at any rate such it is for the Indians), and except for the little brochure *The Worshippers of Saint Cactus,* I had read nothing about it. Everything that happened was simply a diabolical surprise.

Quite unexpectedly I received from Mr. Prosper Szmurło a maximum dose of peyote: seven pills the size of a pea, for which I shall be grateful to him to the end of my days in a way no words can ever express. And it should be added that it was genuine Mexican peyote, coming from a supply belonging to Dr. Osto, president of the International Society for Metaphysical Research. The preparations that I subsequently received from Dr. Alexandre Rouhier (author of *Peyotl, la plante qui fait les yeux émerveillés*), extracted from cactus cultivated, I believe, on the Côte d'Azur, did not match it in ability to elicit visions but went far beyond it in negative effects. . . .

A general characteristic of peyote visions is the presence of a mysterious voice, coming from the "lower reaches of the self," which whispers in our ear the meaning of the images we are seeing and supplies what is totally lacking in the picture itself. . . . Peyote-induced sensations and the strangest of its visions—some are totally realistic—are as difficult to reconstruct as certain dreams in which it is impossible to tell what it is all about or what is happening and which no comparisons can capture, not even approximately, and yet, especially immediately after awakening, one has—almost intuitively—a singularly precise grasp of their contents. Forming strange tangles, the images interlock with the muscular feelings and sensations of the internal organs and thus there emerges an inextricable whole—of an incredibly subtle overall atmosphere, which defies all analysis and crumbles into indeterminate chaos at the slightest attempt to consolidate it. In general, there is a close connection between normal hypnagogic hallucinations and dreams on the one hand and peyote visions on the other—in both, the same subconscious material is symbolically elaborated. Only peyote is characterized by four distinct stages in the total course of the trance, experienced almost identically by all, and then too it produces a certain specific richness of vision with regard to the artistic and decorative side of things which for the most part shares traits with the great styles of art in previous epochs. Herein lies a mystery that has not yet been fathomed, about which I shall later make certain, rather fantastic conjectures. These thoughts arose during the trance itself, when literally overwhelmed by the impact and grandeur of the visions, I tried, in a state of stupefaction more visual than psychic, to explain as best I could why I saw precisely what I did and nothing else. My hypothesis, however, attests rather to the specificity of the peyote vision but fails to explain its essence, which I doubt can ever be thoroughly probed. Physiology and toxicology will be of absolutely no use here no matter how long we endure, and psychology will only be able to furnish a theory of the links between phenomena, but never explain their origin and essence. . . .

If we can put alcohol and cocaine among the *realistic* poisons—which intensify the world without producing an atmosphere of uncanniness—then I would call peyote a metaphysical drug, producing a feeling of the strangeness of Existence, which we experience very rarely in a normal state: in moments of solitude in the mountains, late at night, at periods of great mental fatigue, occasionally at the sight of very beautiful things or on hearing music, provided it is not simply a normal metaphysical-artistic sensation coming directly from the intrinsic Pure Form of the work of art. For in that case it has a different character: it is not terror in the face of the strangeness of being, but rather the soothing justification of its metaphysical *necessity*. . . .

I won't be able to describe everything—out of consideration for the reader's feelings as well as for my own. And I want this book to be read by everyone. But I don't know whether I shall succeed in conveying to the reader all the beauty and horror of what I have seen. . . .

The veracity and accuracy of vision are incomparably greater than in either reality or a world of fantasy. If what I am seeing is a synthesis and transposition of images seen either in reality or at the cinema or in some atlases, how can we explain the incredible expressiveness of the peyote vision, and its three-dimensional tangibility, as compared with the images provided by memory and their combinations, always very faint, fleeting, and never capable of being imaginatively intensified beyond a certain degree of reality. . . .

Peyote eyes seem about to explode from the inexpressible intensity of the feelings and thoughts packed into them, as though they were some kind of diabolical pills. They cease to be dead spheres—all expression resides in the surrounding features and their changes—in which by an age-old convention we claim to see the psychic reality of the mysterious and unfathomable human personality, beyond all evasions and prevarications. Peyote eyes are true "mirrors of the soul"—diabolical mirrors with which the demon of peyote denudes us, making us believe that even in this life it may be possible to know another being's psyche, to fuse with it in total unity in flames of a searing love where body and soul would in truth be absolutely one, even if it meant annihilation. And splendid likewise is the ringing silence accompanying the visions created by the Aztec God of Light—a silence intensified by the unbelievable procession of happenings which, gripped by stillness, flows before us into nothingness. And yet this nothingness is never total. After a peyote trance, something indestructible remains, something higher creates within us that steady flow of visions, almost all of which have depths of hidden symbolism dealing with first and last things. And let no one think I am now singing the praise of a new drug after claiming to have given up others similar to it but whose effects are less powerful. These are qualitatively different matters on a spiritual scale, not only with regard to the intrinsic value of the visual images, but also in that peyote visions are a direct means of perceiving oneself and viewing one's destiny, offering—after taking the drug only once—guideposts to the distant spaces of the future . . .

For fear of outraging public decency I cannot enter into a detailed analysis of these visions. From time to time I like to see monstrous things, but peyote surpassed all my expectations. That one night gave me enough for an entire lifetime.

I am by no means promoting the use of peyote as a new way of "fleeing from reality," I am only pointing out its invaluable contributions if we are interested in starting a "new life." . . .

I end these reflections with the following appeal addressed to all: Smokers, drinkers, and other addicts, arouse yourselves while there is still time! Down with nicotine, alcohol, and all forms of "white lunacy." If peyote turns out to be a universal antidote to all those filthy poisons, then in that case and only in that case: long live peyote!

Report about the Effects of Peyote
on Stanisław Ignacy Witkiewicz
[The following is the original account of Witkacy's first experiment with peyote which he included in *Narcotics* in an expurgated version. He purposely omitted the passages of a frankly sexual nature, which he felt might be offensive although he recognized that without them it would be difficult to convey the true character of a peyote vision. The report, composed at the time first by Witkacy's wife (referred to by her nickname "Nina") and then by the playwright himself, was published in 1972.]

At 5:40 P.M. W. took 2 ground-up pills of Pan-Peyote. After a few minutes he began to feel lightness and cold throughout his body and became afraid of being sick to his stomach. 6 o'clock—yawning and chills, pulse 88. 6:15 feels wonderful, nerves completely soothed. W. takes another dose (2 pills) and eats 2 eggs with tomatoes and drinks a small cup of coffee with just a drop of milk. 6:25 feels a little bit abnormal, as after a small dose of cocaine, pulse 80. The tired feeling after three portrait sittings disappeared totally. W. walks around the room with a steady step and closed the blinds on the windows tightly. 6:40 pulse 72—feels slight, agreeable stupor and lightheadedness. The inactivity bothers him, he's bored and would like to smoke a cigarette. 6:50 W. takes a third dose—stares with tremendous interest at an airplane in flight—then lowers the blinds again and lies down on the bed. Pupils normal, pulse 84. Strange feeling, waits for visions without any results, finally out of boredom smoked a cigarette but didn't finish it. 7:20 got up, took the last pill and lay down again. Starts to feel apathetic and disheartened. After lying down for half an hour, W. got up and felt sick, pulse a little weak, pupils somewhat enlarged, voice changed. Asked for coffee and stays lying down, as soon as he tries to get up, feels sick. 8:30 sees swirls of filaments, bright against a dark background. Next there start to appear animal phantoms, sea monsters, little faces, a man with a beard, but he still does not consider these to be visions, only the kind of heightened images that occur before falling asleep. Someone in a black velvet hat leans from an Italian balcony and speaks to the crowd. Definitely feels a heightening of the imagination, but still nothing extraordinary. Feels better, but when he gets up has dizzy spells and feels "odd," in an unpleasant way, at the same time a strange feeling in his muscles. 9 o'clock begins to see rainbow colors, but still does not consider these to be visions. 9:30—various sculpture in sharp relief, tiny faces, feels "weird," but good. Sees rainbow stripes, but incomplete—the following colors predominate: dirty red and lemon yellow. Desire to forget reality. Huge building, the bricks turn into gargoyle faces, like those on the cathedral of Nôtre-Dame in Paris. Monsters similar to plesiosaurs made out of luminous filaments. The trees turned into ostriches. A corpse's brain, abscesses, sheaves of sparks bursting out of them. On the whole unpleasant apparitions. On the ceiling, against a red background horned beasts. A gigantic abdomen with a wound—the insides turn into coral at the bottom of the sea. A battle among sea monsters. Dr. Sokołowski turns into a cephalopod. Spatial "distortion." Cross section of the earth. Fantastic luxuriousness of plant life. 10 o'clock languor continues. Stupor. Battle among senseless things. A series of chambers which change into an underground circus, some strange beasts appear, interesting class of people in the boxes, the boxes turn into (?). Impressions of two visible layers—the images are only black and white, and the rainbow colors exist as it were separately. Land and sea monsters and frightful human mugs predominate in the visions. Snakes and giraffes, a sheep with a flamingo's nose, cobras crawled out of this sheep, a double-crested grebe with a seal's tail—bursting jaws, volcanoes change into fish. African vision. 11 o'clock terrific appetite, but at the same time total laziness so that eating a few·tomatoes took over half an hour. With the monsters in the background a yellow pilot's cap appeared, then a uniform, then the face of Col. Beaurain in a yellow light. Out of the wild, chaotic coils a splendid beach came to the fore, across it by the sea a Negro boy rides a bicycle and changes into a man with a small beard, and the toys which the Negro boy was apparently carrying turned into Mexican sculpture which, while looking at W., climbed up ladders. A series of female sex organs, out of which spill out guts and live worms as well as a green embryo turning somersaults.

W. Himself Writes the Continuation

Kogda perestanu kushat' pomidory [when I finish eating the tomatoes]. A song. 20 before twelve midnight. *Polosatiye* [striped] monsters at the side. The bottom of the ocean. A shark. Bubbles of gas. Sea anemone. A battle of sea monsters to the left. Anonymous jaws. Previously about 10:30, hairy machines. Abstract creations, machinishly alive, ramrods, cylinders, grasshoppers and their battles. (Marvelous) Anteaters twisting backwards; spiny anteaters. Rodent covered with bristles of that kind etc. Col. Beaurain in a cap at eleven lighted in yellow. Zawadzka, deformed, giving someone a flirtatious wink. 12:10 A.M. Pulse 72. A swelling of time. Metallic and precious stones. Living Indian sculpture (started with gold miniature of Beelzebub). Hellish transformations of stylized mugs and animals (mixed up together) ending in a brood of snakes on a Grand Scale. Coils of snakes turning into monsters. Nina sleeping nearby changes into a mask *from staring at her*, moves her eyes in a horrible fashion (*en réalité* goes on sleeping without moving). A second time—the same thing—monstrous mobile masks.

Narcotics create styles in sculpture and architecture. An elbow with a coat of arms. An arm turned into snakes (yellow and blue), conquered by discoloring monsters with crab eyes. Green snake worlds against a brown background. Worlds. ? Grünewald's Isenheim (Altarpiece) and something like Lucas Cranach. Monsters of this sort mixed up with corpses in a state of decay. The Negro, who rotted before my eyes, evaporated halfway in the form of a shaft of sparks. Often it is all seen crosswise. A cross section of the earth in the tropics. Machines—turbines—the Center of the World and their brakes made out of fur. Monstrous speed. I had the impression that hours (days?) had elapsed—but it was a quarter of an hour. What can you do to enjoy yourself in such a short time? I drew just to "go through the motions," although the lines were something special. But it was a waste of time compared to what there was to be seen. (12:30.)

Snakes too "good to be true." Stylization and colors. Pearly tanks of the Assyrian kings. (I often interrupt the visions in order to write them down.) So many things perish in this whirl. The portrait by old Kossak (hanging in my room) came to life and started to move.

I return to *that other* world. Such a large number of reptiles (colored) are *monstrous*. Higher (metaphysical) acrobatics by chameleons. (How is it that they too do not perish doing those somersaults?)

Again only a quarter of an hour has elapsed. *La plante qui émerveille les yeux*. Brain-strain-storms. The vodka was tasteless. Hunger pains. Total contempt for cigarettes. Mobile china made out of reptiles. Piggish monsters came out of Beaurain's eye. A pile of pigs came spilling out. A stage. Artificial monsters. Pig snouts in green four-cornered caps [those worn by eighteenth-century Polish patriots].

12:55—I am going to try not to write, and to enter more into the spirit of things. I put out the lights as an experiment. I cannot stand not writing it down: a cross-section of reptile machine (of course this is hardly a fraction of what I'm seeing).

Desisterization of doublesharks on water dolthives.

1:02—I put out the light again.

1:15—2nd series of drawings. I roar with laughter.

1:17—I lie down. (No—I pace back and forth and eat sweets.)

1:25—(Drawing with the Mokrzyskis.) Check what the Ms were doing at this time. I shut my eyes for a second—I see an animal behind broken lids. Transformations of animals into people in a continuous fashion *à la fourchette*.

1:28—I put out the light and decide not to write things down. I cannot stop writing. Centuries have elapsed, but by the clock it is 7 minutes after 1:30. It began with the Bolsheviks (Trotsky) and their transformations. Supergenitals in crayfish red colors, sexual intercourse *in natura* and next the *incarnation of sexual pleasures* in various little monsters rubbing up against one another and fighting among themselves, in crayfish red color. Sometimes cobalt eyes flickered on top of filaments. It ended in reptiles.

1:40—Pulse 68. Alien hands are writing. I close my eyes by the lighted lamp. Primeval matter with snakes. It started with a scene from *Macbeth* from the side and from below. A gigantic sister of mercy intersected with frightful genitals seen from underneath. I feel a bit like smoking. I stare at the childhood portrait of Nina. Nina smiles and moves her eyes, but *does not want* to look at me. I have had enough of reptiles. Seals in a sea *thick* as grease. Whole series of brown-green sculpture representing peyote scenes. (Executed in a highly artistic way.) A monastery by moonlight undermined by snakes and a monstrous female organ in a cliff, upon which a violet spark has descended. The monastery crashed down on me into the sea. (Grabiński.)

1:52—Seems that the visions are growing weaker.

2:05—Centuries have elapsed. Entire mountains, worlds and droves of visions. Too many reptiles. Finally a cave made out of pigs—out of a gigantic moving pig, composed of little piggish tiles.

The Chinese knew peyote. All Chinese dragons and all of India come from that source. Artists are the initiated. *Eine allgemeine Peyotltheorie.* Panpeyoteism.

Peyote

the two branches of art

China, India, Persia   America-Mexico, Africa-Egypt

Our navel of decline. Perhaps peyote will resurrect art.

Music and a phonograph from down below spoil the seriousness of the visions. Should I smoke? At times there were red and blue dancing paper figures.

2:11—One vodka and a few tomatoes. Notes. I close my eyes by the lamp. A vision of Gucio Z. *snaked* (by snakes) yellow and black. And then realistically sleeping on his right stomach-side. Headache. Glass visions— criminal ones. Supertramps. The start of fantastic theater. Alcor—the double star—2 stars (160 years a revolution) turned very fast.

2:30—A madman's brain with gurgling eyes in the clutches of a hellish snake-cephalopod.

After vodka sad and gloomy visions. A yellow eye pudent amid soot. *Superhuman* edifices with columns turned into mountain-genitals (big as Giewont) made of shiny pink stones.

2:35—Violet sperm jet straight in the face, from a hydrant of mountain-genitals (down below there are superedifices).

2:45—I eat graham bread and butter. Glancing through the curtained window at unsightly apartment buildings. Reminding me of a certain horrendous view of the Poldeks' apartment building on View Street. Will there be visions? The Poldeks sleep *separately* under one quilt. Poldek on his back and Wanda on her right side, curled up (towards the window). Visions (renewed) of tiny little faces. The thought that Kotarbiński could make better use of this world and my reptiles than Rafał Malczewski or I.

2:53—Superasses keep constantly coming down like waterfalls.

2:58—Procession of elephants and a pearly camel (in a mask) magnificently proportioned (tremendous realism). Eyes peeping at and embracing female organs.

3:00—A little guy of the Miciński type tearing off to the moon and his adventures after landing by parachute in a state of addlepatedness. Elves on a seesaw. (Comic number.) The Queen of Sheba's horny genitals in an astral museum.

3:05—I said "enough visions" and put out the light. Next came cadavero-erotic visions. (*Macabre* number.) A skull (which had dropped down) floating across an abdomen—so hideous that I turned out the light as quickly as I could. Erotic rain of skirted flowers (crocuses). Smiling man with a beard (Valois) enclosed in gigantic ox snouts.

3:10—Hades according to my personal conception. Skeleton in a circular desert and specters à la *Goya.* Goya must have known peyote.

3:30—Trying visions. A battle of centaurs turned into a battle of fantastic genitals. Conversion, but not to any religion, rather in the realm of life. Renouncing drugs. Soulfulness. The crab of iniquity crawled out of the wound in a skull. The partridge-ification of a goshawk. The marvelously wise, goshawkly human eyes grew dull and stupid, became duplicated and flew away in birds' heads beyond the round horizon.

3:45—A Pharaoh similar to me. Processions. Totemistic rites (somewhat goshawkly reptilian). On shields—then floating away in the form of animal spirits. Reptiles in sexual entanglements. Minettes of iguanas.

3:50—Snakes in desert springs. (Realistic number.) Again a vision (repetition with variation) of a madman's brain ulcerated to the point of gangrene (à *propos* no more drinking) and a bird-amphibian face pecking a monster's brain (and holding it in its clutches) lifted up its head in my direction and looked at me lasciviously. Sexual abyss with a blond woolly hippopotamus. Eyes in the midst of it.

3:58—Bristling concepts and from out of these concepts, instead of the truth (it stood with its back artificially turned to me), there came forth a strange animal, and then an ordinary wild pig.

4:05—The birth of a diamond goldfinch. A rainbow-colored basset hound spurted into fireworks of black and pink butterflies on bent pink sticks. Egyptian and Assyrian processions. A female slave behind a column and from out of this there then came forth an unfinished palace tale, drowned in greasy genitals.

4:10—In these visions I saw all my inner wretchedness.

4:15—Transformation of a skeleton into an ethereal body (diamond-like).

4:20—Third series of drawings. I want to smoke.

4:27—Drawings (2) finished (?).

About 3 o'clock a variety of processions in different styles, for example: rococo, present-day, and antiquity. (Mélange of styles as though at the races—seen from below.)

4:30—Crotches from Zakroczym. I cannot be completely saved, since I cannot renounce sex.

Nina's portrait won't look at me anymore, because I have lost my secret power over things. In the dark depths of the coils of my brain the remnants of visions are lying in wait (I have deserved these—the Indians are right, Peyote punishes the guilty).

4:40—Slight headache. Fatigue from visions. Desire for sleep without visions. Pulse 72. Ordinary reality more and more often seems normal, and not horrendous as heretofore. Curving of space slowly vanishes. (Einstein put into practice.)

4:43—Vision of fat old women hanging by ropes in the mountains (Hala Gąsiennicowa). (Vision of unintelligible symbolism.) The Strążyskis in their living room on a sofa turned into a bed. He by the window with his feet towards the window, she on her right side with her head towards the library. Now she woke up, 4:49, he's asleep.

4:45—Realistic eye of Piłsudski—it comes gently out from its eye socket and springs (already ethereal) straight at me through space. It hits some point in the Ukraine and from there swarms of geometricalized, striped black worms pour out onto the entire world.

5:00—The mysterious tale of a lady from the eastern provinces (a blonde), a gendarme, a Russian Orthodox priest, an old man in a nobleman's uniform. English field marshals—one a cuirassier of the guard, the other in a pointed hat—pulling a wagon with a Hindu statue through the rain (punishment). All these reptiles are monsters bred in me by alcohol and cocaine. There was so little of that, and so many reptiles.

5:04—Hideous monster with whiskers, catlike, crawling out of a fatty female organ—being born.

5:08—Grim fleet with faces under the rudders. I have had *enough visions.*

5:11—Rotting foot, the shoe disintegrates. Pink worms, similar to phalluses, crawl out, change into erect lingams. (Foot and shoe gangrene.)

5:18—Ideal young lady slowly changed into an ambling, bubble-shaped horror.

5:20—I think I am the incarnation of the King of the Tatra Mountain Snakes. (Tatra vision.) The Small Meadow in winter, and it ended as a *monstrous* reptile on Przysłup Miętusi.

5:25—I put out the light. Zygmunt Unrug (a heretic), seen in profile, drawn into a vortex of snakes. A shield with a coat of arms grows into a snake and collapses. Alongside, visions of another shield with a lion, his legs astride. Visit to the Sokołowskis in Brwinów. Slinking monsters: chocolate-covered with black and gold.

5:33—Deformation of Nina asleep with her eyes open. Before that, transformation of the pitcher in the corner. I put out the light. The room brighter and brighter owing to the daylight. Immediately thereafter vision of nicotine—small yellow eye in the corpse's skull. Next alcohol—a marvelous hummingbird snake crawls out; and Coco—a woman's eye, white as a pigeon's and from underneath a small woman's hand which grows into white snake reins, prodding and squeezing my neck. White fluffy feminine down and a beautiful eye, a blue one. An empty blister on the leg, protruding into infinity.

5:47—Vision of a deluxe reptile (dinosaur), *pour les princes*. Rather humorous number as an encore. Sunny knight under glass (after a geographic vision with the sun on the mountains from both *sides*). Caricatures of male characters in costumes. An affair of honor involving French officers and wild combinations with a young Russian. Frenchmen and Bedouins on Percherons fill in a well with monsters. General Porzeczko's ulcerated tits.

6:15—Hydrocychnytine. Stinkotine. Music, a lower art, gave birth to itself—but only Peyote could have given birth to such a cunning thing as painting or sculpture, and then it went on its own—just like that.

6:17—I take valerian. Desire to smoke. Mundane quarter-asses barked at by flying dragons (on a cone). Hideous reptile, *bleu acier*, at the bottom of shallow water, flat as a ray without a head, alongside but at the top . . . a snake peeped out from this. Disappearing towers and a gigantic mourner lights the sun of truth—a little metal figure with a bare backside. I, as a little boy on a catafalque, turn into a wild pig.

6:30—I drank the rest of the valerian. I have decidedly had *enough* visions. The total ugliness of naturalism compared to the riches of these forms. Sins against Mother. And here Peyote gave me a vision, although I thought it would not dare. How my wrongs and sins are destroying Mother's health.

6:38—Parade of contemporary masks with duplications and caricatures *in the eyes*, constrictions, contractions, and repulsions. Realistic character of a harum-scarum (scared his harem).

6:50—The Strążyskis start to wake up. Vision of the transformations of a marvelous woman, then erotic tentacular attachment. How much evil there is in me. And I consider myself good. Frightful visions of Mother. Nina on her wedding trip with an unknown gentleman, in a hammock on the Riviera.

7:15—Dozing without *real* visions. Normal sleeping dreams. Franz Joseph and Franek Orkan—one and the same. Marvelously indecent woman gives birth to a monster. Hideous sexual intercourse with a horde of reptiles.

8:15—Morning activities. Fear of the light. However, state still highly abnormal. Pupils somewhat narrower than at the maximum. Fading visions of rainbow-colored whirls of filaments.

9:00—Visions still, but weaker and not so awful. Many visions. *Reptiles.*

9:20—Multiform flat green snake in a shallow pond.

10:00—Remnants of visions.

10:15 to 12:00—Sleep. Then relatively normal state. Slight stupor and spatial disorientation. Weak enlargement of the pupils.

20 July 1928

PART 5: PHILOSOPHY AND SUICIDE
1931-39

N ow nearing eighty, Maria Witkiewicz could no longer run her rooming house, which had always been a financially unsound venture. The hotel went out of business in the summer of 1930, forcing Witkacy and his mother to leave their rented villa and move in with Dr. Białynicki-Birula and his wife, from whom they rented rooms. Debts and tax problems were all that remained of the failing enterprise. Witkacy's mother died in December 1931, and after the Białynickis left Zakopane in June 1933, the playwright was forced to live the rest of his life with two maiden aunts, Mery and Żenia, sisters of Stanisław Witkiewicz. Their villa was old-fashioned, lacking electricity, running water, and indoor plumbing. Quarrels about the rent (five złotys a day) constantly strained Witkacy's relations with the two old ladies. But it was thanks to his aunts' intercession that the playwright received two small grants from the Ministry of Culture in 1936 and 1937 to alleviate his financial distress.

Besides the tormenting love affair with Czesława, the final stage of Witkacy's life was marked by his quest for a father and mentor in the German philosopher Hans Cornelius, and his enthusiastic welcoming of creative talent in younger artists, such as Bruno Schulz and Bronisław Linke. Above all there was the consolation he sought and often found in philosophy, which enabled him to resist a little longer the powerful attraction that suicide had exerted since his adolescence.

An "intensive Renaissance life," the author confessed, had reduced him to a "final stage of exhaustion, madness hanging three centimeters above my empty head." More and more frequently he was overcome by the "loneliness and frightful sadness of existence." But somehow the compulsive creator was always able to make a work of literature out of the worst stagnation and misfortune. Although his output had declined and his tempo of production grown sluggish, Witkacy was still capable of giving slow birth to masterpieces. In 1933 he completed his longest and most politically explosive play, *The Shoemakers*, on which he had been brooding for many years. A gloomy, grotesque drama about boredom and the death of work under oppressive regimes that stifle creativity, *The Shoemakers* remained unpublished and un-produced in the author's lifetime, and it proved his most controversial and constantly censored play in Communist Poland.

The unfinished novel *The Only Way Out* (1931–33) is an extended discussion of art and politics. The sections depicting the painter Marcel in action provide the best account anywhere in Witkacy of the actual creation of Pure Form. *Unwashed Souls* (written in 1936 but not published except for a few excerpts until 1975) is the culmination of his interest in collective psychology and a dissection of the Polish national character in which he accuses his fellow countrymen of caring only for appearances, playing stage roles in life, and living in a world of mythmaking and illusion.

In 1935 Witkacy published his philosophical *Hauptwerk*, as he called it, or magnum opus, *The Concepts and Principles Implied by the Concept of Existence*. Written from 1917 to 1932, six hundred copies were printed, but only twelve actually sold. In his philosophical views, Witkacy abandoned the concept of metaphysical feelings and moved away from his earlier apocalyptic beliefs. He felt that philosophy was not doomed to extinction but would soon blossom as never before and achieve absolute truth. From 1931 to 1939 he wrote over fifty articles on philosophical subjects, and attended meetings, read papers, and became acquainted with Ingarden, Tatarkiewicz, Kotarbiński, and other leading Polish philosophers. "The Congress was very interesting and I was very pleased," Witkacy reported of a philosophical conference in Cracow in September 1926. "Went to a nightclub afterwards and did a solo dance with some awful broads and played several pieces on the piano."

The theater continued to fascinate Witkacy, although by the mid 1930s he had virtually stopped writing dramas. In 1933 the newly formed Cracow artists theater Cricot produced *The Cuttlefish*, his play about an artist in a world threatened by totalitarianism. In a late essay, "Balance Sheet on Formism," Witkacy hails Cricot as a harbinger of the theater of the future. After the fall of Stalinism, Tadeusz Kantor would call his new theater Cricot II to signal its continuity with the Cracow avant-garde of the interwar years, and his opening production in 1956 was *The Cuttlefish*, the first production of a Witkacy play for over twenty years and the beginning of his triumphal return to the Polish stage.

The "Balance Sheet" was a retrospective and yet prophetic self-evaluation of Witkacy's career in which he affirmed his continuity with his father, stressing that in his later years Stanisław Witkiewicz was well on the way to becoming a convert to Pure Form. Even while recognizing his own marginality as a Pole and acknowledging that he had ceased to be an artist, Witkacy was acutely aware of the broader historical forces menacing creativity throughout Europe. The splintering of the avant-garde into various conflicting movements signaled the end of the modernist current with which his whole life had coincided. The end was near. Fascism and communism spelled the doom of art.

An attempt in 1938 to revive the Formist Theater in Zakopane, with projected stagings of *Metaphysics of a Two-Headed Calf* and *The Cuttlefish*, reawakened Witkacy's interest in playwriting. In 1938 he wrote an essay, "On Artistic Theater" (a term he preferred to "experimental theater," which implied something tentative, lacking total faith and commitment), and in May of 1938 he began a three-act drama, *So-Called Humanity Gone Mad* (of which only the title page and cast of characters survive), inspired by his fear of fascism and the approaching apocalyptic war, of which he insistently warned. When he completed the play in May 1939, he could claim, "For two weeks I was an artist." But realizing that this would be the last play of his life, he had to concede, "An artist—I won't be anymore." Witkacy was never able to free himself from the early modernist notion of the demonic, self-destructive artist who must embody all the creativity and chaos of existence.

In the philosopher Cornelius, Witkacy found a revered father confessor before whom he avowed his inner doubts in more than one hundred letters written in German between 1935 and 1939. In 1936 he declared to his mentor, "Either I'll be an artist again (and then quickly destroy myself for good and all) or I'll turn myself into some completely new person." The next year he admitted, "My nerves are already ruined and I feel old age approaching. I led too intense a life and I never spared myself. Now I must pay for it. . . . I feel that I didn't take full advantage of my capabilities and use up everything I had in me."

Unable to afford the trip to Berlin, Witkacy invited the Master to come to Zakopane in the autumn of 1937. Because there was only an outhouse at his aunts', the playwright, apologizing profusely, had to put his honored guest in a neighboring villa. The philosopher's visit had the most beneficial influence on Witkacy's character, according to his own report in a 1938 letter to Cornelius: "I don't smoke, don't drink, and finally am in harmony with myself, since I am not pulling any more erotic dirty tricks and am not lying to anyone or cheating anyone. And it's all thanks to you." Unfortunately, this virtuous, self-harmonious, and abstemious Witkacy felt "absolutely old," uncreative, and doomed to annihilation: "I am psychically and physically exhausted as never before."

As the world catastrophe approached, Witkacy played out a comedy of love on the edge of the abyss. When Czesława broke with Witkacy for the umpteenth time in 1938 and sent back all his presents, the playwright warned Jadwiga to expect eighty kilos of paintings, books, furniture, and clothes, which were soon delivered to her apartment. On the one hand, Witkacy was terrified of losing Jadwiga, who had vowed never to see him again if he lived with Czesława or married her. On the other hand, he could not endure the thought of giving up Czesława. "Her leaving me means the end of life—in her I lose not only a lover but as it were a beloved daughter—she was my creation," he wrote to Cornelius. Witkacy's sense of creativity, fading artistically, became extended to the two women in his life. To his wife he declared, "You are my creation—you didn't exist (at all im Allgemeinen), Kittycat, until you met me, me, me, me. Hurrah!"

In desperation, Witkacy persuaded Hans Cornelius to write letters to Czesława urging her not to leave his friend lest it drive him to suicide. Thus it was that the German monadologist became more and more deeply involved in his Polish friend's love life, receiving long letters in German about his romance with the seventeen-year-old fiancée of the local Zakopane barber, who threatened to cut Witkacy's throat with his razor. The playwright explained that "like Flaubert, he needed a tartlette once a week."

Along with Eros, Thanatos was a dominant theme in the playwright's final years. Karol Szymanowski's fatal sickness and death at the age of fifty-five in March 1937 greatly depressed Witkacy. As he told Jadwiga, "That scoundrel Szymanowski is calling me from the other side of the line." Killing himself now seemed unavoidable.

When the Nazis invaded Poland on 1 September 1939, Witkacy was in Warsaw. He reported to the mobilization point but was not accepted because of his age and ill health. On 5 September he and Czesława fled to the east along with thousands of other refugees. Accompanied by several close friends, they took an evacuation train to Brest-Litovsk, where they spent the night in a hotel. While they were there, the city was bombed by the Germans. Because of the explosions, Witkacy's hearing, already failing, grew worse, and it became necessary to shout at him. The next day they went a few miles on foot, but with a bad heart and weak legs, the writer was unable to continue over bad roads, in the heat of early September, carrying a heavy knapsack full of essential food and clothing. They hitchhiked rides in passing wagons, stopping for the night at peasant farms along the way. Finally they reached the little village of Jeziory, not far from the USSR border. Then on 17 September the Soviets attacked from the east. Witkacy committed suicide that night in a wooded grove. The following account comes from Czesława's diary.

> We went to the woods. We sat down under an oak. Staś began to take ephedrine tablets. "What are you taking those for?" I asked. "My blood will circulate more quickly, it will flow out of me faster," Staś answered, planning to slash his veins.
>
> He dissolved eighteen Luminal tablets and two cybalgine tablets in a small pot. We drank it about 11:00. Then we said good-bye. . . . Staś began to slit his wrist with a razor, but the blood somehow did not flow. He cut the varicose vein on his right leg, but there wasn't any blood there either.
>
> I felt weaker and weaker. I couldn't keep from drowsing off.
>
> "Don't fall asleep!" Staś cried out. "Don't leave me alone!"
>
> After a moment's reflection he announced, "Once you fall asleep, I'll cut my throat. . . . " He intended to cut only one vein. He told me its name. He explained that if a person knew how to do it, then everything would go smoothly, it wasn't necessary to cut one's whole throat. . . .
>
> I started to fall asleep again and when I couldn't sit up any longer, I lay down, hearing and seeing less and less. . . . I woke up during the night. I was vomiting. Staś wasn't beside me. . . . I fell asleep again. When I woke up again it was already morning. His jacket was under my head, he must have put it there. He was lying beside me on his back, with his left leg drawn up, he had his arm bent at the elbow and pulled up. His eyes and mouth were open. . . . On his face there was a look of relief. A relaxing after great fatigue. I started to yell; to say something to Staś. We both were wet from the morning dew, acorns from the oak had fallen on top of us. I tried to bury him by raking dirt over him with my hands. With water from the mug for the Luminal I washed his face and covered it with ferns. I felt frightfully weak. I saw double. Then there were two . . . Stases and I crawled away from him on my hands and knees to get some manuscripts that had to be saved, but I didn't know how, then I returned and sat helplessly on the ground. It was Tuesday, 19 September 1939.

RESPONSE AND REVELATION

■

(1931)

Let us now turn to social questions. Here the complications one faces are simply dreadful. I shall point out only a few fundamental problems seen from the point of view of the "intelligentsia." I have the impression that, as a result of recent postwar transformations, social questions have suffered some loss of ideology. Even in its theoretical aspect, the struggle, which of course in the past was also real, has turned toward the resolution of real issues of a limited nature, while the so-called "great ideas," which so preoccupied people in the nineteenth century and which prepared the ground for various changes in our times, have lost their luster. These ideas are the general subsoil in which grow the many theories currently prevalent, but the struggle itself has become quite concrete: as a consequence of the frightful intricacies of economic life, the "great ideas" have broken down into a large number of limited issues. There are two fundamentally opposed blocs: capitalism and radical (for its time) socialism, i.e., Bolshevism. The struggle between them is no longer a struggle embodying abstract ideas, but a clash between two realities: the one on the decline, the other on the rise.

Because of the long overdue recognition of the bond among peoples, a bond without which there can be no general prosperity, national questions are beginning to recede to a secondary position; yet given the past excesses committed in the name of nationalism, the movement in an opposite direction is proceeding at an extremely slow pace compared to the speed at which it should occur, given the experience of the war. What matters is not the rightness of these ideas in and of themselves, but their practical value. If we confine ourselves to the question of justice in the abstract, there is no loftier idea than Bolshevism, i.e., the most rapid implementation of material equality for all the peoples in the world and, as the optimists hope, the creation thereby of new mental and moral horizons for those who heretofore have been denied them. I personally have doubts about the latter, since social progress by its very nature closes just those horizons it should open. And yet we see against what tremendous odds the struggle must be carried on in order to realize such an idea because of the uneven development of civilization throughout the entire world and the special conditions encountered, for example, in Russia.

Desperately defending itself, the capitalistic world in the persons of its principal leaders has received failing grades in extricating the world from the postwar economic chaos. Capitalism is a kind of gigantic tumor which for quite some time has grown luxuriantly on the diseased body of mankind, pretending to represent it in its entirety, and yet, like every tumor, it has laid waste to the body, from which it has siphoned off the juices indispensable for life—it has not truly taken root in the body, it has not become a necessary organ, and from its phase as a benign tumor, and even for a time as a productive one, it has turned malignant through the secondary processes that it set in motion: rotting and disintegrating itself, it has begun to poison all mankind and drag it down to annihilation. Capitalism went to the wildest excesses, and then for its own selfish goals stirred up artificial national hatreds, provoking a wasteful war that brought only devastation to the entire world, giving in return minimal impetus to carrying out the ideas of political independence, both national and social, in which the noble-minded dreamers of the nineteenth century had wallowed on a theoretical plane. The liberation of some nations from the yoke of others and the creation of two great experimental outposts: fascism in Italy and Bolshevism in Russia—these are the only positive values to come out of the Great War.

Besides, capital became internationalized, and terrified mankind started to create pale specters of international institutions designed to avert in time any approaching calamities and regulate economic life. So far these institutions have failed: "unbridled capital," which like a tumor cares only about growth for growth's sake and power for power's sake and not about production and rational creativity, is incapable of controlling itself, and rapid and constantly exacerbated forms of nationalism threaten the world again with war. Fascist experiments in using a nonpartisan intellectual elite for scientific mediation between capital and labor so as to prevent the destruction of individual initiative likewise appear to have failed. Mankind in its vast capitalist camp has broken loose from its own control, after having created a civilization that has outgrown it, and humanity gambols in a wild tumorous dance on the very edge of the abyss that means final annihilation.

The sole force fighting against unbridled capitalism appears to be Bolshevism, as all other attempts at regulating production have so far proved abortive; not only do we have no idea what is happening at present in Russia, owing both to the essential mysteriousness of the very process taking place there and to faulty information, but also—because this is an initial process geared to the future, experimental in nature, which perhaps no one at present (y compris the sharpest, least biased brains in the field of economics) is capable of understanding, since the phenomenon of Bolshevism is too close to us and given its immensity—we do not have sufficient historical distance from it. Even the negative results of the "five-year plan," the number of people killed and tortured for the sake of establishing a definitive state of happiness for all, the suppression of personal life, and the relentless sucking dry of the individual through excessively hard work—in such dimensions as apparently exist in Russia at present—cannot prevent the working masses of other countries from thinking that perhaps some of the fiascoes and economic shortcomings of Russian Bolshevism, the extremity of personal suffering, and the numerous losses in people, brains, and cultural achievements are the results of the special conditions in which Russia finds herself and of her immediate past, so different from the past of other countries, and that in other circumstances and starting at a higher level for its *point de déclenchement*, Bolshevism might produce far better and perhaps even ideal results.

At any rate, there is probably nothing more that can be expected from the world of capital in its hitherto existing form—whatever positive it had to offer has already been offered. Its civilization is finished, and its continuing dominance, as witness the present economic chaos and the incorrigibility of certain classes despite the lessons taught by the war, is leading mankind to more and more cataclysmic prospects. Our epoch is an epoch so full of surprises that it is impossible to foresee any solution, at least in the immediate future. It seems beyond doubt that we are really finally heading toward the total mechanization and disappearance of the individual, along with his creative energies, in exchange for equable material welfare and social perfection. Such progress cannot be achieved without the sufferings not only of the classes that in the struggle for the future political system must be defeated, but also of those that will start the revolution for the sake of their own future happiness. From this viewpoint, on the basis of what we can assume the approximate state of present-day Russia to be, it might appear that the gradual transformation of society as proposed, for example, by the Mensheviks and the violent *Umsturz* of the Bolsheviks require equally prolonged suffering on the part of the working class. But here the value of ideas enters into play: the working classes of Russia, suffering because of their frantic exertions necessitated by the fact that Bolshevism is surrounded by capitalist powers, know that they are suffering for an idea which is being implemented in reality during their lifetime—and that with their very lives they are creating not only the possibility of a different political system but actually its very starting point. According to the Menshevik conception, the working classes can only organize within a hostile capitalistic political system, while the struggle is waged by their leaders in the legislatures or even in the seats of authority. It is evident that such arrangements cannot satisfy the working masses and lead to contradictions that discredit the very idea of gradually attaining a better future. On the other hand, it is impossible to say how long workers can be expected to exert their muscles and nerves to the maximum without the immediate realization of the Bolshevik political system in its ideal form. It is difficult for an entire social class to live with even the loftiest idea in their hearts and minds but with the foreknowledge that they will be only the manure for future generations.

The views that I have been advancing here are those of a layman in economic matters, and of a layman who belongs to no social class unless it is that of *déclassé* artists and "intellectuals." But such a position is still quite far removed from decadence and nihilism as a way of life. Before I take up the problem, I should like to consider whether it is at all worthwhile in our times for artists and writers—since we must assume they cannot be experts in all the fields, knowledge of which could serve as the basis for any valid opinion in economic matters—to speak up on these questions directly through the representation of reality in their works. For this purpose we cannot rely on so-called intuition—what is needed are the proper data; an able mind simply will not suffice—it would be the same as if a clever literary man set out to solve a problem in theoretical physics intuitively. Gone are the good old days when "national bards" could settle the thorniest question with a single prophetic phrase. That was possible in Poland when the country was partitioned, and the economic situation in the prewar period was childishly simple compared with present-day complications.

And now Russia has already produced a new literature, since life has provided her writers with a new vision of reality and new problems, some of which they found solved by life, but others of which involved them directly as the solutions were being worked out. Some of the solutions are of a purely social and economic nature, while others, related to the former, are psychological. As for the latter, perhaps writers have something to say—but we must stress their total helplessness and incapacity with regard to social and economic questions, all the more so if we are considering the societal future of such a hypothetically complex and unpredictable structure as any Communist government outside Russia, which we must treat as a special case, i.e., a first experiment under special circumstances. Concocting utopias on the subject would in all likelihood result in trashy literature in the worst sense of the word. As for present-day Russian literature, however, given our scanty knowledge of the circumstances of its development, we do not know to what extent it faithfully represents reality, and to what extent it is being produced under the influence of external pressure and fear. If Polish literature, even though not publicly oppressed by anyone, shows such obvious signs of self-imposed abasement and intimidation, then we can assume that these phenomena must be diabolically intensified in a society that finds itself in such a dangerous stage of formation. Whether the human types and problems that Aleksandr Dan discusses in his interesting article "On a New Type of Common Man" are an adequate expression of Russian reality is a question about which, in my opinion, we cannot say anything at this moment, given the theory of the propagandistic role of all art that reigns there.

A writer does not necessarily have to be a disseminator of social ideas, but if he does take them up, he must be absolutely truthful and courageous. That cannot be said about Polish literature today, which is for the most part cowardly and mendacious. Of course, there are extenuating circumstances: such as the tradition of "national bards," the problem of didacticism, the living standards of writers, etc. But that is not much of a consolation—even in those circumstances, it would be preferable if the level of our literature and criticism were distinctly higher and if our writers were more honest and had more courage.

The value of social ideas is measured not by their "idealism" but solely by their practical effectiveness, in relation to all of humanity rather than to one particular social group. The triumphant idea will be the one that offers the best and the most comprehensive solution to the problem of making general prosperity equally available to all. Of course, a completely ideal solution lies in the distant future, when the civilization of our entire globe will be equally available for all, when specialization and an educational program geared to it begun in childhood will make possible the maximum use of each human being in exact accordance with his abilities, and when the mechanization of life and the disappearance of the individual will have reached its peak. We cannot shut our eyes to the losses that attaining this ideal will entail. That is the inescapable law that undoubtedly holds true in all collectivities in the entire universe, and we too must submit to it. The main thing is to be able to draw the right conclusions from history and the immediate past, so that, on the basis of an understanding of the inexorable laws of social development (inexorable in the sense that can be called transcendental according to Cornelius's terminology), further upheavals could take place with minimal losses, which are always the result of stubborn resistance on the part of essentially bankrupt systems defending their existence in defiance of all the lessons of past events. If the transformation of society—in which the individual along with his characteristic creations, metaphysics and art, must be annihilated—is inevitable, then it is crucial that there be no repetition of the errors of the preceding revolutions, which as initial experiments were unavoidable, and that we do not consider the principles according to which those errors occurred as holy dogmas not to be violated.

So now I shall allow myself to make at least a few observations concerning "intellectuals." Just because our so-called intelligentsia is, among other things, indolent, faceless, vacillating, ready for every compromise, cowardly, actually underintelligent, and half-educated (as a rule, rather than in exceptional cases) is no reason for despising the intellectual in the abstract as a person representing intellectual values. Out anti-intellectualism is leading us astray, as is our trust in what is called intuition and our inadequate training in the tools of thought. Hence the writers who once inspiration fails them have nothing to say, hence the lack of "venerable giants," hence all the premature peterings-out and untimely ends of those who started out so promisingly. For some, the intelligentsia is synonymous with decadence. But to inveigh against "Young Poland" and use the term as a "cussword" should be the prerogative of a generation that at least in the artistic realm has reached the level of the creative spirits of that period. Not everything created by the Young Poland movement is worthless when measured against today's communism. Continuity of culture despite revolutionary change would be the ideal. It is completely unwarranted to identify the creative output of Young Poland with the bloated bourgeoisie gorged on workers' blood and preoccupied with aesthetic and psychological subtleties.

Class hatred, which is a valuable stimulus for human progress, should not be indiscriminately applied to unrelated works of art that have originated within certain classes that happen to be hated by other classes. Because Żeromski was not a self-proclaimed Bolshevik is no reason why our Communists should dismiss him, but instead they should look in a more historical and objective fashion (despite passion's value as an element of revolution) at both past and present phenomena and particularly at works not directly connected with the Bolshevik *Umsturz* as such. I have the impression that in recent times literature has stopped shaping life on the scale that it once did, starting in the eighteenth century and continuing up to the war. Literature's role in molding our consciousness is minimal: the newspaper that day after day quite systematically drums into its readers' heads the views of the party that it serves, and the spoken words of political agitators—these are the essential elements in bringing about changes in the way the masses think. Literature has an effect only on the "intelligentsia" and even that on a very limited scale, especially here in Poland. I am convinced that all Soviet literature has more of a social and revolutionary influence on foreign intellectuals than on the masses in Russia and beyond its borders, but that especially and perhaps exclusively in Poland at present the intelligentsia is an element of little value for bringing about essential social transformations—it is passive and listless—and acquiesces out of fear and boredom to any kind of change rather than playing a creative role in bringing it about. Of course, I am not talking about that special group of intellectuals responsible for producing revolutions, but about writers, artists, men of science, about that entire clique known before the war as the "Highly Esteemed" public, a class not easily defined, forming the middle-range intellectual core of society and spreading its tentacles even into the ranks of the upper nobility and for all I know the highest aristocracy and heavy industry. In my view, the concept of the white-collar worker does not correspond entirely to the group that we have been discussing, because on the one hand among white-collar workers there are found types that do not fall into the category of the intellectual, and on the other hand, in other groups— from workers to aristocrats—individuals can be met who taken in toto will surpass by more than one hundred percent the median core mentioned above. The middle-rangers are rather beauty lovers of all complexions, including even those with completely ugly souls, who maintain a certain degree of intellectual alertness. The lower limit of this type would be readers of Maeterlinck, and those who leave the theater with a feeling of pious distaste after seeing a comedy or farce by Stefan Kiedrzyński. The average intellectual level of this class here in Poland is unbelievably low. The task of a bold and truthful literature would be to bring to a boil and a blaze this small inner core of society, often justly despised from a moral point of view, and yet potentially quite valuable. (In any case, in my opinion, under no condition should the most extreme measures be applied to this class summarily, but rather it should be used for higher goals.)

Of course, to some extent my misfortune (and I assume, that of many others) is that my social views, whatever they may be (and under the influence of an almost "active" participation at the beginning of the Russian Revolution, I have undergone strange transformations, shifting from aristocratic aestheticism to the ideology of the Social Revolutionaries, and then of the Bolsheviks, and now recently through a temporary flirtation with fascism to a certain version of communism), do not spring from my very heart's blood and are instead a purely intellectual construction, based on a modicum of training in such matters. Nonetheless, the registering hand of my novels, i.e., the pointer indicating direction and stress, has been utterly misread, and the psychology of the characters who appear in them, which is presented purely intellectually (not emotionally), has been misunderstood and unfairly judged. Analysis of the condition of a world heading for extinction and of the reasons for its decline may be significant for someone for whom literature is only a means of propaganda, but actually everything depends on the intellectual level on which this is done. The next error of those ideologues of revolution who follow the Russian model of communism is their anti-intellectualism, carried out as propaganda for the class called the intelligentsia. Intellectual terror practiced in spheres that have no direct connection to social issues should be excluded from the social program of revolution under any circumstances. As it is, unfortunately, a fair amount of terror is propagated even during peacetime. But anything like compulsory materialist philosophy, as is the case in Russia, must arouse fear in everyone who respects the only truly and absolutely precious human achievement—i.e., the intellect. What is happening in Russia is a degradation of man's greatest pride—i.e., intellectual integrity. The prejudice of our Communists against any form of metaphysics, as something immoral from the Communist viewpoint, strikes me as ridiculous.

It is possible that "metaphysical insatiability" will totally disappear as the mechanization of mankind is progressively instituted, but the deliberate and systematic extermination of that undeniably creative element of individuality as something dangerous is completely unwarranted, all the more so in that it is already on the way to extinction in art and philosophy anyway. Blind hatred for all the works of individualistic culture, because it implies wronging workers, should be eliminated. Preserving as long as possible the positive values of this culture, despite social revolution, should be the task of those who have drawn the correct conclusions from the gigantic experiment of the Russian Revolution. Why should we deliberately carry over the bad side effects of the underdevelopment and underindustrialization of prerevolutionary Russia into societies, that even in the case of a radical revolution can take pains to avoid the errors arising from an absence of general culture and that have the added advantage that change is taking place there on a smaller scale?

METAPHYSICAL FEELINGS

■

(1931)

The common source of religion, philosophy, and art I consider to be what I once unfortunately called "metaphysical feeling." The term still strikes me as essentially correct, but it was unfortunate in that it led to a host of needless misunderstandings in the ensuing battles (which were without much vigor and never dealt with essentials anyhow) over my theory of art, known as "the theory of Pure Form," which many of the uninitiated and even some professional critics identified (the former through incomprehension, the latter deliberately in order to "rip it to shreds") with a desire to create systematic nonsense; it was as such—that is, thoroughly falsified—that my theory was assailed.

In the past I have defined "metaphysical feeling" as the directly given unity of our individuality, and in this instance I characterize the means of being "directly given" as the way in which we are given all qualities: sounds, odors, colors, tactile sensations, etc., including "structural qualities" (the shape of a figure, the line of a melody, etc.). This unity of our individuality, a feeling that each of us possesses to a greater or lesser degree, I called "metaphysical feeling" in contradistinction to real-life feelings, such as love, anger, joy, etc., and I used the word feeling to convey the "popular" sense of something directly given, in contrast to something given us through concepts. . . .

Today I would perhaps not call this unity of our individuality a "feeling," nor add the epithet "metaphysical," so as not to incite against the no-

285

tion all kinds of positivists: from radical, thoroughgoing psychologists to hopeless materialists, who even nowadays can still be found in our midst, if not in the spheres of official philosophy then at least among scholars and the public at large. Not everyone knows that there is a vast abyss between the concepts "metaphysical" and "mystical." Those who like precise thinking but are philosophically untrained and predisposed to positivism (in the above sense) detect something arbitrary and fantastic as soon as they hear the word "metaphysical," which prevents them from seriously exploring a theory that contains a concept corresponding to the term. Little attention gets paid to the definitions I have advanced—instead the aggregate of prejudices and dislikes (phobias) affecting a given individual automatically intervene. That is what happened in most cases with my theory of Pure Form, which in its philosophical premises is based on the above concept.

Today I would simply call this "feeling" the "directly given unity of our individuality" and let it go at that, and I would define as "metaphysical feelings" the emotive reworkings of this unity which at a given moment emerges more forcefully vis-à-vis the other qualities, noting, however, that in my view all feelings, even the subtlest and loftiest, as well as "emotive reworkings," i.e., combinations of a particular feeling of unity with other real-life feelings, are reducible to more or less complex sequences of simple qualities. These include, besides the already mentioned qualities, muscular sensations, sensations of the internal organs, and in general all sensations localized on the surface of or in the interior of our body; these latter can be defined in their totality as a complex of qualities interconnected in a certain way. Such complexes (for example, colors, shapes, or tactile sensations), manifested in regular compounds repeating themselves within certain limits, will also include objects of the external world: "inanimate matter" and the bodies of other living beings.

RELATIONS OF RELIGION
AND PHILOSOPHY

∎

(1932)

Now I maintain that religion is, generally speaking, a construction of feelings arising from metaphysical anxiety, a construction contained in symbols that, in any given cult, are precisely those and not any others, although in the abstract these symbols are, to a certain extent, arbitrary, whereas philosophy, on the other hand, having reached its full perfection, is a construction of concepts—of *necessary concepts*, arising from the same feelings (of metaphysical anxiety), not experienced directly, but transformed conceptually with the aid of concepts provided by common sense. It is immediately evident that any given religion is simply what it is and there can be no question of any progress, except in a social sense, whereas in the case of philosophy we can speak with assurance of progress throughout the entire course of its history, the progress consisting of rendering its concepts more and more precise. The origins of various primitive cults in relation to questions of social organization are beyond the scope of my argument. What I am concerned with is the psychology of the religious feelings of any cult whatsoever once it has already evolved. Here I stress only that I have always maintained, in opposition to the views of Bronisław Malinowski, expressed in his first treatise in Polish on the origin of religious feelings, that at the basis of everything that happens in this sphere there must be acknowledged the primordial fact of the opposition of the individual to the rest of Existence; as a result of this feeling of opposition, the unity of the individual seen from his viewpoint and *the unity of the totality of the world outside him* have inevitably been directly intensified for that individual. Here lies the source of metaphysical anxiety, the further reworkings of which are the symbols of any given cult, symbols either personal or impersonal, which represent certain powers. The impersonal unity of the world is the only basis on which there can be incarnated the figures of particular deities, which thereby become more comprehensible for the human creature and attenuate the frightful and incomprehensible mystery of the world outside him, in which the sole support for the terrified individual has been the existence of creatures of the same species who are similar to him.

THE ONLY WAY OUT

■

(1931–33)

The future now was open—he could lose himself however he wished, he was alone, he could lose himself by finally creating a kind of painting that would be utterly weird—nothing like it in the world, absolutely pure forms free of the abstractness of cubist blockage or futuristic feelings run wild. True painting—what charms lurked in that conception, which had been totally lost during the last decade of the first half of the twentieth century.

As a painter, Marcel considered himself virtually the sole artist in the entire world, for he was the artist in whom all of painting throughout the world—of course, purely artistic, formal painting—found its final expression and termination. Naturally, he exaggerated his own importance atrociously, as do all artists, but there was a grain of truth in all that megalomaniacal raving. There's no denying that those were times when painting as an art faced extinction from one end of Europe to the other, not to mention other parts of the world—it was not hard to be foremost in such a situation. To be the very last gasp of something once as great as painting—is truly something great too in its own way. And moreover, to be able to ruin one's organism and die for something, in a truly interesting fashion, especially in those times, even in a world of delusions and phantasms—now that was a rarity "off the beaten track." He simply could not stop painting; to do that sometimes takes more character than the average jackass may think. . . .

All ablaze, hair streaming, beautiful as a demonic archangel or an angelic demon, Marcel came bounding into the dining room from the veranda. His reddish-blond "locks" hung down over the lightly grooved forehead of a magus, and the flashing of his azure blue eyes was like the reflection of the sky in a foul, muddy puddle—while his lips were twisted by purely existential pain, without a trace of the slightest earthly anxieties. . . . Besides that, Marcel was as powerfully built as a bull and his physical strength was manifest in the springy lightness of his movements; it was clear that this Individual Existence was once capable of breaking the steel runners of skates or of lifting three hundred pounds with one hand. . . .

What bliss to slug down, with a clean conscience, a glass of vodka on an empty stomach—with no regard for the health of either mind or body, convinced that psychophysical self-destruction is the highest goal of one's existence. Only a *creatively self-destructive artist, and no one else, can indulge* in such a luxury. (Beware of using this as a bad example to follow or of trying to become an artist artificially so as to be able to "destroy oneself creatively"—the punishment is nothing less than moral death.)

"Our sole superiority to the antimetaphysical rabble," Marcel liked to say, "is that we artists, by slowly decomposing and dying out, are fulfilling our quintessential mission on this planet—and this is a transcendental principle—encompassing the whole of infinite existence, infinite and Euclidean, I repeat, and not a tiny misshapen scrap of finite existence modeled after their cozy little constructs—I'm referring to one hundred percent scholars—so magisterial as long as they don't overstep the bounds set for them by the presuppositions of their own knowledge."

He swigged down the transparent liquid the way Flint drank his rum, and he planned to kill himself with vodka as Flint had killed himself with rum. Paintings in progress were waiting for him. He was incontestably the greatest (and the last) painter on the earthly globe after that old mountebank Picasso. But no one appreciated him, given the degeneration of cubism, the renaissance of pseudostylized nature in the manner of Zamoyski's sculpture, and the pseudoimpressionistic amorphous blobs of total artistic "nulliters" (from nullity) spewed out over the entire world from the artistic faubourgs of a moribund Paris. At long last Paris had definitively gone to the dogs. Oh, what a relief! Marcel's painting was something altogether new. Here was constructivism of the highest order, in its absolute unexpectedness rubbing shoulders (although not formally) with early surrealism. His pictures were constructions that had nothing to do with "filling up plane surfaces" or with the *échafaudage* of overentelechyized effeters of Pure Form who washed it clean of its subject matter (that's how some lousy bastards garbled the ideas of that smartass from Zakopane, Vitcatius of Krupowa Równia). His canvases revealed "living creatures" given form, for the most part, in two dimensions (without simulating the third, which in the last analysis can be allowed in certain cases), eruptions (not explosions—that's saying too little) and solar prominences—congealed in their onward rush—of a metaphysical volcano located at the very core of a priceless, unique, unrepeatable individual entity (as is every such being—even the most wretched bedbug or microbe). . . .

I think everyone knows Kretschmer's work. My summary of his theory can be found in my book called *Narcotics*.

For a methodical suicide of Marcel's dimensions, what was the use of such preventive, prophylactic, prestallatory little resolves? At the stage of "perishment" at which he found himself, even the loftiest abstinences must have seemed to him what a mosquito's caress is to a tabletop. How was he to flesh out his day? Vis-à-vis the metaphysical powers—essences almost without individuality (under the influence of cocaine even that is comprehensible), guarding the absolute nothingness at the confines of being where Boredom reigns as a thing-in-itself—how was he to justify that random planetary day, amidst a tribe of desperadoes disguised as mammals and Jurassic lizards in stinking rags so as to be a laughingstock for astral spirits watching from their "outpost" (ha, ha) the whole eerie phantasmagoria (*un fantasse-magot-rien*) of the reptilian masked ball? These were the sources. It was from there, from those extreme limits of being, stuffed into a given creature's psychology in the form of extreme states virtually insuring a nonsensical grasp of the eeriness of every single instant, of the unique sui generis monstrosity (words simply fail me) which is individual existence (there is no other kind and never can be)—it was from there that the hideous farce called art flowed, being the creation of little formal constructions in which the horror has been reabsorbed in a feeling of security as happens in a horrible fairy tale for children: all you have to do is put your feet up on the sofa (so that what's lurking underneath can't reach out and grab you) to have the delectable pleasure of being frightened to death by "the Ghostly Barber" from *Tales of Wonderland* or some other "blood-curdling" and "spine-tingling" story. Encased in the armor of art, the mystery has lost its menace and we have been able to caress the monster as though it were anesthetized, forgetting that its fangs and claws are poisoned and that even accidentally brushing against them could lacerate the flesh or cause a festering gangrene of the brain. By creating this veil, or rather this skirt, to cover the shameful private parts of the eternal mystery, life had so far been quite bearable for this tribe of scroungers, stinking cattle decked out in frock coats, sweaters, and dresses, apparently enervated by the sheer anguish of existence in and of itself and contemptuously understanding nothing, and yet eternally happy in their enormous conceit at having fabricated that harmless drug (art), whose effect is only to allay the dread of existence—which is detached from the totality of the psyche—while all the other vital signs during the course of usage undergo no fundamental change, such as takes place if one indulges in alcohol, alkaloids, or states of religious ecstasy.

So Marcel slugged down another glass of vodka to lay a good base for taking the "white fairy" (on first getting up—what a nasty kind of thrill!) and proceeded to the bathroom. He was shaking all over, and his insides seemed to have come loose. Only his heart—truly equine in its pumping power—beat with a slightly accelerated but regular beat, fueling the entire machine with still sound blood, mixed at a rate of five percent with pure alcohol, which was being burned up at a frantic rate, charging the prodigious batteries of his brain with the monstrous energy needed for going into action. The ordinary world was turning into the daily nightmare. . . .

He hastily snorted a huge quantity of coco (a gram and a half in two quick flips of the hand) and set about eating breakfast, which consisted of an infusion of sage leaves and Bébé Malade biscuits. While munching them, he drummed impatiently on the table with his fingers, then felt he was ready to take the plunge. Everything connected with life lost coherence, while all that was perverse and unhealthy lined up in battle array for an attack on the remnants of those normal areas still drowsing in the twilight of the unconscious. How to make the transition from a contemplative state to an active one? With pupils dilated, Marcel stared through the huge window of his ground-floor studio at the day in the throes of growing brighter. Above the dirty white piece of linen that served as a curtain covering the lower part of the window, a magnificent maple tree could be seen spreading the autumnal yellow splendor of its leafy crown like a peacock. Actually it was a sad and banal sight (this sentence describing it is no better), rendered all the sadder by the wan light of an overcast day vainly striving to brighten in the dank autumnal city. . . .

Marcel dashed into the bathroom again to take a cold shower. Only that marvelous "cold, translucent fairy," as he called it—as opposed to the hot variety, i.e., vodka—functioned as an antidote to the partial paralysis of his (what luck) left arm and a certain weakness in the whole left side of his body, which always made itself felt after serious overdoses of "snow." Stimulated

by the cold beads of water, the metaphysical center of his being started making connections with compositions in progress through shifting complexes of
muscular feelings and sensations of the inner organs, especially that inner
sense of touch, which is the unique substance of the primitive, unicellular
self, and the fundamental basis of self-awareness (not as a mood, but existen-
tially) on the part of higher Individual Existences.

Now something eventful was about to happen. How hard it is to rouse to
action the inert, dormant psychological mass. . . .

Marcel emerged from the bathroom a totally new man—perhaps not a
man, but rather a metaphysicalized beast. Now he was truly living, without
any hocus-pocus, in another world—real life had vanished like a speck of
dust blown away by a hurricane. It was all rushing off into the boundless,
blue, stormy distance of remembrance, while at the same time continuing its
duration in that very room. Outside the window, the yellowing maple, *which
seemed to be growing on another planet,* stood there calmly and watched everything unperturbed. . . .

No more stalling. Marcel began working furiously. Suffretka was supposed to come at twelve, and by that time the painting he had started several
days ago had to be finished—this was the last minute for doing it. Every work
of art must be brought to completion at the right time. The process is as
precise as the course of childbirth. The creator's artistic intuition (in this
instance the notion makes sense) dictates that (except for the solution of
purely formal problems) the whole business is to be finished at only that exact
time. Every artist knows infallibly that at such and such a moment a given
project must be begun, and he knows approximately how long it will take and
when and at what particular hours it has to be worked on. If he does not obey
that voice, he is a fraud and a cheat only pretending to be an artist. There is
some truth in the concept of inspiration, despite what is said by overintellectualized and impotent creators who fabricate their works artificially (for whatever ulterior purposes: fame, money, etc.), once they have achieved
recognition in certain circles or perhaps everywhere and such methods of
production have led them astray in other dimensions. But as a certain American president once said: "You may fool all the people some of the time; you
can even fool some of the people all the time; but you can't fool all of the
people all the time." In fact, the act of creation is in all likelihood very similar
to childbirth: something ripe wants and has to detach itself from the substratum on which it grew in order to make room for something new. Failure to
seize the right moment can lead to decomposition of the fruit within the cre-

ator or to stillbirths—to force prematurely the naturalness of this process for the sake of practical matters or side issues leads to serious artistic illnesses and even to complete creative impotence. But one must really be in full possession of this "intuition" and not waste it on account of, say, a bridge game, a meeting with a lady, or an interesting walk, but on the contrary one must do everything possible to foster the conditions in which it can flourish. . . .

So now Marcel was possessed by this primordial intuition and consequently went furiously to work on a composition entitled *The Auto-umbilifica-tion of the Browbeaten*, which only as regards its inessential real-life subject matter had anything to do with this title per se. . . . Of course, the title could be accused of "un-understandability," and justly so—on the other hand, however, in a certain sense everything is understandable, unless our understanding of the term is given a purely logical significance, with precise, rigorous definitions of the relevant concepts: yet one can feel something directly—this feeling may not be synonymous with the psychic state experienced by the "creator" of a given symbol which was not clearly defined a priori, but something will undoubtedly be felt. Words are the nuclei around which there are larger or smaller aureoles of indefiniteness inversely proportionate to the precision of the definition. These constant digressions are unbearable, but then there are so many interesting things (think there aren't, blockhead? Want a punch in the nose?) about which no one has the slightest idea and yet the intellectual riffraff spouts the worst rubbish on the subject, plunging into even deeper darkness the already none too enlightened brains of their entourage. But too bad—it's time to get back to life and (there or nowhere) show what the whole thing means.

This composition like every essential composition in the realm of pure painting (God almighty!) appeared to Marcel as a not yet precisely fixed nexus of initially undefined forms whose directional tensions were indistinctly marked out by their still imperfectly unequivocal resemblance to certain embryonically indeterminate objects. A coil of potential force such as might be found in an unexploded bomb, but already giving a slight suggestion of its directionally dynamic (i.e., vectorial) possibilities. "Verily" the composition appeared to Marcel as he was assailed by a moment of naked and hitherto unparalleled metaphysical dread, when, returning at night from Suffretka Nunberg's, he suddenly felt himself all alone on a *strange and alien* planet, *quite literally*, without any ghastly, disgustingly literary hokum or tricks calculated to affect the reader—and the most average kind of reader at that; he was alone on a sultry summer night walking from the outskirts to the center of town, and his gradual entry into the streets of those districts that were brightly lighted but deserted at that hour in no way lessened his feeling of *absolute loneliness*. And besides he was fully conscious of not belonging to any group, or to any species of similar beings—the feeling was frightful. And what was even more frightful was that the sudden appearance on a side street of an invariably belated (how could it be otherwise under the circumstances) passerby did not in the slightest change his eerie feeling of loneliness and of not even belonging to the human species. It was not a state of affairs that could be summed up in the judgment "I am not a human being"—such a possibility did not even exist; Marcel had simply fallen from nowhere (just as he had popped into Interstellar Space from nowhere) onto a strange and alien orb. It was all equally incomprehensible, but this was incomprehensibility carried to a higher power: as though a grown man had suddenly been born or discovered for the first time that he existed in a particular place—it scarcely matters where—since it was strange and alien in any case. These were experiences that could not be had without narcotics. And in addition to his usual quota of coco, which in the nighttime hours sometimes reached 12.00, he took an additional dose (while at a friend's, an addict constantly working on eucodal) of .08 of the drug *per injectionem cutanea*. This produced the typical transformation of cocaine-induced excitement into the somewhat inanely ecstatic contemplation of the world as something serene and blissful, which is the lot of people taking the above-mentioned narcotic. There he was, Marcel and his walking stick (the malacca cane was apparently not even genuine but nonetheless dearly beloved). The tiny globe earth had shrunk to the dimensions of a piddling little asteroid—you could fly around it in a quarter of an hour— and the town seemed an object "from another dimension" that was spirit engendered: an inconceivable conglomeration of forms without a trace of any idea of practical utility—"the pure form of the nonsense that is objective reality," particularized, but not defined. "Moo and me walking stoock," Marcel said to himself, his joyfulness cool and his inner mood axiomatic. The little man he had met in the street did not belong to this world and by virtue of this judgment (in a logical not judicial sense) he had been banished from it. That was the true miracle. Unfortunately, the miraculousness of such a state cannot be fully appreciated while under the influence of the drug, because one is tucked inside that special compartment, and the price one pays for being enclosed in it is to have an outlook that is inconceivable and inexpressible in a normal state. . . .

Exciting events—everyone dreamed of something happening, even if the exciting events were only such as might be found in the novels of Antoni Marczyński or Edgar Wallace, but actually nothing ever took place in those times, which, for many, seemed to have been cursed by the Demon of Boredom.

Coming back to that refrain: "me and my walking stick" (from then on it was to be a constant leitmotiv dominating the entire future) turned out to be something like this: Earth was an extremely heavy ball made of lead (like a satellite of Sirius—therein lay all its solidity), and he felt almost like a trained monkey balancing on top of the ball that was somewhat smaller than he was. Exciting events—oh, when would something happen? When, oh, when?

Casually swinging his beloved (pseudo) malacca cane, he leaned out into space strewn with myriads of suns from nebulae blazing with astronomical lights and rarefied to the vanishing point as they emitted penetrating rays seemingly "by the bucketful." The horizon foundered—falling headlong into the infinite abyss of fourth-dimensional space: Marcel directly experienced Minkowski's concept à la Whitehead crawling *ventre à terre* at the center point where the coordinates of the fourth-dimensional continuum and its grudgingly acknowledged heterogeneous elements all converged. The moment could not last long—it burst, and in so doing assumed the form of the "aforesaid" composition. When he caught sight of it dimly outlined against the backdrop of starlit darkness (now more real, seen as an earthly sky) above the houses of the Daivur district, the earth became the earth again, an ordinary, everyday dingy hole, and the walking creature turned out to be a man, a repulsive "fraternal" freak, symbol of limitation and infirmity. . . .

Then the world jolted as though it had rigor-mortized. The diabolical importance of the moment and of the art work it produced. For such moments millions are not too much to pay, and if fame and "dough" (hideous Warsaw slang) go along with it, well, then, you know, you're sitting pretty, as long as you've got a clean conscience as an artist (which is asking too much of those overintellectualized pretenders to former greatness in the arts). The importance, the importance—resting there on the knob of his walking stick, only instead of his cheap malacca cane, Marcel was at that very moment holding in his two paws (that seemed to belong to some metaphysical beast out of this world) his own unique composition, perfect in its own imperfection, great in its own greatness! . . .

So at the moment the composition came into being, the whole world—both internal and external—shone forth like a somber nighttime landscape illumined by a flash of lightning that struck nearby—it shone forth and then died out instantly.

But the pictorial vision that lingered on was something truly marvelous. . . .

Marcel was transported, indivisibly and for life, into that other world, and the everyday world (including the "white fairy" and Suffretka) became, in his view, something totally accidental. There is nothing more pleasurable than the specific (characteristic) disdaining of life from the artistic viewpoint. Waking existence becomes transformed into a dream—it's carefree, fortuitous, and nondescript, weightless, light as the fluff of dandelions (*pissenlits*) carried on the wind. But the whole thing has to be authentic, or otherwise it exacts a terrible vengeance—it does anyhow, but *in that case* it's even worse. No one who is not a true artist is allowed to show such contempt for life. In either instance, disdain when carried far beyond any reason found to justify it may lead straight to madness, because someone intoxicated by this strange narcotic (phantasm-producer), which is the by-product of art-making (artistic) experiences—both essential and inessential—loses thereafter (after what?) all sense of proportion in using his existence in this exceedingly strange and alien (although self-chosen) dimension. Everything undimensional, incommensurable, criterionless, equivalent. Nothing to be done, except to wallow in it like a dog in a pile of muck (*dans une pile de muque*). And the qualified and unqualified alike make a practice of it. The pseudoartistic rabble, which is one of the chief ingredients making up the dregs of the urban intelligentsia, is a curse plaguing mankind today, but it will soon die out along with true art and its creators. And besides who doesn't call himself an artist nowadays? In our times even every thief and swindler, not to mention other honest professions, lays claim to this title. . . .

So Marcel finally got hold of his paints and began to squeeze them out on an enormous and (inevitably) elliptical palette. No one in the world understands what color really is—no one except for a handful of people, just as no one except for a few of the chosen knows what sounds are, considered as component parts of purely artistic entities. . . .

At the same time Marcel thought about friendship. Oh, that is something great, a thousand times greater than love, although sometimes, in extremely rare cases, the two go together, and then that is the finest thing of all, indomitable vis-à-vis the metaphysical horror of Existence, but also diabolically difficult if you want to keep it on a high level of veracity, sincerity of reaction (masklessness or uncoveredness), and magnanimous cruelty without a trace of any vile higher-purposeless sadism, perhaps the most repulsive thing to be found in the world, which humans have cultivated in the secret, bestial, excremental chambers of their souls. We indeed have had to pay a frightful price for that slice of brain rind we possess. The colors in a dazzling rainbow on the palette changed from cobalt to ultramarine passing through emerald green to lacquered purples and aniline violets. . . .

Marcel painted like one possessed. Each stroke of the brush was a minor poem à la Słonimski. It had what the French call *touché* of the highest class. The question of form was carried out to the very last elements, which in point of fact means the very first elements—in the placing of each individual dot of color, of even the intermediate "half-degrees" or half-tones.

But who cares about that?

That question is indeed fatal for the next installment of this almost real story (but not in the sense of having any connection with the author's life, as some indiscreet Individual Existences might think). And what actually does happen when an artist is in the act of painting, or putting notes down on the staves, or writing down poetry? What is the conscious content of his consciousness—as for the subconscious content at such a moment, that is a totally different matter. . . .

Monstrous contempt for art shook Marcel to the very core of his being. At the same time three gentlemen could be seen through the open doors of the two rooms in the depths of the corridor lighted by orange bulbs. . . . Marcel kept on painting. In the background the visitors kept slowly drawing nearer—Suffretka devoured each stroke of the brush, since it was due to her, an unconscious, benighted little beast, that this was taking place. Centuries were elapsing, entire centuries . . . seconds, instants.

The visitors kept drawing closer and closer. Cocaine packed years into minutes. How can this be transferred into reality? But actually why bother, if it's right here now—the only difference being that one has to atone for it. Contempt for art: that was something that he, Marcel, had a right to, because he knew perfectly what art was, he was capable of doing it, he saw the end of art clear as day and considered himself the last link in the chain pulling the wagon in which were riding all that ragtag and bobtail of degenerate lizards whose bodies were not adapted to their environment (but with brain rinds burgeoning and differentiated), or in other words, mankind. This chain was already dead—rather it was going dead before one's eyes. As for Marcel, he could not live out his life otherwise—he was not "a painter out of sheer delusion," like eighty-nine percent of Polish painters in the twentieth century, he was a true artist, meaning that he expressed metaphysical convulsions and anguish in purely formal constructions, which likewise acted directly by means of their forms and called forth in the viewers the very same psychic state he had experienced at the time these forms came into being. It is so simple and yet no one can understand it. Incidentally, that is an extremely rare occurrence in our frightful and yet in their own way beautiful times.

From the corridor there came a whiff of a horrendous to-do, as pungent as wet lilacs on a May night after the rain.

The first to enter was the pianist Romek, the king of third-class snobs after the almost total slaughter of the Polish aristocracy during the battle between the PZP and the Syndicalists of the Sorelian kind—he entered and looked dumbfounded.

The painting breathed immobile, congealed metaphysical frenzy. Marcel looked at Romek with what was left of his blue eyes—what was left, because the thin little band of cornflower blue iris had been slowly devoured by the pupil, which dilated monstrously after five grams of coco. On the canvas, encrusted in a kind of diabolical hide, a jumble of forms bursting into infinity roared deliriously. The Marquess of Maske-Tower, greeting no one (as a rule he never shook hands with artists but kissed boxers on the lips and jockeys on the hand), placed in his left eye—which seemed to belong to an antediluvian reptile—a monocle framed in the pubic bone of a female sea hippocentaur vulgaris. Marcel (extremely easygoing in real-life matters when under the influence of cocaine) without undue effort restrained himself from punching him in the nose.

No one thought to acknowledge Suffretka's presence—not even Nadrazil, although he was her former lover. . . . The visitors sat down in wicker armchairs—there weren't any others in the studio. Suffretka served whiskey and soda, but no one thanked her, and they all drank while Marcel continued painting. The paints wheezed and snorted under the brush, as the artist worked himself into a frenzy. The colors, precisely those colors and not any others—more necessary than the most ferociously indisputable laws of physics—flowed as hard blocks of puke through his overstrained brain right onto the canvas, where an invisible matrix, located in that overtaxed brain, shaped them into the congealed explosion of a metaphysical (used in the Schopenhauer-Nietzsche sense) volcano, that is, provided we consider art "a metaphysical activity," in other words, something that goes beyond the fabrication of a narcotic in the normal sense or of any pleasure-inducing qualities. Unless we acknowledge that such a narcotic calls forth a particular state of *metaphysical intoxication*, rather than any states comparable to real-life ine-briations. Undoubtedly there is something like this in art, although one cannot make an absolutely irrefutable theory with respect to all its premises.

Art is the direct expression of the most essential property of existence: unity in plurality. In art this unity in plurality appears to us in a pure state, whether it be in entities composed of simple or complex elements—it makes no difference. The arts share inessential but requisite elements: real-life feel-ings, the external world, conceptual content per se, etc.—what unites them is a common metaphysical content which is expressed in a pure construction that acts directly, in other words, in Pure Form. . . .

Pondering their own beauty, the leaves on the courtyard maple (there are courtyard artists too) swayed in time to the haphazard strokes made by Marcel's pig-bristle brush dripping paints—from the famous firm of Blockx—on the stretched canvas primed with glue made of ground rabbit hide and chalk. Marcel had made a fatal mistake when he failed to switch in time to smooth oil canvases, on which everything is easy to do, and instead remained hopelessly embroiled in paint-thirsty absorbent canvases à la Gau-guin, van Gogh, and our Władysław Ślewiński. But these are professional observations that only painters can appreciate, and fortunately there are fewer and fewer of these in the world.

Marcel began the fatal conversation with the visitors without ceasing to poke at the canvas, which quivered like a thoroughbred horse or a fox terrier who has been told that he is going for a walk. . . .

The monstrous strokes of Marcel's brush (oh, misery, misery, who must one be to devote oneself to something like that and still retain a feeling of one's own value and importance) extracted from (rather than expounded in) the painting some wisps of supramatter in a new dimension. The forms, which he engendered, moaning with metaphysical ardor, were flowing, together with the *nonexistent* objects, into accumulations of pure directional tensions coming from the compositional masses, and they almost burst from the internal pres-sures (each was its own tower of superhuman pressures). . . .

The bulging forms in the middle of the painting *interpenetrated each other, without losing any of their distinctive character*—a climaxing direc-tional tension, like a low blow to the stomach, foamed in a fountain of jets streaming upwards, where cinnabar, in gradations extending to pure white, poured like liquid mush into a heap of ultramarine, ascending in lightninglike zigzags to the apex of a yellow pyramid and consisting of a whole series of interwoven, worm-shaped coils. Marcel's fine-bristled brush now bored into that point, and his face fairly dripped with grim desire for metaphysical self-destruction (as opposed to real-life destruction)—simply to die with a bullet lodged in the brain so as to appease that desire was too little, was something inadequately negative: he longed to hoist the nothingness of the second self, as a *positive value,* onto the Satanic throne built of pure impersonal segments of duration, and then, having seized non-Euclidean space by its quintessential gut, to turn it inside out like a glove or a stocking so that it would become the flattest nothingness, a prop for the unimaginable throne. . . .

Continuing his arguments, Marcel kept condensing the cinnabars, intensified to the bursting point, around a mass of ultramarine belching forth an out-of-this-world blue, while making circular motions with his delicate little brush, movements which remained encrusted forever on the canvas, the way congealed lava in its immobility retains the shape of the eruption or the disgorging that tore it out of the insides of the earth: there on the canvas the fiery interior encapsulated Marcel's entire "self," now immense as some metapsychic Pamir (or something of the sort), and then at times narrowing in its diminutiveness to the dimensions of a Lilliputian piece of hardened turd, accidentally shit by a wretched unknown animal on the tracks of being in the infinite time of the totality of existence.

The Marquess literally frothed at the mouth with delight.

"It is magical, it is wonderful—it is marvelous!!" he repeated over and over again. . . .

Poisoned by the drug ($C_{17}H_{21}NO_4$—it is a miracle that exactly this combination of harmless elements has such an effect on the brains of precisely these creatures and that it is found in some kind of plant somewhere—in *Erythroxylon coco* in Peru, it surpasses belief). . . .

There she was, standing in front of him, that old whore, Art, who had been feeding on his brain, drinking it like the suspended matter in the infernal lemonade of his conceptualizing.

INTERVIEW WITH BRUNO SCHULZ

■

(April 1935)

As a graphic artist and draftsman, Schulz belongs to the line of demonologists. As I see it, the beginnings of this trend can be found in certain works by the old masters, even though in those days they did not make a specialty of it, for example in Cranach, Dürer, and Grünewald. With strange conviction and licentious delight they paint subjects that have an infernal rather than a heavenly inspiration, finding a source of relaxation there with a clean conscience after what must often have been for them boring pieties of a compulsory nature. Hogarth too I consider to be a demonist.

But the true creator of this trend in art (with regard to the subject matter of course, the realistic layer, the pretext for Pure Form) was Goya. Demonologists of the nineteenth century, such as Rops, Munch, or even Beardsley, are his direct descendants. It is not a question of the paraphernalia of demonism (witches, devils, etc.), but of evil itself that lies at the base of the human soul (egotism that makes an exception only for its own kind, greed, possessiveness, lust, sadism, cruelty, love of power, oppression of everything and everybody around), upon which only by proper training can other nobler qualities arise, which, by the way, can be observed in an embryonic form even in animals.

These are the general areas in which Schulz works, his specialty in this field being female sadism with its counterpart in male masochism. In my opinion, woman by her very nature (one can only marvel that she remains *as she is,* having such organs and means of operation at her disposal—marvel, admire her, and praise the powers responsible for the division of the sexes) must in principle be a sadist psychologically and a masochist physiologically, whereas man as a rule must be a masochist psychologically and a sadist physiologically. Schulz has brought the expression of both these psychic combinations to the extreme limits of tension and almost monstrous emotional frenzy. For Schulz, the female instrument of oppression over males is the leg, that most frightful part of a woman's body, except for the face and certain other things. With their legs Schulz's females torture, trample, and drive to sullen, helpless fury his dwarfish, humiliated, and sex-tormented male freaks, who find in their own degradation the highest form of agonizing bliss. Schulz's graphic works are epic poems on the cruelty of legs. . . .

In my opinion, Schulz is a new star of the first magnitude.

BRUNO SCHULZ'S LITERARY WORK

■

(July–August 1935)

A personal confession: I borrowed Schulz's *Cinnamon Shops* [in English translation *The Street of Crocodiles*] on a day I felt particularly tired and planned to go to bed around nine o'clock in the evening, which I did. I kept reading that diabolical book until one thirty in the morning, and then on waking up at five and being unable to get back to sleep, I started reading again and finished it by eight. The entire morning and afternoon I was completely taken up with portrait painting. It was not until nine in the evening, when I went out for a walk, that I began to feel—to put it poetically—rising from the depths of my being the satanic fumes coming from the evaporating cinnamon grounds that had accumulated there during the night. Once the pressure of everyday chores had vanished, something uncanny burst forth from my spiritual crevices, poisoned by that monstrous drug: Schulzean cinnamon. Within me there was heard the gibbering of some unknown beast who began to describe to me, in a cinnamon voice (inarticulate extract of Schulzean venoms), the objective world of a typical summer afternoon which I could see clearly with my own eyes. This world grew deformed in the stream of gibberish, yet at the same time gained power, became "alienated" (estranged), seemed uncanny, shimmered with all the colors of a madman's nightmare. . . .

The Schulzean pulp, as yet preverbal, kept rising higher and higher, flooding ever larger areas of my relatively healthy brain, until I finally saw the ordinary, everyday forest at Antałówka through the eyes of the "King of

Cinnamon" and the "Archpriest at the Temple of Female Legs" and I felt frightened, yet still more marvelously elated.

This is precisely what we expect from an author: he must force us to take a new look at the world—positive or negative, *primo facie* it does not matter, joyous or sorrowful, optimistic or pessimistic, realistic or idealistic, as long as it is new! And this can happen only if the author, besides having talent, is *someone* in absolutely every respect: character, habits, feelings, but most of all, in the case of literature, if he is someone with respect to intellect, if he has his own worldview, and not just a collection of trivial ideas about life held together by some external glue . . . but a *genuine* worldview, which means based on a more or less consciously and clearly articulated view of existence (and not of our narrow little world), in other words, a *philosophical outlook* (or rather a general ontological one). . . .

Of course, the worldview alone does not guarantee, simply by the fact of its being *somehow* formulated, that it will be adopted by the recalcitrant brains in the ambient milieu; a conceptual pamphlet or, for instance, a German "crib" (as our dumbbells call them) is what is needed for pure intellectuals; for the average rabble a special mechanism capable of projecting the author's vision *directly* must be created; in prose this is done by the style and by the author's way of presenting images. . . .

Here is how it works in Schulz: in his "attachment" (too high-flown a word) to matter, in the virtual reverence that he "fosters" (another strange word) for it, there is no trace of materialism in the bad sense of the word: starting from physical materialism (actually a metaphysics worse than the beliefs held by the inhabitants of the Fiji Islands, according to the famous German biologist Jacob Johann von Uexküll) all the way up to vital materialism, which gives priority to material rather than spiritual needs; the latter at least is not connected to the former, except perhaps in a fortuitous, inessential way. Schulz loves matter, which for him is the highest substance, but not in the physical sense (which makes him close to me philosophically); for him there is no opposition between matter and spirit, they constitute a unity: "There is no dead matter—lifelessness is only a disguise behind which hide unknown forms of life"—now this is the confession of a monadologist (or rather monadist) or hylozoist. But the quotation in question would be no more than a rather murky statement, vaguely philosophical, if it were not woven into an entire series of real happenings in which the word "becomes flesh."

Schulz's faith (a "rational faith" in James Ward's formulation) is obvious, since monadism cannot be proved absolutely or demonstrated experimentally (we can arrive at this view by the slow elimination of all others); being drawn into the mysterious lectures given by the father as he sinks into madness and taking part in the strange stunts he plays with cockroaches, birds, little girls, and the female cook, Adela, become our direct metaphysical experience; we feel our link to the universe, not because of some sort of inscrutable transcendental oneness, but on account of the author's love for all living creatures, and consequently for seemingly inanimate matter, which can only consist of living creatures and nothing else; otherwise it would not have found a mode of being for itself, or even existed at all; it would merely be, as the idealists believe, the sum total of the categorizations (?) of our experiences. Schulz is a realistic monadologist—idealist monadism, such as Husserl's, is in comparison a cheap solution, although there is a certain greatness in deriving the world from pure consciousness, without the use of the concept of body as a special complex of hyletic elements. Only a monadism that acknowledges corporeality and the interaction among monads can attempt to constitute truthfully the world of inanimate matter based on a statistical calculation of actions. Schulz's remarks about "reverting to the roots of existence," to "the metaphysical core," to "the primary idea" (i.e., unity) in order to "betray it" and turn it into "the Regions of the Great Heresy" express in toto the necessary duality of Being, without which existence is unimaginable. Ignoring the threefold duality: unity in plurality, "I" and the world, and temporality and spatiality, gives rise to all the erroneous monistic systems, from materialism and pure psychologism to the hypostases of the idealists who, aspiring to the seemingly higher regions of ideas, make use of the half-baked concepts of a philosophy of life.

Realism of matter implies spatial realism, but for Schulz the artist, not the philosopher, there is a strange contradiction between the reality of our closed everyday space and those for us imaginary spatial levels that stretch out into infinity; the latter notion can be seen in the concept of space in Schulz's short story "The Gale," and even in the last chapter of *Cinnamon Shops* relating Father's experiences in the shop. Despite its relativity, clearly stressed in an extraordinarily beautiful form, time for Schulz is no less real than space, as duration which when directly experienced constitutes a unity with extension.

The father's experiences on the borderline between body and spirit clearly prove the essential unity of these two worlds, seemingly opposed but uniformly expressible in psychological terminology, in the language of qualities (Cornelius's elements of qualities). The father's brother (the uncle?)

transformed into "a bundle of rubber tubing" expresses this monism in a tangible fashion. As the sum total of living beings, inanimate matter ceases to be alien and hostile to us: the miracle of transformation is an ordinary, everyday occurrence—in the constant process of eating, drinking, breathing, the inanimate becomes animate. This miracle would be unimaginable were it not for the fact that essentially the difference between inanimate and animate is the difference between the collective and its individual members. Schulz's profound statement that "the morphological scope of matter is limited as a whole and a certain quota of forms is repeated over and over again on various levels of Existence" is immensely important for the monadistic conception, which would not be possible if we accepted an infinite scale of perfection and consciousness on the part of monads (one of Leibnitz's errors) and infinite transitions between different species of monads. The latter concept implies, in the most virulent form, actual infinity and shifts the sphere of mystery to an area that may be totally free of it. I think that without such a cleverly veiled philosophy Schulz would have been incapable of creating his magical style, which transports us directly, in the very process of living, into a different dimension of apprehending reality. In an interview in the *Illustrated Weekly* I called Schulz a phenomenon just this side of genius, if he is not in fact quite simply a genius in embryo. This is no trite superlative, if by genius in art and literature we mean an individual who to the highest degree of intensity combines the following elements:

1. A worldview that has not been acquired secondhand, but that has sprung from the innermost guts of its creator.

2. An intellect sufficiently powerful so that his worldview can be presented conceptually or at least symbolically.

3. Talent, that is, the ability to create sentences which are syntheses of images, sounds, and conceptual content in almost homogeneous amalgams, provided that these are sentences whose arrangement of words, imagery, and sound patterns (in other words, form) is not a repetition of any previously known form in literature. I believe that Schulz possesses all of these qualities. . . .

Schulz has in prose what Miciński had in poetry: the ability to create alloys in which image and sound plus the conceptual aspect, both of itself and as the source of imagery and sound patterns, constitute an absolute unity: they create new composite qualities. That is why I consider some portions of Schulz's prose to be short compositions in Pure Form. . . .

For Schulz the chief element is the image, and I maintain that up until now there has never been such a master in Polish literature and, who knows, perhaps even in world literature. . . . Like meteors, Schulz's sentences illumine new, unknown lands, which are usually submerged in a sea of banality and which we, deluged with mediocrity, are not able to perceive. . . . His words are condensed pills which expand inside us—like the cotton soaked in fat used to poison rats in that hideous fashion—with an excess of content crammed into them under enormous pressure, spreading far beyond the boundaries of the prose itself and creating for us a metaphysical vista on the world, a vista on the ultimate Mystery of everything in the universe, without which no great literature or formal art is possible.

Besides artistic values, Schulz gives us purely practical values concerning life, and for certain of these we must be eternally grateful to him. . . . In my opinion, these include the following:

1. A feeling of the highest, immaterial pricelessness of life, which it is so hard to maintain in a state of intensity in the ordinary course of everyday life with all its cares and complications. This feeling is a priceless treasure in and of itself, and whoever does not have it is a true beggar, despite all his other good qualities. This feeling comes through directly in almost every sentence, whereby Schulz with a kind of outright metaphysical lechery paws the tiniest nooks and corners of his beloved reality. But this has nothing in common with hackneyed sensuality or aesthetic gourmandise: it is *a genuine grand passion* which he also "instills" in us.

2. Out of this supreme love there grows a feeling of the ultimate unknowability of the object of our affection (as is always the case with true love), paralleled by the incomprehensibility of the very feeling and of the individuality of which it is the content. The most profound essence of Being is inexhaustible and limitless: we do not know what our own existence is, nor that of the world; we do not know what we are, nor the sense of our being in the totality of becoming. The Ultimate Mystery—expressed in primeval concepts not subject to definition—shines through the most ordinary everyday activities. . . . Schulz gives us this, and if we try to imitate him in this "insight" of his, we shall live differently, and even dream differently, once we have really got into his relation to reality. . . .

For Schulz, given the immensity of the Mystery of Being, madness and a normal worldview are equally valid—who knows, perhaps madness is automatically closer to it; a brain that has burst from the inability to absorb the Mystery versus a brain that has confined it in an inadequate symbolism of signs limited in their meaning? . . .

Schulz is the only writer who has given a real description of the purely personal enchantment of the dream, which is in principle untranslatable into general symbols: he objectified the dream (see *Cinnamon Shops*, for example), made it intersubjective and intelligible for all in its "auto-individuality." . . .

Schulz expresses the "Inexpressible" *explicite*, with the ease of true inspiration, with the simplicity and sincerity of a child. His writing is devoid of third-rate symbolism, puzzling passages, innuendoes, false vagueness: thus Descartes's philosophical ideal, *clair et distincte*, has been achieved in prose, and yet the Mystery remains intact, unattainable in its depths but glimpsed through the necessary veil of ideally lucid phrases. . . .

With Schulz we travel *everywhere*. Through his eyes, the earth is one of the strangest stars in the universe, and not a place of dirty business deals, underhanded schemes, abject poverty, exploitation, and degradation. But this is not the resignation of those who cannot enjoy life. In Schulz's writings we find a glimmer of hope that this invaluable strangeness can be shared by all: under what conditions still remains to be seen. Perhaps Schulz will explain it to us in his future works. After all, each one of us dreams about suddenly waking up on other shores, about changing the grayness of his existence, about taking a plunge into the unknown. . . .

■ ■ ■ ■

And lastly, will he have strength enough to carry on and maintain the same form—even to bear himself with dignity if he should have to face a hideous, unsavory death?

UNWASHED SOULS

■

A Psychological Study of the Inferiority Complex
Carried Out According to Freud's System
with Special Attention to Polish Problems

1936

Introduction

The present work is not meant to be a systematic theoretical exposition but rather a summary of several theories—not my own, by the way—and a report on a series of psychological observations I made on myself and the people around me, and then I shall attempt a historical explanation of the phenomena noted in the light of Freud's theory, with particular emphasis on the inferiority complex (*Minderwertigkeitsgefühl-komplex*).

I owe my acquaintance with Freud's system, i.e., psychoanalysis, to a friend of my parents (and to some degree a friend of mine, the great difference in our ages notwithstanding), Dr. Karol de Beaurain, to whose memory I dedicate this book with a feeling of deep gratitude, respect, admiration, and good will. For many years I did not duly appreciate what this earliest pioneer of Freud's principles in Poland had done for me in an indirect way.

Interested by my dreams, he suggested to me in 1912 a regular "practical course" in psychoanalysis, to which I joyfully agreed as a kind of "novelty"; but I entered into this experiment not without a critical attitude and some slight mistrust. I won't describe here the details of the treatment, which in any case was not designed to cure me of anything in particular, since, despite the opinion of Rita Sacchetto (the first wife of the sculptor August

Zamoyski), who never referred to me other than as *"dieser geisteskranke W."* [this mentally ill W.], I am a relatively normal person.

For Dr. de Beaurain, beyond the personal feeling he "entertained" for me, I was an interesting "experimental guinea pig" (*ein Versuchskaninchen*)—plus the fact that this exceptional man, undervalued here in Poland, wanted to give me something of himself, of his profound knowledge of people and life, increased a hundredfold by the powerful machinery of the theory created by Freud, who likewise is not everywhere duly appreciated as one of greatest geniuses and benefactors of mankind in our epoch.

In a certain sense, Dr. de Beaurain wanted to save me from myself. Quite possibly it worked out well for me that he did not succeed in doing so, since if I had "resolved" (as the psychoanalysts say) all my complexes, I would probably have had to give up work in my specialties, i.e., in literature, painting, and philosophy, or at least change its nature radically—stop being myself to some degree. And I must stress that despite all the negative judgments about my work, it is particularly what I have done in philosophy that has personally given me a great, great deal (independently of what it may have been able to give to others or to contribute to knowledge), and without it, despite my share of strange adventures and never having been bored, I would consider my life, which—at least until now—I would not exchange for any other (not even the life of the emperor Pu-Yi), a barren wasteland. Here I am especially referring not so much to art and literature as to *philosophy*; I repeat, *until now*, because at the thought of tortures, which I have so many times been fortunate enough to escape, and which, after all, I never deserved, I invariably go cold all over, and if such things were to be carried out on me (may it never happen!), I do not know what tune I might sing then.

It is said (to return to the previous subject) that all work known pompously as "creative" stems from complexes which have not been disentangled and that it dies down once they are resolved, the way a mountain stream dries up in its riverbed in summer. Whether that is the case would have to be established with total certitude; and since such an extremely complicated experiment cannot be repeated in exactly the same conditions (redoing someone's life with and without psychoanalysis), the answer to the question can therefore never be completely certain. We can talk with some precision about curing someone of a given complex in the light of a number of similar cases, but despite innumerable observed instances, nothing certain can be said about something as unpredictable as creativity, especially in the artistic realm. At any rate, even if in rare cases the elimination of a pathological complex—this notion I shall soon explain more exactly by means of examples—might prove detrimental to "creativity," in the majority of cases involving people considered "normal," who are not committed to any special creative or particularly artistic work, the cure can only have beneficial effects. Of course, practiced on a large scale by dilettantes, psychoanalysis can have fatal consequences and lead to serious nervous disorders. In fact, it is easy enough to pry into someone's psyche, but the real trick is to ease his suffering and make a proper synthesis of the exploratory analytical work. It was just this part of the program that I did not pursue to the very end with Dr. de Beaurain, for reasons beyond our control, and that is perhaps why my psychoanalysis (so far) did not have as beneficial an effect on me as in principle one might have expected. This was made clear by certain events in my life that happened immediately afterward and that for many years distracted my attention from this field; and when I took it up again intellectually, it was rather in a somewhat ironic manner, which is immediately evident even in some of my plays. But it is not true that I ever totally disparaged psychoanalysis, as has been imputed to me along with anti-Semitism and god knows what else. To be sure, these are matters of little importance, but since I intend to write in high praise of this science, and since among Poles a fundamental change in convictions often leads to strange imputations of self-interest or even dishonesty, I therefore considered it fitting to add these few words of clarification relating to the distant past.

The fact is that even though to some extent I employed psychoanalysis in my introspection and my study of others, in a crude fashion be it added, and even made use of its terminology, for many years this field of inquiry remained in a somnolent state for me—despite the superficial application, it was all lifeless and seemingly petrified. The book that brought about a true revolution in my thinking and fundamentally changed my attitude toward myself and toward others, opening unsuspected horizons for me (as a leptosome-schizotyme—at the present moment I can almost say a "former" schizoid, because since then I have become pyknicized), was Ernst Kretschmer's *Körperbau und Charakter*, published by Springer in Berlin (1921). At this point I shall not enter into a detailed account of the theory advanced by this brilliant psychologist and psychiatrist, whose above-mentioned work should absolutely be known to all reasonably intelligent people, but especially to those whose task in life is leading the masses, and for whom the material of creativity is living man in a state of becoming, i.e., those charged with *education* in the broadest sense of the term—from the village schoolmaster to the summits of state power. Here I shall give only a brief summary to encourage those capable of understanding the import of Kretschmer's work to become personally acquainted with it.

The General Principles of Freud's Theory

Laymen who understand nothing about psychoanalysis accuse Freud of psychological erotomania and of reducing everything to the erotic, and even of wallowing in filth for its own sake and psychocoprolalia or something of the sort. I maintain that the charge is false. Freud devotes exactly as much attention to the erotic as it deserves. Like it or not, the erotic is one of the crucial aspects of the famous and as yet totally undisputed triad of fundamental life forces: hunger, fear, and love, the latter understood for the moment, without any sublimation, as the simple urge to reproduce and to preserve the species, in which individuals are passive victims of a life force transcending them, created for distant goals beyond our ken and locked into the world of inanimate matter with a simply terrifying power. . . .

Fear is a great autocrat and hunger a mighty ruler, but eroticism is also a power to be reckoned with.

Quite justifiably, Karol Szymanowski used to say in his unforgettable little voice, as subtle as that of the metaphysical ruler of a land of hyperephebi out of this world: "You know, for me the erotic is something so diabolical that, you know, it is simply shocking . . . "

Freud is in no way wallowing in, to put it delicately, erotic indecencies but quite the contrary: he is trying to enlighten the uninitiated as to the subterranean sexual currents of the subconscious so that they can free themselves from their dark, anarchic influence, and once free, use this newly attained energy for "higher goals"; Freud is concerned with creating just such a conscious transformer, because subconsciously it has always happened that way: from sublimated (and even inhibited) erotic feelings there has originated all that is most essential in human creativity. And there is no reason to suppose there is anything degrading for human creativity in seeking its source in that realm. It is an empirical and historical fact that that is where the sources are to be found. It was only a question of articulating the hitherto mysterious and obscure mechanism of these transformations.

Freud's alleged paneroticism should be understood as follows: in the primitive organism, consciousness is only consciousness of the body, with very short and indistinct snippets of memory of the most immediate bodily "sensations." The cells of the lowest order multiply by division. The entire body of the cell takes part in the process, starting with the nucleus and ending with the outer layer. This must be accompanied by very acute positive bodily sensations—otherwise, the cell might not "want" to divide at all, just as we might not want to devote ourselves to certain practices. In what fashion the transition to the two sexes takes place is something I do not know. The fact is that the cells began to draw together (as the spermatozoon does with the ovum) and to unite instead of to divide in order to produce a separate being or a multiplicity of them. This bodily joining of cells into larger units is immensely significant—as a result of the high degree of joining and at the same time of differentiating there arises the multiple organism, which, moreover, due to exact conjoining of cells surface to surface during the process of accretion, possesses—as duration in and of itself—a single "psyche," or consciousness. This is, as it were, the basic "daily miracle of existence," of which we and all living creatures are examples.

And we can ask the materialists: just how could a living organism emerge from inanimate "little balls" understood in the broadest possible terms, extending to such entities as electrons and accidentally interacting or colliding fields? This must be satisfactorily explained or else materialism is, in a sense, a joke. And certainly that is the case, because many biological phenomena cannot be explained by any materialistic spatial schema.

But we cannot ask how from many cells, which are after all organisms possessing rudimentary consciousness, there can emerge a multicellular organism possessing a collective duration for all the cells, a single consciousness, which does not simply include the individual cellular durations; that is precisely the primordial fact, the sole truly real fact, infinitely more real than all physical facts, which we must somehow take into account, to the extent that that is at all possible with regard to a general view of the totality of Being. Quite possibly this is the supreme primordial fact leading to monadism, a fact that is at the basis of the totality of Being, both animate and inanimate. Biological monadism is a theory according to which, being unable to reduce individualized animate matter to inanimate matter, we assume that everything is composed of living entities, from which on the strength of a statistical calculation of their actions we can constitute inanimate matter.

Returning to the previous subject: every organism must therefore defend itself (self-preservation), avoid dangers, feed itself, i.e., perform yet another daily miracle of animate existence: the transformation of inanimate to animate matter—and also fulfill the reproductive urge. This urge is something like an embryonic form of what we call "the spirit," that is, of those elements that are not the actual sensations of the body and its memories, in other words, an embryonic form of image-making elements, and further, in us (human beings), of thoughts (arranged into a "purposeful" whole, rather than being complete chaos). For us chaos is something almost unimaginable, by virtue of the principle of limitation and recurrence, i.e., that nothing can actually be infinite or absolutely new. In the organism seen "from the side" and "from the inside," i.e., in its sensations, there must be a certain order: not such a perfect or absolute order—illusory in any case—as reigns in the inanimate matter surrounding us by virtue of the law of Large Numbers, that is to say, statistics, but at any rate a kind of order, in this case biological and psychological.

The point I want to make is that if for the time being we disregard fear and hunger, the first as temporarily having no reason for occurring at a given moment, the second as being temporarily appeased, then what we have left is the erotic as *a constant, latent, potential substratum—lurking in the inmost bodily sensations—for all the "experiences" of even the most primitive animate being.* Only immediately after being appeased does this primal feeling in any clearly pronounced form disappear for a very short time; except then, this feeling is constantly present within us, seeming to lie in wait, as an energy-laden potentiality constituting an integral part of our corporeal personality, of what we actually are intrinsically, in all that we experience. Please do not think that I am inciting all the washouts of the world to universal erotomania. But it seems to me that the state of reproductive proclivity is, in its diverse variants, the most constant background and even very often the dominant note in the total affectivity of each individual. That is why Freud, in my opinion, shows profound insight when he looks to the erotic for the origin and motive force of almost all the "higher" experiences of the individual, even of such a complicated individual as our relatively intelligent contemporary man. On such a foundation grow all the products of the human spirit, as transformations and sublimations of the primal feeling of the individual and, beyond this simple feeling, of his desire for a higher affirmation of the very fact of his existence.

Here is the essential point: affirmation of one's existence. It is not enough simply to exist, unreflectively, passively, negatively; one must manifest one's existence more expressively, in the face of death and the surrounding nothingness which is a sort of backdrop for all beings, the way interstellar space is a sort of backdrop for the existence of stars, planets, comets, and our own bodies. It is necessary to objectify one's existence, to affirm it and confirm it somehow in eternity, in a subjective eternity or at least an eternity for the species, finite, illusory, "psychological," relative. This purpose is served by the reproductive instinct, whose impact goes beyond the individual being, beyond the ephemeral "I" of a particular entity and in which there is actually transcendence of a limited individual, an Individual Being, beyond his inexorably limited duration.

This desire to endure at all costs is expressed in all the fallacious theories of the immortality of what is called "the soul," which as a "substance" without a body no one has ever seen or will ever see, because the body joins with the soul, or more precisely with the temporally continuous individuality, to form a unity. Given the fundamental law of existence—the principle of limitation, which is the sole basis of our existence—we must acknowledge as futile the search for a way to vanquish the metaphysical dread of existence, which in reality is absolutely invincible. That is why in all our acts by which we attempt, through creativity broadly interpreted—from life to abstraction—to build an illusory bridge connecting the hopelessly doomed individual to eternity, we must recognize derivatives of the erotic instinct, and certain of its transformations, because in fact the erotic instinct represents the primary victory over individual evanescence which is the lot of even the lowest creatures. That is why I believe Freud is right to consider all creativity a transmutation and sublimation of the reproductive instinct, in which on the most primitive level one individual creature turns to another, seeking help in the suprapersonal transcendence of feelings when faced with the absolute loneliness of living beings hopelessly enclosed in their impenetrable individualities. . . .

The Role of the Individual in the Evolution of Society and the Tragedy of the Downtrodden

In their superb book, *Des clans aux empires: L'évolution de l'humanité* (La Renaissance du Livre, 1923), Alexandre Moret and Georges Davy describe in an uncommonly interesting way the highly mysterious process by which the origins of individual power emerge in the primitive, almost totally *communistic* clan. The first embryonic ruler, as we see him in the Australian tribal *alatunia* (magician), is a rather amorphous figure.

According to Frazer (whose *Golden Bough* I know), everything starts with the public sorcerer; we know that magic is the most primitive form of religion, dealing with powers that are still virtually impersonal. In my view, these powers provide the foundation for all "the rest" of existence, i.e., everything that is not "I," to which in a certain sense I stand in opposition. I mention in passing that I am an opponent of the reduction of religious feelings to feelings concerned with everyday life, which is what Bronisław Malinowski did in his *Primitive Beliefs and Forms of Social Organization: The Problem of the Genesis of Religion with Particular Reference to Totemism* (Cracow, 1915). That is the supposedly scientific approach (for me it is "pseudo" scientific), which consists of disallowing from the outset as a basis of research any more or less clearly defined metaphysics, meaning in actual fact ontology. But sometimes it is precisely this purportedly scientific approach that leads straight to the creation of the most pernicious metaphysics, since it is false as well, the most perfect example of which we see in the tragicomedy of materialism, renewed today on a grand scale in a slightly modified form by the Wiener Kreis [Vienna Circle] school of philosophers.

Besides, in every country there are a certain number of reasonably intelligent pseudoscientific materialists won over by the Vienna Circle, which is establishing branches throughout the entire world. As I have tried to prove in all my writings, there is a need for metaphysics, in the sense of general ontology—the only thing that matters is *what kind.* . . .

It is not possible at one and the same time to bring about both a higher level of culture and general happiness for all. First, the former is achieved through the sufferings of the oppressed—there must be human pulp on which to grow the splendid flowers offered by the great individual benefactors of the whole—and only then is the latter possible, based upon increasing self-awareness on the part of the masses as well as upon setting the great individuals (but of a different type than before) to conscious work for the improvement of all mankind.

I am not, as might appear, some kind of "spokesman for obscurantism"; on the contrary, I hold the most radical social views (which could be characterized as a special brand of socialism but not, God forbid, a communal variety); all that concerns me is whether the process of creating ideal happiness on earth—that is, the elimination of poverty and material inequality and, at the same time, the preservation of a high cultural level—might not take a fundamentally different course. I have come to the conclusion that there is no such possibility. This, it seems, is the tragedy of every species (IEP: Individual Existences in the Plural) in the universe.

All that matters is for the period of false, hypocritical democracy—providing an equal start for everyone but in actual fact involving the most hideous form of slavery—to last as short a time as possible. Unfortunately, we cannot transmit our achievements to the moon of Jupiter, where there may be emerging a form of humanity comparable to our own at the period of the French Revolution. Nay (as certain people are wont to write and say), we are quite incapable of learning even the simplest lessons from our own history. Instead of the revolution from above, which could bring happiness to millions without any bloodshed by means of a single decree signed by a ruler aware of his responsibilities, all we see at every turn is the violent overthrow of such rulers, who with strange obstinacy have been clinging desperately to their illusions, and class warfare, which is evidently a necessary evil, quite unavoidable in this "vale of tears."

It would behoove the ruling classes finally to come to their senses and initiate the revolution from above while there is still time, at least in those cases where they have not yet been replaced by rulers of a new kind, coming from completely different social and psychological backgrounds—this is the crucial point. Since they already have concentrated power in their hands, without having had to make any effort to acquire it, the revolution from above is simply child's play: a few decrees, that's all there is to it. But the misfortune of rulers of this sort is that—after needlessly spilling rivers of blood, setting civilization back, and destroying what is known as the cultural heritage—they have to be thrown out on their ears, although they could have been blessed for all eternity as the benefactors of mankind. To have the power and not to use it for the betterment of the majority of the people in society, and to support an international clique of exploiters and maniacs on behalf of the power of capital for its own sake, is sometimes unintentional but nonetheless a crime.

But the revolution from above is evidently an unrealizable utopia, for statesmen are first and foremost people incapable of learning anything from the past that could be applied to the future, unconcerned about the general welfare in the broadest sense of the term, and even if not concerned with the personal advantages that power brings, still obsessed with illusory points of honor and dreams of imperial might, unaware that the earth is burning up under their feet. "Who knows, perhaps I won't be forced to step down during my lifetime," is how each and every one of them thinks, either out of general principles or for purely personal reasons. But general principles and personal reasons sometimes become inextricably intertwined, and "unwashed souls" are known for their ability to find all sorts of justifications, more or less convenient for them.

It is quite easy to identify with a general principle while "eating langouste in a top hat" (that is, with one's own head in the top hat, not the langouste's—no need to belabor the point, as a certain old count used to say); it's harder to do while locked up in a stinking jail cell being eaten by bugs and systematically smacked in the mug: there are convenient principles and inconvenient principles. To realize that a principle is inconvenient and yet to put it into practice is an act of heroism. There are few heroes in prominent positions on our earthly globe: there are either sincere adherents of the old dying world acting for the sake of delusions, which as a matter of fact have long since fallen into oblivion, or there are cynics. These delusions seem still to be needed only by the exponents of that rotting tumor, capital, for their atrocious death-rattling machinations.

There's no help for it, the revolution from above is, it would appear, hopelessly utopian, and arousing and inciting the ruling elite to action—which I am trying to do here on an exceedingly small scale—is a hopeless and thankless task. . . .

Even before the war, in 1912 and 1913, I came to the conclusion that the price mankind must pay for perfect socialization is

a) the end of religion as a "primary metaphysical approach" (in any case its role as time-honored educator of mankind is coming to an end in a natural fashion);

b) the suicide of philosophy—as a general system toward which we are tending, rather negative in its results (limiting the frontiers of the Mystery implied by the impossibility of defining all the concepts of the system and therefore by the necessity of admitting a priori concepts), and which will reconcile the apparent contradictions implied by existence in each conceptual formulation;

c) the decline of art, which having prematurely exhausted all its means of producing effects must come to an end either by repeating what has already been done or by indulging in total perversity, delirium, and disorganization of its constructional forms.

Of course, for the above mentioned reasons, I used to be in a state of despair, scarcely having gone beyond my aristocratic worldview, buttressed by philosophic skepticism acquired from contact with the system of Cornelius, whom I have been studying since the age of nineteen. Now, after having renounced art and written my philosophical *Hauptwerk* (1917–32), I have come to terms with all that as with an unavoidable historical necessity, and I think that everyone should make a similar adjustment and then there would be heaven on earth. . . .

I myself am a totally areligious person and even in my childhood, except for some attempted compromises, I never was a believer. I speak of these matters quite impartially, respecting every belief that leads to genuine progress and creativity.

The history of Poland is a tragic history of hideous errors (caused by weakness). Since I lack the proper training, I shall not enter into a critique of these mistakes. The first fundamental error was the adoption of Christianity and, in general, of culture from the West instead of from Byzantium; this was the initial mistake, which warped all our history and national mission, and all further blunders are simply a consequence of it. . . .

The French Revolution marks a basic step in the evolution of mankind as the rise of the modern nation-state from the totem clan. The only event of equal importance is the Russian Revolution, an experiment on a fantastically grand scale, marking anew the beginning of the end for the fraudulent era of democracy and the domination of capital. It does not matter how (in detail) the experiment is realized: whether right now, or only after some hesitations and transformations; what matters is that a beginning has been made and there can be no turning back. Russia is paying for this experiment by her terrible sufferings, but she can rejoice that in the world today greatness is hers alone. . . .

I have never been able to read much on the history of Poland because I always felt choked with indignation and shame, all the more so in that I, like all my fellow countrymen, was a product of that awful historical machination—I have experienced its effect on my own life. But I must say that thanks to some hard work on myself, and thanks to Kretschmer, Freud, and Dr. de Beaurain, I have at least succeeded in warding off certain things. More recently I have had much food for thought in the spectacle of the Russian Revolution from February 1917 to June 1918. I cannot call it anything but a spectacle since unfortunately I watched it as though from a box at the theater, not being able to take an active part owing to my schizoid inhibitions. I observed that unparalleled event at absolutely close quarters, as an officer in the Pavlovsky Regiment, which began the Revolution. Later I had the honor of being elected by my wounded soldiers from the front (I was in only one battle, at Vitonezh on the Stokhod) to the Fourth Company of the Auxiliary Battalion of that regiment, the same company that actually started the Revolution. I owed that honor to my own weak negative qualities: I did not smack my soldiers in the face, or swear at them *po matushkie* [——— your mother]. I gave lenient punishments and was reasonably polite—nothing more; 300 men, enclosed in a huge, round regimental stable, fought for several days against the whole of tsarist Russia. That unit had the privilege of going ahead of the first in parades, and then came the first, second, and third. I simply consider as an unfortunate cripple anyone who has not lived through the Russian Revolution at close quarters. More detailed accounts and explanations will find their proper place in my posthumous works (volume 14, 1978). . . .

The basic psychic trait of almost every Pole has become perpetual discontent and perpetual self-inflation beyond one's abilities, and the need to live beyond one's means both physically and spiritually where feelings of importance are concerned. . . .

The complex symptoms of this malady can be summarized as follows: *Appearances are more important than reality and, given the absence of long-range perspectives, enjoying oneself and being superficially creative is more essential than fulfilling difficult and often thankless tasks that involve long-range planning and thinking of the next generation and of generations to come.* . . .

It took me a long time to realize exactly what makes a city like Warsaw so diabolical: the feverish haste of superficiality (rather than the tense, authentic speed of essential work), everything "slipshod" (instead of being properly done), the makeshift and the "slapdash" (because there is no telling what tomorrow will bring).

Material uncertainty tomorrow, ideological uncertainty the day after, and still worse, the day after the day after, is to some extent widespread throughout the entire world: the whole hypocritical period of democracy is something makeshift and ephemeral. The only peoples and groups and even individuals who will have a say in the organization of a better future for mankind are those who at this horrible time of fluttering pulses preserve (1) a maximum long-range stance, (2) a faith in the enduring values of cultural efforts perhaps unavailing in the short run given the frantic pace of the whole show, and perhaps for the time being undertaken without hope of reward, in the broad sense of the word, encompassing not only money but also "fame," and (3) a stubborn belief in the highest values—at present obscured by the general cynicism—revealing the organizational and socially creative talents of the human species. Because what passes for social creativity today is mainly sawdust that will be blown away by the first gust of wind announcing the fierce hurricane of social change on a grand scale, whose (poetically speaking) far-off murmur and burning breath (as before the mountain gale strikes) can almost be heard and felt coming from the darkened horizon of the stormy future. What I have in mind is the economic organization of the entire planet to insure the dignified coexistence of all peoples without loss of their individuality, an organization comparable to the coexistence of the organs within an organism.

The real trick would be to know how to avoid the makeshift as the house was burning down and be able, for example, to install an electric door-bell with one hand while with the other dousing the flames with a small coffee mug. And that is more or less what contemporary man must be like if he wishes to withstand the onset of future transformations, which may begin at any moment unless the white race of muddle-headed geniuses dies out by committing collective suicide during a prolonged new war. But now it is the turn of the yellow and black races—*schwarz-gelb*—who are the sole object of any possible faith, since no one can put much hope in whites any more. Mankind will survive, but it will be polychromatic, and whites may have to travel in special railway cars labeled "white people" (as is now the case in America for negroes, who must ride in cars labeled "colored people") in an ideally governed black-and-yellow State (of work) for the Entire Planet. But these are desperate measures. Perhaps the healthy animal instinct of the species will make itself heard and speak above the heads of our super-subtle, impotent statesmen and diplomats in top hats, alerting brains not yet degenerated that it is the eleventh hour for the brainy elite, if there really is such a thing, to bring about a bloodless transformation without lowering the general level and without destroying the already attained cultural achievements.

The Russian experiment may help mankind reach this kind of awareness; although not fully instructive, because it is taking place under abnormal circumstances, the Russian experiment should give much food for thought, but so far—curiously enough—it hasn't. . . .

Despite everything, I deeply believe that the lie will not prevail and that better times socially are coming, only at the expense of art and philosophy, and well, a slight setback to culture (oh, can't be helped—everything has its price, and social perfection is no exception), unless present-day world states-men learn fast and institute by decree a radical transformation of society from above. Because in the last analysis what purpose do these rulers serve? (Roosevelt is possibly the first of a new type of statesman, but that still remains to be seen.) Things cannot go on this way. Why do those gentlemen consider themselves empowered to have humanity in their persons commit collective suicide because of their shortsightedness, their class egotism, and sometimes, it seems, quite simply their lack of intelligence? Because I can scarcely believe that only an overwhelming nostalgia for bygone days directs their thoughts and plans, nor can it be ordinary carelessness and blind desire to hold onto the stinking little tail end of an irretrievable past fading into the distance. Things are not that bad. But if we observe the conscious slide into the abyss, we must conclude that this is the work of superhuman international forces, only seemingly directed by human beings, which have escaped from our control and "gambol" through the world without any real goal, like cows in the spring. These are the forces of international capital, which was once a healthy organ and produced our present civilization, but which with the passage of time has turned into a malignant tumor. . . .

The Atmosphere of Cities

In the past I have reflected many times on what constitutes what we call the atmosphere of a given city, which ensures that in one city we feel awful or wonderful—quite independently of such self-evident factors as the architecture, the composition of the city as a whole (in case it is small) or in its parts (in case it is too large to be absorbed easily in its entirety), the degree of intensity and the nature of its traffic—all elements that influence our relations to a given human conglomeration but that can easily be eliminated from our judgment of it through proper analysis and abstraction. Well, such "imponderabilia," which I had not noticed before in my capacity as a leptosome-schizoid wrapped up in myself (or rather in the artificial transparent ball of my aristocratic-artistic worldview), suddenly became apparent to me once I went beyond a certain point in the process of pyknicization, which I succeeded in doing—as a result of my radical triumph over the use of tobacco. I had not seen these factors because *en ma qualité de schizoïde* I was completely cut off from other people and did not understand their highly differentiated natures. Such a discovery may seem banal to many of my pyknic readers—but for me it was epoch-making, as was everything else at the time of that abrupt change in my character and frame of mind. Now what determines the imperceptible differences among cities, what gives such vivid and yet such hard to grasp traits to all our impressions in whatever place we happen to be in, *is the general character of the mutual relations among its inhabitants.* If we live somewhere for a long time, we completely lose the ability to react to a given state of affairs: the best way to observe the phenomena of a moral atmosphere is by a change of place and a move to unknown parts of town.

I think that the basic relation of one Pole to another is mutual contempt, if not natural contempt, then artificial contempt—which is still worse. . . .

Well, here in Poland everyone puffs himself up so as to be able to look at his "fellowman" with contempt. I maintain that eighty-five percent of our compatriots, in addition to their regular diet, draw sustenance, even gain weight and grow chubby from contempt for their "neighbors." For most members of our society it is every bit as necessary as breathing. If they are not nourished by contempt for others, such people will wilt, fade away, dry up, and expire miserably. I shall return to this problem later as it appears in other guises—for the time being what interests me is the street. To start with, one can always try to discredit a person who says things like that, as I am now doing: "You have a persecution mania aggravated by megalomania and you are only imagining all that. You're always turned in on yourself, hypersensitive, hyperirritable, morbidly proud," etc., etc. . . .

I admit that given my character and social standing I have been particularly vulnerable to that kind of treatment. But contrary to what one might think, with age, despite many bitter experiences, and those frequently with people I considered my best friends, all the bitterness that I may have felt to a slight degree in my younger days has completely left me. I react to the worst examples of swinishness with relative calm because I have fathomed their secret mechanism. And whereas previously I would in many cases have suspected treachery, ill will, sadism, or a conscious desire to humiliate, now I see only an unfortunate guy fallen prey to his own pathological complexes and playing three-fourths of his minor and even his major dirty tricks absolutely subconsciously, solely to make up for, by some miracle, his inferiority complex, convinced that he is the noblest of human beings under the sun. And in reality he is noble, by his very nature, but he has a small unwashed soul, about which he is absolutely ignorant and he has no way of washing it and takes no steps to remedy the situation.

Coming back to the subject: I noticed that walking through the streets of Warsaw exhausted me in a strange way. I would leave the house hale and hearty and fairly satisfied with what I had accomplished, I would go where I felt like going and where nothing bad could befall me, but I would reach my destination peevish, discouraged, and out of sorts, as though I had a slight hangover or had become depressed or even physically reduced.

As the proprietor of a large "mugs-made-to order" firm, or in other words, being a psychological portrait painter, I have the foible of being uncommonly interested in the human mug. Simply walking down the street, I have always had to record every face I saw: ingurgitate it, digest it quickly, define it "intuitively," and spit it out; "every face" is an exaggeration, but certainly every second or third, and our country does abound in mugs: profoundly mendacious, intriguingly masked and bizarre, complicated and ravaged by life—one must give Poland credit for that. After a quarter of an hour of such strenuous walking I was done for: all my joy in life and nonchalance would leave me, the mugs had poisoned me with their clearly and not so clearly expressed contempt. I also observed how those people looked at one another—it was the same story: looks of contempt that were taciturn, muzzled, venomous, or insolent, overweening, "lewd," arrogant, blustering, pugnacious (nice expressions, eh?), and obscene—always obscene and malodorous. Then I stopped observing faces and—"Lo and behold!" (as the poet said)—my fatigue vanished, my carefree attitude and feeling of satisfaction suffered no interruption in the street, and I took along with me wherever I wished my sense of well-being unimpaired. I had discovered the mystery of cities: the *mal occhio* is no joke—people do drain and suck one another with their looks, just as they can inspire one another with energy and courage. . . .

The Nitwit's Smirk

My voice sounds as faint as a mosquito's buzz in comparison to the banalizers' megaphones, but the fact is that I issued warnings many times against various things: the excessive acceleration of life, the decline of the theater and literature (as a result of sucking up to a public that grows more moronic from one day to the next), anti-intellectualism, and the threat of total guanification of people's brains. No one was even willing to discuss these matters with me. When the ideas that I had developed entirely on my own began to penetrate to us in the form of Spenglerism and Huxley's literary caricatures, even those circles that had previously scoffed at my predictions began to grow somewhat *bedenklich* [suspicious] about these matters. That's the way it is with everything: harass homegrown originality but welcome the same thing several years later when it comes from abroad. Słowacki already wrote about this phenomenon, and the situation is getting worse and worse. Of course, the nitwit's smirk is just as much a manifestation of an inferiority complex as every other bit of self-puffery. I call special attention to it only as a singularly virulent but on the surface and in small doses supposedly harmless form of dealing with others, at which we are so proficient, *nous autres Polonais*. I know in advance what the reaction on the part of the smirking nitwits will be to what I am now writing: "Mr. W., deservedly unrecognized because of the slight value of his works and embittered on that account because of a lack of certain amenities of life that money brings, pours forth his bile in this fashion, seeking revenge on those who refused to let themselves be taken in by him."

LETTERS TO MALINOWSKI, 1935–38

■

WARSAW

15 OCTOBER 1935

Dear Bronio:

I'd like you not to feel lonely and abandoned in this misfortune that has struck you [the death of Malinowski's first wife] because I'm apart from you; you always have in me a constant friend from the old days. Did you get my registered letter sent half a year ago and the book of philosophy published by Mianowski?

I hug you with all my heart and great sympathy.

Regards to the children.

Your Witkacy

If you can, write to Warsaw, 23 Bracka St., Apartment 42.

Did you get our photograph from the days when I lived with my family at the Ślimak cottage?

Come to Poland.

My intuition tells me that it will do you good.

2 OCTOBER 1936
CRACOW

Dear Bronio:

I just attended a philosophical conference where I even enjoyed (within my dimensions) a modest success. Memories of former times came back to me. Well, now, there's a certain limit in not answering letters, beyond which in actual fact people stop existing for one another. I'm afraid we're reaching that point.

Through an oversight my publisher, Kasa Mianowskiego, failed to send you a copy of my (philosophical) *Hauptwerk*. *Has it finally reached you on the second try and also a reprint from* Przegląd Filozoficzny *containing my polemic with* Kotarbiński? These are rather serious matters for me. (Incidentally, I'm undergoing a devastating personal crisis; after five and one half years of being in love, the only woman in my life and I have had to part as of 2 August 1936—the most dreadful thing that's happened to me since Janczewska's death.)

4 October 1936 (continued). First of all, I must tell you that any sort of communication with Tymbeusz proved to be impossible. Poles living abroad tend to mummify in a bizarre way and are unable to accept new realities. Tymbeusz is a prewar mummy with all the defects. I'm sorry that that's the way it is, but we couldn't breach the gap between us. Besides, I feel a decided antipathy for his wife, Zofia de Schomberg.

Now, I wanted to ask you *en ma qualité de monadiste*, whether you— since you know Wildon Carr—couldn't suggest founding an international journal of monadology, which would bring together all the monadologists, who at present aren't very numerous. There's Wildon, me, Stern, some Serb, and that's about it. But I think monadology has a future. I could send Carr my book (there's a summary in German at the end).

Then I asked you to send me postcards with likenesses of Carr, Russell, Whitehead, the late James Ward, and Wittgenstein. I'm writing about them, and yet I have no idea what their mugs look like—and that's a matter of importance to me. Couldn't you make me a present of your *Argonauts* and of Russell's *Analysis of Matter*. I'm financially strapped. (If, by chance, you've failed to answer an offer of an honorary doctorate from Harvard University, then I forgive you for not responding to my letter.)

I have the feeling it would do you good to spend a couple of months in Poland just resting and doing nothing at all.

I'm about to leave for Zakopane; if you decide to write, send the letters to my Warsaw address: 23 Bracka Street, Apt. 42 (in case you come to Poland the telephone number is 277-18).

Many heartfelt hugs—I don't think there would be any problems of communication between us.

Your Witkacy, the Little Squirt from Zakopane

Enclosure No. 1—Form letter to be filled out.

P.S. Once again my sincerest thanks for the Du Maurier. But you must have someone who can take care of many of my requests so that you don't have to spend your time on them.

(Regards to your daughters from their far-off Uncle Vhit Katz.)

Congratulations on your recent honors. Despite the insinuations made by the Tymbeuszes, who bored me to death with incessant chatter about you, I am *not* jealous of your fame and success.

Stop driving yourself so hard, or you'll come to a bad end.

Do you still smoke? I haven't smoked for *four years*!

Enclosure No. 1

DAY   1936

Dear Staś:

I received your letter of 3 October 1936, for which many thanks.

1) I did not receive your *Hauptwerk*, and also the brochure. (If you did not, cross out the appropriate noun.) For which I thank you.

2) I did (not) talk with Wildon Carr. He does (not) agree to found a journal. Do (not) send him your book.

3) I do (not) enclose the photographs of the philosophers at the same time.

4) I do (not) enclose as a gift my *Argonauts* and Russell's *Analysis of Matter*.

Heartfelt hugs.

Your (Signature—it can be illegible if you are in a hurry)

Please have this letter sent by your footman to:
S. I. Witkiewicz, L. S. from Z.
23 Bracka, Apt. 42
Warsaw

26 OCTOBER 1936

Dear Bronio:

I am touched that such a notorious nonwriter of letters has written to me. I'll straighten out one misunderstanding right away: I'm not in the least interested in the autographs of those guys, only in their mugs. Since I'm writing about them, I'd like to see what they look like.

Too bad that you can't find a way to come to Poland—I have the feeling it would have a wonderful effect on you. I hope that once you return you'll finally answer the questions I posed in my letter.

I am currently in Zakopane and constantly look at Olcza from the window of my room. At the moment I am writing about Carnap. I am on friendly terms with several Cracow philosophers (Kotarbiński, Ingarden, Metallman, and Szuman—actually the latter does not know much about philosophy) and I correspond with them and with old Hans Cornelius, who despite our conceptual disagreements considers me his *best* friend at a distance.

After 15 November I'm going to Warsaw, where I'm to give a lecture at the Philosophical Society. So write me there.

My sincerest thanks.

I tell you: come, or we'll croak without ever having talked over the important things.

Thanks again and a heartfelt hug.

Your

Staś

11 MARCH 1937

Dear Bronio:

I'd like to know once and for all whether our relationship is still valid, or whether I should consider it terminated. I sent you a form to fill out and I got a letter from Oslo with a promise of things to come. I sent an explanation that I'm not interested in getting autographs of Whitehead, Carr, Russell, and Ward, I only want their likenesses. I asked you for Bertrand Russell's *Analysis of Matter*—I desperately need this book, it's out of print, and I'm out of money. I asked you for *The Argonauts*, which Limanowski pinched from me. No sign of any reaction on your part.

But you're writing to some former girlfriends. Have Tymbeusz and his wife been "intriguing"?

If I don't get an answer to this letter in a month, I'll cross you off the list of people who mean something to me.

Please write whether I should consider our relationship over, or whether you'll do what I'm asking you to.

I'm enclosing a "childhood" photo of us (17 and 19 years old).

Your Witkacy

Answer by registered letter—be a dear.

Address: Zakopane 3

Antałowka, the Witkiewicz house

16 MAY 1937

(Formerly) Dear Professor Malinowski:

I'm sending you this paper as a farewell gift. I don't think it is very beautiful on your part to destroy such a lifelong friendship as ours because of "intrigues" and gossip. Nevertheless, it is a "sorry" fact, as we poor Polish people sometimes say.

May God protect you from pickpockets.

Yours formerly

S. I. Witkiewicz

[Original in English, here slightly corrected for intelligibility; a poem, entitled "To Little-Squirt Friends," accompanied the letter.]

[16 MAY 1937]

Old Pig—I did not know that you are serving in the Polish Army and that you have such a nice dog.

Accept my congratulations.

[Original in English, here slightly corrected for intelligibility; written on a photomontage made from illustrated newspapers.]

[16 MAY 1937]

Don't you think that by declaring our old Tymbeusz a future genius you can compromise your authority in the opinion of later generations? That you have not sent me a copy of the Polish translation of your bloody book is swinishness of the highest sort (other instances I have forgotten already).

My best wishes to you, to the Duchess of Kent, Her Majesty, the Queen of Greece, and to that old fool of ours, the Emperor of Bessarabia.

Yours truly

Vitcatius
Antałowka
Zakopane 3

[Original in English, here slightly corrected for intelligibility.]

[16 MAY 1937]

Allow me, dear Professor, to give you this last mark of my life on this planet.

Not quite your former friend

Vitcatius

Please show this to your friends, the Count and Countess de Schomberg.

[Original in English, here slightly corrected for intelligibility.]

**ANTALOWKA, ZAKOPANE
25 JULY 1938**

Dear Bronio:

Thanks for your letter. I haven't written because I wanted to write you something cheerful, but it's getting worse and worse and I've decided (in the near future after I finish a few things I'm working on) to bring my life to an end a *bit* prematurely, because it's high time.

The woman who was in love with me and who for the past seven years meant everything (as the saying goes) to me has abandoned me; in part, it's my own fault (some slight infidelities, which she found out about from others) and she won't even listen to my explanations.

I'm in a terrible state. I'm suffering almost as much as when we went to Australia.

Perhaps some "miracle" can save me, but I don't anticipate anything like that.

"I have cooked my goose," as the British say.

So I'm saying good-bye for now, my dearest friend, I give you a hug and thank you for everything you have done for me.

(I'm not saying what will happen as an absolute *certainty*, but it's 98% sure.)

Your Staś

22 SEPTEMBER 1938

Dearest Broneczek:

My sincerest thanks for your letter. I've come back to life, unfortunately not thanks to my own strength (although I kept going for half a year miraculously "leaping from one dry spot to another over the quagmire" in the midst of atrocious tortures), but only thanks to the fact that she first deigned to write to me, then allowed me to talk to her, and finally has returned to me—but I'll never be what I once was for her.

As for myself, I'm totally "reformed" and I'll hold on for certain as long as she doesn't leave me. She is truly an exceptional being. I was 100% finished, emotionally, tormentologically, and mentally, and if she hadn't come back, *giving me the possibility of moral reformation*, I wouldn't have been able to go on living.

For the time being I'm continuing with my work and I'm waiting for whatever happens.

I want to end my life in a way that will make sense of it.

I'm very sorry that you're still unwell and I'm distressed that you won't be coming to Poland. Won't we see each other again before we die?

My wife (who is a miraculous specimen of her kind) dreams of meeting you.

Heartfelt hugs and all my gratitude and friendship.

Your Staś

I'm enclosing a letter from the person mentioned in my letter. I haven't read it.

I don't know if I wrote you that Cornelius (Ilans) visited me last year.

BALANCE SHEET ON FORMISM

■

(March 1938)

1. Personal Confessions

First of all I must point out that since I was sixteen years old, that is, more or less since 1902, I have been a formist in theoretical matters and actually an advocate of Pure Form. Already back then I had worked out the fundamental tenets of this theory in discussions with my father, who was a proponent of realism in painting, although at the end of his life he had modified his views to such an extent that had they been consistently developed further he would have been led to acknowledge Pure Form. I was concerned with the reinstatement of painting in the ranks of art, a position it had lost in the age of realism, and with putting it on an equal footing with music, about whose "superiority" to realistic painting there was much talk then among musicians. . . . I strove consistently for the realization of my theory in practice, not programmatically and at all costs, but by a course of natural development from naturalistic, yet compositional landscape painting, through compositions markedly burdened with literary content and portraits, already at that time conceived psychologically and not naturalistically in a corporeal sense, up to the last compositions from the year 1924, when I completed my artistic work in painting, having realized that further efforts in that direction would be fruitless, quite apart from any success or failure it might bring, to which I have never paid any attention. *Selbstlob stinkt*, as the Germans say, but that notwithstanding I must emphasize, in answer to objections of "consciously belying" my theories in actual practice, that despite a lack of success with my artistic painting I have not changed and will not change my beliefs; how I would respond to physical torture is the only thing I cannot answer for: perhaps in that case I would repudiate both Pure Form and biological monadism, but it certainly would be contrary to my convictions. I wrote about Pure Form even before the war, but I did not publish any of those essays. My first book, which I began to write in St. Petersburg in 1917—*New Forms in Painting*, published in 1919—is out of print. The following are still available: *Aesthetic Sketches* and *Theater*, the latter being the book in which I present the theory of Pure Form in the theater. The theory arose spontaneously, as did my first works for the theater in 1919, without any outside influences. At present I do not consider myself an artist in my role as painter, according to my definition of art. The psychological portrait, ranging from the accurately drawn likeness to the wildest psychological caricature, is an applied art, not a pure one. On the basis of the paintings that I did on my return from Russia in 1918, I was accepted by Pronaszko and Chwistek into the group of formists, which had just been organized then, and I exhibited along with them, for which I owe them my profound gratitude, since that was a short period of time during which I did not feel isolated in my work.

2. General Questions

It is a mistake to claim, as many have done, that everything known as the new art was a pure hoax, which for that very reason had to end in failure. It was in fact as a result of the hectic nature of our contemporary life—of what I called "insatiable craving for form"—artistic perversity, and the general decline of individuality in the course of social evolution that the revival of authentic Pure Form in painting had to end precisely that way and not some other way, despite the absolute sincerity of the artists taking part in the movement. Art in general is coming to an end as embodied in the new art, whose last gasp, surrealism, is already something in essence not purely artistic, despite the true greatness of some of its manifestations (here in Poland, for example, Bronisław Linke); what is coming to an end is not a certain unimportant branch of painting, as the realists think, but rather it is painting itself which is dying in its most essential form, in its inevitable development. The fact is, however, that the new art, despite its brilliant beginnings, never produced works equaling the greatness of those by the old masters. Many of our most promising painters as artists (in contrast to the realists) stopped short in their development without having carried their art to its ultimate consequences. I won't enter into the reasons for this state of affairs, which seems to me incontrovertible. But in any case these reasons do not reside solely in the indifference of our society to art, which is likewise an incontrovertible fact. The reasons lie much deeper than our experts on art think: it is a universal phenomenon occurring everywhere and has its origin in profound psychic and social transformations, which we are experiencing even here in Poland far from the main currents of life. . . . Nonetheless, it must be stated that we were right from the theoretical viewpoint and the essence of painting was and is the creation of formal constructions, and not the imitation of a slice of the external world in its randomness and chaos. The situation is quite different as regards the theater, which still has something to say and has not yet played itself out in its most recent forms. It is with joy that we should, as the saying goes, welcome the founding of the theater Cricot in Cracow, which is not, I gather, an experimental theater (despite the name) where unfocused energy is expended without any awareness of what the nature of theater is, but rather the beginning of a creative, artistic theater, which each of our cities should have alongside the others unless our theater is to die an unnatural death, rotting away, while still alive, in its own odorless sauce.

APPENDIX

CONTEMPORARIES AND MODERNS
COMMENT ON WITKACY

If you take into account that this "author" is eight years old, you've got to admit that he's got an awful lot of talent! Lope de Vega wrote his first play when he was ten years old—Staś was seven and a half when he began. If he keeps on at this rate and continues to write as much, then undoubtedly his works will be numbered in the thousands.

Stanisław Witkiewicz, 1893

Supper with Staś, who is brilliant and in rare form. . . . I feel dominated by a sense of inferiority which undermines my relations with Staś. . . . His style—on the one hand, it fascinates me, and on the other, it disturbs me. I am unable to resist his influence.

Bronisław Malinowski, 1912

Finis amicitiae. Zakopane without Staś! Nietzsche breaking with Wagner. I respect his art and admire his intelligence and worship his individuality, but I cannot stand his character.

Bronisław Malinowski, 1914

He is a degenerate individual, equally removed from true art as from life, a perpetual embryo crazed by megalomania.

Leon Chwistek, 1914

Witkiewicz is by birth, by race, to the very marrow of his bones an artist; he lives exclusively by art and for art. And his relationship to art is profoundly dramatic; he is one of those tormented spirits who in art seek the solution, not to the problem of success, but to the problem of their own being.

Tadeusz Boy-Żeleński, 1921

We are dealing with a painter of great talent, even of genius, who compels us to admire the boldness of his line and composition, the variety and freedom of his technical means, the richness of his colors. . . . Witkiewicz as an artist is connected to realism, and even to naturalism—above all, he is so connected by temperament and blood. What impels him to formism are his own theories of painting, emanating from the subtle brain of a theoretician and metaphysician, for whom the real forms of being cannot suffice. In this split, in the ceaseless struggle and strife between these two creative elements, lies the mysterious and evocative power of Witkiewicz's talent as a painter. He is creating his own style in painting. Between him and his "young" contemporaries, whatever we call them—futurists, formists or expressionists—there is nothing in common.

Kazimiera Żuławska, 1924

341

The antinaturalistic, deformed, often monstrous portraits by Witkacy displayed in the exhibit are not caricatures. They can aptly be called psychoanalytic portraits. Witkacy bares the psyche, bringing to light the hidden, the quintessential psychic traits of his model. But he does not do this to amuse himself or anyone else with the sight of his fellow man ridiculed, stripped bare, rendered helpless, but rather he uncovers the tragic grandeur of the human self.

Stefan Szuman, 1932

The very fact of individual existence here on earth implies irony, trick playing, sticking one's tongue out like a clown. Here, I believe, is the common ground between my *Cinnamon Shops* and the world of your creative work in painting and theater.

Bruno Schulz, 1935

Thanks to the author's kindness, I read several of Witkiewicz's unpublished and unperformed plays in typescript. Perhaps they contain faults, flaws and shortcomings. But the uncommon originality, the uncommonly consistent method present in his originality, and the uncommonly fruitful and vital results of his method along with dozens of other first-rate qualities expressive of Witkiewicz's truly great individuality not only successfully compensate for the "shortcomings" but moreover turn the supercilious and disdainful experts into jackasses devoid of any perceptive feelings. Since there is no possibility that the already depleted brains of the elderly *Kulturträgers* could understand, we direct the attention of the young *Kulturträgers* to his works.

Witold Gombrowicz, 1936

Witkacy belongs to those creative artists who despite even considerable popularity during their lifetimes must be forgotten and discovered all over again after many years because Witkacy's popularity was connected rather with the eccentricities in his life and with what in his creative work was the least valuable—and not with his enduring achievements in the realm of ideas and artistic creation. . . . He had a tragic gift for running down his own accomplishments. . . . It will take many years for the legend still alive today to die out, connected as it is to his character and only then will it be possible to find the true value of his work.

Bolesław Miciński, 1941–42

Witkiewicz was a self-taught philosopher who had never been trained in a good college, and he lacked an adequately thought out and consistently applied method. However—and I am strongly convinced of this—he was more of a philosopher than many of those who looked down on him, treating him at best as a philosophizing literary man rather than a scholar. He was a philosopher, above all, because he pondered issues with which he lived, in which he was personally interested, and which moved him deeply. These were not issues merely taken out of literature or something that just happened to belong to his professional field. . . . In philosophy he found a way to calm the storm that nevertheless did not cease to rock the foundations of his being.

Roman Ingarden, 1951

Poor Witkacy, a demon in his relations with women and a programmatic depraver in intellectual matters, was at the same time so infantile that he could not live apart from his mother and depended on her in all respects until her death. Equally infantile was his never-sated passion for mystification and the reactions to it he hoped to provoke.

Jan Lechoń, 1953

Witkacy, Witkacy, and once more Witkacy. He is such an interesting writer. He should have a theater devoted to him, and we want to become such a theater.

Tadeusz Kantor, 1961

His significance . . . transcends the limits traced by one historical moment and one language. . . . It is possible Witkiewicz was not dialectical enough and underestimated the resourcefulness of our species. . . . Yet Witkiewicz was hardly wrong, it seems to me, in his realization that something strange had happened to religion, philosophy, and art, even though their radical mutation did not equal their disappearance.

Czesław Miłosz, 1967

CHRONOLOGY
STANISŁAW IGNACY WITKIEWICZ
AND BRONISŁAW MALINOWSKI

Witkiewicz

24 FEBRUARY 1885.
Born in Warsaw in the Russian sector of occupied Poland, the only son of Stanisław Witkiewicz, painter and author, and Maria Pietrzkiewicz, music teacher.

JUNE 1890.
Witkiewicz family moves to Zakopane because of father's tuberculosis.

27 JANUARY 1891.
W.'s christening. Helena Modjeska, his godmother, present. Educated entirely at home because of his father's dislike of schools as mediocre and conformist. Draws, paints, and plays the piano from an early age.

1893.
Writes *Cockroaches* and publishes it on his own printing press as volume 1 of his *Comedies*.

1899.
Fascination with locomotives which he begins to photograph.

JULY–AUGUST 1900.
Spends vacation in Lithuania. First absence from home and beginning of correspondence between father and son.

1901.
Takes part in his first exhibition of paintings in Zakopane (two landscapes from Lithuania).

1902.
Writes his first philosophical essays.

1903.
Receives his secondary school certificate by examination, as an external student.

Malinowski

7 APRIL 1884.
Born in Cracow in the Austrian province of Galicia in partitioned Poland, the only son of Lucjan Malinowski, professor of Slavic philology at Jagiellonian University, and Józefa Łacka, a good linguist and cultured member of the gentry. Attends the classically oriented Sobieski Gymnasium in Cracow. Weak, sickly, with poor eyesight from tuberculosis, M. is frequently absent from school and is tutored at home. The Malinowski family rents a house in Zakopane, where they spend part of each year. Beginning of a lifelong friendship between M. and W.

1898.
Malinowski senior dies. Mrs. M. devotes herself to her son and his education.

1899.
Visits Montenegro and travels to Egypt for six months with his mother because of his poor health.

1902.
Receives his secondary school certificate as an external student and enters Jagiellonian University (Cracow), where he studies physics and mathematics and is influenced by the positivism of Ernst Mach and Richard Avenarius.

345

1904.

Visits Vienna and Munich and then Italy; first meets the composer Karol Szymanowski and becomes friends with Arthur Rubinstein, then visiting Zakopane on a concert tour. W. senior moves to Lovranno with Maria Dembrowska.

1905.

Starts to attend the Cracow Academy of Fine Arts against his father's wishes. Travels to Italy with Szymanowski.

1906.

Interrupts his studies at the Academy of Fine Arts and returns to Zakopane. Going back to the Academy, lives with the Malinowskis in October and November. Moves to his own apartment after a break with M.

1907.

Sees Gauguin exhibit in Vienna. Visits Paris from late January to mid April, where he discovers the nabis, fauves, cubists. Pursues studies in Cracow and turns from landscapes to portraits and grotesque charcoal drawings ("monsters").

1909.

Continues his studies in Cracow. Becomes involved in a two-year love affair with the modernist actress Irena Solska.

1910.

Writes *The 622 Downfalls of Bungo; or, The Demonic Woman*, an autobiographical novel about his affair with Solska and friendship with M.

1911.

Goes to Pont-Aven in Brittany to study painting with Władysław Ślewiński (former pupil and friend of Gauguin). Spends the last two weeks of July in London with M., while Mrs. M. is also visiting. Definitively abandons his studies at the Academy.

1904–5.

Reads Frazer's *Golden Bough*, which inspires him to become an anthropologist.

1906.

Continues his studies in philosophy of science and completes his doctoral dissertation, "On the Principle of the Economy of Thought." Visits the Canary Islands with his mother.

1908.

Awarded a Ph.D. in philosophy from Jagellonian University, with special distinction *sub auspiciis Imperatoris* and receives a gold ring from the Emperor Franz Joseph.

1909.

Studies at the University of Leipzig with the psychologist Wilhelm Wundt and the historian Karl Bücher.

1910.

Visits Zakopane in the summer; moves to London and becomes a student of Charles Seligman and Edward Westermarck at the London School of Economics and Political Science, where anthropology has recently been introduced as a discipline.

1911–13.

Writes articles on Frazer and on totemism for the Polish ethnographic review *Lud*.

1912.

Lives with his mother in her boarding house in Zakopane. Undergoes psychoanalysis with a Freudian analyst, Dr. Karol Beaurain. Does many charcoal drawings and photographic portraits of M. First uses the name Witkacy in correspondence.

1913.

On 17 January becomes engaged to Jadwiga Janczewska. In August exhibits several dozen pictures and thirty-three drawings ("monsters") at the gallery of the Society of Friends of the Fine Arts in Cracow. Has last meeting with his father (in Lovranno).

1914.

On 21 February Janczewska shoots herself because of an emotional imbroglio, probably involving Karol Szymanowski, then staying in Zakopane.

1912.

Comes to Poland in February and stays for a year. Lives with W. in Zakopane in the first half of March, then moves to Cracow, where he lectures at the Polish Academy of Sciences on "Tribal Male Association of the Australian Aborigines" and "Relations between Primitive Religion and Social Structure: A Theory of Totemism." Returns to Zakopane in August and is inseparable from W.

1913.

Leaves Zakopane in January for Warsaw, where he spends two months before returning to England in late March. Lectures at the London School of Economics and publishes, in English, his first book, *The Family among the Australian Aborigines.*

M. invites W. to accompany him, as a draftsman and photographer, to the meeting of the Congress of the British Association for the Advancement of Science to be held in Adelaide, Australia, in August. M. comes to Zakopane in May and returns alone to London, where W. joins him at the end of the month. They depart on 10 or 11 June on the SS *Orsova* and arrive in Colombo 28 June. After a two-week stopover in Ceylon, they sail on SS *Orontes* for Australia from Colombo on 11 July, arriving in Fremantle on 21 July. Spend two weeks sightseeing in Western Australia. After learning of the outbreak of World War I, they travel by ship, the *Orvieto*, to Adelaide for the start of the conference on 8 August. 10 August M. goes with a group of anthropologists to visit a settlement of aborigines of the Marrinyerri tribe at Milang on Lake Alexandrina, where they see natives perform dances, throw boomerangs, build huts, and weave baskets; W. stays in his hotel room and writes to his parents about his superstitious fear of the hour, twenty minutes to ten. On 12 August members of the BAAS go by train to Melbourne, where the congress continues its meetings. 19 August official conclusion of the BAAS Congress. From 21 to 25 August M. and W. stay in Sydney, with short excursions to Canberra, Murrumbidgee, and Yanco. 25 August M. lectures at the University of Sydney on "A Fundamental Problem of Religious Sociology." They travel by overnight train to Brisbane, where they remain from 27 to 30 August, with excursions to Nambour, Gympie, and Ipswich. On 1 September M. and W. visit Toowoomba, where they quarrel about Poland and the war.

FALL 1914.
Returns by train to Sydney, where he waits at the Hotel Metropole for a ship to Europe; as a Russian subject decides to fight in the tsarist army against the Austro-Hungarian Empire. On 5 September leaves Sydney on the *Morea*, which stops in Melbourne and Adelaide, before leaving Australia on 10 September.

Returns to Europe on the *Morea* and via the Balkans and Odessa reaches St. Petersburg by the middle of October and, despite lacking documents, is accepted in officers training school on 29 November.

5 SEPTEMBER 1915.
Stanisław Witkiewicz dies in Lovranno and receives a hero's burial in Zakopane.

1916.
Finishes officers training school in five months and serves in the elite Pavlovsky Regiment; made a lieutenant in the infantry in January; seriously wounded in a battle at Vitonezh in the Ukraine on 17 July. Receives the Order of St. Anne, fourth class, and is hospitalized from 28 July to 11 September, spending the rest of the war as a convalescent on frequent sick leaves.

FEBRUARY 1917–JUNE 1918.
Witnesses the events of the Russian Revolution, primarily in St. Petersburg. 6–31 March 1917 serves as elected head of an auxiliary battalion. While on leave, February-March 1917, visits Karol Szymanowski in Kiev. Interested in joining Polish legion then being formed in Russia in anticipation of Poland's achieving freedom. With Tadeusz Miciński goes to Shchukin Gallery in Moscow, where the fifty Picassos in the collection make a lasting impression. On 15 November discharged from the army. Lives on Ofitserskaya St. in Petrograd with Leon Reynel.

Returns to Brisbane. As an Austrian subject is nominally interned by the Australian government but receives financial support for his research. Spends the next five months doing fieldwork in New Guinea, first at Port Moresby, then on the island of Mailu.

1915.
M.'s *Primitive Beliefs and Forms of Social Structure* published by the Polish Academy of Sciences in Cracow; read in manuscript by W., who is acknowledged in the introduction. In June M. starts a ten-month field trip to the Trobriand Islands; by October has learned enough Kiriwinian language to dispense with an interpreter.

1916.
Returns to Australia in May; publishes "Baloma: The Spirits of the Dead in the Trobriand Islands" in *The Journal of the Royal Anthropological Institute of Great Britain and Ireland*. Receives Doctor of Science degree from the London School of Economics.

OCTOBER 1917–OCTOBER 1918.
Makes second field trip to the Trobriand Islands. Ends *Diary* (begun in 1914). Death of M.'s mother.

1918.
Returns to Poland in July; in Zakopane joins the group of painters known as the formists, exhibits with them, and begins playwriting with *Maciej Korbowa and Belletrix*, dedicated to Irena Solska.

1919.
Writes *The Pragmatists* and publishes *New Forms in Painting*.

1919.
Marries Elsie Rosalyn Masson, daughter of Sir David Orme Masson, professor of chemistry at the University of Melbourne. They have three daughters, Józefa, Wanda, and Helena.

1920.
"Introduction to the Theory of Pure Form in the Theater" appears in *Skamander*. Exhibits extensively. From January to June writes nine plays and an operetta, dedicating *The New Deliverance* to Karol Szymanowski.

1920.
Returns to England and lectures at the London School of Economics; goes to the Canary Islands for his health. Writes *Argonauts of the Western Pacific*.

1921.
Writes six plays, including *Gyubal Wahazar, Metaphysics of a Two-Headed Calf, The Water Hen*, and *The Anonymous Work*, dedicating the latter to M. Premiere of *Tumor Brainiowicz* at the Słowacki Theater in Cracow (the first of W.'s plays to be performed). Writes and lectures on the theory of Pure Form in the theater. Premiere of *The Pragmatists* at the Elsinor in Warsaw (two performances).

1921.
Considers returning to Poland and applies to Jagiellonian University for a teaching position; asks W. to find out about living conditions.

1922.
In August and October visits Poland with his wife and two young daughters, but declines chair in ethnology at the university. In August, in Zakopane, has first meeting with W. since Australia. Publishes *Argonauts*, with a preface by Frazer. Moves to Italy for three years in November.

1923.
Writes *The Madman and the Nun, Janulka*, and *The Crazy Locomotive*. Marries Jadwiga Unrug; publishes *Theater*, a collection of his theoretical writings.

1924.
Abandons painting as a pure art and devotes himself to portraits. Writes *The Mother*.

FALL 1924.
Receives a permanent appointment at the London School of Economics as a reader in anthropology.

1925.
Successful premiere of *Jan Karol Maciej Hellcat* at the Fredro Theater in Warsaw. Designs and directs the double bill of *The New Deliverance* and *The Madman and the Nun* for the Theater Society in Zakopane. Writes *The Beelzebub Sonata*. Begins writing *Farewell to Autumn*, an antiutopian novel containing an account of a journey to the tropics. First meets Bruno Schulz.

1926.
Successful production of *The Madman and the Nun* and *The New Deliverance* at the Maly Theater in Warsaw. Directs Strindberg's *Ghost Sonata* at the Formist Theater in Zakopane.

1927.
Publishes *Farewell to Autumn*. Premiere of *Persy Bestialskaya* (now lost) in Łódź. Begins writing *Insatiability* and *The Shoemakers*.

1928.
Publishes *Rules of the S. I. Witkiewicz Portrait-Painting Firm*. Premiere of *Metaphysics of a Two-Headed Calf* in Poznań. Experiments with peyote and its effects on creativity.

1929.
Meets Czesława Korzeniowska, seventeen years his junior, with whom he will have a close though stormy relationship for the rest of his life. Finishes *Insatiability* in November.

1930.
Publishes *Insatiability*. Renews acquaintance with Bruno Schulz in Zakopane.

1931.
Publishes many articles on philosophy, culture, and literature. W.'s mother dies 3 December.

1925.
Publishes "Magic, Science, and Religion."

1926.
Makes his first visit to the United States on a Laura Spelman Rockefeller Memorial Fellowship. Undertakes field trips to the Hopi people of Arizona. Publishes *Crime and Custom in Savage Society* and *Myth in Primitive Psychology*.

1927.
Made professor of anthropology at the London School of Economics; publishes *Sex and Repression in Savage Society* and *The Father in Primitive Psychology*.

1929.
Publishes *The Sexual Life of Savages in Northwestern Melanesia*, with a preface by Havelock Ellis.

1930.
Comes to Zakopane in August; W. finds him "odd and Anglicized to the core." The last meeting of M. and W.

1931.
Becomes a member of the Polish Academy of Sciences.

1932.
Publishes *Narcotics* and a second edition of the *Rules of the Portrait-Painting Firm.*

1933.
Finishes Part 1 ("Friends") of his philosophical novel *The Only Way Out* (never completed), begun two years earlier.

1933.
Serves as a visiting lecturer at Cornell University.

1934.
Completes his last surviving play, *The Shoemakers*, begun seven years earlier. Reads Bruno Schulz's *Cinnamon Shops*, which makes a "staggering impression."

1934.
Participates in the activities of the International African Institute and visits students working among the Bemba, Chaga, and Swazi tribes in eastern and southern Africa.

1935.
Publishes his major philosophical work, *The Concepts and Principles Implied by the Concept of Existence*, in an edition of six hundred copies, of which twelve were sold.

1935.
Publishes *Coral Gardens and Their Magic*. Becomes a British citizen. His wife, Elsie, dies after a prolonged illness lasting almost a decade.

1936.
Publishes portions of his major work of cultural criticism, *Unwashed Souls: Studies of Social Manners and Morals*, written the same year; participates in a philosophical congress in Cracow.

1937.
Depressed by Karol Szymanowski's death, W. predicts that he will die at fifty-four, during the war, foreseeing a coming world catastrophe. Invites the German philosopher Hans Cornelius (with whom he had been corresponding since 1935) to Zakopane.

1938.
Attempts to organize a Society for an Independent Theater in Zakopane and hopes to stage *Metaphysics of a Two-Headed Calf*. Writes a three-act play, *So-Called Humanity Gone Mad* (lost).

1938.
Writes the introduction to Jomo Kenyatta's book *Facing Mount Kenya*, prepared as a diploma thesis under his supervision. Goes on sabbatical leave to the United States, where he remains until his death.

1939.

Completes *The Psycho-physical Problem*. At the outbreak of World War II on 1 September, goes to a mobilization point but is not accepted because of his age. He and Czesława leave Warsaw on 5 September and flee with other refugees, heading east away from the advancing Nazis. Commits suicide on 18 September in the wooded village of Jeziory (now in the Ukraine), the day the Soviets attack Poland from the east.

1939.

Appointed Bishop Museum Visiting Professor of Anthropology at Yale University, then tenured professor.

1940.

Marries Anna Valetta Hayman-Joyce, who paints under the name Valetta Swann.

1940–41.

Studies peasant markets among the Zapotec of Mexico in the Oaxaca Valley, assisted by his wife.

1942.

Dies of a heart attack on 14 May in New Haven, a few weeks after completing *Freedom and Civilization* (published 1944). Buried in the Yale University cemetery.

BIOGRAPHICAL NOTES

FELIKS BERNATOWICZ (1786–1836):
Author of sentimental romances and the historical novel *Pojata, Daughter of Lezdejko; or, Lithuania in the Fourteenth Century* (1826). Went mad at the end of his life.

TEODOR BIAŁYNICKI-BIRULA (1886–1956):
Trained as a doctor in St. Petersburg. Practiced medicine in Zakopane, where he became a close friend of Witkacy and participated in his experiments with drugs.

TADEUSZ BOY-ŻELENSKI (1874–1941):
Satirist, poet, critic, and translator of French literature. One of the founders of the Green Balloon Cabaret. As a theater critic, hailed Witkacy's originality and helped get his plays staged. Murdered by the Nazis.

LEON CHWISTEK (1884–1944):
Philosopher, logician, mathematician, painter, and theorist of art. Member and chief theorist of the formist painters, 1917–22. Close friend of Witkacy's from 1894 until 1919, when philosophical and aesthetic disputes led to hostility and polemical attacks by W. Appears in *Bungo* as Baron Brummel de Buffadero de Bluff.

HANS CORNELIUS (1863–1947):
German philosopher and professor in Munich. Epistemologist admired by W. Visited Poland in 1937 at W.'s invitation.

ROMAN INGARDEN (1893–1970):
Philosopher and theorist of literature and art. Member of Husserl's school of phenomenology and of the Warsaw Circle, similar to and in contact with the Vienna Circle of logical positivists.

STEFAN KIEDRZYNSKI (1888–1943):
Author of popular comedies and farces in the 1920s and 1930s.

TADEUSZ KOTARBINSKI (1886–1981):
Philosopher and logician. Member of the Warsaw Circle. Co-editor of the 1957 memorial volume of essays about Witkacy's life and work.

ERNST KRETSCHMER (1888–1964):
German psychiatrist. In *Körperbau und Charakter* (1921) advanced an influential theory on the correlation of physical morphology and mental typology, contrasting the

thin, long-limbed schizoid, predisposed to schizophrenia, with the short, thick-set pyk-nic, subject to manic depression. Kretschmer's theory of psychic biotypes accorded well with Witkacy's techniques of portraiture in theater, fiction, and the visual arts.

JAN LECHOŃ (1899–1956):
Poet and critic. Judged all of Witkacy's work negatively. Committed suicide in New York.

BRONISŁAW LINKE (1906–62):
Painter and sculptor. Enthusiastically praised by W. in 1936 and chosen as stage designer for the projected Zakopane Independent Theater in 1938.

RAFAŁ MALCZEWSKI (1892–1965):
Painter and writer. Son of Jacek Malczewski, Polish symbolist painter of the Young Poland movement. From 1917 lived in Zakopane. Exhibited with Witkacy and worked with him on stage design for the Formist Theater 1925–27.

TADEUSZ MICIŃSKI (1873–1918):
Symbolist and protoexpressionist poet, playwright, and novelist. Considered by the young Witkacy as his Master. Appears in Bungo as the Magus. His Basilissa Teophano (1909) called by W. "the greatest dramatic work of our epoch." Murdered on his way back from Russia in 1918.

HELENA MODJESKA (MODRZEJEWSKA) (1840–1909):
Polish-American actress, celebrated for her Shakespearean roles. Moved to the United States in 1876. In love with the beautiful Helena, Stanisław Witkiewicz thought of emigrating but lacked the necessary money. Witkacy's godmother.

ANDRZEJ PRONASZKO (1888–1961):
Painter and stage designer. One of the founders of the formists.

ZBIGNIEW PRONASZKO (1885–1958):
Painter, sculptor, and stage designer. One of the founders of the formists and a lead-ing theorist of formism. Brother of Andrzej.

ARTHUR RUBINSTEIN (1886–1982):
Pianist. In 1913–14 frequently in Zakopane, where he met Witkacy and established a lasting friendship.

BRUNO SCHULZ (1892–1942):
Writer and artist. Taught drawing and crafts at the gymnasium in Drohobycz (now in the Ukraine). Witkacy was the first to champion S. and to promote him as a writer of genius. Friends since the 1920s, they met often in Zakopane and Warsaw. Shot on the street by a Gestapo officer.

WŁADYSŁW ŚLEWINSKI (1854–1918):
Painter, resident in France from 1888. Friend of Gauguin and follower of the Pont-Aven school. A major influence on Witkacy, whom he met in 1906 during a sojourn in Poland. W. spent several months with S. in 1911 at his home in Doëlan in Brittany.

IRENA SOLSKA (1875–1958):
Actress, star of the Polish modernist theater. Active career from 1896 to 1938. Married to actor-manager Ludwik Solska, divorced 1914 and remarried. Had a love affair with W. in 1909. Brilliant reciter of futurist poetry.

STEFAN SZUMAN (1889–1972):
Professor of educational psychology in Cracow. Author of works on psychology and aesthetics. Close friend of Witkacy.

TADEUSZ SZYMBERSKI (188?–1943):
Minor playwright and author. Close friend of Witkacy's in the period before World War I. Appears in *Bungo* as Tymbeausz. Malinowski dedicated *The Sexual Life of Savages* to him. Moved to France in the 1920s.

KAROL SZYMANOWSKI (1882–1937):
Composer of orchestral and chamber music, operas, and ballets. Visited an aunt in Zakopane in the early 1900s where he met W. Friendship continued in Russia and then again in Zakopane in the 1920s and '30s.

WŁADYSŁAW TATARKIEWICZ (1886–1980):
Polish philosopher, aesthetician, and historian of art. Close friend of Witkacy.

JADWIGA UNRUG (1891–1969):
Witkacy's wife. Granddaughter of the painter Juliusz Kossak.

ALEKSANDER WAT (1900–67):
Futurist poet and author of fantastic tales. Witkacy painted his portrait several times and wrote an essay about his work.

AUGUST ZAMOYSKI (1893–1970):
Sculptor. Returned to Poland in 1918 after studying abroad and moved to Zakopane in 1919. Joined the formists at the suggestion of Witkacy and exhibited with him. After 1923 lived in France and Brazil.

STEFAN ŻEROMSKI (1864–1925):
Major novelist and playwright, concerned with national issues and problems of social justice. A longtime friend of the Witkiewiczes. Witkacy painted his portrait several times.

SELECT BIBLIOGRAPHY
(MOST-RECENT EDITIONS)

Individual Works

Bez kompromisu (No compromise). Edited by Janusz Degler. Warsaw, 1976.
Czysta Forma w teatrze (Pure form in the theater). Edited by Janusz Degler. Warsaw, 1977.
Jedyne wyjście (The only way out). Edited by Tomasz Jodełka-Burzecki. Warsaw, 1980.
Narkotyki: Niemyte dusze (Narcotics: Unwashed souls). Edited by Anna Micińska. Warsaw, 1975.
Nienasycenie (Insatiability). Warsaw, 1982.
Pożegnanie jesieni (Farewell to autumn). Warsaw, 1983.
622 upadki Bunga, czyli Demoniczna kobieta (The 622 Downfalls of Bungo, or The demonic woman). Edited by Anna Micinska. Warsaw, 1972.

Collected Works

Dramaty. Edited by Konstanty Puzyna. 2 vols. Warsaw, 1972.
Dzieła wybrane. 5 vols. Warsaw, 1985.
Pisma filozoficzne i estetyczne. Edited by Jan Leszczyński and Bohdan Michalski. 4 vols. Warsaw, 1974–78.

Paintings, Graphics, and Photographs

Franczak, Ewa, and Stefan Okołowicz. *Nie-czysta Forma: Witkiewicz i Głogowski fotografie.* Cracow, 1985.
———. *Przeciw nicości: Fotografie Stanisława Ignacego Witkiewicza.* Cracow, 1986.
Jakimowicz, Irena. *Witkacy, malarz.* Warsaw, 1985.
Jakimowicz, Irena, ed. (with the assistance of Anna Żakiewicz). *Stanisław Ignacy Witkiewicz, 1885–1939.* Warsaw, 1990.
Krysiak, Maria, ed. *Asymetryczna Dama.* Łódź, 1991.
Micińska, Anna, and Urszula Kenar, eds. *Witkacy: Wiersze i rysunki.* Cracow, 1977.
Piotrowski, Piotr. *Stanisław Ignacy Witkiewicz.* Warsaw, 1989.
S. I. Witkiewicz: Photographs 1899–1939. Glasgow, 1989.
Sztaba, Wojciech. *Zaginione obrazy i rysunki.* Warsaw, 1985.

Correspondence

Malinowski, Bronisław. *Listy do Bronisława Malinowskiego.* Edited by Tomasz Jodełka-Burzecki. Introduction by Edward C. Martinek. Warsaw, 1981.

Witkiewicz, Stanisław. *Listy do syna.* Edited by Bożena Danek-Wojnowska and Anna Micińska. Warsaw, 1969.

English Translations

The Anonymous Work and "A Few Words about the Role of the Actor in the Theater of Pure Form." In *Twentieth-Century Polish Avant-Garde Drama.* Edited and translated by Daniel Gerould. Ithaca, N.Y., 1977.

Beelzebub Sonata: Plays, Essays, Documents. Edited and translated by Daniel Gerould and Jadwiga Kosicka. New York, 1980.

Insatiability. Edited and translated by Louis Iribarne. London, 1985.

The Madman and the Nun and *The Crazy Locomotive,* with *The Water Hen.* Edited and translated by Daniel Gerould and C. S. Durer. New York, 1988.

"On Pure Form." Translated by Catherine S. Leach. In *Aesthetics in Twentieth-Century Poland,* edited by Jean G. Harrel and Alina Wierzbiańska. Lewisburg, Pa., 1973.

Biographical and Critical Studies

Cahier Witkiewicz. Edited by Alain van Crugten. 5 vols. Lausanne, 1976–84.

Crugten, Alain van. *S. I. Witkiewicz: Aux sources d'un théâtre nouveau.* Lausanne, 1971.

Danek-Wojnowska, Bożena. *Stanisław Ignacy Witkiewicz a modernizm: Kształtowanie idei katastroficznych.* Wrocław, 1976.

Degler, Janusz. *Witkacy w teatrze międzywojennym.* Warsaw, 1973.

————, ed. *Spotkanie z Witkacym: Materiały z sesji poświęconej twórczości Stanisława Ignacego Witkiewicza (Jelenia Góra, 2–5 marca 1978).* Jelenia Góra, 1979.

Dialectics and Humanism: The Polish Philosophical Quarterly 12 (1985). Special Witkiewicz issue.

Dziechcińska, Hanna, ed. *Literary Studies in Poland/Etudes littéraires en Pologne,* XVI: *Stanisław Ignacy Witkiewicz.* Wrocław, 1986.

Gerould, Daniel. *Witkacy: A Study of Stanisław Ignacy Witkiewicz as an Imaginative Writer.* Seattle, 1981.

Kotarbiński, Tadeusz, and Jerzy Płomieński, eds. *Stanisław Ignacy Witkiewicz: Człowiek i twórca: Księga pamiątkowa.* Warsaw, 1957.

Michalski, Bohdan. *Polemiki filozoficzne Stanisława Ignacego Witkiewicza.* Warsaw, 1979.

Micińska, Anna. *Witkacy: Stanisław Ignacy Witkiewicz: Życie i twórczość.* Warsaw, 1991.

Miłosz, Czesław. "Stanisław Ignacy Wikiewicz: A Writer for Today?" In *Emperor of the Earth: Modes of Eccentric Vision.* Berkeley, Calif., 1981.

Pamiętnik Teatralny 3 (1969), 3–4 (1971), 1–4 (1985). Special Witkiewicz issues.

Piotrowski, Piotr. *Metafizyka obrazu: O teorii sztuki i postawie artystycznej S. I. Witkiewicza.* Poznań, 1985.

Polish Review 18 (1973). Special Witkiewicz issue.

Przegląd Humanistyczny 10 (1977). Special Witkiewicz issue.

Puzyna, Konstanty. "The Genius of Witkacy (Stanisław Ignacy Witkiewicz)." Translated by Bolesław Taborski. *Gambit* 9, nos. 33–34 (1979).

Sokół, Lech. *Groteska w teatrze Stanisława Ignacego Witkiewicza.* Wroclaw, 1973.

———, *Witkacy i Strindberg.* 2 vols. Warsaw, 1990.

Speina, Jerzy. *Powieści Stanisława Ignacego Witkiewicza: Geneza i struktura.* Toruń, 1965.

Studia o Stanisławie Ignacym Witkiewiczu. Edited by Marian Głowiński and Janusz Sławiński. Wrocław, 1972.

Szpakowska, Małgorzata. *Światopogląd Stanisława Ignacego Witkiewicza.* Wrocław, 1976.

Sztaba, Wojciech. *Gra ze sztuką: O twórczości Stanisława Ignacego Witkiewicza.* Cracow, 1982.

Sztuka 2–3 (1985). Special Witkiewicz issue.

Teatr 6 (1985). Special Witkiewicz issue.

Theatre Quarterly 5 (1975). Special Witkiewicz issue.

Witkiewicz: Génie mutiple de Pologne: Festival Witkiewicz (Bruxelles, Novembre 1981). Edited by Alain van Crugten. Lausanne, 1981.